La Vieja

A JOURNAL OF FIRE

OTHER WORKS BY DEENA METZGER

FICTION

A Rain of Night Birds
La Negra y Blanca
Feral
Doors: A Fiction for Jazz Horn
The Other Hand
What Dinah Thought
The Woman Who Slept With Men to Take the War Out of Them
Skin: Shadows/Silence

NON-FICTION

From Grief Into Vision: A Council

Entering the Ghost River: Meditations on
the Theory and Practice of Healing

Intimate Nature: The Bond Between Women and Animals
(with Brenda Peterson and Linda Hogan)

Writing For Your Life: A Guide and Companion to the Inner Worlds

Tree: Essays and Pieces

POETRY

The Burden of Light
Ruin and Beauty: New and Selected Poems
Dark Milk
The Axis Mundi Poems
Looking for the Faces of God
A Sabbath Among the Ruins

DRAMA

Dreams Against the State
Not As Sleepwalkers
Book of Hags

La Vieja

A Journal of Fire

(this is not a novel)

Deena Metzger

Afterword by Laura Simms

Hand to Hand is a community based endeavor that supports independently published works and public events, free of the restrictions that arise from commercial and political concerns. It is a forum for artists who are in dynamic and reciprocal relationship with their communities for the sake of peacemaking, restoring culture and the planet. For further information regarding Hand to Hand please write to us at: P.O. Box 186, Topanga, CA, 90290, USA. Or visit us on the web at:

www.handtohandpublishing.com

Donations to organizations have been made to replenish the trees that were used to create the paper in this book. We also wish to acknowledge the RSF Social Finance AnJel Donor Advised Fund for their support.

The I Ching readings quoted in this book are from Stephen Karcher's *Total I Ching, Myths for Change*, Sphere, Little Brown, 2008. The poem "Wolf Leave Tracks Now" is from *The Axis Mundi Poems* and *Ruin and Beauty: New and Selected Poems* by Deena Metzger.

This is a Literature of Restoration Book.

Layout and Cover Design by Stephan David Hewitt
Author Photo by Jay Roberts

La Vieja, A Journal of Fire. *Copyright © 2022 Deena Metzger*
ISBN: 978-0-9983443-6-2

Printed in the USA by Hand to Hand Publishing

"Our home which has to be defended like a holy relic."
Alexei Leonov, Russian astronaut

PREFACE

April 8, 2020
The Year of Covid-19

L a Vieja first appeared to me in October 2017, the way characters do, suddenly, a complete stranger, seemingly fully formed, if obscure. Writers' lives are composed of such meetings. She wanted a writer; I wanted a character. *Bashert.* If I tell it the way it actually happened, I was in Santa Cruz, California to give a reading of a novel I had just published. While I was celebrating the book, I was also disconsolate as I had no idea what the next one would be. The day after the reading, I sat down to write and La Vieja appeared. It was the oddest experience. I saw her, and, in a limited but very particular way, recognized her—she was La Vieja—no doubt, who else could she be? And also she was undefined. Exact and indescribable. But vague as her appearance might be, the intentions she announced were extreme and daunting, and a writer—the Writer, she asserted—would inevitably be significantly affected by her, La Vieja's, choices. I braced myself.

In the past, in order to write what had insisted itself, I had had to master fields of knowledge and history, astrophysics, Mayan cosmology, climatology, the Conquest, and more. I didn't choose these pursuits. Characters arrived and I was obligated to accept them and their histories. Ultimately, they didn't choose their lives and so neither could I. Not fate but summons. Naturally, I had to do research, had to see where they came from, what had shaped them, what had bitten them hard. I often traveled to those sites which were fundamental to the characters' development and where their stories originated. I think those journeys, or the habit of them, began to prepare me for La Vieja because I learned that every story is precisely rooted, has its own genesis. So, from the beginning, writing and pilgrimage were linked in my mind because the sites I had to explore were saturated with human events and most often, tragically, conflict. The land bears the burden of our conflagrations and ambitions. When you are on a former battlefield or a mass grave, you know. I came to consider the importance of place and speculated that to know anything fully required feet on the ground.

When La Vieja appeared—she didn't knock at the door, you understand— the distinct consciousness, from which someone like La Vieja could emerge, entered my sphere with her, neither invited nor resisted, not only into the room, but into my mind which rearranged itself to accept her perceptions. It accessed me as smoothly as fjords, green and blue, intertwine as they merge descending toward the sea. Although I had been entirely autonomous, well, at least since the previous novel, I was once again reeling with the on-slaught of a unique intelligence and perspective that promised to disrupt the familiar landscape of my own life and I anticipated the enormous task of incorporating and integrating her perspective.

She didn't want to tell me her story until this moment. She has zero interest in telling me anything of her past, or even present. I never learned more than snippets. What she wants is for me, for us, to know where she was going, why she must be there, and for me to bear witness to it and transmit it.

You know, in some ways, she is like a spirit. Maybe that is true of every character who inhabits a writer. For me, the writer, to transmit to you, the reader, the very essence of a character, I have to embody her and allow myself to be formed around what is most essential.

She was going to a place. That is what I was to understand and, happily, I did, in an instance of clarity, like fierce light breaking through parting storm clouds. She was going to the forest, to the woods, to land, and in that moment, without saying more, emphasized that our natural abodes, our biologic locations are as critical as any social construction. Whatever story was going to emerge could only happen there. This story happened there and could not have happened elsewhere. The same for the origin of characters. By that bend in the river, by that Sycamore, no, Juniper, at that time of day, when the midsummer light streaming toward sunset slanted just so through the Pinion branches, when the cones were ready to give up their seeds and the Bears were approaching in the center of a storm. Place is alive and specific and communicates outside of language. The imagination yearns for substantiality. Indeed, I didn't always know this about place and time, I assumed human culture formed us; I didn't know it was Earth. But, I did know enough by the time she appeared to understand what she had brought with her made it possible for La Vieja to seek me out. It would have been far too much for her to explain such to me in addition to everything else that would, as was said in my time, "bend my mind." We had to have an intuitive understanding even though I couldn't fully divine where she was coming from, or how she came to be.

La Vieja came with an entourage of exact experience which in a moment altered, became other than it was. Just as I thought, "Got it," whatever it was dissolved. The unmistakable deep yellow scent of dandelions became faint, the texture of the tight yellow blossoms instantly become the gossamer tufts floating away in the lightest breeze. It was immediately apparent how unique a person she was, and ungraspable. La Vieja was always precisely who she was and in another moment, she might appear differently in every respect. She appeared short, then tall, muscular, then svelte, seemingly fragile, then surprisingly sturdy, and was of no identifiable ethnicity, religion, race, culture, nation. She spoke English but you wouldn't say she was born in Cornwall, New Orleans, Bombay or Brooklyn, but that she spoke the way you spoke, whoever you are, and so called no attention to herself. How can I say it? Identity was immaterial. To impose such would diminish her. While it was certain that such a being didn't just spring out of the air, she came from place, time, circumstances, none of these were or would ever be revealed. They weren't hidden. They just weren't. It was perplexing; she had no history and was not without foundation. It wasn't that her face changed but that each time it might seem different from the time before although you would not remember how she had appeared earlier, but only that she was now exactly herself and indescribable. When I tried to imagine her, I felt her determination, the power of her resolve, her intense commitment, but not more, and these impressions were as strong as the features of her face might have been.

There was one feature, however, that was consistent and definitive no matter how she presented, these were her eyes. They took in the light, of course, that is what eyes do, but they cast a light around her as well. So that's how I knew her, knew it was her, by her eyes. She missed nothing she gazed upon in all the 11 or 12 dimensions. Of the great forces that must be reconciled to have a unified field theory of the universe, the most difficult one is gravity, the one that binds us to the Earth. Her eyes, piercing green, had gravity.

In the beginning, our connection was tenuous. I attributed it to my inability to grasp her story well enough to write it and my inability to dismiss it and go on to another. A writer's classic dilemma. But here is the mystery. When La Vieja came to me in Santa Cruz in 2017, she had announced herself as a recluse. I was intrigued but could make nothing of it. Though I had over the years successfully entered a character's experiences far different from mine, this time, I didn't and so she faded out of sight. I was preoccupied with my life, with teaching, with the increasing urgencies of our times and, I suppose, with worldly business. It seemed she had wanted me to acknowledge the necessity of her choices and, more extremely, share them. At least I think that is what she wanted, and I wasn't up to the task. I recognized the conditions she was entering, but I didn't cross the divide between us. Yes, I went on silent writing retreats regularly. Yes, I was writing this text on such sabbaticals, but I always returned to the world. I had never considered being a hermit; I was always engaged. She and I had connected but not enough for her life to flourish on the page. This did not interfere with her pursuit of her own life though it happened out of my view which alerted me to her extraordinary independence. I should have known, but nothing prepared me for such understanding, that when a character presents herself, she is an autonomous being and may not be ignored. The second time she appeared, I succumbed.

Before our first meeting, La Vieja had decided to take up residence in a Fire Lookout in the Sierras in California. She had entered solitary in order to see and intended to remain there. She wasn't planning to return to ordinary life, to being blind, the condition, she maintained, in which most of us live. Coming to this refuge was a soul commitment. I don't think it was her idea. I assume she had been guided here or maybe even transported. She didn't think in terms of her own will. She hadn't thought about herself personally when she made the decision, if she made a decision, when she transported herself to those mountains. Nor did she think of anything practical: how she would gain provisions over time, communicate, if at all with others, keep up her relationships whatever they were or had been. How she would act if she became ill, how she might meet loneliness, possible depression, danger, injury, even how she might face dying alone were not her concerns.

Rather she ensconced herself immediately in the story she would be living, as if having birthed her, manifested her, it nevertheless contained her; she had emerged from it and remained within it, her dwelling and her fate, without there being any contradiction between the two. It was a story which required solitude to be fully realized—that much she knew. This is what else she knew, or thought she knew: though she had left human society, she was not detached from human life. To the contrary, she had come to solitude for the purpose of investigating the times without obstacle or impediment and maybe, in ways she couldn't imagine, some good would come of it for all of us and for the future. What if anything the story would reveal was one objective. That the story would exist was another. This later she assumed was realizable, if dependent upon me.

Then circumstances changed. All our circumstances. Many things had happened in the more than two years since we had first met. Global warming has proved itself to be a misnomer and climate change is rapidly escalating toward climate dissolution. Wildfires blaze everywhere, also floods, tornados and drought. Extinction is rampant. Global agitation, physical and spiritual. A few heartbroken and unshrinking observers of what is have begun to consider climate collapse as imminent. Some people petitioned for the rights of trees, rivers, mountains, so they could be protected and some of us agitated for the recognition of the crime of ecocide. Then Covid-19 appeared, a spectre, a plague, another warning.

La Vieja got my attention when she entered my studio again. This time, she spoke in a common language, in a way I could not fail to understand. Her appearance was a rebuke, reminding me that I had failed our accord. She had come, she said, to alert me. She was going to sequester herself at the Lookout for the rest of her life. Sequester. That was my word she was using. I began to use it when Covid-19 arrived and so her use caught my attention and allowed me to open to her.

Some say being sequestered is like being imprisoned but clearly it is not. Late Middle English: from Old French *sequestrer* or late Latin *sequestrare* "commit for safekeeping." For safe keeping. She, I, you. We are here together for safe keeping. We are here together sharing common circumstances. Are we here together to keep each other safe? La Vieja might say, we are here together to keep the world safe.

La Vieja was not anticipated. Nor was the text that began appearing on the page, a text I seemed to be writing while simultaneously, or after a second's delay, reading for the first time, not as if I had just written it, but as if I were a reader discovering an unexpected plot line in a book by a familiar author. I followed it, slowly and carefully, wary, letting it unfold and more than often dismayed as I became completely lost in territories and characters that I did not know but couldn't abandon. Every sentence a surprise. Yet, when I tried to step away, I felt as if I would die. As if the writing were oxygen and if I didn't continue, it would run out.

Running out of breath is the defining circumstance of this time. Covid-19 attacks the lungs, takes our breath away. As does deforestation, the rapidly diminishing forests of the world. As do the increasing wildfires. As did Derek Chauvin when he murdered George Floyd whose last words, "I can't breathe," alerted and awakened us to so many other such deaths which hadn't been validated.

I took a breath and the next words of the text appeared, and I wrote them down and took another breath, grateful, and continued, writing and breathing. Continued haltingly but gratefully. Over time, the pace accelerated although I was always pushing into the void, the unknown, and later what seemed to me the unknowable.

The Advent of Covid-19 was both a chance occurrence and a divine intervention. We started calling the virus, Queen Corona. Reeling, we tentatively considered how we will have to live differently when we emerge from this global imposed retreat, every person on the planet threatened, no exceptions, in response to this species-threatening illness.

La Vieja returned or made herself known again, at the moment that Covid-19 began flourishing worldwide, explaining that she was choosing isolation, seeking deep silence where she could address the necessary questions and listen while maintaining her perspective. La Vieja came into radiant view under the dark light of Queen Corona.

It is unnerving to discover that this text, which began years ago and which I have never fully understood but could not abandon, is exactly for this moment and these conditions. The prescient La Vieja, was sequestering in her Lookout, and four and a half weeks after sequestering myself, I see that her intrinsic concerns and those imposed upon us meet the urgent call to all of us for awareness.

Covid- 19. What do you do when you have an illness that may kill you?

You go into retreat to ask: How must I change my life?

The old and familiar question "How shall I change?" transforms into

"How must I change?"

After great scrutiny of one's life and the manner in which we are living, possibilities appear: Live every moment as if this is your last moment to act on behalf of all life, not only your own, not only your species. When all life flourishes, may yours flourish as well. Through such a prayer, our species might align again at last.

* * *

Tonight, April 8, 2020

Awareness and technology align and the form of this text becomes possible. I yield to the subtle tutelage of La Vieja who occupies the continuous present—what was and will be intermingling with what is or what might be—and insert, as needed, a comment or an event, in what was written before, or continue an earlier text in a future time. We have no choice but to present this as a linear text, one word following another, as if it were written this way, but it wasn't. It's like a mind-map shaping a balloon. Accordingly, the writer is sometimes required to locate us in the moment when the writing or observation occurred. So this section purports to be written on April 8th 2020, (when much of it was indeed conceived and recorded), twenty-one days after we went into lockdown in California under the euphemism, Shelter in Place. But it is inserted as the beginning of a text that began in November 2017. (And, truthfully, I am rewriting these words of beginning in August 2021.)

Why do we need to know this?

Because an old woman is making a toilsome effort to live alone, utterly alone, in a remote area near the crest of a rugged, uninhabited mountain not yet burned to ash in the recurring conflagrations. She is aspiring to see, to see the sweeping range of what we must grasp, *we* must grasp, of our precarious circumstances, human and non-human, organic, stony and inanimate. Additionally, how we got here, that panorama from history and then deep time, including all the different scenarios of where we are going as we charge into the future so rapidly, we rival the speed of light. A future, which if we do not reverse our course, will resemble predictions of a continuously expanding exhausted universe, where whatever has not decayed is aimlessly drifting away, isolated, disconnected from everything else.

Alone. The wind comes up sharply and sweeps the dry leaves and needles on the deck into other configurations. La Vieja doesn't step away from peering into the dark west and only raises the zipper on her parka. She doesn't write anything down, but a clear picture occurs fleetingly in my mind and then smudges. Could I identify her in a police line-up? I could not. At this moment.... No, I could not.

I began perusing this text, which, again, I barely remember, in November 2017 and continued with a remote devotion, to find it has—dare I say?—mantic qualities. And so, I feel the necessity to superimpose or insert this Preface and will continue to both edit the original text as it demands by its nature while also, when appropriate, comment or enter the text as these days and times and whatever this book is to become, demands. When the certainty of a future for our species and all species is in question, when the past's bedrock assumptions of eternity are turning to gravel, and everything, everything, seems like it is coming to an end, I say with a slight nod to laughing at myself, that this book to the contrary seems to have a future in mind. Why say this? Because it wants to exist in and for a future. La Vieja, who is seemingly without any wanting, wants it.

This text is seeking its own precise completion, to be manifest in this specific present moment. For present moment has its own particularity and this one has been born out of the horror of what we have done to the world.

The human species is jeopardized, we have menaced all life. As a consequence of so many beings having gone extinct, the human is now suffering common jeopardy whether by chance, retribution or revenge.

We are destroying everything through our passion to dominate while to our confusion a very littlest one is taking us down. We do not know if I or you or the species will survive. We hope our ways of life that are so cruel, so rapacious, will undergo the necessary and anguished transformation for Life to survive. This is the challenge. How dare we resist it? How can we fail to take it on?

Who is asking this?

La Vieja is asking this of us.

Oh, there is one more thing.

Fire.

PART I

1

It is not a matter of writing for others, but for oneself, but oneself must also be the others, so elementary, my dear Watson.

Julio Cortázar,
A Certain Lucas

Something is coming from Elsewhere, if we listen. That there is an Elsewhere and energies reaching toward us from it, at a time when everything—everything—is threatened with extinction, eases me. And I/we have to assume that while this story I am/we are able to observe, comes here in this form, there could also be so many other communications to others from Elsewhere in so many different forms. To you also. Why not?

Actually you have had such inexplicable communications. We all have. In the old days, before we the set the world on fire, people lived according to the spirits who spoke to them individually and together, so life was in balance or they knew how to adjust it kindly when it went off kilter. But later, attending such communications was forbidden. And so, when we receive a transmission, it's frightening, in part because it forbidden by the churches and dismissed by government, so we set it aside and disdain those who still live listening deeply to the voices. And still, the voices speak and some of us listen.

Yes, such gives me hope that we might meet this moment. Maybe the story is designed to remind me, and you, that Elsewhere exists—and is entirely benevolent. What if the spirits are reaching out to us with assistance, or insight, to remedy this seemingly irredeemable tragedy of the full throttle attack on Earth, on all life, on existence itself, for which there looks to be no solution? Why would an old woman like La Vieja inhabit a Lookout if it were not to detect a fire in time for it to be put out?

About Elsewhere, it doesn't mean the story that follows is divinely inspired. I mean there are mysteries which ask us to yield to them. What characterizes this as a transmission of some sort is that I didn't conceive it. I mean, I didn't/couldn't have imagined it. I could not. I mean what we don't know or understand may turn out to be veritable, more so than what we Westernized humans assert is certain.

I prayed for this story, that is for a story, and these are the words that are coming. I am trying to follow it because one doesn't bargain or refuse a gift at the end of one's life.

La Vieja

One should have his abode where one can see all things from the point of view of solitude.

Lankavatara Sutra

L et's begin again. Let's pretend you're reading a story. Just a story. Because you like stories, let's pretend this is one. Maybe you like stories because they inform and entertain, but also because they can be dismissed. After all, this story is only about a few people, a few of billions, and the characters aren't even real, are they? Custom asks you to think, it's a story and the writer imagined it, made it up, and it's arbitrary.

But maybe it isn't. Maybe some stories are living entities.

The imagination always takes me by surprise. Sometimes a story appears out of the blue, relating events or considering issues for which I have no experience and yet, somehow, what appears on the page is accurate, frighteningly so. Sometimes, writers don't know the characters at the beginning, or what the characters know. Writers may not know anything about what will be appearing on the page, what will be relevant from their own lives or experiences to inform their characters' lives, may not know where the story is going or why it's been given to them to tell. And yet we write, not foolishly, but informed, I think, by awareness from other realms. We are compelled.

After writing for sixty years, I am still perplexed by the process. A character enters my mind, a stranger; a guest appearing like wanderers or beggars who may really be angels. A knock and I, the writer, open the door to the company I will keep for years. I have no choice. Maybe there was an agreement made before I was born and, accordingly, something wants to enter. Someone. From the other side. Like La Vieja.

So that's what we're in. We. Since you're reading this, we're in this together. Even after being at this for so many years, I am being schooled as I set this down. I have been given a gift; this story is coming alive in me. But not as if it were planted there. It arises from a dynamic, constantly changing, common field of knowing, an analogue of the original primordial soup or the process of abiogenesis from which creation emerges.

This story, this putative fictional event, is appearing as a strong memory just seconds after the episode has occurred. The event occurred somewhere where I was and was not consciously and I experience it sometimes as memory and sometimes as an occurring event. And sometimes as a demand. La Vieja appeared and so I was called outside, picked up my computer, and sat down by the row of Eucalyptus trees, before the stupa or cairn where we have buried the dead. Now, try to put these fragments together in a coherent whole!

The trees were planted before I moved here and self-seeded into a grove over the years, their trunks smoothed of their aromatic bark by wind creating various niches of affection by the ways they cluster, twist and bend toward, around and upon each other, continuously rearranged by rain and wind, cold and heat, dark and light. Across their latitude, the horizontal of a string of shredding white prayer flags quiver, the Tibetan letters faded from the effort of carrying the prayers. The prayers are conveyed as the cloth flaps in the wind and also as the flags shred and offer themselves up.

Birds, dull streaks of gray, brown, indistinguishable blue, cross in less precise lines to the feeders and back again to their nests in the brush beyond, to a tangle of Oak, Sycamore, chaparral leading to the mountains, which are gray today, and the sky, equally gray. The wind is up, and so the flags are beseeching while the long graceful branches they traverse glide back and forth ceaselessly in no discernible pattern. It is all gray, and it is all—still —alive. The wind increases, the flags rise and flutter, the prayers became more adamant in the colorless wake between the just past rain and the descending dark. We added our own prayers as we hung the prayer flags, but now they're out of our hands. We pray for the Earth. May she be restored, may she thrive, may all life flourish, *Mitakuye Oyasin*, all my relations. We add that Lakota prayer which if we, the non-Indigenous, understood and followed would restore the Earth and then all prayers would be answered. So the prayer flags ruffle and tremble with the extremity, not of the wind alone, but of the need.

One of the prayers, I am sure, was for a character to come and a story so that my last years wouldn't be deprived of what I love best, and what I hope is true, that writing is my given purpose.

When I review my life as a writer, I recognize an original edict to correct the assumption that the human is separate and autonomous and that creativity is inherent in an individual and belongs to that person, was born in *him* by chance and is *his* property. Increasingly, those who hold this belief, also believe they have a right to profit from this gift and also from whatever else they are clever enough to get their hands on.

Over the years, I gradually understood, no, over the years I was gradually *given* to understand, that there are other ways of knowing that arise from the heartmind which is the primary form for all beings and includes the human except for that dominating segment that withdrew from the natural world and, grievously, has brought us to this impasse where, all who have succumbed to this way threaten all life by their ways.

La Vieja's appearance requires me to delve into the mystery of being a writer, wanting to set our relationship, mine the writer, and yours the reader, and hers, La Vieja, straight, as I receive her story with the obligation to transmit it.

To speak of this changes the nature of this text just as our origins dictate who we will become. There is no reason for these energies or forces to be invisible except to enhance the false notion that the writer is an autonomous creator who owes nothing to anyone but herself. And so, we must open a path in the direction of interdependence even or especially while engaged in this singular activity of creativity.

To begin with, we are not defining this genre, not accepting the convention that insists that a novel must be only this but not that, or a text must be this and not that. La Vieja asserted her intention to yield to other voices and other realms without pretending otherwise and I have to do likewise. There are no familiar words for this phenomenon because Western culture confines literature to a realm outside the reality of the marvelous, avoiding the spiritual and cosmological implications of such events, denying the substantive relationship with the universe beyond.

But even though I am writing yet another such novel or imaginal text, I am still perplexed by the obdurate mystery of these visitations and it is as now my task to relate the path to the story as the story itself.

Mind, memory and story, all are outside of us and also, we are in them. The imagination is not only within me, but is without. The imagination is not mine, but is an instrument of perception or discovery, like having a good eye and is also the field, the reality in which we exist.

I wish I could make things up, but I don't have the skill. What I am able to do is listen, listen deeply and try to fold the inexplicable into language. And if this is the last, or one of my last novels, fictions or texts, then you see how essential it is to speak of a lifetime trying to understand what I have written, thinking I understood it. While I am experienced enough, I am not able yet to grasp the full meaning and implications of the creative process: The imagination is an instrument of perception or discovery and also the imagination is a real place.

Who am I? I am the writer and so the narrator. The writer is always the narrator whether disguised as another persona or not. I am relating the story as it makes itself known, the entire book changing each day, a boiling, writhing form until it is fixed in its final form by the act of publication.

Sometimes the book seems to have its own energy, almost its own will, but why say almost, when that is exactly how it is: story is autonomous. Interestingly enough, because the story or stories have agency, I am slightly removed from them, an observer even, of the character La Vieja. I observe her, or what she allows to be seen, what she deliberately reveals, but she for the most part seems uninterested in observing me. She is embedded in her life, in the story, and I am outside of it, watching. She is independent and I am intertwined. This is not fantasy or science or Cli-Fi, this is realism, call it magic realism if you wish; this is how things are.

Why speak of all this? Because how the story appears is as important as the story. The way the story manifests is also the story.

This is what just happened: I started a retreat on March 3, 2020 to write and consider the imminent collapse of all the global natural, social and political systems. We were supposed to be on a plane to South Africa and Botswana to reunite with the Elephant people whom we had met many times. Then we read that a terrible drought was gripping Southern Africa. How could we go on safari when animals and people were starving? We postponed the trip, counting on the monsoons to return. Then Covid appeared and grounded us at home.

I was lost. How were we—how are we—going to meet the accelerating chaos? Wisdom, if it exists, was elsewhere. No one I knew had sufficient answers for this time. If we did, we wouldn't have come to this juncture.

So, I addressed the spirits through the I Ching by asking this question:

"As a response to everything, climate dissolution, extinctions, the collapse of natural systems, Covid-19, what shall I pursue during this retreat to guide me when I emerge?"

The answer:

20 Contemplation or Viewing

"…the hexagram can be understood as picturing a type of tower characteristic of ancient China.

"A tower of this kind commanded a wide view of the country .... The hexagram shows a ruler who contemplates the law of heaven above him and the ways of the people below....

"The root of the term suggests visualizing in all aspects.... King Wen, spiritual father of the Zhou built such a magical tower at Fen, watching the skies and consulting the Intermediaries from a ritual platform raised high above the ground.... He was waiting for the appearance of the "Mandated Star," waiting for the command of Heaven... to be implemented below."

That's La Vieja, I thought. I got the chills at the startling appropriateness of the response. The hexagram speaks to me, the writer, who has had to withdraw, and to the character, La Vieja, who from the first moment of her manifestation withdrew to a Fire Lookout (a Tower) for the last years of her life. When Covid-19 arrived, La Vieja was no longer just a single character who had chosen isolation, but one of billions. The novel was coming to life beyond our little imagined world.

Here is the mystery. We are, as it were, in Creation itself. In terms of the story and characters, it is as if an entire view of another coexistent world, or several coexistent worlds, each perhaps only one nanosecond behind this one, is being made visible—the inhabitants, their pasts and present, their location and their horizons coming into plain view, moment by moment. But now with the analysis from the I Ching, the supposedly stable and real world that brooks no interference or control from outside influences, is also penetrated by forces outside itself which winds all events into a common field of consciousness, the lived, remembered, imagined, revealed, all intertwining. The worlds are distinct but exist in such close proximity that they also sometimes blend, one into the other. Though so far, I never know more than the particular that is revealed, I trust that what I am seeing is true, meaning it is happening, is happening even now, and happened. I am remembering and remember seeing it. But I don't know where it is going. At least, I don't think I do, at least not yet. I mean that here we are at the beginning and I don't know any more about what is coming than you do so that when we get to, let's say, page 148, which is beyond what I have so far written, I will only remember up to that moment in the history of this writing.

Why is this important? Because there are myriad consequences of every occurrence in the universe, we cannot calculate cause and effect as every action is composed of more elements than we can discern and compute. Every moment is as dense as that particle which exploded into creation from which we and all things descend. And that's the point (sic). An event cannot be described by math alone as it also results from the jiggle of resonances and relationships embedded within and influencing from without, and is by its organic nature boundless, unfathomable, immeasurable.

My task is to look hard at what is before me, allowing nothing to obscure my 360-degree view of this world as it burns nor to discredit the reality of the lives of these strangers who are presenting themselves to me, or to us, for reasons I don't know. Maybe that is why I am here, neither celebrating nor bemoaning the life I have lived, but determined to see if we can find ways to save beauty from the myriad threats arising every day.

* * *

La Vieja glanced down from her Fire Lookout and saw two people at the base.

* * *

Something else has to be said here. Until this moment, I have been occupying a familiar role as a writer, despite what I have written and purport to believe, that the book is given and I have to accept it and bring it to life, while hedging my bets and secretly assuming that I can at any time stop and desist, can leave this writing, begin another, or not, because I am uncertain of how to do this and equally unsure if I like what I am reading on the page.

But the conjunction of the I Ching reading with the plot, or what I know of it, the virtual communication from elsewhere means that this is a mandate given without right of refusal. I can feel it happening, in this instance, can feel myself being taken even as I am giving myself, can feel myself becoming the one who has received an edict, can feel the certain identity shift to the one who is writing this book.

Who am I?, I asked earlier without knowing I would come back to it again this way. I am the writer and narrator, I answered but with a bit of distance, a fact related to role. But no, not now. Now the answer is I am the one who is writing this book. That is who I am. I am nothing and no one else. My heart must open to it. I can only write it from the heart that seeks what must be known.

In the I Ching relating the ancient story of the Zhou line of kings "that establishes an order that renews the time, under which communication with the spirits is re-established and the blessings once again flow for all in a golden age."

In the I Ching, the good king goes up onto the watch tower with an open heart, with a heart broken open, to survey the territory on behalf of the people. La Vieja had done the same. So this must be my mandate too.

Am I writing about her or is she here to show the way?

* * *

The good king goes up onto the watch tower and so does La Vieja. For him, it is a yearly ritual but La Vieja is considering this for the rest of her life. She rented it from the Forest Service for a year. The ranger was amused and had worked hard to turn his wry smile into welcome as he handed her the key and she handed him cash which also caused him to raise an eyebrow. She could have commented or explained but she didn't. Any attachment would become an impediment, even just an exchange with the ranger. His responses were familiar, developed from years of being the interface to the woods for the public, the one who opened the gate to a life that was increasingly forgotten and he wanted them to—well, if you asked him honestly—he wanted them to enjoy the woods but, more importantly, he wanted them to behave. If he were personable, that goal was more easily achieved—he was benevolent, but also, they would feel he was watching. In response, La Vieja was neutral. It was not strategic, it came from her focus. She signed papers. She agreed to notify them if she left for any length of time. They would have to know if she were there in the event of fire or another catastrophe. By agreeing to critical issues, she avoided other entanglements. It was known that those who had occupied Lookouts in summers were loners, not infrequently writers, so what might appear odd behavior and a desire for solitude were not so very odd.

"Water?" the Ranger asked.

"Sufficient." She said and he understood she would get more if needed. Food as well.

Usually believing he would not be needed was a relief, particularly in the late spring through early fall when there was an onslaught, but she was an old lady and he felt responsible for both his grandmothers. It was how he was raised. When she entered and they made eye contact, it was immediately obvious he was not to stand up even though she refused to sit down and so now, he didn't stand up from behind his desk when he made his last attempt to connect with her, "I could come up and carry the water up," he said in a low enough tone not to be intimidating. What he expected, occurred. She refused his labor.

"If I can't carry the gallons up over time but still quickly enough, it won't be right for me to live there. You'll hear from me if it doesn't work out. If so," and now she was taking it all into her own hands, "you'll hear from me and I'll return the key." It was done. Later, trying to explain her to his colleagues, he somehow couldn't remember anything about her, not even what she had been wearing, or the used car she was driving.

"She sounds like a phantom," one said.

"Her cash was real," the Ranger responded but checked anyway. It counted out in hundred dollar bills.

* * *

La Vieja turned off the engine and, key in hand, ran up the stairs, through the open trap door, onto the deck and circled it. Though they were above 5,000 feet the trees did not seem sparse to her yet. To the south and west, she could imagine she was in a tree house as she looked down toward the ground, the layer of leaves and needles, brambles and underbrush, gnarled trunks, branches, twigs, the forest itself. Rather than circumventing the cabin below before she ascended, she inspected where she was from above, following the direction of the eastern stairs leading down to a small meadow with an articulated path in the midst of brush, leading into the dark woods. Immediately, she knew that would ultimately be the direction she would investigate on foot when she felt confidence. She glanced down at her feet, the boots would serve her. In the meantime, she had the task of combining physical vision with spiritual understanding, and learning to see. Would she find a spot and stay there or follow the light and then the dark? It was her mandate though she didn't necessarily understand it. Well, she had, she faltered even to herself, the rest of her life to figure it out.

* * *

As the writer, I know so little about these early moments because she hadn't contacted me yet and then she did and I began writing but I was preoccupied until Queen Corona came and said, even to me who thought I was so aware and conscientious, "Stop and listen." It dawned on me only then that La Vieja was one of the voices I was obligated to hear. Well, really, I am dissembling. I don't think I ever articulated that to myself but rather, finally, sitting outside alone day after day after day at the edge of the wild park, and our circumstances causing me to be alert every moment to fire, allowed me over time to hear her differently. So, yes, I was setting down what she was transmitting and that couldn't fail to change me big time. Because by the time we had an agreement that I would be the scribe and give it the attention it deserved, which was everything I had and then more so, I began to understand that her motivation was juxtaposed with my own anguish about the surging degradation of our world, coupled with my stubborn insistence since childhood that we could set it right.

When the teletype from her inner world began, she was settled into the Lookout and as you might consider, she had no interest in conveying what were for her the wearisome details about moving into the Lookout and the first days or weeks or months. All I had then was her increasingly sharp focus and her reliably reluctant memory. Also what she couldn't report was the progress of her perceptions though I felt over the months that she was fine-tuning her instrument so that gradually she was able to see farther and clearer. I felt this because it was what I was aspiring to and such ambition had to have come from her. She may have been learning something, but I don't know what it was.

The entire process of writing this text was a puzzle. Even when one's book is partially autobiographical, the writer's stance always has a little re-move. Looking at myself from my own eyes, I am the subject of the writing and so it must be seen objectively to some extent. While no one could be more different from me than La Vieja, on the other hand, she was determined that I develop the means to validate what I was setting down and the only way to do so was through my own experience. Can you imagine a character coming to you and saying, "Don't write that down until you know it through your own experience?" Well, what if she had been a skydiver? In fact, this was more daunting.

And there was Queen Corona positioned next to me, to both of us, I imagine, to everyone I know, hissing, "Be still and listen." Then not quite under her breath adding, "Change your life or we're going to have to return with higher stakes. We're not letting you guys and gals take the world down if we can help it. Covid and I and others that you know and some you have not met have some tricks up our sleeves."

We had gotten their warning earlier in so many different ways in the last years, but we can start with the Australian bushfires September 2019 to July 2020 when we were sequestered. Three billion animals had died. During just one of those catastrophes, the Currowan fire had burned one million two hundred thirty acres, and people had had to run to the sea to take shelter in small boats not to be burned alive.

Long before the time of sequestering and the drought in Africa and the bushfires in Australia, I was prepared to recognize climate dissolution and the urgent need to change our lives, my life. Then the abject isolation of the pandemic enhanced the sorrowful intensity of the time. How alone if not lonely she must have felt. She didn't say. Well, I don't think she wanted to reach out to me as a friend, only to dispatch.

But my own feelings were refined by La Vieja's circling and circling the deck, which from the heat of fire season rising and then turning, twisting, began to feel like whirling, like *dhikr*, the trance of such deep attentiveness that one can begin to understand what is coming to us from beyond. I spent more and more time alone and peering out, there at the southeast corner of the field bordering the park, the Oaks and the Laurels, trying to protect them, calling for rain and calling for rain and calling for rain. And if I were in such a state—for after all, I heard cars and food was delivered, or I went out masked and over-cautious to purchase it, and I had running water, electricity from solar and propane and a woodstove and lots of wood, mostly from the land, from trees and limbs that had fallen— I was ok and a phone ring away from help if I needed it. But, La Vieja? She could contact the Ranger's station but I doubt she would do so, no matter what.

* * *

It was late at night in the Shasta-Trinity wilderness. It was dark and there were stars. She had no lights on. She was outside, walking around the deck, stopping and gazing in whatever distance called to her. It wasn't silent, the forest was alive with other beings who lived there, and were fortunate to feel safe, unless it was hunting season. It wasn't hunting season. Not for anyone.

She might go to sit at the bottom of the stairs, to be closer to the creatures, sometimes the pain of being without an exchange with another being was crushing.

La Vieja

(The Writer had improvised this because I can't imagine otherwise. Or maybe if she had to hunt for food each day, it wouldn't be so hard. Many people across the world choose to live entirely alone. La Vieja was working on the cabin, making repairs, whittling, wasn't that wooden flute on the shelf her carving? I was struggling with trying to imagine how it really was, day in and day out, for her.)

It was a quiet night, the Earth was not endangered by her lights, and so she went down to the bottom of the stairs and listened to the creatures. It was quite late and still safe when she returned and lay down on the bed to sleep. In the morning she would wash, maybe even go down to the creek that was still running and bathe, and change clothes, wash others there. She always slept in her clothes so she could be instantly ready for whatever.

The sun came up, heart-red and she began her rounds again. Then she would do chores around noon. But as she had left to sleep, she needed to do her rounds and realign herself with all that is.

* * *

La Vieja glanced down from her Fire Lookout and saw two people at the base.

At first, she thought some hikers had found their way to the cabin. Then, she saw that the two people below were among trees she didn't recognize along the foundation of what appeared to be a Lookout but quite different from this one on her land. It was quite distinct from her Lookout and yet there it was, too. Vertigo. She recognized them although she had never seen them before. Their entire pasts and, even, some of their futures slam-dunked into her awareness—and so mine.

* * *

The two fade in slowly, one reality yielding to another, time adjusting. I don't think that they see La Vieja but have their own reasons for staying below. Something is impelling them. A force they cannot resist, like a scent which is a determinant of action. And then I hear it too, and so does La Vieja, though it exists in another geography and perhaps in another dimension of time. It is a grunt that is associated with an essential force composed of fur, moisture, bone and a unique and reliable intelligence that knows its environs the way it knows its own body—Bear.

They are staying below because of the Bears. They do not want to go up into their cabin to escape the Bears. They want to stay below for a greater certainty of being with the Bears.

*   *   *

I understand now. I have been brought here through La Vieja to witness a possibility and give it language without retreating from the motion, like the possibility of an expanding universe seeking an equilibrium, retracting on behalf of restoration.

We are here within the manifestation of a synchronous moment. How can we make this real?

2

The animals are speaking to us, through us and with us. They are coming to us, not only in our dreams but in our lives. Perhaps in those moments of their disappearance and endangerment, they are offering themselves in ways known in the past....

Linda Hogan, Deena Metzger, Brenda Peterson
Intimate Nature: The Bond Between Women and Animals

La Vieja is living within one dimension and I am within another. The dimensions interpenetrate without altering each other, the way time and space coexist. Sometimes we are distinct and one communicates with the other by acknowledging we are viewing the other from outside and sometimes we each know everything the other knows. Then we are two discrete beings, momentarily one consciousness.

Physicists aren't certain if there is a fifth dimension, and if it exists is it tucked within the other four and, therefore, invisible? If it coexists with our three dimensions, can it with effort and technology be made visible? Einstein believed in it and the Kaluza-Klein theory supports it. String theorists postulate many more than the five. Some hold the dimensions exist within quantum physics but not in our world, but I am definitely in this world and I am asserting that La Vieja is as well, however I don't know if we, including you the reader, are tucked into her world with the two she has seen at the foot of her stairs, or do they occupy another reality? I don't have an exact map of our worlds yet, or understand or can describe with authority its dimensional geography. But La Vieja exists, as does her world.

At this moment I am on the patio where the prayer flags are hanging, looking out toward the bowl of low mountains that surround this dwelling. While writing, I am listening to the birds who have returned this year, a brief then fleeting chip-chip of Towhees, the screech of Blue Jays, the haunting chant of the Mourning Doves. I could score it, could give the Towhees the flute, a piccolo, fife or penny whistle to the Blue Jays, and the clarinet to the Doves, another wind instrument to reproduce the raspy lyrical twitter of the Red Finches, but for now I just listen to their songs, punctuated by the conversations of the Crows and Ravens who come here during mating season. The excited adolescents caper on the winds, alarming the Finches, more interested it seems in the ruckus they create than the eggs they might filch from the nests. At first, I thought the Mockingbirds had disappeared but they had taken up residence in the citrus orchard among Bees and Bluebirds. But the Acorn Woodpecker, Ash-throated Fly-catcher and Golden Crowned Sparrow do seem to have disappeared and their place in the scale emptied here, if not everywhere. Every once in a while, I spy a Thrasher as if traveling through and no longer making his home in the brush of the Plumbago among the blue flowers.

I once imagined an Animal Orchestra. La Vieja and I might have met through this vision. Had she read my mind, it may have confirmed to her that I am capable of transcribing her story. She may have recognized common interests. Or perhaps I picked up the idea of the Orchestra from her. No. I think this is the only time I transmitted to her.

I, or we, pictured human musicians gathering in the woods, each one having selected a single animal who had gone extinct, or was threatened and on the verge of disappearing. Then with voice or instrument, the musicians were to go to the depleted woods to duplicate the exact missing notes and their place on the scale, their timbre, rhythm, expression, re-musicing the forest so that, I hoped, we hoped, that not a single tree or animal still living who heard these sounds would doubt that the animals were returning and so begin to make their way toward the song that had been absent for so long. This would offer such a jolt of well-being, that the entire woodland would brace itself for a future it hadn't dared consider was possible, jarring them from the assumption of their fast approaching demise. Maybe even the disappeared animals would be drawn back, their bodies rematerializing in the hope of welcome into the most sublime composition of all, countermanding the exodus of the animals who, according to the Elders of so many different traditions, were leaving, had left planet Earth for other spheres, at the very least vacating their material incarnations.

Music is not just sound. Music is a conversation, an action through alliance that occurs between beings. We think of it as a human expression but rather we learned it from the Others as they consistently coordinate the Earth and the spirit worlds through their song. So much more than personal exchanges, music is the essential connection. You think it is electromagnetism, gravity, chemical bonds, the strong nuclear force or the weak nuclear force, or even love or power that holds the universe together? It's music.

It is the music of the Others, the Birds, the Animals, who, with their songs, bind the world into the connectivity from which all life emerges and which is necessary for it to flourish. Long strings of sound winding through the air, catching on each other in chords of relationship, tying one life to another to another, weavings of many colors of sound on the loom of creation. And then in the sea, the great epic recitations of the history of the world as the whales recount it, singing their song sagas in order to keep us, all of it, alive.

This symphony of the Animal Orchestra is more than imagination. I heard it and saw it in my mind and then I saw it as clearly as if I was overlooking the scene. And in a way I was, from the virtual Lookout I have learned to inhabit from La Vieja.

La Vieja's Lookout is real while mine developed from thinking about her choices. It combines the view I imagine is La Vieja's blended with the real view looking from this land to the surrounding low mountains that form a bowl around it.

From the beginning, I couldn't fully control what I was trying to visualize. Yes, I was visualizing the processions but I was unable to avoid the earlier jarring sight of the awkward humans gathering at the various parking lots ringing the sanctuary where the animals had all once lived. How bumbling we are compared to animals, each one of which, every one of them, is lithe and graceful each in their own way. But humans! Look at us getting out of our vehicles, sorting our stuff, putting on sunglasses, vests, hats, stuffing repellent, alarm whistles, sandwiches, apples, thermoses, mugs, cameras, hats, compasses in our pockets, shouldering backpacks and fanny packs to hold whatever might be needed, removing instruments from cases, or slinging the cases over a shoulder, while simultaneously trying to decipher the individual map designed to reveal the area where a particular animal might have congregated or denned. Then, shrugging to let the weight settle and setting out.

I waited. La Vieja waited. Yes, a joint endeavor that became a foundation from which we pursued our common concerns in our own distinct ways. It became a wordless initiation that led to wherever it is we are going together.

Watching from her aerial view, perched above the trees on the catwalk circling the Fire Lookout, La Vieja also saw each person cautiously taking first steps to find the place it was thought the last creatures they were invoking, had been before they had disappeared, then tentatively sounding first calls. While the humans were following as best they could the injunction to take on, to be inhabited by the disappeared animals through their music, few managed the beings' original innate comfort in their native environment. Each human had to make her, his, their burdened way. There is no marked path any longer for the disappeared as the animals haven't walked here in their own ways in so long and might not follow where Others, the remaining non-humans had continued treading.

The two-leggeds were moving slowly, so very slowly, listening for the animals, the birds, for each other, wary, at first, some fearful of exactly who they were calling, afraid they would actually come, and then yielding to anticipation, letting their musical training focus their concentration and tune them to what they were hearing, natural sound and instrumentals. Each one finally sounding into their ancient designated position, allowing themselves to slip into the animal mind that was embodied in sound and hope, finding one's place among the scored and the spontaneous, the two-leggeds and the Others, the one note and the lyric, the extinct, the threatened and the survivors, drawing closer to each other to drink it in, the sound becoming richer, more complex, denser, louder, first because the two-leggeds became more confident, bolder, and then because the animals did gather and began vocalizing without inhibition, trilling off each other until the river of sound was flowing again. A new form of a revival meeting.

Not willing to expect magic, still secretly imagining the Orchestra, we could not avoid hoping for what those of us had also begun to understand what was occurring on the planet, desired the end of extinction, the end of the plagues of bark beetles and locusts, dying forests, tinder dry grasses, rampant desertification, poisoned waters, bleaching coral reefs, melting glaciers, forest fires, deadly floods, increasing frequency and intensity of hurricanes and typhoons, unbreathable air, death in the winds. Desired, hoped for the reversal of the grim warnings in the collapse of all living systems. We did this together, probably at the same time, but maybe not, and, you understand, without awareness, each of us, of the other.

La Vieja's motivation? She loved life. Her love was unquenchable, despite all. She cultivated memory, she sought restoration. This odd species we watched gathering was remembering when they, like the others, had been singers, not individual musicians, but each of them consistently and constantly singing, all together now.

Looking down, I recalled the first flicker of the Animal Orchestra. It was from an article by Bernie Krause, a musician and soundscape ecologist, who said that birds and animals located themselves by the music they created together. When a bird or animal disappeared, they were all confused, or better said, de-ranged; the community of animals diminished and began to fall apart from the loss of the species and their song. No glue. Additionally, the din of the human world was already invading and drowning out all song, all music, all beauty, adding to the poverty and intensifying the speed and extent of the decline of the natural world and human existence as well. The ultrasonic screech of a deer whistle sounding as soon as a car travels 35 mph, pervading over a quarter of a mile causing animals to freeze, and given the amount of traffic and the speed on most highways that traverse forests and remaining strips of the natural world, causing a kind of perpetual paralysis.

From the human perspective, perhaps the social chaos, turbulence and violence, the greed, corruption and hate-mongering, these derangements, are also caused by the loss of the music of the natural surroundings: perhaps two-leggeds need to tune regularly to Earth music for their survival, to be part of the universal composition. No doubt the rising levels of physical and mental illnesses among humans and domestic animals are related to the increasing extension of their dulled, equally hysterical, disconnected, atonal lives into every aspect of existence. Maybe humans are directly suffering as much from being deprived of the natural environment and the resulting meaninglessness as from the invasion of alien toxins from noise, chemicals, and electronic imbalances.

The intent of the Animal Orchestra was to restore balance through music or restore music for balance. Perhaps such an effort would have a medicinal effect on humans as well. Though I had many musician friends, it never came to pass. Some years later Bernie Krause's book, *The Great Animal Orchestra*, appeared. Though he was the one who had recognized there had been a universal, continuous animal orchestra, he didn't try to reproduce it with human musicians to see what might happen from the effort to recreate the original composition. He didn't even project recordings of the missing into the devastated territories except when he used recordings of humpback whales feeding to help lure Humphrey the Whale back to the ocean from where he had wandered up the Sacramento River in California. Krause is a scientist and an artist. Still such an event seems not to be his way. There were many related exhibits and performances, some held in museums, as dead a space as extinction itself. These were designed for the education, entertainment and interest of humans and not for the wild where some, albeit gravely threatened, companions of the disappeared still reside.

* * *

La Vieja could read my mind, it seemed. It was because of such experiences, that she had come to me, trusting the environment was sufficiently fecund and safe for her story to be grounded and emerge. Accordingly my imagination was no longer *my* imagination but was the substance of the field we both could enter. It seemed the Animal Orchestra was perceived similarly by both of us and we could not, and should not, try to determine its parentage. How do I know, maybe she planted the idea originally? Ownership or credit were not conditions she sought, and I was carefully and steadily relinquishing notions of such and more. She had no past of which I was aware and I was stepping away from so many assumptions of my upbringing. Giving up ownership and acknowledgement were just the beginning.

* * *

When La Vieja looked down from her perch, away from the Animal Orchestra of imagination but to Bears who were clustered below in the stories she was living, La Vieja wondered if she had called them with her sorrow or whether they had come to her by their own intention. Did it matter whether she had unknowingly called them or they initiated the contact? There are certainly many different ways to summon the animals or, likewise, to be summoned.

When she had first approached me, when she had indicated her intentions, and alluded to having lived with wolves, I wondered if she had come to me because of my relationship with Elephants.

We had dreamed them and then we had met in the African wild in 1999 and on many occasions afterwards in ways which indicated intent on their part as well as mine. It was incontrovertible. Our meetings indicated openness to exchange and perhaps even longing on both our parts to affect some mending of the torn world through our improbable connection.

Are we, aren't we, responsible for our dreams, I began wondering? Are the dreams of our own making or rather are we the recipients of sacred events? What entitles us to enter the other worlds they reveal?

Over time, I came to know the Elephant people's music. Over time, I could hear it through my feet as they did, rumbling silently to each other across vast distances. Even now, I am hearing their anguished cries, the death songs of more than three hundred and fifty elephants around water holes in Northern Botswana succumbing to what might be a neurological affliction whose cause remains unknown on Saturday, July 4, 2020. The dying Elephants have been communicating their plight to other Elephants in Chobe, where I pray the Ambassador I first met in 1999 is still alive, and those we met later, the Matriarchs in Mashatu, Namibia and Thula Thula and even the Master Teacher in the desert of Namibia and beyond to all the Elephants we know, and further still, until all the members of the species know and are mourning while contemplating their next moves for survival, seeking and preparing to yield to another strategy to keep them alive. Because I was so broken by the news, I understand such heartbreak can't come from reading the news but only directly from the Elephants I know, sending across the African continent and across the Atlantic and across the continent of the United States to land here on the west coast so that I can howl with grief, but only after I have screamed a rage so sharp for all the harm done to them, all the massacres, so that no perpetrator in the vicinity should be able to survive it. My great gray people dead, splayed out, tusks gone, heads down on the Earth. Aiieeeeee!

Helena Kriel answered me from South Africa when I asked her about the multiple deaths. "When a Rhino is shot, it falls and there lies like a human. And a tear comes out of its eye. I've seen a rhino cry, they cry," she wrote. "They weep at their unjust death. They weep. At the injustice."

La Vieja did not know Elephants, but she had said that she had known Wolves. She had lived with them, she indicated. Hybrids mostly, yes, but not only hybrids. Full-blooded Wolves. She knew their music and how lonely they were without the chorus that brought them into sound, each finding their own distinct and varying arpeggios, shifting from minor to major and back so as to keep the harmonics synchronized with the individual sounds, accompanying each other without neutralizing and then, as with the local Coyotes, a Singer emerges to lead the pack in an interchange with the other clans to whom they are calling or signaling to a member of the pack who is away from home—the voices, their compass, the pack, true North.

Down below La Vieja's Lookout were the Bears. She knew Wolves but she didn't know Bears. And yet here they were gathering visibly and in-visibly, just outside the perimeter of the Fire Lookout.

It was all open to the wild. Not that a fence would keep the Bears out if they wanted to enter. They could pass through the way they could slip from one dimension to another or cohabit the field of consciousness that had allowed me and the Elephant Ambassador to communicate so precisely that I had come by his instructions to the exact place at the exact time we would meet that first time in 1999 and then again and again and again—the same place, at the last hour, of the last day—until my last visit in 2017.

It looked like the Bears were settling in the way an idea approaches soundlessly and settles in, makes a home inside your mind and then you tend it the way you tend your life because it has become a part of you. Below La Vieja in the proximity of Léonie and Lucas, whom you haven't met yet but will, the Bears are gathering.

3

Traditional Native perceptions of animal nature represent a type of thinking and attitude, dramatically different from those of Western science. In the Native way, there is a fluid and inclusive perception of animal nature that makes less of a distinction between human, animal and spiritual realities. These realities are seen as interpenetrating one another. This is a view held in common with evolving descriptions in quantum physics.

Gregory Cajete
Native Science: Natural Laws of Interdependence

Two people, Léonie and Lucas, are seated below. Below their cabin. A few minutes ago, they were considering climbing up the stairs to their Lookout which, invisibly, is parallel to or interpenetrating La Vieja's, though also quite a distance, 300 miles, to the east. But something got their attention. Their hackles rose, invisibly, then fell. They heard the same grunt she heard. Probably heard it before she did.

Although newly acquainted, they simultaneously eased, Léonie is leaning back into Lucas as he settles against the pine so that the Bear senses he had the freedom to approach or not as he wishes. As Bear *wishes*. They consciously open to his choice and this reception exudes from them like an aroma so that even La Vieja can smell it 40 or more feet above and 300 miles away. It is not an invitation; they are not willful. This response is neither active nor inactive. His fingers almost tighten ever so slightly on her body, enough to confirm their bond without altering their energy, but he withholds the gesture. The Bear, he knows, would perceive even such a subtle move diverting their focus to each other and all would be lost. Still, there is a tsunami occurring because Lucas is also at this moment falling in love and the movement of these two distinct, coexistent and co-extensive plates is causing upheaval. And here comes the Bear into the current. Léonie is afraid even to lick her lips which are drying with anticipation, afraid she will inadvertently communicate this faint discomfort which implies a momentary focus on self rather than the other.

Unbeknownst to her, the Bear perceives everything but is unperturbed by their human distractions, whether manifested or undeclared. He has assessed the situation. They had been thinking their recent meeting was fated but this with Bear even more so. Where did she learn to be in Bear's presence? Oh yes, she has always dreamed Bear as you will learn soon. And he? He hasn't revealed this yet to Léonie or to La Vieja's intuitive knowing and powers of observation.

It only takes two ambassadors to make a covenant. Reassured by the calm in the forest, Léonie allows herself to turn her head to glance at Lucas whose profile is not yet familiar to her. Dark amber skin with golden highlights along his raised cheekbones. He has a large vision which can encompass her, the Bear and their location at the same time. And so she trusts him, his undivided but complex, attention. And the salmon he brought for their meal and as much again as an offering which he will drive far into the woods away from human habitat to a river to leave for the bear. A mystery gift from which he hopes he will have eliminated his scent.

"What do you want from the Bear?" she will ask him later.

"His intelligence," he will say. "I want to establish a bioethics that privileges him, not only includes him." Now we know his engagement with animals. "I want him to teach me how to do it." Damn, he thinks, that habit of speech, "to teach us, I mean, to teach us how to live."

* * *

July 4, 2020, 4:12 a.m., PDT, Planet Earth
"The Bears have come."

These words awakened me at 4:12 a.m. They asked me to accept a reality that challenges non-Indigenous humans. The Bears have come to La Vieja through the two who are below her, and in the ways her reality and mine intersect I am privy to her field of awareness, and so they have come to me.

Reflexively, I want to humbly refute this, as they didn't come to me, not in the ways the Elephants came or I was able, actually, to be with them in the wild, trunk to hand. Contact. Communication. Not in the way they came to Charlie Russell, the great and unparalleled Bear whisperer.

But, still, I can't deny what I just heard. 4:12 a.m. I hear these words and they repeat, again and again. The line startles me awake and then doesn't let me fall asleep again. The reality is startling and changes everything. If this is true—I have to accept it is—then we live in a world entirely different from the one we are trained to accept as real.

"The Bears have come" is what I heard. Meaning, "We are here." Meaning, pay attention and be respectful. Meaning, refusing to accept this out of false humility is an abdication of responsibility for a relationship that is critical for this time.

* * *

Two years ago, I put a Bear Crossing sign on the fence at the entrance to this land. It's a prayer, I said, hoping the Bears would return to this area for the first time since 1916. Coexisting would allow us to begin to make amends for thousands of years of cruelty which have turned a pacific species into one which is wary, on alert, territorial, protective and, when necessary, aggressive. Here come the two-legged murderers, the hunters. They deny us food. They kill us for sport. They shoot our babies in their caves. Watch out. Protect the little ones. We ask the Great Bear God, "How did You allow this to happen?"

Tonight I recognize that coming to La Vieja, coming to Léonie and Lucas, the Bears have come to me. We are in it together, the Bears, Léonie, Lucas, La Vieja and I. This is not a novel or a memoir. This is a record, as accurate as I can render of how it is, of how things are in the real world. In this world, the Bears are present, alert intelligences, coherent species, waiting for the barbarian two-leggeds to come to some inner order that will prevent the destruction of all life. Yes, the Bears have come but they are down below, and it is Léonie and Lucas who will meet them. Still, La Vieja up above, elevated so to speak, the Bears below will not be set apart.

Perhaps, despite her great longing, it has taken so many years for La Vieja to divest herself of the ways she had been trained, to consider the human a species apart, that watching from this perch is all that an old woman can do. She can watch and praise but if she descends the stairs as she longs to do and stands there too while the Bears approach, they would know she is not ready enough, her history prevents her from taking what would be the necessary step, to stand still without fear, to approach without approaching, to open without imposing, to yield entirely to the other beings who did not separate themselves from the divine intelligence which permeates all things.

Will La Vieja yield to the Bears the way I yielded to the Elephants?

The way, even now, I am hoping to yield to the Elephants?

To yield?

To follow their injunction: Yield to their knowing. Yield entirely to their knowing.

How do you do that?

I am trying to find out.

What are you trying to tell us?

That longing, not desire, is a holy path.

4

What you remember is saved ....
What you remember saves you.

W. S. Merwin
from "Learning a Dead Language"

I'm a woman of a certain age, as they say, living alone though most of my peers do not, at the end of a disheveled road that looks as worn and traveled as I do. My life is not so much a ride as the circumstances of someone who had been ridden.

I didn't think of myself as the old one until La Vieja appeared and I looked in the mirror—also of my soul—and clearly, I am. I have been nominated by an invisible tribunal and I know not to refuse. What I mean is that La Vieja appearing was a sign that I am not a young chicken any longer. I admired her fierce integrity, choosing solitude, living alone in the woods, daring winter and fires in order to put her aging to some use. I knew immediately I am not there, am not where she is, but I have to know something to be able to receive her story. It has to land somewhere. Where? I asked. Do we have any common ground and if not can I acquire a landing field for her? I have to be willing to understand what she is communicating to me, at least to set it down accurately. In order to do that which she awakening in me? What does her presence demand? I don't know the answer to that. Part of the knowing that comes with age is knowing what you don't know.

It's odd what is happening between us. She lets me know what I need to know so I can put it in language and tell her story and so I am directly influenced by her presence and it shifts me even if I don't quite know how. How could I not be affected by being privy to her thoughts and experiences?

I have to embody them in order to know their reality so that what I write is true not arbitrary.

I knew a woman once who claimed to channel Kwan Yin. She said women lined up to meet with her so that she could direct the great river of Kwan Yin's kindness through them and they would be healed by the direct energy of such insight and deep loving. They left healed, they attested, energized and inspired. But she was bitter. She said that it exhausted her to do this work. She resented having to respond to all the calls, she wanted to be free of having to serve, she wanted to return to her work as an animator, which required nothing of her but her skill at drawing. She wanted to be free of Kwan Yin. She refused to accept that the spirit of Kwan, passing through her, was bringing great healing to her. Once admitted, she would not ever cease the work. So she wanted it to pass through without her feeling the benefit she was transmitting, without being in the flow of compassion every moment she was gifting others. But she couldn't maintain distance indefinitely. Over time, she took down the barriers and her life shifted. When La Vieja appeared, I thought of my friend. Whatever came through me from La Vieja I vowed to accept.

What she knows of me, I don't know, other than I might be the right person to do this for reasons of my history; the Animal Orchestra or the Elephants are good examples; they may be how I qualified. I don't know what she knows and, frankly, I don't think she cares. There's an extreme discrepancy. I am entirely fascinated with her and she cares not a fig for me. Does this bother me? No. I am not interested in myself compared to my fascination, obsession even with her. So I am quite happy to eavesdrop, participate in surveillance, or listen for her transmissions, her psychic version of texting.

Much of my life has been spent this way, hearing voices or instructions, listening deeply and living accordingly. Only this time, I know who the sender is and so while this juncture in my life is not categorically different from earlier ones, it is critical since time at the end of this human or earthly cycle is reaching the vanishing point. I am very aware that La Vieja has appeared at this time of Covid-19, when we are definitely at a crossroads. I am also aware that she arrived when I put out a call for a story when nothing else was on the horizon. Accepting what came is a way of saying yes to a mandate that is vague and demanding while also facing aging and death simultaneously and not only my own. This is what she brings.

La Vieja

I am not the only one facing death and when I die it will be timely unlike so many, too many, you, possibly, who are facing unnatural deaths not in their time. The Earth is dying; too many may not live their full lives. We have blood on our hands.

La Vieja appeared and prompted me to ask: What does an old woman do at the end of her life? What does she do when all life is threatened?

> "An individual may be told she, he, is to die and will accept it. For the species will go on. Her or his children will die, and even absurdly or arbitrarily—but the species will go on. But that a whole species, or race, will cease, or drastically change—no, that cannot be taken in, accepted, not without a total revolution in the deepest self."

That's Doris Lessing writing in *Shikasta*, speaking to us from the grave.

My father died in a dying language. Heartbroken that he couldn't protect what he loved. Not ordinary heartbreak. *Hartzveitig*. That is how you say it in Yiddish. My father sat at its deathbed, urging it to breathe, to continue, to rally, to procreate before it left. He breathed into it, gave it his own breath, would have given it his last breath if it would have revived the language. And maybe he did. Maybe, subliminally he gave it up when he heard the news of the Challenger exploding on the TV in his room, unable to speak to the nurse to tell her that what was on television was the last thing a dying man wanted to hear. Yiddish, is what he wanted to hear.

He wouldn't have been concerned that the Challenger had exploded though he was dying and these were his dying companions. His vehicle was language and would have advised them to accept a similar voyage for their lives. He knew, regretfully, that another mission would be scheduled and that disturbed him. That we wouldn't know that the Challenger's failure that played and replayed, accompanying his dying, was a message that we had done enough harm on this planet and had better rectify it rather than going out to explore and populate the pristine universe with our current gift for havoc.

He had no words to tell the nurse or me to turn off the TV as he was looking for the passageway to God, the God he had sought his entire life and didn't want to miss this opportunity, finally, for connection. I was standing by his bed which at the end of his life resembled the crib we inhabit at the beginning, holding his hand, and not focused on anything but the reality that I was losing my father and wanted him to feel comforted by my presence. I didn't realize until much later that after spending a lifetime trying to shed all the impediments that his daily life insisted he had to attend before the holy, he certainly did not want his soul to arrive contaminated by the dregs he had worked to avoid. Maybe, as he exhaled that final breath which set all the alarms and bells off, he had breathed into her, into the *mamaloshen,* into the language, into Yiddish so she could go on a little longer, dancing and singing for God. Ecstatic.

What would I give my breath to so that it could survive, thrive? Maybe if I give it to the wolves and they survive and thrive, and nothing—which means no one—will ever interfere with their hegemony, then everything will be restored as a result, Elk, Deer, rivers, Salmon, grasslands, trees, all of it. I don't know how to do that. I would if I could. Wanting something like that may be why I am here, not hobbled in senior living, but peering out from a virtual lookout, tuning to La Vieja as she tries to see far into the past and future to give her breath to save creation. Only she doesn't talk about it in such terms. She's just living in the Lookout and looking around. But I believe I can read into her silence.

This old woman, La Vieja, maybe she follows what the myths say. Maybe she goes out to the edge of the world, as far as she can go to see if she will be granted a vision. She has no interest in preserving her own life. She has every interest in collaborating with whomever will join her to reverse the condition of beloved Earth.

It's an old story, someone goes out, risks his or her life on behalf of someone or something else. She hopes to bring back a potion or a vision. However, La Vieja knows that this time such a gesture will not be sufficient. No, we all have to go out in our own way and return to conjoin our offerings in a splatter of colors from which creation might be restored.

This is one of the offerings of the old woman, La Vieja.

* * *

So, where is the end of the known universe? Where does an old woman go? Her perch is on a rise some feet above the tallest trees on this highest ridge. It's 5,000 feet up. The Lookout itself is up another flight of stairs so nothing blocks her 360-degree view. When I began writing, I had to pay close attention to where she was and what I could glean of how she lived there alone. I was definitely influenced by her courage and willingness to live alone. I didn't have the courage myself, but I could live it vicariously, through her.

* * *

One day, I imagined it. I did everything I have learned to do to give myself entirely to the experience. In my imagination, I was living at such a Lookout but I couldn't maintain the fantasy for too long. I entered and was expelled and entered again and expelled.

OK. Here I am at the top, after many trips down and up again and everything sorted and in order, I know now from here that I will never return to my old life.

You have to understand. This is my, the writer's, virtual lookout. I would like to have the strength and fortitude to live in La Vieja's Fire Lookout for some weeks, months, the rest of my life in order to see, now, when hopefully I can discern the terrain of this time. But I don't. Not even for a single fire season. I didn't apply. I didn't want to hear the laughter as I tried to qualify. A woman? Very few women have been allowed into the club.

The first fire lookout ranger was a woman and then it became a formal position and the men took over for the most part though for a period of time there were a few women at it still, not with male partners, but on their own. And then none again.

These, I imagine are the questions one encounters when applying for the vanishing positions as the daily surveying has been taken up by small planes, helicopters and drones:

Can she bear solitude for long periods of time?
That I can do.
Can she deal with mice droppings?
Reluctantly.
Is she focused enough to look for signs of fire every hour and wake up to do so during extreme fire season?

Positive.
Meet a bear face to face?
My pleasure.
Drive a 4x4 up a non-existent road?
Sure.
Haul up water?
If I must. I just did.
Fix a hole in the roof? Lift, axe or chain saw a large fallen tree?
Unlikely.

Nevertheless, here we go. I am beginning to climb. It's hard and I am tiring, as I might have had I walked from a long distance to this most remote Lookout and then climbed these stairs at this altitude to the wooden deck which I will circle before entering the small rooms I will inhabit forever, for where indeed will an aging woman go afterwards?

I won't be able to do this unless I can imagine my way, struggling up toward the entry to my future sky house, walking along the planks of the surrounding deck saturated with fire retardant. I stop there. We're facing east. It is late afternoon, the leaves and needles on the trees below are beginning to turn gold.

I am very, very tired. Only midway. I will certainly be fit when I can do this every day. Biology demands it. The outhouse is below and a ways. A small shelf extends from the banister where I can put down these packages, rest, get my binoculars out of the pocket of this (traceable) down vest and have a preliminary glance at my local habitat before I stretch to see the entire globe at once, because that's the goal, isn't it? Take a sip of water … and then … continue up?

Or withdraw?
Climb.

*   *   *

Since I met La Vieja I have begun preparing for dying. I think she wants to be entirely aware at her age and to let nothing block her view and so I consider how to do the same. The view of what is and what was and what will be. To see across the still living treetops into the dispersion that we call death. It has taken me eighty plus years to come to such a perspective and only by trying to read her mind. I think she believes it is her final job to observe from the vantage point of farsight and age and then to tell what she sees. No. I don't think she is going to tell what she sees. That's my job but I'm not there.

Here's the problem. She's there and I am just writing. She is really there and I am not, but I am telling it as best as I can. Someone has to.

I call this, Bearing Witness. It's the necessary step at her age toward living mindfully: Bear Witness. Engage in rigorous scrutiny of self and world, past and present. Remember. Be ruthless about your regrets and many failures. Be ruthless about our culture's many failures. Then vision. Restore what has been wrongfully injured, eradicated and despised. Restore the natural world in its luminous and limitless complexity. The job of the elder is to remember how it was once before we destroyed it. To remember and to restore. To remember and to restore. I am trying to live up to it. It's a hard task.

"It'll kill you" she says.

I guess that's the idea.

I met her and that's why I'm here. I also searched a long time until I found the perfect Fire Lookout where it would be my work also to be awake. When I consider the circumstances, not La Vieja's story but the story I am in with her, it seems obvious that I came to this Lookout at the behest of the Invisibles who have been with me for my entire life though I was not always aware of their presence. But they did put their mark on me early on as my first memory is of a figure of light.

At the foot of my crib—a woman composed entirely of light. Her substance was light. A body of light. A luminous woman. She said nothing and did nothing. I opened my eyes and met her eyes, composed of light, and full of light. Something I needed to know in order for my life to progress as it was determined it could. Light is. Knowing this, I determined to live accordingly. The woman of light appeared and obligated my entire future.

I have told this story before and there may be many retellings of old stories in this manuscript. There has already been much repeating and there will be more. It is deliberate. Part of being old is repeating, is retelling the stories, not because you're dotty and can't remember you've told it before, but because you're a little wiser than you were when you thought everything had to be new and original (and so discardable or forgettable). As one ages, one learns which essential stories have to be told again and again so they will never be forgotten, so they can be passed on to the next generation to forge a life. And anyway, they are never the same story, no more than you are ever in the same stream.

I will need, we need, a really large view in order to bear witness. Here are the stairs to climb for the far view. They're formidable. If you really want something, then you have to make an offering and that usually means some sacrifice. It isn't an offering if it is easy. If you're rich, don't only give money as an offering; it won't count. (But do give money, a lot of it, to restore justice.)

After the civil war had decimated Liberia, a village woman told us she had dreamed her husband would be captured and killed by the rebel forces. She understood the dream came as a warning. In order to prevent this fate, she had to make a sacrifice.

"What is a sacrifice?" we asked.

"A sacrifice is giving more than one can possibly afford."

Those of us who are dreaming the climate collapse are being warned of what could be coming. The dream spirits or the earth spirits want a sacrifice. And what is the sacrifice? Giving more than we can possibly afford. Giving more than we have been giving. Giving differently than we have been giving.

How do we know what to give?

La Vieja has gone to her Lookout to find an answer, her answer. And I am listening to her at this virtual Lookout to discover what my sacrifices should be.

The task La Vieja has given herself is like writing this book. I will only find out what it is going to be while listening to her and then writing it. She will only find out when she is there. Plans and outlines limit the possibilities, make for a predictable story. It won't help us now. We have done everything we know how to do. The predictable or the already known is not our way. I can't see where I'm going when I start out and continue blind every step of the way. When I come to the end then, there we are: the end. Surprise!

I am looking at the slight curve of the highest branch of the closest tree below that is attempting to reach to the sun. There has never in the history of the world been a branch such as this, nor a tree like the one from which it springs, yes, springs because it has bounce in the wind and sometimes when night falls on it hard, it dips and flows like water. Never before and never again will such a being leap to the heavens in awe of the holy, the sun and the dark light.

I may know something when this undertaking is well underway or not until it's over. Or never. I might never know as there are no guarantees that one leaves this Earth in a blaze of understanding, one's last chapter summing everything up. Had I really thought that might be the case? It's a writer's folly, if she expects that everything written over the years will organize itself into a final revelation that makes the entire damned journey worthwhile.

Uh-oh. Truth telling: Sometimes as I begin this, I don't know which one of us is speaking, whether it is me, the Writer or La Vieja. I tell myself it could be either one of us but I know she's so far ahead of me and she's real and my perch is imagined. Still why try to distinguish us except that I have to remember that we occupy different spaces—and that may not be correct either. So let's not effort to distinguish us as we are immersed in the same field, that mysterious realm I first experienced with the Elephants. There is no other explanation for the ways we communicated or met over the years but that we permeated or were permeated by a reality formed by interconnection or inter-penetration.

Confession: Earlier, this manuscript had a different name because I was unwilling, too shy, embarrassed perhaps to consider a title like *La Vieja*. It wasn't vanity that kept me from writing about the old woman but rather the opposite. I was afraid it was vanity to claim to know anything of her. No matter which. My feelings are unimportant. I am also an old woman. I am facing that. The times are grim. I was born shortly after the descent we are in began with WW I. I was born just before Guernica caused some in the Western world to realize we were losing our ethical compass though so many had known this forever, since 1492 on this territory, far, far earlier in other places, Europe, for example.

I was born at the time, three years before the Hitler-Stalin pact. I knew what I was getting into from the beginning. I came in with a purpose and now at the end of my life I am asking myself—Am I meeting my mandate and my soul's commitment?

Whew! That's a question. I haven't spoken those words to myself before. Ever. I have asked myself and others, again and again, What is your calling?

I haven't asked, have I met—am I meeting—my soul's commitment?
Have I?
Am I?
Excuse me. I have to stop and take a breath.

Begin again. La Vieja is living in a Fire Lookout in the Sierras. And I am on a virtual retreat, sometimes trying to imagine being where La Vieja is. But I am not. I am in Topanga, California, where the mountains meet the sea. For 180 degrees, I do not see another house as I look onto the hills, to the patches of grasses, Chamise, Sage, Bay Laurel, Black Walnut and Scrub Oak. Montane chaparral. The parkland is wild and dense, and very vulnerable to fire. My perch is a dry corner where the earth is so hard it takes a pickaxe to make the smallest indentation to plant something as it is caliche, and when it rains, it is equally thick, heavy, impenetrable mud.

Today, the wind, which has increasingly taken up residence on a daily basis, is swaying the Eucalyptus trees on the patio where the ones who built this cottage must have planted them. The Diné (Navajo) must have a word for this exact wind event. The Jays are at the bird feeders and dipping their bills into the water at the bird bath. A Goldfinch has come to the Buddha fountain. Two Squirrels clamber up the bougainvillea and the red bracts flutter to the ground.

It is too hot to have a fire in the woodstove and too dangerous to have a fire in the firepit next to the Buddha fountain. A candle can substitute for a sacred fire if it must. A sacred fire, a call to the spirits, an affirmation of the life force, the heart of the world. I will have to keep it lit within me because fire has been abused and has become rageful. Queen Corona and La Vieja say it is time to stop. Stop and be present and ask while everything is in the present moment of the continuous presence, Am I/are we fulfilling our soul's commitment at this moment?

* * *

Looking out from this vantage point, it is still likely I am already seeing it as you are and at the same time, unlikely that I will ever sight the fire that is/will take us all down. Likely I/we will remain helpless before it, will not see it because it's everywhere and continuous although it is not the eternal light.

Two concurrent events—the virtual lookout among the trees, maybe in the Sierras, and this place of lockdown in Southern California. For the moment, I am carrying my bundles and making my way up the remaining stairs. I've transported 80 glass gallons of water up these steps, gallon by gallon. In the winter, I will melt snow.

I never imagined myself, as have some friends, men and Buddhists particularly, as a hermit in a cave with paper, pen and sake, sliding poems over the boulders and out with my last breath although I did long to be a crone at the edge of the forest, whom others come to visit when conventional approaches to a great problem do not serve and they are in need of another point of view, in need of someone who remembers.

I fantasized an old woman living a contented life with some old Dogs and maybe a Goat alongside me. More desirable, a small Wolf pack, two Foxes, male and female, a Mountain Lion at the perimeter, the inevitable murder of Crows, an unkindness and conspiracy of Ravens, all of whom will provide the company I need as my eyes sharpen or dim. Maybe this hermitage isn't far away from that crone image.

5

I know you are reading this poem which is not in your language
guessing at some words while others keep you reading
and I want to know which words they are.

I know you are reading this poem listening for something, torn
between bitterness and hope
turning back once again to the task you cannot refuse.

I know you are reading this poem because there is nothing else
left to read
there where you have landed, stripped as you are.

Adrienne Rich
From "Dedications"

Despite everything I have written so far we are living in the assumption that there will be a future, and there may not be. No matter how rigorous I am, I can't face extinction and annihilation. How do I write this sentence so that we understand what is being said, the implications and consequences? Why is it being repeated again and again? Because it repeats again and again, the way an atrocity, enacted or witnessed repeats in the traumatized mind, in the veteran who has continuous traumatic stress disorder which is not a disorder, but a grave injury. Extinction is the unhealable wound.

* * *

Topanga is my real lookout. If I walk outside to the meadow and go up the incline to the east, I will not only see the sun and the moon rise, but will have an unimpeded view for several miles in all directions from this high ridge of the canyon in the Santa Monica Mountains. Toward the south is a wilderness park of 10,600 acres or 16.5 square miles and below to the west, one road divides the canyon for fifteen miles ending in the suburban flatland of the San Fernando Valley and beginning twelve miles to the south at the Pacific Ocean. When I stand here, I can see far back in the past to the Wooly Mammoths, Dire Wolves· Sabre-toothed Cats, Short-faced Bears, Horses and Pterodactyls making their way from these heights down to the sea. Mastodons are romping in the waves the way Elephants like to do when they have a chance, wading out to meet the Whales as they did before white humans settled Cape Town. One of the last places Wooly Mammoths survived was St. Paul Island in Alaska because it is said there were no killer humans there.

From this lookout, I can see back but I can't see forward. The smoke in the air obscures the view to the future.

Wooly Mammoths. Elephant ancestors. I have been finding my kin, looking for my People. Family, not only within the narrow kinship network of blood and DNA, but the larger but not less connected field of relatives. Elephants, Wolves, Bears. These I am certain about. It's an old road we have been walking and burning up behind us. Yes, standing here, I still have a long view back and a standing need to watch for fires. I am staying here until I die.

* * *

It isn't quite a year since I was packing my car in December to drive to Alameda when I read that the Topanga Coalition for Emergency Preparedness had posted potential evacuation plans on their website. "If the Skirball fire jumps the 405 Freeway and starts heading west: put whatever you will want to take with you by the door and place your car in position to drive out of your house at a moment's notice." It was the requirement to have the car ready and pointed south that alerted me. There was room in the car and I quickly added two copies of each of the books I've written, the crystal necklaces my mother strung which I have been keeping for my children and grandchildren and an Eagle feather, my sacred prayer pipe and, at the last minute, the skins I sleep with, Wolf, Bear and Buffalo. A drum. I took a Bear fetish, several Elephant fetishes, the Tanzanian Elephant goddess with her skirt of cowry shells that you pray to when all else has failed, a turquoise Eagle fetish, an Eagle whistle, the fan of Owl feathers that an

Elder made for me, and an Inuit Mantic Owl, her wings/arms spread to protect the world. To protect the world....

And so it seems right that I choose to inhabit a virtual Fire Lookout at this time in my life. Fire season, which used to mean September and October, starts in June and can go until December. I don't know, it may never cease, given climate change and drought. And so we are always on the lookout. Lookout! Fire! Or Fire! Look out! Perpetual alert.

* * *

A virtual lookout and also not a virtual lookout. Imaginary as my climb to the Lookout may be, it is also not virtual. A call and mandate, wherever and whenever they are realized, are the same and so equally arduous and challenging. I adhere to the understanding that the imagination is a real place and to be respected as such. So this is a test of a creative ordeal. I expect I will encounter sufficient cold and physical hardship and at least as much loneliness, disorientation as needed to first dissolve into chaos and then to be reconstituted in the hope of attaining the clear vision that solitude can offer.

Being healthy and of sound mind, the quest is to examine the past and the initial calling and to see what I understood on the life journey and what I might need to be complete. What I have the capacity to realize I couldn't have imagined when I was young and formed by that luminous figure of light standing silently at the foot of my bed in Brighton Beach, Brooklyn, NY, USA, planet Earth in May of 1939, the month Germany and Italy announced the Rome-Berlin axis, Churchill signed the British-Russian anti-Nazi pact, and Hitler proclaimed he would move into Poland.

Four months later, Germany and Russia agreed to a non-aggression pact and my father collapsed in a catatonic state and had to be carried home, his stiff body maneuvered through the side entryway, stepping in, turning left two steps past the door to the basement and up one step and right up three steps, and left into the hallway and left again to the living room, where the three men set him down on the green pinstriped velour couch. Seeing he was home, noting his apricot satin chair with the smoking table alongside holding the round brass ashtray and the wood container filled with Camel cigarettes, a book of matches nearby, becoming aware of his desk (which is now in my living room, facing the Eucalyptus trees) facing the window to his garden with the cherry tree laden with sour cherries that month of August 1939, underneath which was the card table where he set his papers early morning, every weekend morning, to write and then observing that I was studying him, curious and concerned, my father recovered. Only to re-experience the trauma again and again, days in a row, for the next six years. Over time the horror of what was happening seeped so deeply into his understanding, it acted as an antidote to his fear and he roused himself, as I am doing now, to write.

Co-incidence of events: the appearance of the figure of light alongside the great darkness that took my father and the world down. As if the horrors occurring on the Earth were occurring in his body. I brace myself: the glaciers are melting, so is the ice in Antarctica and Greenland, the barrier reefs where all fish life is sustained are bleaching, the temperature is rising drastically, 132 degrees Fahrenheit in Furnace Creek today, methane is being released from the melting permafrost, the seas are polluted by mountains of plastic and microplastics and microfibers are poisoning the earth and the air, and it is said they will end the viability of human male sperm by 2050. The Pacific is radioactive, the water ways are polluted with every pharmaceutical we take and excrete forming a highly potent toxic cocktail. There are too many supersites to clean up or count and a variety of manufactured electronic waves are destroying the fine electrical balance upon which life depends.

* * *

It doesn't come from the south. It comes from the north. The Fire starts within or just outside of a Superfund Radiation site. An electric transformer breakdown—the same cause as that of the Camp Fire. The Fire erupted and spread so fast it was suggested we evacuate voluntarily within the next few hours and I obliged. Perhaps it was the killing of our beloved 21 year old Noel Sparks by the Thousand Oaks Vietnam war veteran that told me danger is everywhere and I didn't need to use up the resources for a rescue when there was nothing of the fire I could see from this perch that I couldn't see from an urban setting. The radiation released is invisible, is as undetectable as is any concern in the aftermath of the ongoing danger to everyone within a hundred miles, as invisible as any responsibility we are taking for these fires, these grave woundings of the ecosystem upon which we depend.

6

> At no time in our history have we looked toward the natural
> world, especially toward the social behavior of animals, to under-
> stand that we are a species in evolutionary transition and that
> we are out of control. We have focused on separating ourselves
> from animals rather than looking at them as models that have
> been molded and shaped by five hundred million yeas of bit-by-bit
> development. Until we are able to get over ourselves, we will pro-
> ceed down the path of a technology-driven arms race that may in
> the end be just that: the end. Understanding the common denom-
> inator of human behavior could, in the end, save us from our
> own technology.
> To think this way requires hope.
>
> Benjamin Kilham
> *In the Company of Bears*

I watch the old wolf, Shoonaq', who is fourteen and content to lie on a mattress on the porch, watching the passing wildlife, Quail, Rabbit, Coyote, Bobcat, and, these days, growling at anyone who tries to pass across the boundary of the land marked by a chain-link fence that opens to allow passage up and down the narrow road, but only now because of the pandemic to those invited. She almost never challenged anyone before, certainly not with a growl, but Covid-19 has arrived, and the entrances to the parks are closed. We live at the end of the road; Shoonaq' is guarding the territory, enforcing the edict.

Shoonaq' was watching the territory until she passed on 6/23/2021, her legs collapsing under her after such a long life.

From this perch, I can see across a broken field of fire to Africa. Every area has fires burning that we have set: pilot lights, chimneys, smoke stacks, stoves, cigarettes, lighters and matches struck, candles lit for the living and the dead, churches alight with prayer, synagogues with eternal flames, houses, apartment buildings burning, factories exploding, blast furnaces making steels and welders bending metals, furnaces burning coal, woodstoves and natural gas heaters, forges, barbecues and thousands of Bunsen burners in laboratories. Not to mention the fields and forests burning and at this very moment of writing this, Thursday, July 25, 2019, there are 1,639 active fires in the US, and lightning is striking the Earth 100 times a second while a tiny asteroid is burning up, bright as the full moon, before it falls to the ground. And here comes the sun.

* * *

January 6, 2020
Epiphany. I was alarmed by the fires this summer when I was writing this chapter, but six months later greater alarm has been sounding. On January 6th rains finally began to fall in Australia where three billion animals have died due to the catastrophic bush fires which burned 18.6 million hectares and it seems one billion shell fish died in the sea in the extreme temperatures of this week's heat wave. We are in The Fire Next Time.

* * *

Where am I? I am not at the Lookout or the virtual Lookout. I am in my car on that road that is the only entrance and exit to the canyon. For fifteen miles, the cars are not moving. After I wrote the above paragraph, I looked out the window of the studio to see smoke billowing up and then a helicopter circling overhead and heard the sirens of fire engines. Then as the phone started ringing with the local emergency alert, I grabbed the dog GentleBoy, my purse and passport, this computer and flew down the road, not sure I could get out the only narrow road to the main highway where a van had exploded and set fire to the brush between the main road and my house. Three squad cars and a cop on a motorcycle sped past me to warn all the residents on this canyon inlet as I turned left on Highway 27 (only one lane in each direction) toward the ocean and pulled over to the side of the road reassured by the presence of many fire trucks and police vehicles. A neighbor gave me water and a cup for GentleBoy. And here we are. I didn't leave the canyon. Where is there to go? I want to be with the trees with whom I have lived for 38 years! If I can't fully protect them, I can be with them in their fate.

I acquired this house on April 1, 1981 after driving up the precarious, narrow, muddy road to view the property. The brick patio was flanked by the Eucalyptus trees. I sat in the living room that dreary rainy afternoon and thought, "I can look at these trees for the rest of my life." And I have and so I cannot leave them now.

In a few hours, we are assured, the fire will be out and I will be home and then I will return to my perch. Truly, we can't give up the overview, even if we have to leave the area. In other words, let's not pretend the world isn't on fire.

In response to the fire, I could feel the roots of the Eucalyptus trees alongside my patio withdraw from the burning soil five hundred feet away. Then I perceived the distinct movements of the jacaranda, the peppers, the oaks, then the orange, lemon, grapefruit trees in the orchard, closer to the fire, almost as close as the walnuts. Then against my will, I felt the alarm of the trees of heaven which, propagating by extending their roots and rising from them, feel particularly vulnerable.

These were subtle gestures, a slight recoil, a miniscule increase in the gnarl, like watching a vein in the back of an old hand contorting in time lapse photography, then the hairy tendrils reached down more deeply than they usually do to garner whatever water and minerals were in the soil from about 100 feet of the trunk. The root systems responded differently but in unison as the different trees have root systems at different levels. The black walnuts we planted were at the front lines but they are also the hardiest in relationship to the fire. Even if they burn, young though they are, only eight years old, they might have some resilience and can recover and begin growing again like their neighbors up the hill, the scrub oaks.

Those people who had evacuated and were gathered alongside the road were talking among themselves about how tired they/we are of being evacuated. We had all spent eight days away from our houses last November, though some had sneaked in the back way after it looked like the Woolsey Fire was not going jump into the canyon. It was dicey to come back into a threatened canyon without electricity or phone service. You had to tune in to clues we as modern people no longer rely on but which nevertheless seem to resurrect even as some of the trees would. There was no way of predicting who would live and die no more than we would know if or why a certain house would remain standing in a grove of other houses all of which were taken down.

I stood apart from the clutches of conversation trying to listen to the non-humans who were threatened by the very slow rise of flames up the hill. There was no wind, fortunately and we had a few hours before sunset and, at the very least, the inevitable breezes that would occur when the temperature fell and the warm air rose, preceded by that absolutely still moment, the freeze frame before the shift, before the birds pick up again, before the dark hints at its approach, before the wind fans the flames and carries the embers where it will. No wind and no traffic now and so in the seething spaces between the long spouts of chemical pink fire retardant drops, there appeared very brief and intermittent silences in which a sensate mycorrhizal tension before possible oblivion is detectable.

The singularity of a slow and languid fire was rising up while the complexity of soil withdrew into itself, feeling the threat from the heat, from that hunger which was fed by what it devoured, and wondered if it, and so its symbiotic partners, would survive. Wondered? Considered? Contemplated? Soil did that? Having no awareness of the nature of the non-human, we do not have language for the indisputable visceral tension that arose when such a fragile and careful balance as they had maintained together, from season to season, year after year, was threatened. When it was only in relationship that they could be.

And then, as if the sky had opened, which indeed it had, but from a metal mouth and not a filament of cloud, but still rain, hard, narrow and violent fell upon the fire and extinguished it. Again and again. What did they think, those tender microbes, those delicate hairy filaments, around which in this imperceptible reflex to survive, a single particle of sand or soil might rearrange itself as the life under the earth adjusted to what might be coming—and the strange onslaught of fire and water—bam, bam, bam.

And now a remarkable intersection of worlds, as the dictionary consulted for synonyms for "endangered" yields only "endangered as related to vulnerable, plant life, plant and flora". And, similarly, "threatened": "words related to threatened, *adj.* (of flora or fauna) likely in the near future to become endangered."

That which is considered to be fixed, like words on a page, or definitions written in stone, becomes malleable and responsive to hidden thoughts. Nothing fixed then. And how could anything maintain rigidity in the presence of water and fire. Or earth, as that moment revealed. Or, air, that is, or wind. Of the elementals then. Nothing fixed and everything in movement.

I ascend to my lookout. It isn't a lookout so much as a listening site. I am listening deeply to what is beyond words. I watch the meeting of fire and water. How did the fire originate? A car, a combustion engine, an imprisoned fire, an old spirit's bones turned to oil is taken from the earth and burned and, in turn, it burned the earth. So much oil burns that the rain disappears. Earlier the rain was in the sky but now we have to fetch it from the ocean in a metal scoop; it comes down like a pillar of salt. The water disperses as does the fire. Still they interpenetrate each other.

We are not of such interconnections, though we should be, we once were. I waited in my car at the foot of the burning hill. A van had overheated and exploded and set the hill on fire. Later, I drove up the road in my (hybrid, but still) 4x4 to my house. We are a species apart with our inanimate if sometimes mobile carapaces. The fire was naked and I was not.

* * *

I return to my perch, to scan the broken field of fire in front of me all the way to Africa. Behind me, the Pacific Ocean is burning, invisibly, with radiation. But there is only one ocean and that ocean is everywhere, on the Earth, in the clouds, in the mist that pads on its spirit feet through the canyon as the sun begins to set. The ocean is also in the clouds and the rain, and in the water you drink and release, and so it is in our bodies, yours and mine. One ocean despite the illusion that the hemisphere, like a great god, seems to have parted the waters as they cannot be divided from each other no more than a series of locks that control a surgical scar on the Earth can connect them.

From this perch I can see far but I can also see close. The sun is a white light overhead. GentleBoy has just scooped out a shallow cool bed under the Eucalyptus trees. A neighbor suggested I cut down the grove of Eucalyptus trees, the very ones I moved here to be among and all the pines, the holiday trees that we planted as well. The neighbor expects they will become 150-foot-high living torches if a fire strikes them. But I cannot cut them down, even though the environmental purists have cut down the magnificent arcade in the newly designated state park that called us to a long walk and is now bare, flat, empty and of no interest to songbirds or humans. The righteous ones keep up a monotonous complaint about the immigrant trees and the indigenous Coyotes and Cougars, all of whom they want gone.

I didn't want to leave the trees when the fire started two weeks ago. I felt the same way yesterday, when writing, yet again, as I do now about fire, and saw smoke billowing up, traveling on the ever-present wind from another direction this time, from the southeast corner of the park in a direct line, 2.5 miles, from seven burning acres to this land. I packed the car again, just in case, as I had before, adding water and a dish for the dog and the same box of the books I have written, and settled down to wait. The birds gathered so I filled every feeder with seeds and every basin with water and we waited together—the Blue Jays, the covey of Quails, about thirty of them, the family of four red-headed Woodpeckers—the last I have seen of them—several couples of Mourning Doves. Then the fire was quenched.

I texted my friend, Sharon Simone. I am in solitude but I don't want to be alone with this and so walk a fine line, the fire line, between solitariness and camaraderie. Sharon is a Diviner. I want to know what she understands from this second fire event in a few days, occurring each time when I was writing about fire, about being on a Lookout, about watching for fire.

She writes:

> In response to the fire text just now: I looked at FIRE above the MOUNTAIN: (In other words, she reads the landscape and translates it into a hexagram from the I Ching)
>
> ### #56 Sojourning At The Borders: A Quest
>
> You are outside the network on a quest of your own. Mingle with others as a stranger whose identity comes from a distant center. Adapt to whatever crosses your path. Be willing to travel and search alone. You are on a mission of real importance. It will turn the expansive awareness of the whole into a stabilizing inner restraint.
>
> Circle of Meanings: "A seeker and a quest, the wandering sage who establishes relations with the shadow lands; journeys, voyages outside the norms, staying in places other than your home, exile, beyond the frontiers, soldiers on a mission, those who "travel the roads." An inner field that supports changing awareness.
>
> #55:56 Pair: **Abounding And Sojourning** display the hidden connection between the New King who receives Heaven's Mandate and the Wandering Sage who sojourns

in the Shadow Lands to make the new connections. ELE-
MENTALS.

One more quote FROM #56:

This is a REALIZING figure, part of a zone of radical
transformation when the Bright Omens that guide people's
lives become Flying Words that carry them across the
threshold of life and death. It is an experience of the Cen-
ters of Power in the stage of the symbolic life when we
must deal with power and our responsibilities to the human
community.

Every line resonates. I am, La Vieja is, we are outside the network on
quests of our own. We have to be willing to accept the solitary quest which is
in part a search for *expansive awareness of the whole.* Does she not have a *mandate,* this *wandering sage,* who has appeared here? I don't know about the *sage*
in myself, but La Vieja in her *wandering* or in her *aloneness,* in her solitariness
is seeking wisdom though she wouldn't say this herself. And here she is
leaving the familiar, *wandering, seeking,* and daring herself to explore *the
shadow lands,* the darkness of this time. And this takes us into another way
of being, the way we used to know, when the spirits and the beings who
are always connected included us, the two-leggeds, before we pulled away.
And now she dares to cross that *border* again, *to make new connections.* Welcome,
La Vieja.

This is my second day of silence but really the first. I came to this
Lookout to spend 17 days in solitude. On day one the fire broke out but
today has been quiet, except for another car fire which did not set the hills
ablaze. The stillness in my heart as I give up speaking and connecting to
the human world, seems to be echoed by the stillness of the land, except
there is also an emerging concert, with every species winding its own song
through the lyricism of the others. The resonant longing of the Doves and
the honeyed insistence of the Quail, pierced by Blue Jay. Here comes the
silent Hummingbird whirring in the flowering blue and the thub-thub of
the Thrasher drinking.

I am standing here looking for signs of life and vitality that advise us
what we must divest from and what we must protect. An unexpected memory rises. It comes from a time when I began to recognize animal intelligence, seeing evidence of what our culture assumed were only human be-

haviors. Walking through a rainforest in Costa Rica, I had seen four black Guans perched on a branch, their feathers the color of night and their faces the color of sky. They nodded to us as we stumbled down a darkening path lit only by Fireflies. They were peacefully observing the last rays of the setting sun. It was, we were certain, their evening ritual. Their meditative presence had reassured us. Perhaps their greeting implied we would be welcome in their nests of leaves if we were as faithful to ceremony as they were.

Soon night will fall here. Let the new moon rise in the sky that is fjord blue and clear as the North Pole. There is Orion. And the Pleiades. A world is dying but perhaps it can be reborn. Let it be summer solstice and new moon. We will not light a bonfire here though I have seen such at the Arctic Circle when the sky turned black as the light was born. There was a pile or pyre of what no longer served which was topped by a small fishing boat, twenty feet long. It no longer served the old man who had built and used it and wouldn't serve a younger one even if there were enough cod to make fishing worthwhile. It was a few hours before the solstice itself which would be at 3:30 a.m. but there would be little difference in light so far north except the sun that had slid behind the mountains was appearing through a wide pass in the rocky scimitar of land reaching to the sea when dark clouds stampeded the small slit causing night to slam down. For an instant, the stars were visible and startlingly brilliant, as if in another reversal, the frosted crests of the icy winter sea were in the sky but then in a few minutes they were wiped out again or rotated by the sun's sweep upwards, and the constant light of summer was restored.

I have spent my life among the elementals, and so I know fire and light, not their irrelevant physics or chemistries, but the way you know a being, its character, its spirit and soul, its deep nature, its heart. Shall we then, in our hearts, burn the old year, our old lives, our benighted uncivilization and begin again? And when we do so, what essential activity is engaged by offering the past to a conscious fire? Can we cooperate in the restoration of balance between flame and rain?

Perhaps, I am not up here looking for danger so much as seeking the return of an old companionship our peoples once knew. We met with the Bushmen each morning when they came to a retreat in Big Bear, California, just before they won legal access to their own land but I don't know if they were in fact able to return. We got up just before dawn and sat by their fire, smoking cigarettes, watching each other's red glow. They told stories and we told stories. But we didn't speak among ourselves, and certainly not to others, about the moment we danced the rain prayer together until the first drops began to fall just prior to being called to the opening session of the gathering when the rain would come generously that month of the terrible drought. There was nothing to do but to skip and leap into the meeting hall, our clothes wet, our skin shining with moisture, all eyes bright. You don't speak of such things, but you note that the spirits received our prayers.

Years before, I had dreamed a rain dance, and as I was young, I violated the covenant which I hadn't known I had made. Maybe I wasn't responsible for the weeklong torrential rain and terrible flood but, secretly, I had to take responsibility so that I might learn how to deal with power and from then on be humble and cautious, only following spirit's call without naively initiating what I thought might be a good idea.

Because the Bushmen were there, because they are rainmakers, it was possible to consciously remember the rain dance and so bring forth the possibility that it might be successful and a good thing for all, the humans, the non-humans, the trees, the Earth. I think the spirits wanted us to recognize that the Bushmen had kept up their relationship with the sacred and that such devotion might result in a connection between the spirits, the Earth, the rain, all the beings who benefited, and also with the humans. When you pray for something, the prayer has to be secured by a durable bond with the spirits that you have tended for years. The genuineness of the relationship can't be feigned—because the spirits know. We all prayed together, but it was their prayer, thousands of years old and based on reciprocity and a divine contract, which brought the rain.

Yes, as a young woman, I had dreamed a rain dance. Then I did the rain dance. Harm came. The first principle—first do no harm.

Ah, here we are tiptoeing toward the future and Lucas' concerns. Lucas? You will meet him soon. He's a physician, not doing harm is his concern, is a vow that he's taken.

Many years after the first debacle, but when I was older and wiser, I that did the rain dance again. The first violation had taught me not to utilize such powers and I refrained for many years. I had learned never to invoke the energy of the elementals without clear instructions in the moment from the spirits yet the possibility remained in my awareness as the times of drought increased. Non-Indigenous do-gooders without elders, a community and a culture to support and restrain, can cause great harm. This time I had permission from a Native American elder.

I was visiting a medicine woman at Lukachukai. There was a terrible drought. We spoke about it. I offered the dance. She thought about it. Only, if she made the request ... I would. She did. I went out into the field, away from the hogan and began. Soon there was lightning flashing in the far distance. When it began to rain lightly and after my gray silk blouse was soaked, she came to me gently and called me to the small fire we had set together. It was good to be warm when the rain was falling at the perimeter of our shelter. "A female rain," she said. "That's what we need. No more." The rain came because of her devotion.

* * *

La Vieja walked out to the rail, even though the rain was streaming from the dark clouds. There in the distance, lightning struck a pine which flared skyward, one fire descending and one fire rising up. After thinking about it she lowered the hood of her rain jacket.

* * *

You understand by now, that as this is being written over a period of years, I often go back to what was written before and continue, perhaps for weeks, before leaving for another roost. While writing this text, I am oriented, not to chronology, but to time itself as it wiggles and waggles back and forth although we insist it travels in a straight line and without wavering and without hindsight or foresight It doesn't matter whether the two small fires, the Cheney fire and the Palermo fire succeeded each other within two weeks, which they did, or whether they occurred in separate years, and blended in thought if not in literal reality with the Woolsey Fire although it itself had incorporated several other fires and didn't need any more heat or conflagrations. Keeping everything separate and distinct seems unimportant because when we meet, we dissolve in the field of each other, time flows like a river splitting and combining in all directions.

More than anything I wish you could see the light of the setting sun on the thin red bark of the Eucalyptus that is one of six sprouting trunks from a single core, the shaggy, craggy bark of the twisted core to the west, and the naked core to the east, all in all six sisters shapeshifting between girls, snakes and species.

*   *   *

I didn't know that the path to Elsewhere when one is my age is not direct, but can circle or traverse the realm of the elementals so we can see what is most essential at the very, very end.

7

It is believed that animal nature helped to create humans and
that animals have always served as humanity's mentors in coming
to know the nature of the world.

Gregory Cajete
Native Science: Natural Laws of Interdependence

I had wanted to meet Lawrence Anthony when I learned of him and
the wild animal preserve he had founded at Thula Thula in South
Africa. Later, he had gotten the understanding or the message, the
gut knowing, the insight, the urge, the great idea, the light bulb going off,
that as the Americans were invading Iraq, the animals in Saddam Hussein's
zoo needed care or they would die terrible deaths, the best of which would
be being eaten. Immediately, he boarded an airplane and made his way to
Babylon, that is Baghdad, shrewdly engaged American military support,
protection, trucks and food that allowed him to save many of the animals
that Hussein had collected in the Baghdad zoo. I wanted to talk with him
when I read in his book, *The Last Rhinos: My Battle to Save One of the World's
Greatest Creatures* of his being "drafted" by Joseph Kony of the Lord's Resistance Army who controlled a preserve which had just become a war
zone. Kony invited him—if a demand from a warlord made directly by
one of his associates can be considered an invitation—to broker peace
under UN auspices between Kony's forces and the Ugandan government
in return for Kony protecting the last Rhinos who resided there, already
critically endangered by poachers. Anthony traveled, as required, unaccom-
panied and unarmed to Kony's secret camp and forthwith did broker the
deal which, however, did not last long because the Ugandan government

would not be receiving funds from the US unless it was at war. And it needed the money.

But what had truly drawn me to Anthony was that he had spent all night, each night, for several months directly outside the boma enclosing the Elephants he had rescued so that they would begin to trust him, would perceive with their extreme sensitivity who he was, and over time accept that he had brought them to his land in order to save their lives. He understood when they first broke out of the makeshift enclosure he had erected, they were suffering the trauma of being removed from their own sacred land after a rancher threatened to shoot them because they were, in the local farmers' words, vandalizing their crops, notwithstanding that they were just seeking food for themselves and their little ones where they had foraged for hundreds of years. And so they were transferred by truck to a strange place and confined until they accommodated, (capitulated), and until a large enough enclosure was secured. Anthony and the Elephants bonded finally and found true ways to communicate across the species barrier, Lawrence Anthony and his ranger reaching out, hour after hour, to Nana, the Elephant Matriarch, and later to Frankie who, when the two small herds merged, became Nana's lineage holder, dharma heir.

When he died very suddenly, in Johannesburg, hours before he received a major award, the Elephants came to his house to acknowledge that they knew and to mourn him in their ceremonial way, an act they also understood would reveal their true nature to the world through him. And so, even though he died before I could meet him, I had to go and be on his land and in his presence and with the Elephants whom he had befriended. But I would not have gone without an invitation—I would not. And it was not, as you must understand, an invitation from Anthony or his people.

* * *

I asked the ranger at Thula Thula if he could take me to a place where it was likely that I would meet the Matriarch as she made her daily rounds. He hesitated, wary of imposing upon her in any way. "We will go where we go," he said, "and she will be there or not." We began to argue, although I was impressed by his adamant concern for the Elephants above the desires of a visitor.

Still, I said, "But you don't understand. I'm only here in answer to her invitation." He was very dubious though trying to disguise the level of incredulity he felt, and, naturally, I didn't have a letter or any proof. She had written on the wind or drummed their invitation on the earth in the ways her people are able to sound the alarm when culls occur and are perceived and understood precisely, even 100 miles distant. Even farther. Elephants' ability to communicate is not limited by science's ability to trace and verify the message.

"Why did she invite you?" the ranger asked as if sincerely entering the conversation.

"I believe a distant relative of hers suggested it. We've been meeting regularly in his territory over almost twenty years. He was the one who called me first and I came. Well, I am not sure he called *me*. It is equally possible, that he and his people, put out a universal call, and I am one of those who responded. Who knows who else received and who answered which call from which Elephants and where they met, if they did, and how? But I am the one who has lived this particular story for twenty years.

"I had been traveling with a group of people and we ended up at a certain tree at the side of the road across from a shallow pond pooling out from the river, and this became our ongoing meeting place every time we returned. A bird had landed on the tree while we were looking to meet whomever would appear. As it happened, the bird, a Fisher Eagle, Chapungu, was sacred to my friend who was driving and he refused to leave as long as the bird was there. Ultimately, the Elephant we now call the Ambassador, showed up. We had exchanges. I had brought my people and he had brought his."

"How did you know it was him?"

"You couldn't mistake the circumstances then, nor since, even though they vary from year to year. The fact of the meetings is incontrovertible; they play out like improvisational theater pieces that progress to tell a story from each of our interactions and we are all parties to it. I wasn't alone as an observer or participant. There were witnesses. Professional, unbiased and skeptical. They each played a role."

"And so he told you where to go next?" The Ranger was testy.

"Oh no. Eighteen years later, she sent us the call. Of this I am also almost certain, because this time, I received very particular instructions regarding etiquette, which I had never received before. Nor could I have as I didn't know the first time whom I was going to meet, only that an overwhelming longing for such a meeting was instilled in me which I could not resist no matter the effort and cost. I had told my traveling companions, 'I want to sit in council with the Elephant people.' And so we went where we might meet them and then he came."

"Is that why you went originally?" The Ranger was going over the territory again as if I hadn't spoken of this, trying to find the loopholes, the fantasy that he could then dismiss. Patience was required to navigate this exchange.

"Yes."

"And he was there waiting?"

"No, he wasn't waiting. We waited for him. You see, given the way we humans are behaving in relation to animals and the Earth, we had to make significant gestures to show we were trustworthy. It wasn't enough to come from the West Coast of the US, we had to be willing to wait. And so we did. We came looking for the opportunity to have an exchange. He came at almost the last hour of the last day. He was testing us. Of course, he was."

The Ranger's discomfort was increasing; the story is so unlikely. He must have been thinking, this woman is mad. But if it were a true story, he was obligated to bring us to her, and also if he brought us, the gesture implied his endorsement. Despite his overwhelming skepticism, he would have to accept the consequences. To do so, he had to be willing to trust us, or at least give us the benefit of the doubt and also to admit and follow his great hope that what I was relating was possible. If real, this situation had incredible implications for inter-species communication particularly because it was occurring at Thula Thula where Anthony had pioneered such a connection.

Assessing a situation, deciding whether to trust someone or not, predicting behavior, negotiating tense circumstances were skills the Ranger honed because he guided people in the wild, but he usually didn't have to apply them to what his passengers in his vehicle said about Elephants they didn't know; constraining their behavior was task enough.

I continued telling the story in as casual and sober way I could.

"Oh no, he certainly wasn't waiting for us." I laughed, accepting being cross-examined. "We had to go out each day for several days and look for him. We had to find the place where he might be."

"It could have been anywhere?"

"Yes."

"And you didn't have any way to recognize him, so he could have been anyone?"

"Yes."

"But it sounds like you met him. Did he just turn up?"

"We were running out of time. It was the last day and almost the last hour we could be in his area. We were leaving the next day. And we still didn't know where to go. Our hunt felt increasingly futile, and even foolish. We had come such a long distance.

"Then, as I told you, my colleague, who was driving, saw something, saw the bird, the Fisher Eagle, his totem which indicated that we must stop where we were. Whether or not it was the place, he wouldn't go on. He turned off the engine. In his mind, we had been brought to this place for reasons we couldn't anticipate. We had to wait and be open to whatever came to us. He was no longer looking for Elephants. He was in the sacred place of the Chapungu bird and he was exulting in its presence.

"Sometime after we had parked under the tree, I saw an Elephant far down the road along the river and prayed it was him. In my innocence, I prayed that I could call him to us telepathically, without recognizing that it was he who had called us a far greater distance from the US to Africa.

"He walked so slowly to us; it must have taken a thousand days. This was one of my first experiences that time does not exist in the way we presume it does. It took so long a time because we were being prepared to see who was before us. And then a similarly infinite time passed while he allowed me to gaze into his eyes and penetrated mine so that we could step over the line, which has separated us for thousands of years. We entered into a profound and inexplicable silent exchange."

"What did he say?"

"To translate into English would diminish what occurred between us. We speak entirely different languages, each arising from different histories, world views, circumstances and experiences. His lineage, ancient compared to ours, was developed painstakingly over millions of years. Accordingly, his communications would be far more difficult for us to comprehend. In his presence, I quickly knew that he did not need language in order to communicate and that my words, being limited by my culture, would diminish our connection."

"He wasn't limited?"

"Not by his languages. He didn't use language.

"He came very, very close to me. I felt no harm would come. History was written on his face, the distances he had traveled, the dangers and their tentative resolutions. He let me see this and was cognizant of what I was able to perceive. We looked into each other's eyes, each of us entirely open to the other. Clearly, he was leading; I was trying to follow. Time stopped and passed simultaneously. Left to time as I know it, what would have literally taken eons occurred within our comparatively few minutes together. Our half an hour equaled infinity. I was grateful that in such a short period of time, we were able to grasp that he is a peer. More than a peer. I felt the enormity of his presence, intellect and agency. He was orchestrating our meeting. I was grateful that I could respond. I believe the purpose was for me as a two-legged to fully understand and accept our common denominator as distinct and equal beings. I fully accepted, though he would not insist upon it—he is too great a being to do so—that he had rank and I did not in this interaction. Perhaps we are not peers. More likely, we are, as the Kogi say, merely the young ones and he and his people are the Elders, the Elder Brothers.

"I don't know how to convey what happens within one when we are open to a great Presence. It was Epiphany, January 6, 1999. Later, remembering this brought awe, disbelief and then a little humor to relieve us of the enormity of the event. But before that, when I was beginning to glimpse what was occurring, I did speak to him in my mind believing he would understand my language, that he had that capacity.

"I said, 'We both come from a Holocausted people and so, I promise you, your people are my people.'"

"So do you think he understood?" the Ranger asked.

"Well, over the years, he came again and again and again. He came every time we returned to that place. He understands more than I understand. I only know he called us. What sphere of intelligence does this reveal? I can't assess it. I don't understand it.

"After about a half hour, I glanced as my watch. It was exactly time to leave the park before it closed. He must have known this as he leaped up in the same moment, spun around and disappeared into the bush. Although forbidden to be outside a vehicle, we all jumped out of the pickup and collapsed on the ground. Several of us were weeping. But we were late and we had to recover quickly, mount up. We set out regretfully and slowly.

"And then ... and then ... and then ... his people started coming down from above the hill and from among the trees behind us, little ones and matriarchs, great bulls, small groups, a small migration. They arranged themselves quietly and with great dignity facing us alongside a mile of the river road. Not one of us had ever seen such a lineup before or since, nor any photos of such. We did not know if the flood of animals had finished but we knew that one must never come between a female and her young, and yet we could not find another way to go except along the river way they were occupying. And so we set out trusting that our perception was correct: they were waiting for us now. As we proceeded, there was no danger although there could have been. There was only our slow and careful procession and their subtle but undeniable acknowledgement that we had come a great distance and, perhaps, most importantly, that we had heard and felt the call—the longing they had instilled in us. That we saw who they are. That some humans have the capacity to recognize the presence of the gods when they appear. Our understanding of the nature of the world was shattered by this beauty and now we live in Mystery and awe. Whatever occurred it came from beyond and was beyond us and remains so."

The Ranger fiddled with his intercom as I probed the brush with my camera. He needed time. Then I began speaking again.

"That first meeting was almost twenty years ago. We have met since. And now we are here. We heard a call again. This time we could discern who sent it. It brought us here. As we were preparing to come, we learned there is a protocol to be followed. We hadn't known this but could have anticipated it if we were wiser. We received instructions, and this is what I am trying to explain.

"We have been instructed upon arrival to go with you to a neutral place that you know and wait for the Matriarch to appear. When she does, I am to introduce myself and my people, briefly describing our history and intent. You know how this is done with a minimum of words, if any. We will open ourselves fully and she will read who we are. Then, I am to ask permission to be here and to be among them. We, my people, Cynthia Travis and I, are to pledge our willingness and commitment to honor her and her people's sovereignty, to take nothing from her or her people and to commit to protect them—from such as we are—as best we can. Nothing less will gain us entrance to their domain.

"I understand," I continued to the Ranger, "from your hesitancy and caution, that you are trustworthy in relationship to her which is what matters most. She knows that you will be the one to bring us and has probably arranged it. Still, it is up to you, though she will as we travel find us on her own if that is her intention. Each one of us has to meet issues of trust. These are such times." He turned away from us and looked out at the road. We sat still, waiting. Then he started the truck again and we continued touring the area without any signs of Elephants that day.

We went out early the next morning and the Ranger parked in a field that they often traverse in such a way that we would not be blocking their familiar path. They could, if they came by, greet us or not as they wished. Drought was taking its toll and they might go anywhere to search for water. This spot was on a little plain above the valley even though they were more likely to find hidden springs with remains of mud, if not running water, below. The sun rose high and it was very hot. We had to wait a long time, and we expected as much. Then they came slowly through the bush.

Nana walked regally as she does, and we were aware that she saw us and was taking our measure. She did not stop but walked around the Rover so that she could examine us from every angle. It had a canvas roof, but no windows and we were completely exposed. Her people were following her. She may be slightly apart, but she is never away from them. And then, equally slowly, we saw her deputy, Frankie, the Matriarch-in-training, approaching. Frankie stopped and waited searchingly. Nana was behind me and as this was her choice, I did not turn around, but proceeded as I had been instructed to introduce myself and the others. I told her that we had received their call and were honoring it. If she and her people were willing, we would like to be among them for several days so that we could learn whatever it is they wish us to know, that we would honor the transmissions received and consider deeply what we were called to do. I told her we were not anthropologists or the equivalent for the animal world.

Frankie nodded in her way and encircled us as Nana had done, clearly giving the little ones permission to explore us with their trunks, and then they left. Over the next days we met again and again. As has been the case each time, there is no way we could predict or anticipate what might occur, the way daily events ultimately conjoined to translate into direct communications.

One day, Frankie and her extended family surrounded us as they had the first time. We had our eyes locked on each other. There was tension in the air and I could feel that the Ranger was wary though he didn't say anything to us. He hesitated before he turned off the engine, kept his hand near the key and did not lean back in his seat as he had in the past. I was not afraid but concerned that I, we, might miss something in our ignorance of their ways. Then Frankie seemed to twitch with impatience and left my side to go to the other side of the vehicle where she caught my eye again as I turned to her. I knew this was a critical moment but not how to meet it. Then she spoke directly into my heart. There was no pretending her words weren't clear.

"Do you know," she asked, her eyes piercing, "how hard it is to be the matriarch for my people when I can't find water for them to drink and I am unable to leave this preserve to search for it? If, it exists anywhere at all. If your people haven't consumed it all."

There was a complex back story behind her inquiry. She acknowledged that she and her people had been given sanctuary on this land and otherwise they would have been shot where they had been living because farms had been established where they had foraged and they tried to eat what they could, what was there, what belonged to them, but now they were facing the consequences of their imprisonment. She was not able to exercise her major responsibility to lead them to food and water wherever it might be.

On our arrival, a group of guests had been greatly delayed for dinner. When they arrived, they said they had stopped to free a baby Nyala from a mud hole. But in only a few days, the mud had become dry and cracked. It had not rained for a long time. Our water was being trucked in from Richards Bay and the Native people on the hills surrounding the valley of Thula Thula were demonstrating, burning tires, blocking the roads because the water infrastructure promised them by the candidates in the last election had never materialized.

"She sometimes gets testy," our guide said, "it's probably time for us to go."

"No," I said, "she spoke to me," hoping he would understand that I couldn't leave until she did. When she, herself turned and led the younger Elephants to a grove of ripe fig trees, we stayed some distance watching them in happy camaraderie with each other, and left as well. When we were almost down the hill toward our encampment we saw that Frankie and Nana were leading the herd down the hill, but rather than keeping to the road as is their habit, they were walking parallel to us, slightly behind, with slow deliberation.

"Do you ever come to the camp?" I asked. Our guide seemed distressed. "They are enacting their water witching skills," he said, concerned. "They are walking along the buried water pipeline and in some hundred feet they will come to the only place the pipes go above ground to bring water to the lodge for the guests. Once, at a similar time of drought, they broke the pipes to get the water."

That afternoon, the Native villagers had commandeered the water truck headed for the Reserve. Frankly, we all cheered them as the action forced the government to deliver the water that was rightfully theirs. Now the Elephants stood very still facing the employees' and the guests' tents. Their behavior was not threatening, but it was exquisitely articulate.

Frankie stood closest to my tent. It looked like a casual choice. No one else noticed how precisely she had positioned herself. She stayed there a long time and seemed to be pointing at the pipes with her trunk and then she slid her foot back and forth until she had shaped a foot width trench very close to the pipe. I was sitting on the porch looking at her, imagining her sliding her tusk under the pipe and raising it up, then raising her trunk higher until the water pipe broke and the water ran into the furrow which quickly became a stream. Had she planted the image in my mind? I wouldn't have conceived it myself.

Francoise Anthony, Lawrence's widow, joined us for drinks that night. She drank a dry sherry and I had an Irish whiskey, neat. The contrast between our indulgence, the Elephant's anguish, and the Native people's desperation was obvious. But the Elephants had invited us, had directed us to stay here, and were revealing their unhappy situation to us. Francoise's deft avoidance of the subject of rain and water was, in itself, eloquent. But somehow, it had also been decided that Thula Thula would fill a few water holes for the Elephants. (And the Native people had won assurances that municipal water, enough for their needs would be delivered to them as needed.)

Once this was guaranteed, we watched the Elephants leave in a slow and ponderous way, each step, usually so silent, a statement which we learned by the time dessert was served included advising us that they did not want to drink from metal tanks. That was made clear from the way they had stood by the water holes even as the tanks were being filled. Standing without moving was the language they seemed to have developed so there would be no confusion about their intent. They had been confined in a boma, they had yielded to human will, they had made peace with Lawrence Anthony. But he was in the clouds now and still there was no rain. They were wild, but they were not aggressive animals unless they had witnessed a cull, unless the young ones had seen the matriarchs slaughtered by AK47s fired from helicopters, unless the young bulls had no elders to guide them, unless they were fenced in, unless they were confined in a zoo or made to perform in a circus, unless they were tortured with bull hooks and electric prods. The combined two herds living at Thula Thula were pacific in nature, but, they wanted us to know, from the tension that characterized their stillness, that they could, if they remained without water, take us down.

As we were finishing dinner, a guest who had retired early to take a shower came screaming into the dining area, in her robe with a towel wrapped around her red hair. When they could make out what she was saying, two guards ran off to her tent and ultimately we learned that when she turned away in her outdoor shower from the wall to the trees, she saw a Cobra with its head raised staring at her. She leaped toward the doorway and ran to us. Even a Koperkapel gets thirsty, the guards informed us when they returned from banishing it to an abandoned termite mound they thought it would like. Calmer and assured the Snake would not return, she described the water pouring down on the stone footing, the relief from the heat and dryness of the safari ride, and the terror she felt when she turned to see the cobra with its flared head looking at her or at the water, she couldn't tell. She hadn't turned the water off—the cobra must have drunk its fill. Fortunately the precious water hadn't run too long or perhaps other animals had taken it in as had, most surely, the roots of the trees.

Each night afterwards, we nodded to each other as we separated to sleep, indicating that we would pray for rain, not only for the people, who were suffering among other afflictions, our privilege, but, particularly for the Elephants and the animals. Whatever I knew about calling rain, I kept to myself.

On the very last day, we set out to say goodbye to the Elephants on the way to the airport. The weather was awful. No, the weather was magnificent in that everyone's prayers for rain had been answered in an ongoing downpour the day before The ponds, the pools, the mudflats, the streams, the roads were all flooding. The Ranger reluctantly agreed to try a precarious road but he would only go so far because we had gotten stuck in the mud the night before after the rain and we couldn't risk it. On the other hand, these were our last hours and so he had to try though he doubted that we would find them. We and he had become comrades and were clear about the need to enact reciprocity with each other and all the beings we encountered. He accepted now that we had consistently been greeted by the Ambassador or other Elephants in other areas on the last hour of the last day. The road was muddy and almost impassable, filled with debris. We went slowly, the ranger always wanting to turn back and equally determined to have a final exchange. He was following an intuition, was taking this high and narrow road because now, he was compelled. When we had only minutes to stay until we had to set out for the airport, when we could go no further and reluctantly came to a stop, yielding to fate, we heard faint hums and rumbles, unmistakably the sounds of their communication with each other. Through the silvery mist beginning to shine with intermittent points of light, we saw their great gray shapes silhouetted against the mountain and were filled with gratitude as they turned toward us in acknowledgement. Yes, it was the last hour of the last day that we would be there, and we realized that their relative in the other country, the Ambassador, had told them that meeting, in whatever way, on the last hour of the last day would confirm the magic and great mystery we had entered together over time and space. They had needed reassurance that we would make the effort to find them, needed to know, as much as we did, that it was possible to dissolve into a field of common consciousness on behalf of a future in which we all coexist and thrive. We had come as far as we could, had hit a dead end of mud and a slight landslide which any being would recognize as impassable. They had seen us come to this point. They turned toward us. We greeted them in our hearts, offered tobacco which by now they knew was our sacrament, turned the Rover toward the highway and our departure to resume a life we could not escape despite the harm to our souls and to their lives.

* * *

Even as I write this story, having told it so many times, I am shaken by its reality. It shatters all my, our, assumptions about the world. Yes, this happened. This really happened. I, with others, experienced this connection with the Elephant people several times over twenty years. It stunned us every time. We do not pretend to understand. I am left with questions I ask again and again. What is the true nature of the world in which such things happen? And how, then, shall we live?

* * *

Just three weeks after we were in Thula Thula, having just returned to the

States, I learned that armed poachers had stormed the well-guarded Rhino orphanage connected with Thula Thula, a refuge and rehabilitation center for Rhinos and other baby animals who have lost their families to poaching, had held the staff hostage, ripped out the security cameras and shot two 18-month old white Rhinos, Impy and Gugy. The caregivers were savagely beaten and one woman was raped. Both baby Rhinos had their horns brutally removed. One had died after being shot but the other had been defaced while still alive and had to be euthanized.

The night of the poaching, Frankie came to me. I don't know if it was a dream or a visitation and can't distinguish the two. She stood in front of me as she had in Thula Thula, assessing me and challenging me to meet her. I was ready to enter the pain she was carrying, put up no barriers against her ongoing awareness of the possibility of annihilation even there in Thula Thula.

I wasn't back in Africa. Still, she was with me. I was aware of her long tusks resting on the bed the way she had rested them on the hood of the truck. It was for these, I needed to understand, that her people were being slaughtered and brutally so, as it had been for the horns that the little ones had been massacred. The gross absurdity punctured my heart as she could have easily done had she attacked. It was for these, but she wasn't giving them up. Elephants in Namibia were being born without tusks, not just females, the males as well. But if she were without her tusks she would be severely limited in her ability to perform what was necessary as an Elephant and a Matriarch. It was with these that she accessed groundwater for the herd, warded off attackers, protected or rescued little ones. Her tusks were large and carried a huge price.

Our encounter lasted all night, maybe several nights. Elephants can walk very slowly or run 25 mph even up to 40 mph if required and seem like they are walking. So this proceeding went very slowly. Proceeding? Was this a trial? Oh yes.

She didn't speak to me but rather it seemed that she opened her mind and drew me in at the speed that I could go so that I was increasingly exposed to her inner cognizance, the world she inhabited and could not escape. Reminding me, she was in prison and disempowered and it had not been her choice to trade her former life for safety, a relative term. It wasn't that she said this, or that I heard it, but that I had to allow my own mind to disappear and be absorbed into an other's. Then as the stillness in me deepened and my own thoughts and context dissolved, I was no longer in her mind either but she had passed me on to another and then another Elephant so that the field of their understanding was made plainer to me than I could have imagined. And when the transfer came to a rest, I was in the savannah, which I also knew from many visits over the years. Assessing that I could bear the pain of it, she entered me into the Elephant people's constant awareness of imminent annihilation by human hands.

Fear, matriarchal fear. I was immersed in it. I was in a lake overgrown with algae. There was not enough oxygen for the beings that live there. Almost drowning in it, but not. Unable to escape from it. Keeping my trunk above water. A heavy burden. The fear that I might be taken, any time, by a round of bullets from an AK47 delivered from a helicopter, ongoing terror for the species' extinction. How would they go on without me when I carried the topo map of our two hundred year migration route, the local water map, above and under the surface, survival knowledge developed over millennia (though only rudimentary in defending against the many ways humans attacked) and a deep tactile memory of how it had been once? Once. Before.

There was nothing I could do to safeguard myself and protect myself from my own death though I was considering the danger to the herd if they lost me and what I could do to break out, what I could transmit to them before I died. I felt all of this even as I remembered how I had protected the herd before, what it felt like to be continuously wary, considering what I would do, could do, if danger came. And then it came, and then I plowed forward, my great gray weight plunging, despite how confined I had been, like a tornado bearing down, the others behind me.

I was entirely in Elephant mind and then somehow also in two minds at once as the woman in me queried the Elephant, also in me, "When you carry the gift and curse of such sentience and intelligence and are helpless, do you pray, as humans do, for an unlikely miracle?"

There was no answer but when I was fully restored to myself as human, I prayed for her, and particularly to the Tanzanian Elephant Goddess with the cowry shell skirt, who accompanies the other Elephants on the altar; and so the night or the nights passed.

* * *

From this perch, I do wonder if Elephants pray. Prayers imply a division between the penitent and the divine. The Elephants know. Are in the field.

Are of it. The Mystery of no distinction simultaneous with individual awareness.

I could feel in the way that specific feeling is a specific intelligence that the Elephants know the ways trees know. The way Earth knows. I could also feel the level of fear that the invading human presence had introduced, unknown until then for fifty million years. They had not had enemies unless weakened, ill or were a baby alone which was unlikely. Each Elephant is considered so precious that when illness or accident takes their lives, profound mourning rituals are enacted. But now death is everywhere and nothing relieves the Matriarch's newly primal fear of abandoning the herd to slaughter. She didn't fear her own death. She feared that her death would be accompanied by so many others.

On March 25, 2021, The African Forest Elephant was listed as Critically Endangered and the Savannah Elephant as Endangered. The species is endangered. The Matriarch knows her people may become extinct.

I pray that the savannah Matriarch's death will be a natural one at the end of a long life, with a Matriarch in training, like Frankie, alongside her preparing a rain of leaves and blossoms and calming the herd that is already walking around her, their orbit winding the old one into the vortex taking her to the other side.

* * *

In mid-January 2021, Frankie, the Matriarch, died of liver disease. She had sought out an isolated place to die and was found on January 15. Nana partially resumed the matriarchy, but reluctantly. Frankie's daughter may assume the role, but it is not certain. There has been no equivalent Matriarch in training.

* * *

In Thula Thula, the Elephants have gathered at the foot of the hill where the orphanage is, listening to the howls of mourning, human and non-human alike. They stand still until after the police anti-poaching teams have left. They witnessed the humans putting the little one out of his misery knowing he had witnessed his mother's similar death and did not leave her body though he was weakened by agonizing pain, lack of food, water and the plenty of grief. That is where he was found when he was taken to the sanctuary.

From their distance, they will wait while a ditch is dug for the two little bodies, while the raped woman is bathed, wrapped in soft hand-woven cloth, tended to carefully by the remaining staff and neighbors; her brothers from one of the surrounding villages standing guard now, enraged. They will discover which of the gang members of Mpumalanga did this deed. In the past, the local judiciary has been very lenient with the Rhino poachers. This time, the brothers say, there will be no mercy. The poachers showed none, they will receive none. Within six months, 365 poachers will be arraigned. While these are the locals who are trying to feed their families since their Indigenous ways of life have been totally destroyed through colonization, the Imperial profiteers are not among those to be fined and sentenced.

The Elephants begin their slow circle of grief below, winding ty-phoon-like with greater and greater force, gathering all sentient beings into the inescapable center. Without my awareness, they gather me in. Frankie appears where I am sleeping and awakens me in more ways than one.

* * *

La Vieja knows this story. And so she stands at her perch searching in all the directions, seeking water as the fires spring up everywhere around her, feeding on the trees.

PART II

8

WOLF LEAVE TRACKS NOW

The animal looking out of the bars
is relieved to know she is an animal
but nevertheless, they have put her
behind bars,
when they look at her through bars
they become the bars, so to speak,
look how they spread themselves out
between the dark poles.
She does not want to be those bars
but she is behind them nevertheless.
She is pleased she is an animal,
but she also knows
she is behind bars,
she,
who would not know?
how to construct bars,
or why,
she is an animal,
that is what she knows.

She is the animal
that is
what she knows,

she knows
the animal,
she knows.

La Vieja

There was a clearing in the woods that Léonie believed had been made by the animals and belonged to them. It challenged the assumptions she was supposed to inherit about territory. When she was there, young as she was, she knew two things: the land didn't and couldn't belong to her and she was safe there. Safe, without possessing. Safe in a territory that did not belong to her or any human being.

She didn't know how her parents found it, how they could have driven and then walked not too far as she was too young to hike and too old to be carried, but still far enough to come upon a circle within a grove of Jeffrey Pine and Juniper where they built a fire without anyone else around them. The campsite had to be fairly near the road and yet there were no other cars, no hikers, no tents, no other fires. Pristine wilderness. Her father dug a fire pit, surrounded it with stones and they built a small pyre from wood they had brought and with the kindling they found nearby without damaging, they told themselves, the shelters of the beings who lived there, some of whom were too small to see and so might be displaced by the human family's desire for light, warmth and beauty. Everything, she learned, was fired by desire, including fire, which is desire itself. There was no one else around—that is no humans—for all the time they were there. How was that possible?

They never went to the place again and after some years her mother didn't remember it, so maybe the dream she'd first had there was more extensive than she remembered. Maybe Léonie, who was a dreamer, had dreamed the sojourn there too, not only the dream that remained with her for her entire life. Dreamed the drive, dreamed getting out of the car, putting up the big tent under the trees, and her pup tent close enough to reassure her parents, though they also knew she would sleep outside of it, and far away enough from them for her to dream. Even then, though it perplexed her parents who never seemed to want to part from each other, she preferred solitude. Maybe they never went to the grove, maybe she dreamed all of this and then dreamed the dream within the dream.

As she thought back to that time, she realized she had to qualify everything because of how imprecise the English language is, in that it only acknowledges humans as persons, when it had become clear to Léonie over the years that this was a gross misunderstanding of the nature of reality. "Bear, Bear, Bear," she said to herself. So even solitude which implies being alone only means to be free of human interference in order to be in active relationship with all the non-humans, the other peoples, and oneself.. Each of these relationships supporting and informing the others.

Unlike her friends and everyone else she knew, she did not dream people. Her dreams were always about animals when she was young, animals and those other beings she called stone people. She meant that there was a quality of presence to stones, rocks, boulders, cliffs, mountains, that she did not understand but could not deny and this was particularly true in her dreams where she so often created little villages of stones which then came to life.

As for her dreams about animals, they pleased and unnerved her. Everything she learned and experienced, especially to the rough silk of the Bear mother's fur, thrilled her. But she also felt as if she were spying on them, because she had no other way of knowing who they really are and she wanted to know, wanted to know even more than she wanted to know who she was or would become.

In her dream, she was creeping toward the others watching in the dark, the way animals sometimes gather at the dark fringes of campsites to observe the humans who have entered their territory without asking permission, without making an offering, without appreciating that it is occupied and has been for hundreds of thousands of years. Millions of years, the Bears say. Three million, they say. She dreamed them and they watched her. The dream, it seemed, was a place where they actually met each other. She dreamed the particulars of their preferred territory within another territory, a field comprised of their common consciousness, a sphere of being, a little world.

She would know they were near her even without seeing the fire's reflection in their eyes. It wasn't fear that alerted her; she was never afraid of them. It was comfort. Being among those who belonged to this territory was intensely reassuring to her.

She was cautious in her movements for if she turned too quickly, she would startle them and they would disappear. Survival mode. If they slipped away, gone was the agate evidence, their amber light. Gone the dream if she startled awake to prevent them from knowing she had been engaged in surveillance. Did the animals suspect she was an intelligence agent? Unwitting perhaps, but guilty. A phantom memory chip had been embedded in her brain from birth or before. Perhaps she had arrived on the planet with this affinity for the other. At best or worst, she was a double agent, but the entire enterprise was so mysterious, she didn't know who or what she was unconsciously serving. From her perspective, her dreams were a bridge to the animals, to the real world in which all life coexisted in dynamic relationship and she was, if temporarily, included. It had once been this way—these interconnections had once been as natural as one body of water melding into another.

Yet, what assured an animal now—the cloak of darkness, the containment of solitude, the ability to hear the night, a life away from humans—was undermined by her approach, involuntary though it was. Léonie apologized each morning for the audacity of her dreaming but that did not alter the dreaming or her gratitude for the experience.

She entered their territory in her dreams and inscribed her observations on her memory, a permanent record for the length of her life. Over the dreaming she had no control, much as the animals had no control over her intrusions and her species intruding without impediment into their lives which she, given she was dreaming, could enter from anywhere to wherever they were hidden. From the beginning she was at odds with what she loved best and struggled to do what was increasingly urgent—to protect the animals and the non-human world from herself and her kind. Her unkind kind. The dreaming and her concern companioned each other.

The dream was so primary and repeated so many times, she understood when she was older and still dreaming it that it was her origin dream.

Within the dream, her parents had taken her camping and she had fallen asleep by the fire, the flames and shadows flitting over her face. In the dream, she slithered forward on her belly, the soles of her bare feet reflecting the fire and her face toward the dark where yellow eyes in a circle, like stars in an ellipse in a dark sky, maintained the boundary between the worlds. But when she arrived at that periphery, between the light and the dark, between her area and theirs, hoping to join the dark shapes darker than the dark, she did not feel welcome. Quickly, she turned around and saw there were strange shapes, another circle of seated black Bears around a fire. She scuttled to them and swiftly she was with them, all of them seated facing the fire. Simultaneously, their eyes were focused on her. What did they see? she wondered. Had they been, were they, dreaming her?

When the Bears saw her mother and father seated by the fire, her father stirring the ashes as he liked to do, stirring the flames with a poker he had brought with him—as he could bring anything he wanted since they had driven to the campsite, could fill the van to the roof if he wished—

what did they see? Invaders, Léonie thought. The Bears saw invaders. Surely, they were wary, not curious, but rather suspicious and cautious. Surely, they were not feeling kindly and were more alarmed than intrigued. But they did not attack the small group. They knew only too well what would happen to their tribe if they did. They did not keep written records, but they knew their recent grisly history. Recent, that is, 500 years. They didn't have to remember before that. Before that they were able to live in right relationship with all, including two-leggeds. They had made agreements that had been trustworthy for thousands of years. But these invaders attacked everyone, the Indigenous, the Bear, Buffalo, Wolf, Deer, Turtle, Eagle peoples and the Tree people as well. "Timber!" they yelled, and another tree came crashing down. These foreigners were routinely untrustworthy; they respected no one, did not keep agreements, they did not honor treaties, even the ones they originated. The invaders were cruel, devious, voraciously hungry for food, land and power. They were ill. They had lost their minds and were heartless, but they didn't know this. These invaders even developed stories about how much the animals, the Natives and even God loved them. They thought they were as good as divine. But the animals knew otherwise. The animals knew the Divine. It was their nature.

Her mother must have put a blanket over her, but she felt the comfort of dark fur, the firelight glancing off the long silken hairs, her own secure heaviness, the contact between earth and limbs so familiar and exact. She was not lost in her own body, she was cognizant of the pebbles, twigs and soils and their own awareness of themselves as she was simultaneously mindful of her own existence. Somehow without the disorientation of transport, she was in one perspective and then another, like an electron leaping from one position or ring to another position or ring though there isn't really movement as it disappears and appears, exactly in the manner that was occurring to Léonie who was lying by her tent, was scooting toward the fire, was seated in the circle, no longer herself but never more so.

This dream first occurred when she was young and then repeated in various forms. She never disputed it or the similar ones that followed which were generally indistinguishable and so were, perhaps one dream. One dream or one made several by repetition. She yielded to their familiarity, their constant presence that could have been understood to challenge her early reluctance to keep records, to actively remember. They were. A fact. Part of her nature like the arch of her bold brown eyebrows, her skinny brown legs, her blond hair; she resembled her grandmother, Mere.

Her blond hair—she was no Goldilocks; she disliked the book. When she had sufficient language, she denounced it. A gangly white woman invading the home of other beings. Breaking and entering, using force and deceit to get what she wanted, whatever she wanted, devouring what she could and entirely casual about the theft and property damage she caused. No charges filed. No amends made. No apologies. No remorse. No restoration.

Imperialism. Léonie had to be an adult before she understood the parallel in the world. Or it took the story, Goldilocks and the Three Bears, for her to realize that this quintessential Western fairy tale described a long history of global, national, personal conquest that was somehow considered divinely sanctioned. Although not all people indulged but even so, too many, human and non-human, were the victims of such violence. This story wasn't about human privilege, but rather European or Western privilege. Indigenous cultures told other kinds of stories about their origins and their relationship with animals, the way Turtle carried the world on Her back, the way Coyote created the stars, the way Spider saved the world from being burned up by the sun, the way Bear and a young woman had married and had cubs.

She always liked the stories, like the one she was dreaming, where it was not such a bad idea for the human to become an animal. This direction was more likely than the animals becoming human—they had no interest in that. Like the Silkie myth. The Seal woman would not have become a human if the man had not stolen her fur garment and imprisoned her in his house and his life. Finally, after she had children, she found her skins and, despite all, put them on and went back into the sea. Léonie loved the story and savored the end when the woman slipped back into the heavy smooth fur that shaped her body and her mind, and slipped with great relief into the cold water, feeling the ocean everywhere upon her, between the sleek hairs, so smooth and heavy, sensing the currents moving alongside her, and another mind, a watery mind that extended beyond her and was part of everything around her, returning to her and restoring the wonder in which she had lived before. That cold and fluid slide, finally, into the deep, into the welcoming, penetrating waters.

Was the Bear mother that she was dreaming or sitting next to, or both, giving her back—if only for a short time—her own rightful hide?

Yes, back to the dreams. She was wary about remembering them though they seemingly wanted to be remembered.

Remembering is not the right word. When she was re-experiencing the original dream or a variation, when the formative moment repeated, it was as if to confirm her intrinsic identity. When she was within the formative moment again, she was outside chronology, that is without a line from here to there, outside of linear progression, but within a sphere of relationships ballooning from a point, first in another realm, and then a point of contact in this realm. This was not a recurring dream; this was being re-united with a point of creation, present and continuous. It was dizzying. She was in a vortex of constant emergence. Because in the dream she was also remembering, or rather was within all the other dreams and their persistence in the continuous presence. She was not alone in the dream as she was always accompanied by animal others who were distinct and yet with whom she was fused, animal others whom she became and into whom she was incorporated.

When she was older, when she was an adult and the dream or the dreams persisted, her perplexity about them repeated as well: Am I real in the dream, or am I a fiction? Are the Bears real or are they fictions also, and if so, did I invent them? Or might I have been, might I be continuing to be a fictional manifestation of their dreaming, their minds, their desperate activity to inform and correct our behavior and insert another reality to preserve themselves? Does this dream come also on behalf of the stones, the trees, the weather, the soil itself? Is Bear the guardian of the real world and is that why they come to me?

These are human questions. Bear, she thought, does not think this way. But, Léonie grunted to herself and laughed at how preposterous she was and that this half-life of dreaming enhanced rather than diminished the power and wisdom of Bear. How did she know that Bear doesn't think this way? Maybe these were Bears' thoughts!

As the dreams persisted, her mind was honed by them. They formed her so directly, she sometimes thought, she was parented by Bear, or conceived by Bear. That must have been, must be the way of the Big Bang—from an invisible spark, an infinitesimally small point, came the both immediate and ongoing emanation of an entire universe. The Bears dropped an ember, a point of light into her night mind, she explained to herself, and a world of understanding ensued so luminous it was as if all the extinguished Bears had been restored. Restored, a great light of wisdom, despite the fact that the Earth is dying, that the animals are suffering greatly at our hands, are living lives as increasingly desperate and unnatural as are our own, that we are killing them off, that they are going extinct.

The human she was thought the Bears watched her when they could, whenever she entered their territory, for they were not permitted close into hers, not in her back yard, not in the swimming pool had she had one, not taking water from the garden hose. Her parents would allow it but not the neighbors. The wilderness park rangers cautioned against having bee hives, planting fruit trees in Bear territory that might attract Bears, although the Bear had lived there originally, free to hunt honey from the wild hives and eat berries and whatever they wished that the Earth provided them. The park rangers warned against feeding the birds because Bears liked bird seed, against putting out water for the wild, though the humans were draining the aquifer, saying the Bears and other animals could find their own water whether or not there was fresh and unpolluted water remaining in their territory, whether the water had been stolen by Nestlé for its toxic baby formula which undermined a human child's immune system and also the mother-child bond, whether the water had been stolen and bottled because the local water was too polluted to drink, and whether or not the humans had set their land on fire and used every drop of remaining water anywhere to put it out.

She did not know if they could observe her in her dreamtime, when it seemed she had carte blanche or the power to go where she would without impediment. She was not a lucid dreamer, this was not her will, she was not invading by choice., she did not believe she was entitled. Still, she was seemingly programmed, another hidden camera, like those placed everywhere so that no animal had privacy nor had autonomy over their own precious animal lives. But, she assumed they watched her whether or not she was aware of them that they had also absorbed her into their field.

She did not think they chose many humans but assumed that they watched some who were allies and others because they were dangerous and required a steady sentry's gaze upon them. These objects of their scrutiny did not enter their field, were not admitted into their consciousness but rather the Bears set up an impenetrable wall that prevented the potential enemy from knowing what the Bears wanted to withhold.

(Recently, Léonie read that two burrowing owls have been caught rejecting the hidden camera that was recording their underground lives. It made Léonie smile that they could take control of their habitat and she shuddered at how little ability anyone or any being had to be free of observation and scrutiny.)

The Bears, she believed, did not believe those two-leggeds would change their assumptions or behaviors if they knew more about the Bears and who they really are. After all, the Bears were well aware of how those two-leggeds treated each other, treated the natural world, and treated those Bears they brought into their proximity either to exploit, experiment on, or keep in a state of perpetual observation. Tortured to become dancing Bears. No, the Bears were not going to reveal anything of themselves to these aliens. But to Léonie…? She believed they put up no barriers and so everything she saw was sacred and this intensified her reluctance to record the dreams.

* * *

We're back at the campsite, either in real (by contemporary cultural assessments) life or in the dream. What's the difference? There may not be a difference. In this instance, it is morning and she awakened with the dream on her mind. She did not tell the dream when her mother asked, as Melissa always did ask if anyone had dreamed that night. The girl did not want praise for being a dreamer. She did not want her mother to write down the dream. She does not want to have records kept because they can distort the past, present and future by specifying what will be remembered and what will not, what is notable and what will be ignored. How impossible it is to see the whole picture because the human perspective is miniscule and distorted. And so memory could well endanger the Bears.

* * *

We could be at an impasse. Léonie, as a child, did not want a record and intrinsically, the writer's work is to provide the record or, obviously, nothing here would exist. And so, we continue in contradiction.

It hadn't been clear to me until this moment, that I could be at such extreme odds with the character who has come to me or has been given to me to bring into the world, to the character who found me in order to do exactly what she doesn't want done.

* * *

Not speaking in human ways has advantages, Léonie thought. Animals are free in every moment because when memory is linked to nature, it is fluid. Also, animal memory is not calculated, does not engage in strategy—though it may be strategic in terms of survival—and animal memory doesn't lie.

Aside from what she remembered there was the understanding that came to her without her awareness, in the ways human children learn intra-uterinely, that she had animal understanding which could not have come, she believed, from any other source but the mysterious teachings that occurred in the Bear's winter den of gestation and birth. No Bear missed that darkness that was outside the body but inside an earthen womb.

* * *

The Kogi Indians, who managed to escape the Spaniards and Western civilization until very recently, live on a unique pyramid shaped mountain the Sierra Nevada de Santa Marta, in Colombia. It is the highest coastal mountain in the world, and has almost every ecosystem and 7% of the Earth's biodiversity. Léonie would learn when an adult that they raised selected children in the absolute dark until they were nine years old, or even older, eighteen, so that when they were brought so carefully into the light and into the sight of the wondrous beauty of the Earth, they were ready to take on the role of the Mamas, to govern the community with compassionate and wise hearts, and protect, which is their ultimate work, the heart of the world. That's what the dark provided. That, Léonie, is what the dark offers, Bear taught her. That's what the dark also offers Bear.

* * *

After dreaming the dream again and again Léonie was more confident in the dreaming. The fire dimmed and burned out and becoming cold, she leaned up against the mama Bear who was next to her. The night enfolded them like a dark cave. Maybe the Bear lay down. Maybe they were sleeping one against the other in a sheltered area that would hold them for three more months. The cubs had spent the first two months in utero and then they exited. All this was happening in the dark, in the deep winter sleep. When the bear cubs are born, they are furless, like Léonie is. She leaned against the mother as if she were a cub. The cubs will suckle the mother while she sleeps. Léonie took in the knowing as if it were milk. She dreamed it again and again as if they were in the cave together for months and as the dream repeated for years.

When Léonie emerges into the adult human world, she will continue to think like a Bear. And she will know that Bears think. She will also know they have large hearts for that is how generously she was being raised, all the secrets transmitted. They did not have to sign a contract. Léonie is and will remain trustworthy despite being a two-legged. The Bear knew this. Léonie extended herself against the Bear's belly and it seemed that the Bear's front legs came down and embraced her, pressing her against the Bear mother's swollen teats.

What is the Bear mother thinking? What instinctive intelligence is theirs, what wordless impetus that we, if we felt it, would call love? Maybe so much more than and distinct from what we experience. Love seized her as she tried to protect this frail being against the harm that could come to her from almost anything—cold, wind, fire, rain, insects, falling branches, other animals—anything at all. Bear Mother doesn't think in sentences or narratives. Here is a small creature. Here is her large body. She wraps herself around the cub and if she could have drawn her back into her womb, she would have done so.

In the real world, where dreams are also real, such things happen. In such a way, we are able to live real lives.

Melissa, her mother, must have understood something of what was unspoken but still occurring because she was also overtaken with a desire to embrace Léonie, press her hard against her chest and protect her against all alien influences. But she did not. She knew such an abrupt gesture would be entirely unwelcome.

"Sometimes I think you are raising yourself," Melissa said, marveling at how different her child is from herself.

"Not quite," Léonie answered intending to assure her mother and not wanting to lie.

Some of what Léonie knows comes from the dream Bear, but some seems innate to her. Not common sense but almost as if she was born so, as if she came in with it. She could feel it and didn't understand why if commonly accepted, why people thought research was necessary to support or deny what Léonie saw as evident. Self-evident. But then, Léonie also recognized that most people thought there was a universe of difference between themselves and a Bear or any other animal, while Léonie found more differences between herself and other humans.

Once she learned that humans hunted Bears to "harvest" the bile from their gall bladders subjecting the animals to unimaginable lifelong suffering, she disassociated herself from humankind. Sometimes they didn't hunt for the Bear, but bred Bears and confined the cubs in crush cages which they grew into, remaining within their tiny walls for their entire lives of ongoing torture, an open wound in the gall bladder where the bile was syphoned out. Léonie's heart contracted as if it were similarly confined. It didn't contract, as one would assume, to being hard-hearted, no, on the contrary, she suffered what the Bears suffered. She was one with them in all ways, in their rampant beauty and love of life and in their unspeakable, unceasing suffering.

Most people she knew thought animals were simple, living by habit and instinct, by which the humans meant without thinking, reasoning, planning, without—many believed because it served them to believe it—without an ability to suffer, without an emotional range, but living in the narrowest present without a developed sense of past or future. They did not ascribe to animals the particularities of memory through which humans assumed their own identities were formed. They did not think in terms of animal intelligence. But Léonie knew the Bear remembered where she had denned the year before and three years before that and she would return or choose another based on her foreknowledge of the weather that was coming, her intuitions about the cubs she was gestating, her assessment of the nature and mood of the other Bears and her concerns about safety from humans.

Léonie also knew that the Bears remembered which humans had hunted them and abused them and which had been respectful and without fear. They remembered the way their land had been, generations before, and saw what had become of it over hundreds of years and how it was now and the difference and what caused it. The breadth of Bear mind allowed her to know, feel, experience all of that, all of it, now. Léonie did not think a Bear mother could birth and raise cubs without knowing all of this and more. And she would only allow a mate to mount her who knew this as well because she knew the gene base her children needed to survive.

For Léonie, the dream was happening in the moment, this moment, not happening again, but present and also precognitive, for wasn't she sitting now among them and having made, hadn't she made, a fire for them? The dream was not a dream but a real event that was happening, would happen, had happened. All at once. She struggled…. No, she struggles to identify the divisions that seem so apparent to everyone else. For her, the past, the present, hope or concern *are*. She might say, for clarity's sake, are *one*, but actually she is saying that the past, the present, hope or concern, the future *are* and this is the source or foundation of Bears' wisdom. Even here she is struggling to translate Bear perception into what is a foreign language for Bear, the one that arises in Léonie as her birthright but is incapable of communicating what Bear knows.

The past, present and future are all one, or her location, like the electron, changes so rapidly, she is hurled from one place to another or they meld and appear as one or she is in two or more places at once. Prescience and being present intermingled or intermingling.

Here is the dilemma. She can't speak of the reality in which she exists in the language given to her to describe experiences that aren't hers, or the Bears, but are assumed to be universal. The Bears, like Elephants, the Others, communicate through tools intrinsic to another reality, one she hopes she understands somewhat or hasn't forgotten. How can it be that all the Beings speak the same or similar languages, but one? The Being she is, supposedly. She is brokenhearted because she is outside the sacred language.

And to whom is she relating this story of the dream, and the fact of the dream and the life of the dream, her life, Bear's life, the same? She who also lives in time, human time, knows that the clouds come and go, that the sun rises and the dark leaves flutter in the wind, that the Bears had territory and habitat and now do not, that they had lived a golden life of salmon and glistening salmon berries and now are wary, hungry and bitter. She knows that. They know that too. All known and coexistent. The details, every detail of the sparkling water breaking into light over stone and the flash of salmon and spray as present as the dull water and the weary fish and scarcity and guns, helicopters and terror.

La Vieja

* * *

This is her origin story. It happened when she was seven. But in the moment of the dream, she was both innocent and ageless. When you step out of time, you remove yourself from a reflexive chronology that imposes a narrow view of cause and effect as the determinant of reality and then the sequence of events does not hold ultimate meaning. Rather reflection allows one to discern an origin story, a central event, a pebble of meaning, activity and possibility dropped into the lake of being from which ripples flow out toward a future, while simultaneously a magnetic core draws event, possibility and meaning back to the heart center. Her entire past leading to this moment, and this moment determining her future. An origin story from a tiny point, infinitely massive, that is expanding toward myriad lakeshores until it manifests in narratives and simultaneously draws such narratives from outside itself and Elsewhere back to the heart core. This is the sacred motion intrinsic to life.

* * *

She was sleeping in a down sleeping bag on a pad facing the fire. The dancing shadows of flames on her face described the fire's life. It was a small animal that her father had coaxed out if its hiding place, blowing on sparks and cinders, his gentle caress of the kindling urging it to flare. And so it did with a tiny roar announcing its acquiescence, its willingness to come forth. Eager.

Léonie could not contain her instinct to play, to roll a smooth stone toward the fire, have it land in the coals, blacken a little and then roll back to her. She was an animal too, fire was an animal, they were one species. She rolled one stone from the cache she had collected before lying down toward the fire. It entered the fire pit and stayed there. Disappointment. She rolled another. Disappointment. She closed her eyes to allow fire to speak in waves of heat and dark. The stone heated, red hot, white hot, and there was a burst of energy, sharp as flint, and, yes, the stone rolled back to her. She had to wait for it to cool before she could pick it up and examine it. "You have come back to me," she whispered as she took it to her lips. It fit her palm exactly. It would never leave her, she vowed and kept her promise to keep it with her, in a pocket, in a purse, on an altar, when home or traveling. Because she was faithful, it became one of her totems—a sign of being fire's child.

Then she was further away from the fire. There was a circle of boulders around the fire that served as seats. She had been moved outside the circle into the cooler dark where no sparks might singe her sleeping bag. Behind her, darker shapes of trees were swaying in the slight wind. Between and behind them the topaz lights which had comforted her went out one by one. And then she saw a line-up of black beings who eclipsed the fire that glinted between them, coronas glowing around dark fur. These parabolas of dark and light were not her parents as they had retreated to their tent, but other beings for whom, though she only sees their shapes and how still they are, she feels an explosive attraction that she can only imagine is what others mean when they say *love*. And so she lays in longing, grateful for their presence, if saddened that she is so far away as twenty feet or so which seems infinitely distant. Between the smoke from the fire and the distance, she cannot smell them.

Then as if longing were transport, she is beside them. Maybe she is dreaming this and maybe this is not a dream. Both. The shift leaves no trace as if the air has not parted. She is sitting as erect as they are, her small shape between their larger shapes, the one to her right larger than the one to her left. She is part of a Bear family or an ancient stone circle marking solstices, the passage of the great fire. Her tiny body covered with fur or granite. Not so tiny any longer. She settles into herself and settles into the earth. Distinct and diffuse. At one.

And then again. She moves slightly in life or in the dream, she cannot tell the difference and the distinction, if there is one, is unimportant. But still she wants to know if the Bears continue to exist when she turns her head, wants to see if they will disappear. But also, she wants to be with them more than she wants information. This is a divide between two minds, one that belongs to Bear and all the other beings and one that belongs to the humans who meticulously separate themselves from the natural world. One is concerned only with being together, with relationship, sees any separation as dangerous to all life, and one values its own individual thinking above all. Her thoughts continue but she doesn't move her head. When she is in the wilderness, as she may be now, with her parents asleep in their tent, and turns her head—if the Bears disappear—where do they go? Do they appear anywhere else? On another ring, in another circle, in a site of their own? Are any Bears left where they are safe from our probes and observation? Or, better yet, does she exist only because the Bears will it so.

* * *

School did not interest Léonie because she wasn't interested in human behavior and it seemed to be the central concern for her teachers and her friends. It's true. Melissa, her mother, was often irritated when Léonie evaluated or compared everything to how she thought the putative Bear or animal would respond.

"And don't tell me they're psychic too," Melissa was often exasperated.

"They know what they need to know and sometimes that's the future," Léonie retorted.

"And how do they gain such knowledge?" Melissa's question was more challenge than inquiry.

"Because they aren't lost in their own heads but live in the natural world and learn everything from each other." By the time, Léonie said this, she was a teenager and formidable.

"Do you think my being a librarian is being lost in my head then," her mother felt challenged, "and what good will knowing about Bears do you when you're my age and trying to support a kid?"

"Bears don't have libraries." It was a non-sequitur. They both knew it and understood that Léonie was trying to understand what was beyond her. The questions were also beyond Melissa and there they were facing the unknown together. Melissa took the hairbrush from the top of the cabinet and began brushing Léonie's abundant golden ringlets.

* * *

Animals don't have libraries, schools, newspapers or radio stations. Without such resources how do the animals know the start and end of hunting season? How do the animals know when the season begins when Western humans do not know without being told? How do they know to jump the fence to be safe in the nearby preserve when hunting season begins? Without a news source, animals have been able to calculate where food might be, for whom they might be food, and what the weather promises, short term and long. They have had to develop extreme sensitivity to human behavior and the harm likely to come to them from the newly arriving two-leggeds, those who were settling the area and making it uninhabitable and those who arrived suddenly, stayed for only a short time but were even more dangerous as they had no inner restraint, no overview or consideration for others to prevent them from taking everything they possibly could back with them. The two-leggeds, from the Bear's perspective and experience, had only two things on their mind: plunder and killing.

Melissa's friend, Roger, lived on the Mogollon Rim in Arizona. He was a hunter and depended on Elk and Deer for his family's winter food. All summer long, the Elk lived in his yard which backed onto the mountain and the state forest. He'd stand on his back porch and aim the bow and arrow at them as they bedded down in the hot afternoons, practicing, never shooting. They paid him no attention. But the day before hunting season, they disappeared. Each year. Sometimes he would scout them but usually failed to find where they had scattered but he sought them only out of curiosity. After living in such close proximity, he couldn't shoot his neighbors and had to find Elk he didn't know to hunt for his winter food.

Melissa would not have believed Roger if she hadn't seen this herself.

"How does he explain it, Momma?" Léonie asked.

"He says he and the animals are in a relationship. He says they have lived alongside each other for so long, they can read each other's minds, posture and sweat. Beyond that, he speaks of how grateful he is that his father and his brother and he built this cabin so that he gets to live in it now that his father has passed. He says, he doesn't want to live anywhere else. He says, he can't." Melissa paused, "I guess you would like to live there too."

* * *

In Africa, I had my own experiences of the precognitive sensibility of animals as Melissa had through Roger.

Map lines carefully surveyed and established delineate the no-hunting areas from the hunting areas of the Selous, a wild animal preserve in Southern Tanzania. The area was named to honor Frederick Selous, the noted hunter, who donated (as if they belonged to him) 524 mammals from three continents, all shot by him, including 19 Lions. Overall, more than five thousand plants and animal specimens were donated by him (his property) to the Natural History section of the British Museum. In catalogues for the world's largest animal specimens hunted, Selous is ranked in many trophy categories, including Rhinoceros, Elephant, and many ungulates. He also hunted in pursuit of big game in Germany, Hungary, Romania, Scotland, Sardinia, Turkey, Persia, Caucasus, Wyoming, Rocky Mountains, Eastern Canada in 1900, Alaska and the Yukon.

La Vieja

When you drive through those areas, the animals remain at a distance, careful not to approach you the way they do easily a few miles away where hunting is always prohibited. The animals do not have access to the maps and anyway reading maps is not their way of knowing. Unlike humans, they do not need maps. The animals know!

It is not uncommon for animals to be able to predict danger that may be coming to them though we do not know how they do it. And we will never understand how they accomplish this until we are willing to accept the fact of animal intelligence and agency, respecting the languages they speak so different from ours.

Suddenly, there are many Whitetail Deer at Fossil Rim Wildlife Center in Glen Rose, Texas, according to my friend, Krystyna Jurzykowski, its founder. The Deer are native to the area but are not part of the herds at the Wildlife Center which was created to protect and preserve endangered African animals. So it must be October or November. Hunting season. A host of two-leggeds get a permit to kill. Some hunt to eat; some are just interested in the trophy Bull. You can buy a permit or perhaps you enter a lottery for permission to kill, without having to explain why you want to kill. The thrill is assumed.

We don't know if it matters to the prey whether it will be eaten and every one of its parts used entirely and with great respect or whether they are taken for the demonic fun of it. Perhaps the prey know which hunters have made offerings and said prayers on behalf of the hunt and the food they will have for their families and which hunters got drunk the night before their adventure because it's just a big party, this killing. The Stag will not benefit from the offerings, but the ways the family lives which makes offerings and prays does affect all the beings who will be connected through this deed, and so the offerings may well incline the deer to let his life be taken. It was different in the old days, when the Indigenous people had agreements with the animals. But today …? Today, we don't know if the Stag thinks tactically anymore. But it would be good for the world if we accepted that Deer have complex minds and it is our limitation, not theirs, which obscures their thinking from us.

Perhaps the animals sense that the mounting desire among the two-leggeds to kill other living beings has come to a head and tomorrow they will swarm the area with their lust and weapons. The animals do not seem to need to read the death applications; they sense what is imminent; they know. They know in Arizona and in Texas and they know in Africa and everywhere and act to protect themselves accordingly. Bear permits and Deer permits are issued at the same time. The Deer know, the Bears know and Léonie knows. She feels their knowing in her body and so she understands that bodies can be organs of understanding. The Bears have transmitted this knowing to her; she learned it in the dark.

Léonie learns more from the animals than from her mother. Extending her field of respect and connection creates a different mindset and another world manifests. Everyone survives in this world because it depends upon everyone's survival. Melissa watched her daughter from the proximity permitted to her. She wanted a world in which her daughter would thrive and the current political and environmental trajectory would not provide it. Melissa is concerned because she knows what her mother, Mere, suffered, caused in part by her father who, in a turnabout or to make amends, saved the mother and brought her to the States. Now Melissa's daughter seems to know something she, even as a mother, doesn't know. Well then, trust the light-filled beauty who exited from her body in a blaze of wonder. The mother tousled her daughter's hair and hoped that such a miniscule gesture of approval will matter.

* * *

During the Liberian civil war, 1999–2003, the Elephants knew they could not survive another war, especially when the guerilla forces were bivouacked in the forest. They left Liberia, crossing the border to Guinea. We know that one Elephant warned a man that he needed to take his family and flee the country, which he did, but we don't know if that Elephant left herself or just dissolved into the dream world until she reappeared in another dream when it was safe for him to return to his village after which she continued to guide him, telling him where and when to build and farm.

How do I know this? The Elephant Dreamer told me himself. Several of us were sitting together, drinking coffee, smoking a prayer pipe filled with Elephant tobacco, a good smoke, though you might think of it as dung. The stories flowed between us like the smoke that took our prayers for the Elephants and the villagers to the spirits.

When he was a young boy, the Elephant Dreamer said, he had been walking alone in the jungle, when he heard an Elephant crashing toward him. Greatly fearful, he started running, but fell. The Elephant came up to him and stood over him, running her trunk over him but without touching him. He was terrified. After a time, the Elephant went away and the boy started running again only to hear the Elephant running after him again and coming closer. Not knowing what to do, aware he couldn't outrun the animal, the boy quickly climbed a tree, not realizing that his new perch would bring him eye to eye with the Elephant reaching toward him with her partially raised trunk. Cornered and terrified, he reached desperately for the Koran which he always carried in his pocket and began reading aloud. The Elephant stood very still and listened to the boy who continued, increasingly confident that the huge animal understood and was grateful for the sacred knowledge. That, the Elephant Dreamer said, was the beginning of their lifelong friendship. "I always remember," he said, "to perform the ceremonies and make the offerings that my grandfathers performed so that the villagers and the Elephant people would live in harmony. From now on, when I pray, I pray for the Elephant's family as well as my own. And when I meet the Elephant, I always read to him from the Koran."

"The Elephants returned from Guinea," the Elephant Dreamer said, echoing what the Superintendent (Governor) of Lofa County, had said in 2006 when he had called to consult with us about creating a working relationship between the villagers and the returning Elephants, "when hostilities ended." The Elephants apparently could discern the exact location of the land borders, albeit arbitrary, between Guinea and Liberia. When peace was declared and supported by the United Nations forces, many of the small herds who had gone into exile returned to their old homes.

War changes everything, even the land. Everything is out of balance so that the people and the animals are no longer sustained in the old ways. They vie with each other for sustenance.

When a widow demanded that the Elephant razing her field leave her the last cassava plant to sustain her and her children because her husband was killed in the war, the mother Elephant shuddered with reluctance, but backed up. The widow held her ground and stared defiantly as the large gray animal, unwillingly consented, turned and so very slowly, walked away. The two had come to this agreement by recognizing their individual possibilities and limitations. The widow was bound by her little plot of land, she could not harvest beyond it while the Elephant, the widow explained, could browse what might be left in the wild. The widow will make offerings and give thanks and somehow this will increase what is available in the jungle. She will tell the story of the Elephant's generosity and the story will flourish. As a result, kindness will be extended to the Elephants and other animals and laws will be passed and observed to protect the forests and the animals who live there. That's what the Elephant understood and why she backed away. Or maybe, she withdrew because she knows what it is like when one's children are hungry. Ellen Johnson Sirleaf was President then and restoration was possible after the civil war.

September 2020

The Elephants are returning to Liberia again. The writer hopes it is a sign that peace is coming to the country. But our friends in Guinea say it is more probable that civil conflict will break out in Guinea again so the Elephants are leaving. The Elephants returning can be a sign of peace or may be an early warning about danger. When the Zos, the Liberian medicine people, look to the spirits for signs they are habitually seeking early warning signs.

A great change has come over the wilderness and the nature of the animals is changing as they try to accommodate. Some are increasingly coming to resemble the two-leggeds who invaded North America from whom they had always differed extremely. Desperate, the animals are hunting the hunters.

August 21, 2019

'The Lion Man" who owned a Lodge and preserve was killed by his own (caged) lions. On July 5, 2018, a pride of Lions ate the poachers seeking to kill Rhinos. The headline to the news story is: "Lions kill suspected rhino poachers who sneaked onto South African game reserve." I sit with the headline which implies that the Lions knew who they were, made a judgment, and attacked them. Ate them, of course. But food was not the primary reason, justice and protecting the wild was the reason.

The animal remembers who shot her mate. As if it just happened. And so it has in the continuous present. The mate, his death, the killer, present! The animal knows what to do in this moment. We think about what we have done. About coming to consciousness, remorse and being forgiven. We want to be forgiven. But if you killed her mate and the Elephant sees you coming again, beware. You don't see her mate still on the ground in his agony of the continuous present, but she does. She knows you are a danger to all life and doesn't want you to exist and repeat your deadly actions. An Elephant will recognize the perpetrator of a cull thirty years later and show no mercy. She has to protect her herd. He, the son, knows he will be shot but he will act because he sees his mother still lying there on the ground and despite the Hyenas, Vultures and Marabou Stork that are keen to devour her, she will, for him, be there forever because of what you did. And then you also shoot him for setting things right and he will join the eternal presence of pain. But you won't see that—you will be blinded by your fear or your desire for approval, admirations, forgiveness, love and respect.

* * *

Léonie is grateful that her actions in her dreams are respectful; she wants only to act on behalf of the animals. She wants them to live. This is another reason she doesn't tell her dreams. What if she dreamed the extremely endangered Rhino and someone followed her in the dream and found the hidden animal? What if they are tracking the Bears? She does not want any harm to come from her dreaming. It is better to forget and live in the moment even though she cannot forget, but she can live as if she didn't remember, as if the dreams never occurred. But she is a dreamer, she can't forget the dreams; she has become who she is through the ways the dreams have shaped her.

* * *

"I don't look like anyone I know," Léonie tells her mother.

"You look sort of like me and sort of like your father. Both of our colors blended into the most beautiful skin tone there has ever been. Could have been otherwise, you could have come out looking different from everyone as you're a mutt from a long history of mutts on all sides of the family."

"Is that a good thing?"

"The best," her mother was certain, admiring the blond curls against Léonie's bronze skin.

"Did you marry Dad for his blond hair?"

'You mean, did I marry Dad for you? To explain your future blond curls? Maybe I did to insure the persistence of your blond curls which all our people have. But then, he did the same. My name is Melissa and he wanted a honey child. And so did I."

"And your mother, why did she marry Grandpa?"

"There was a war."

"Is it always a war that brings people to other places?"

"War or famine," Melissa sighed, accepting years of resignation to this knowledge even though her life had been protected from such realities by her grandfather's decision to protect her grandmother from them.

"Always was that way?"

"Lots of war. Lots of famine. That's what the books say."

"And before books?"

"Before books, I don't know. I am a librarian, I only know books. But your grandmother would have said, 'Let's not talk about it. There was war so there was hunger. But we're here. It's over. It was so long ago.' I wish you had asked your grandmother, she knew the old stories but she didn't tell them to me."

"Is that true?"

"I don't know. Maybe she didn't want to speak of her past or she thought I wouldn't want to hear the stories and they would skip to you."

"But I don't know the stories."

"Yes, you do."

Léonie stared at Melissa as if coming upon a mirage from which, nevertheless, water was flowing, who was saying, "The stories skip a generation and then they land. Maybe they have a different cast of characters, but they are the same stories."

"Melissa! Is that true?"

"We don't know what's true except you're my honey child and that's true."

Her mother's name was Melissa and she knew that Bears loved honey. There was a puzzle at the core of her life.

PART III

9

> One might not be able to 'squeeze meaning' from a stone, but
> a stone, presented with an opportunity, with a certain kind of
> welcoming stillness, might reveal, easily and naturally, some
> part of its meaning.
>
> Barry Lopez
> *Horizon*

We are at a library. The library is on a slight hill and in the far distance is a range of mountains like the Cascades. Beyond the automatic glass doors are three sets of curved, wide stone stairs angling down to the street corner meant to resemble the tide coming in. The way the fading light falls on the edges of the cut stones we might imagine the froth emerging from and withdrawing into the darker waters. The librarian's desk is behind a curved wall that extends a third of the way to the two-story ceiling and partially into the room so she does not see him enter and he does not see her at first.

* * *

Whether they remember the moment in the same way or different ways, they both remember the moment. He did not say, she did not say, whether they remembered the moment in the same way or different ways, only that they both remember the moment.

The first sentence implies they have a future. The second sentence implies that indeed the moment occurred. This is their origin story. Not a dream but it still seems like it. And when he remembers it, when she remembers it, like her dreaming, it is happening now.

When is now? Now. Now and always. All of this in the extensive and continuous presence of his remembering, her remembering, their origin story. Their meeting. This moment.

* * *

Lucas approached the research desk cautiously, or better said, shyly. He was used to searching on his own for whatever he needed. He was reviewing the habits of his early academic training, taking a card catalogue drawer to an oak desk in the common research room, feeling the quiet company of fellow researchers while sorting through the slightly yellowing cards, touching what others before him had touched with the same sense of hope and curiosity. The silent camaraderie which had extended into the classroom and that he had expected in medical practice, had so rapidly eroded that he never opened his own office or pursued a specialty other than ER.

But he had come to a library, why not the medical library at the University which was not so far away? Why a municipal library, sizeable as it was? He wanted to find what the people should have available to them. He wanted to enter into the conversation that should be happening in the community. He was engaged in researching ethics. Ethics are of the people, not professionals. Such an understanding is the core of ethics for him. He was already dreading what would not be available to him here and so not to the general public.

From the time he had entered medical school until finishing his residencies, the heart of medicine, as he had pursued it, had hardened. Intimacy with patients was considered old fashioned; family practice was disappearing; he opted for ER teamwork—the docs, nurses, aides, techies, they were still all in it together from beginning to end. ER had to be a community effort and that sustained him. A group effort so much more so than elective surgery which also relied on others but identified a hero. ER had few lone heroes though specialists were called when needed. Rather, ER depended on an ensemble that was well trained, technically proficient, able to triage, and agile as any troupe of performers entering a new city and having to adapt to different languages and ways of thinking. Every patient, in his view, was a foreign culture and success in meeting it meant being scrupulously attentive to the foreign language while willing to enter the unknown—and not know—while trying to adapt to the situation whatever it turned out to be.

When Lucas had thought of becoming a physician, he thought first of being a core member of a small town, like having a large family and being involved in each others' lives. His doctor had had his office in a wood shingled two-story neighborhood house. Climb the front steps and turn right into his office or turn left into the physician's home. When it was warm enough, patients could sit on the porch, on the two-person swing or the rocking chair near the playpen where one would also find the blocks, the various dolls and animals that belonged to the doctor's children. Correction: "patients," but only for this instance, more correctly the neighbors who happened at that moment to be in pain and in need of his services though it would be as likely that they had had dinner together the night before and the doc had suggested the neighbor come in so they could get some tests. That was how Lucas had imagined his life. As a child, he had often come to the doctor for a childhood ailment and when he had had a high fever the doctor had come to him.

Having this in his background, he was alien to the impersonal world that was developing as quickly as an aggressive metastasis. Everything he had ever cared about had been hands-on. So, he was glad to have walked into the library rather than doing the research alone and online though it would not be the same as in the past. This time he would not be making his way to a section in the stacks which he knew well, where books familiar and unfamiliar stood next to each other creating families of interest, that's how he saw it, who invited him to add a book of his own to the shelf one day, or to browse and praise among those not long to be strangers.

No longer. Certainly not in the field of bioethics which logically should be the most intimate but its entanglement in law rendered it remote. Most of what he was seeking was in periodicals, newspapers or medical journals and would not be in a paper card catalogue if one still existed here. Most likely, he would have to peer into a computer, even in this setting. He disliked doing so.

The only possible advantage that he saw of the computer in the examining room was that he was seated on the same level as the patient when in the past he would be standing, writing in the chart which was on the cabinet top by the swabs, cotton balls, familiar tools of hygiene and healing. His doctor's cabinet top had looked the same. It was also an advantage to stand so he could easily move around the patient and use his hands as diagnostic instruments. A feeling of peerage was possible, if they were both seated, he told himself. But not really. Moving around, leaning against the wall, touching the patient established a relationship because he was equally touched. The patient was aware of the doc's deep listening to the heart, lungs, belly sounds, the voice, to what was being said and what could not be spoken but was discernable through different forms of attention.

* * *

I have to interrupt this monologue. This is the Writer, again. Lucas Jay isn't a writer and it is no surprise that he introduces himself in this way. He wants to engage your interest through his sincerity. As I don't know him well enough yet to present him to you, I've had him convey the details he thinks are essential, what we think someone has to know in order to know him, the way each of us has a story that must be conveyed for trust and intimacy to occur. He wants you to know the kind of physician he is and that contemporary medicine, medical care is in decline, is dangerous and corrupt. He wants you to hold this understanding from your own experience in tandem with what you learn about who he is, his origins, and what he thinks.

As you most likely understand, he and Léonie came to me the way La Vieja came but without the personal connection I have had with La Vieja. I was still desperately lonely for the unexpected community that gathers in a book and learns to coexist, to depend upon, enhance, affirm the existence of each other and so I gratefully ensconced him in the heart of my imagination. Then I asked him to assure me that the three of them who had gathered were capable of coexisting in and enlivening a text.

"We belong together as no others" he insisted though the story had not begun and they did not know each other. "Our story will occur and so it has already happened. You can write this memoir of ours in any tense you find appropriate at any moment as you may be recording it, even its future, in past tense, in the present and past tense, that is, after the event."

The imagination is a real place where all the worlds are real and simultaneous even if determined and validated by different laws.

* * *

In the old days, he would have been charting as he found necessary so that he would remember—he, not anyone else—and if necessary, so that he could make a referral in his own way to a colleague. In his world, he was determined to practice medicine as best as he could in the old ways. There was no way to code what was truly important from what the patient was saying, and he found it insulting to dictate his notes in the patient's presence in a form that satisfied the insurance company and hospital record keepers. Since there was no choice if one wanted to practice medicine in a hospital or in a medical group but to go along with the system, the good physicians he knew took the bitter medicine and found ways to compensate for its side-effects of alienation and its limited understanding of the conditions they were meeting. The obsession with keeping records for financial purposes was dominating his field instead of encouraging the physician to focus on the event itself and do whatever true healing required.

What mattered to Lucas was looking at the person before him as he was listening to the patient's story, noting how he/she presented the injury or illness, and then used his hands to translate pain and anguish into particularities that might be eased.

"Is the pain here? Or here? Ah. And how would you describe it? And now? And now, what are you feeling about this? What would you say is causing this discomfort?" And so on. Not looking to MRIs or CT scans or even ultrasound at first. First his senses and then his extra senses and then the particular knowledge conveyed by his hands. It all came to him at once and he had known this since he was a child.

And then, the story. The patient's story. The pain, the condition, the symptoms, when did they occur? How did the patient receive them? What did the person think? Why might this have occurred, why now, why to this patient, what might heal it, how did it relate to what was going on around the patient, at home, at work, in the community, environmentally, in the world?

He recalled a woman's eyes filling with tears, but not because of his medical skills. It was because he had asked her what she thought was ailing her and why. She knew exactly why and no one had listened to her before. Having come to a diagnosis together, they proceeded to collaborate on a treatment.

If the patient was someone who might still be connected the ancestors, he might ask, "What does your grandmother think?"

"She isn't with us anymore."

"Yes, but what does she think?"

And so the patient might say or speculate, because the patient had secretly consulted the grandmother who was even wiser now that she was on the other side and was spending her afterlife taking care of the living relatives. When everything was told, the family stories, the grandmother's opinions, then they would both laugh, or all laugh depending on whether other family members were in the room, when likely, someone else would add something about the way they understood what was happening and Lucas took that in as well.

"You're running late," a nurse would say as the end of each shift approached and he would always answer surprised, "Oh, I didn't know. I'm soooo sorry. I'll stay late."

"The next shift will be coming in soon," the nurse would protest, and Lucas would stare at the huge clock on the wall as if seeing it for the first time and as if his attention to it as a sentient being—maybe it was, how would we know?—could change the position of its hands at will.

"And what about me?" the nurse continued, but grinning—knowing she or he would stay late too, had known it before coming to work, last week as well, and knew it would recur tomorrow and the next and the next. It was the price, never too much, for team work and respect. "You know we are the only ER in this county that doesn't respect time."

"In this country," Lucas noted agreeably. "We should get a medal."

Family legend had it that his grandfather had been a bone setter and continued serving his village even when physicians in the city began using X-rays. "How did he do it?" he asked his uncle, who much older than his father, and still living on the island where the two had been born and who never went to war and was intact, and was responsible for maintaining the story, true or not.

"Well, he saw into the body," his uncle stated matter-of-factly. As a young boy, Lucas thought he literally meant with his eyes and kept trying to penetrate beneath the surface of physical objects. But perhaps the grandfather could see with his hands or had developed other senses and Lucas began to pursue whatever entrances he could imagine that with permission would not be intrusive. He was fascinated by the enigma of shape which implied a boundary and the fact that knowledge demanded openings. Though he was a man, he wanted to be entered as well, to be revealed. To open, to reveal, to be revealed, to enter another, to respect, to understand. In and out were koans he was always considering.

The card catalogue had been traditionally housed in a beautiful piece of oak furniture. An article on the website of the Smithsonian Institution regarding the card catalogue's demise noted that the cabinet now served to hold wine, white wine on top.

This library had been modernized too. There was no catalogue. There were computers everywhere. Lucas was lost. He hadn't been in such a library often enough to find it familiar.

He walked gracefully, bending forward slightly as if reaching toward someone or something or humbling himself and yet he also seemed entirely upright. Inner and outer postures modifying or supporting each other. Standing at the desk, he found himself silent. The woman sitting there looked up at him, assessed his restraint and asked in a very kind and earnest voice: "Can I help you?"

He did not regard her question as gratuitous or professional. He contemplated the question, cocking his head, ever so slightly, birdlike as if to scrutinize her. No, he was scrutinizing her. Was he nodding? He was considering the question. It had been genuine. Can she help him?

Nonplussed, his quiet and equally sincere response was, "You already have." He looked at her without encroaching on her privacy. On the surface, he was simply observing the kind person who offered him help without revealing that he was skilled and practiced in interpreting the slightest sign—as was she.

Her eyes watered slightly and she flushed and looked away. The subtlest energetic exchange has been detected.

The next move was also up to him. They were both in unexplored territory. He had only a second or two.

"I am researching bioethics and access to the field is daunting. So, yes, I need help. But as the field is often concerned with whether people are being kind to each other, you have just brought it to life."

Years of practice, innate sensitivity and perhaps his lineage combined so that he could accurately assess what was before him in seconds. He waited for her response though certain of what its tone might be.

"I think I may know how to open the field to you though I don't know yet what in particular you are looking for."

He liked her voice. It had a quiet vibrato. Bees returning to the hive, honey running.

"Yes," he said, "But might we have a cup of coffee and a pastry together later. I will be tired with low blood sugar. And perhaps you will be so as well." Maybe they had had a far longer conversation than is indicated here. His invitation could easily be considered presumptuous, but she did not think it was.

Summer. He was wearing a white linen shirt, not formal but not informal either and tan slacks, a narrow brown leather belt, dun leather shoes, not quite moccasins, not quite loafers. He is lean, his skin is smooth and tawny. He is rather bald, the very top of his head shining as if having deliberately created a tonsure, the hair below dark, almost black, also shiny and very wavy; if a few inches longer it would curl. This classic cut is so natural to him—is it why he appears both humble and devoted? She guessed he was about 35 years old. She was off by a several years. He was older, is 40. Somehow medical training and working as a doc hadn't aged him. He was not wearing glasses. Oh yes, he was wearing frameless glasses, not obvious at first. Like a desert landscape or a magnificent animal seen against rock and sand, he seemed to be of a piece, in all ways integrated with himself. The way an animal still comfortable in his own terrain walks, runs, confident and without the need to assert himself. His presentation—no, his being without presentation—is still imposing, yet restrained, a remarkable combination, and, yes, intriguing. She cannot identify his history except that it is unlikely to have been metropolitan for generations.

He was neither aggressive nor passive. This is what puzzled Léonie who was considering how to respond; his manner appeared untroubled, that is, calm but weighty. Untroubled but serious in these years when everyone, it seems, is stressed, the entire country, maybe the entire globe, unnerved. Untroubled when everyone who had come to her desk recently had been visibly distressed, burdened, driven by a quick need for information more than a need to understand. Untroubled is not accurate. He is deeply troubled but not flustered by it. The ER has taught him well, has trained him to meet crises. She looked again; he only appears untroubled, because his extensive concerns are not personal, are not for himself and his reflexes are to respond on behalf of someone else. So much to register in a minute. And she is also well trained to do so. Who *is* this man? she wondered.

It has been a long time since she has been interested in knowing who a man might be. Who is he? The question didn't leave her. And what animal would he be, if he would be an animal? This is her way of knowing. His species eluded her, as if he and her thoughts were running from her and then it was obvious, as the speed of not knowing increased, she noted that he could maintain this speed for a long time, that running is his nature, not sprinting but the long-legged extension over the ground for hours, yes, it was so clear, he is a horse, a wild horse. He is a Przewalski's Horse, though not stocky still the same coloring, And she thought, but mystified by her thoughts, the same energy. A Przewalski's Horse, yes, not a mustang. And why not? Because Léonie wants him to be a being whose existence is being restored and not a mustang who is living under increasing threat. She doesn't want him to be someone under constant siege, but rather someone who will thrive. She is so tired of the ways extinction is burning up the land, she wants, if only for this moment, the experience of life in its fullness.

If ER has instructed him to be aware of nuanced communications, twenty-five years of being with, of dreaming Bears, have trained her to be exquisitely sensitive to humans. Bears, she discovered are far more capable of reading human motivations and states of mind than any human has ever been to reading Bears. Bears have the laser ability to see through human pretenses while humans rarely know when the Bear is bluffing, particularly if they meet in the wild, the Bear's territory. They are in her territory; she thinks he is being straightforward. And there is his horse presence, this rare horse who was extinct in the wild and then restored through breeding the few who were in zoos or preserves. Now a few are reintroduced and living in small family herds in Mongolia. And some in France, of all places. Actually, Leonine and Lucas are sniffing each other with the highly developed skill and precision with which animals determine who is in their territory and what their intentions might be, and this, without a word or common language.

"Let us see if you be can helped to get on track with your research." She structured the sentence deliberately.

He noticed. "Let's see" would have had a different tone. "Let _us_ see...."

"Then, perhaps, we can consider your invitation again at 8:45. Someone else is scheduled to close the library tonight, so we could leave at 9 pm." He is already counting on _we_.

She is not apprehensive, detects no hidden agendas or repressed energies. Shortly, she will be further reassured by what he is seeking to study— she will spend the next hours searching for documents relating to his current ethical concerns. Is it always assumed that Judeo-Christian thought, Western medicine and Western science have hegemony in medical ethical issues? She senses he is also asking, "Should they?" Then he wants to know how African, Asian, Latin American patients or those from the Pacific Rim might have different ethical concerns in hospitals or getting treatment than those of European descent. He takes notes, gathers the references, and goes to the next items on his list, long enough to occupy him for several years.

Are animals persons and what individual rights might they have in regard to science and research? Is it always necessary or right for science and research to be first and always concerned with human rights? Is it ethical to experiment on one animal on behalf of another? What precedents exist to meet conflicts between human, non-human and environmental concerns?

"I think a four-year dissertation is brewing," she notes though the statement is also a question.

"Oh, I have done that," he smiles. "Not again, please. Unless," now he catches himself. He better not press ahead or he will lose all traction, if he has any at all, with her. But it is too late.

"Unless?" she asks.

"Unless you want to be my committee."

"I'll pass," she says. He hopes it isn't a death sentence.

Their search will take them to a wide field and questions she never had the occasion to consider with someone else. Because of the animals, she is entirely engaged. She may learn how horses think from him. They are herd animals, so they were already in *we* territory even if he didn't language it from the beginning. And Przewalski's Horses bond with unusual attention, seeming to like to live flank to flank, or groom each other head to flank. She is curious about what might transpire between these two species—both of which Bear and Horse live here on this continent as well as in Mongolia.

She has to return to his investigation, to what he wishes to discover. It does not seem as if he is considering a particular case but rather preparing his mind for what he might have to consider and meet. She imagines discussing what is not privileged over a drink. Their exchange is productive.

He smiles believing she is interested or at least, he feels that he has not sabotaged the evening. "8:45?"

She nods. Relief. But adds, "We'll check in then." She still seems interested in meeting later, even though she is slowing things down. That's his observation and that's a good thing in his estimation. But he can't resist, following with, "I can't imagine that I will rescind the invitation or that my reasons for offering it will change." He privately notes that she spoke in the plural and he is still responding in the singular. He notes her *we* and his *I.* Damn his gender conditioning. He will learn from her. He hopes to have the opportunity. He doesn't speak automatically in communal terms; he has been raised in the United States where he was born. But he could speak otherwise, his grandparents, his grandmother and that grandfather would have had that instinct, but he falters, "I yield to your uncommon sense and will be happy to extend the invitation again at 8:45." The sentence has been uttered; it is too late for him to correct it. "Let's yield to your uncommon sense …" he might have said.

At exactly 8:45, he approaches her again, "What shall we do? Might we get a cup of coffee?" He feels he has gotten it right. The invitation is not as formal as before. She accepts with a laugh and a toss—he notes for the first time—of tight blond curls. Then she suggests a meal and a drink rather than coffee as it is late. Damn. In trying to be moderate, he missed that she might not have eaten since starting this shift. He is accustomed to not eating, not sleeping. It goes with the territory of his profession. And consequently, although he is observant, there is a lot he has missed. He has not noticed what she is wearing. He has not looked to see if she is wearing a ring. She isn't. That is, not an engagement or wedding ring. A ring with three ovals of turquoise on her left hand extends to her knuckles. He does see that she is wearing a silver Navajo bear pendant. Maybe, he doesn't see this at first either but thinks he saw it because she always wears it, and ultimately he is aware and thinks Bear, of course. Her nails are filed, not polished. Vertigo calls him to put his hand on her desk to balance himself. She likes the square brown hand. To her it seems steady.

This is the 21ˢᵗ century, the USA, Planet Earth. They were both born here in an environment of fear and suspicion so their exchange should not play out this way—his ease and her openness, and the sense they both have that they understand each other and that this necessary exchange is only a formality, but it is happening in this place at this time in America.

They will have dinner in a small late-night restaurant. *Enchiladas* with *salsa verde* and *chiles rellenos* this time. They decide to share the dishes.

"Cheese or chicken?" he asks.

She raises and drops her shoulders, not helplessly, but indicating the choice doesn't matter, or both are the same, or she is not vegetarian or vegan, which is what he needed to know if he were to order, or that she wants to see what he will do. He orders cheese.

The restaurant is called Milagro. She goes there regularly as much for the name as for the food. The name may be proving itself. They won't go out to a restaurant tomorrow night but they well might on Monday night. And the next night and the next. Unless he is working the ER night shift, which he does frequently but not tonight and won't for long. Over time he is already thinking he will change to days, Tuesdays, Wednesdays and Thursdays. When the small hospital staff is stressed, he will cover Monday as well, which is a hard day for patients and physicians after the weekend. From time to time, but irregularly, he takes extra days which can't be planned in advance. He likes to come in when the winds are high like Santa Anas, Sundowners or Diablos and he gets to see how weather can make everyone a little crazy and he can reassure some patients that they will be sane when the winds calm down.

Tomorrow, she will ask him if he thought the food was good the very first time they ate there. He will laugh and say, "You will have to ask my mother."

Their meeting should not happen this way, not at this time in American history, not in this violent country, not where trust is entirely eroded, not where conflict and suspicion are the rule, not where any woman is potentially endangered rather than protected by every man she meets, officers of the peace included.

But she did not do a background check, she did not ask if he has an STD—he does not—she did not wonder if he has a gun. To protect her? To coerce her? Negative. She did not check Facebook to see if he has a page—he does not have one—or the hospital website where he supposedly works—where he does work— or his references as a Medical Ethicist. She did not leave a note for her colleague about her evening plans with the information connected to his library card. She did not consider that he might be a serial killer or a sex trafficker which is the world we are living in now.

* * *

Soon they will have a conversation about trust. Léonie's parents never locked their doors and so Léonie didn't when she began living alone, but her friends convinced her to start. When did people begin locking their doors? When did they stop trusting each other? Vietnam, she thinks. When we did the unthinkable. She thinks we because her father thought this way about Vietnam. Then, she had heard her grandfather speak of WW II. He had said "We witnessed the unthinkable but didn't comprehend what we were seeing. Until, the end. Until the bomb." Her grandmother said nothing but if the conversation went on too long about the war, she left the room.

That was it, she is thinking, as she watches Lucas who is both a stranger and entirely familiar. So that was it. After the Bomb, people began to lock their doors. How could it be otherwise after what we had done? First we had to imagine it and then we had to do it. The Death Camps and then the Bomb and so My Lai was inevitable. So people began locking their doors. But not her folks despite what they saw and not her grandparents. No surprise Léonie thinks looking at this man who she is going to trust, that she locks the door to her house and her car and probably so does Lucas. She decides she will not lock her door so he can enter as he wishes if he turns out to be who she imagines he may be. It is all speculative, the food hasn't even come yet.

"What are you thinking?" Lucas asks.

"I am thinking about locking doors, about when I didn't lock my doors and why I lock them now. I am thinking I don't want to lock them anymore."

He laughs. He guesses he will have to stop locking his. This makes him laugh again.

But the Bears do not laugh. The hunt is ongoing. They cannot lock their dens. They have no safety.

*   *   *

5,000,000 or so Native Americans survived the five hundred year hunt. The majority were killed by the European invaders through massacre, biological warfare, armed conflict, land theft, starvation, cultural suppression, reducing their numbers from 18 million at the time of the conquest when the Europeans arrived to an estimated 250,000 in the late 1800s. 18 million compared to the few thousand who invaded? Native Americans have never been safe in this country since 1492. By rights of origin or majority, we should be living under their laws and government, ruled entirely by the Great Law of Peace of the Haudenosaunee, the Iroquois Confederacy, the welfare of the Bears, trees, and people assured by ceremony and a great love for the seventh generation who will not be known by us, by anyone, will not exist, if we don't change our ways.

* * *

In truth, we don't know whether Léonie's and Lucas' bonding took place over a few hours, a few weeks or months or even before they actually met for the first time. This description is accurate to the dynamic, to what they were immediately imagining, to the ways they instinctively stepped toward each other and away from convention. Most importantly they would both confirm that it is accurate to the field they have stepped into and the raw and bare nature of their connection. The details are not important and distract from what is essential. Two people meet in another time and place, irrefutably real, at the edge of a singularity. They will be taken by the whirlwind that is just just just—there. And then...?

After the food comes, she thinks about his research interests and so of Biotic Ethics. Thinking she does not want to colonize the universe, doesn't want her species, that is the human species, to spread like a virus through the cosmos, destroying whatever doesn't please or conform to our ways, ignorant that survival depends on the inter-relationship of all beings, whether we understand it or not.

* * *

As this text is being edited, two billionaires have set off for space, inaugurating private adventures and further threatening the lives of the remaining mammals and the natural world. The beings most in jeopardy have not been consulted.

* * *

There were once 50,000 Grizzly Bears in the US—now perhaps 1,500. She wants the original numbers of Bears of the extant eight species worldwide to be restored in the wild. This would mean the restoration of forests, original habitats, other wildlife, waters. The effort to restore the Przewalski Horse is nascently effective but they need to be entirely free, to run wild without any limitations, and they need the land to do it. Infinite herds across the plains? Unlikely but greatly to be desired.

It has not been more than two hours since they left the university library and he is thinking that he may have met his soul mate, and before dinner is over he will think he has (finally) met his match. She, having a sense of where this might go, is cautious about "signs and wonders," has no time or interest in flirtations, wants to be certain that they are aligned on what matters most to her at this time, this means the fate of the Earth and the natural world. She is thinking she will really have to stop locking her doors or give him a key.

Léonie is thinking that a female Bear is only concerned about meeting males in the woods when it is *the* season. She likes thinking in this way, about the relationship between time, weather, climate and activity. In her study of Bears in her spare time at the library, as well as in her direct and dreamed observations, she has learned that in summer a male may become a predator when the female is in estrus. If she has cubs, she will not want to conceive and will fight to protect them. In that instance, they may well fight to the death. He wants to plant his seeds in her and she wants to wait for another year, until the cubs are independent, intent upon protecting her little ones who carry another genetic line than his. A man is seated across from her. One reason, she is thinking about the Bears is that this is a biologic event for her. It's summer. For the Bears and for Léonie. Come October, they, Bear, Mama Bear, Baby Bears may all be foraging, safely in the same field. Léonie too? Lucas?

Léonie is imagining Mama Bear fighting a male Bear on behalf of her cubs. Then her mind switches or expands, imagines Mama Bear alert to the threat to the little lives from hunters, settlers, habitat destruction, climate change, fires. You think she, Bear Momma, doesn't know? You think she doesn't understand? Léonie knows she knows.

Léonie could begin, "The earth is burning, there are wildfires everywhere, ice is disappearing ..." to see how Lucas will respond. Or she could dare to begin with what is always weighing on her heart, what is driving her mad: "The animals are going extinct. What kind of life will it be without them?"

"No life."

He hears "extinct." Whether she says it aloud or not, he hears it. Of course, he wants to embrace her, to reassure her, to protect her. It is an old cultural habit, more than 5,000 years old. It could be considered patronizing but he has the history to know colonization and decolonization in his own body and skin and his reflexes are not of that kind. He hears "extinct" and a voice in him shouts, "No!"

She startles. Nothing has been said aloud but she is engaged by hearing his certain if silent resolve to meet her and whatever she is carrying and to meet the tragedy aside from her concerns. She has met her partner. The partners have met each other. He also has an agenda. A life calling. A destiny.

Something is rising up in both of them as powerful as estrus or musth.

Let's not pretend we know what is happening here either within each one of them or between them. Between, meaning in the space amidst them and also between as in joining them. Or what common field is being formed from what is emanating from them? What is being created from them individually that is absorbing them back into it? What magnetism pulls them to each other that becomes a potent field that holds them both? How are they being altered by having met, by being drawn to each other? There is something between them that is now essentially their own, in the way they are each their own person. Also, the field they are creating and occupying, that it is creating them, is not a field of a nuclear couple, it is … she doesn't have words for her thoughts. He is still unknown to her though they are rapidly becoming of each other. In the way she had been with the Bears when she was a child. They hadn't had to speak in order to enter a common current in which they remained both particular and dissolved. Each individual drop of water and the stream, then the river and then the ocean, and then the entire Earth's currents and tides. And in my body, she thinks without thinking. I could drown in him, she thinks while he is thinking water is life. *Mni wiconi.* They are in agreement.

Nothing has been said. No thoughts explicit.

Lucas leans toward Léonie ever so slightly. Has she spoken yet? He is concerned, as he was from the moment he first spoke to her in the library that he will dominate the conversation, because he is a male and this is how men are trained to be by this culture. Also because it was his research, his concerns that they have already attended for several hours. Their connection will collapse of its own weight if he continues. He knows himself, and his contemporaries, and how they are influenced, well enough to know that he is a social and also biological being. She is not a woman—no woman is—upon whom a man should impose his will, his desire or his certainties. He leans back a little further than he leaned forward and settles against the dark red leather of the booth. He will wait.

She has a Bloody Mary, the rim of the glass thickly frosted with salt the way she likes it. They know her here and how to prepare what she favors. The waiter had been amused to take the order from the man and quickly composed his face. The man has ordered a glass of ice tea. Léonie is going to test Lucas by telling him what she holds most intimately in her heart. She is going to continue with "Extinction." The test is whether he will understand. The test is whether he will respond in kind. But he already has responded, he has thought *mni wiconi*. She knows what it means: Water is life.

She is so confident that he is trustworthy, she speaks at the outset of what she would not reveal to her mother or anyone else. She says, "When I was seven, I began dreaming of Bears. Essentially the same dream has come to me again and again over the years, changing slightly in response to my growing older and to their reality that is being conveyed to me. They are going extinct. They know this and live in fear and terror, immediate and unceasing. In the dreams, they know this. In the dreams, over time, the number of Bears who sit in a circle with me diminish." She repeats it for emphasis. "In the dreams, I sit in a circle with Bears but over time the circle became smaller." She does not tell him yet the greater secret that in the dream she has sometimes become a Bear. She does not tell him these are and are not dreams. She doesn't say these are real Bears, that is Bears that also live in the four-dimensional world she and he are occupying. And she is permitted to coexist with them in another dimension which is also real but requires a key to enter. The key is not a skeleton key, a mathematical formula or a hadron collider. The key and the dimension are of the Bears' making. They turn it.

He listens to her with seriousness, understanding that they are about to cross another singularity although their relationship is just beginning, may not even have begun. That this is occurring within moments of their first significant exchange is challenging but no more so than entering a village where the people are of another culture and language altogether. And he has done this several times and so has the Writer who also knows what it is like to enter a village in a foreign country and be greeted, though essentially a stranger, by drumming and dancing. These first moments are such between them, especially as there is no means to prepare, destroying any assumptions he or she might have about anything. For Lucas it is as if he has fallen from a boat into the ocean and has to swim and there is no chance of being rescued. He is not going to be saved from her. He is going to swim or drown in her. Most likely both.

The territory is not only unfamiliar, it is of another world; he is entering quantum physics land which has intrigued him though he has always had to live in a Newtonian universe, or that is how it seemed. No one called him to quanta before. Naively, he reaches for a buoy to hold on to for these waters are far too deep for an anchor. He wants something outside himself to give him buoyancy. Strangely, he wants law. He doesn't want to believe that everything they value is outside the lives they are called to live. He goes to work. She goes to work. He drives a car. She drives a car. He wears shoes that are manufactured in a factory, maybe in a foreign country, maybe by a child or an impoverished woman—he looks down— so does she.

This is quantum but the laws of physics are not going to help him. He needs something stabilizing, a ground to hold him. He is an ethicist. He goes to law. He would prefer natural law to human law and now is he relying on one that partakes of both. This is a crazy way of meeting the moment, it is entirely outside of linear thought, but he has found a foothold, something to think about, a law, a real law, one on the books, and he is using it to sustain him; he grabs on to it.

Rivers and Mountains have been given legal standing as persons. This is a new development but it is based on an old Supreme Court case that was greatly influenced by a strategically placed essay in the Southern California Law Review and brought to the attention of the Supreme Court Justices: *Should Trees Have Standing: Towards Legal Rights for Natural Objects.* Should trees have standing? Thinking of this case and everything that has come from it, gives him confidence in the future, in possibility, and so in this moment. The tree is like the tree of life. There is a memory rising in him and he suppresses it. Hard. Without realizing that is what he is doing. To do so, he drops into an old way of thinking. It only lasts a few seconds, if that long. Time in the mind is different from time lived. But still, it is a departure and he knows this.

In his mind, in his thinking, it is ethical to treat animals like persons. Therefore, it is unethical not to. Most ethicists do not go so far as they remain faithful to privileging the human. But, in his mind, they are persons. He is safe. He can honor the Bears she is describing. He can navigate these waters.

"We have lost our moral compass," he says. He enfolds her within his understanding. "Maybe we lost it thousands of years ago or five hundred years." He embraces her insight and anguish. But in that gesture, he takes her into himself and she is no longer independent but neither is he. Now, he will have to learn how I remains I in we. And how we is an energy that allows for I to be particular.

She is thinking about Bears and he is climbing a tree. This will not do. Can he become a Tree? Will that unite them? This is not the right direction. He must try to understand Bear. He finds he is rushing toward understanding; he is swift. He is galloping toward it without understanding why he is speeding so. He can hear in her intonation that she means Bear and not bear. But he hasn't met Bear. Except for what he has read. Until he learns more from her, bears will remain inside him, and inside him they cannot be Bears, they are confused with the human concept of, the human understanding of bear. Science. A science bear is significantly different from Bear which is more fearsome than extant.

Somewhere in the forest, Bear twitches in her sleep. They were so close to standing alongside each other. Bear stands up to her full height, walks over to the Jeffrey pine that towers over her and raises her forefoot high, scratching down the bark. The claw mark is ten feet high. Bear does not give up on the man because she trusts the woman, but, in defense of her little ones, she leaves her mark. Just so he knows. This is an unusual moment. This is her, Mama Bear's, territory. She has sought it out and is protecting it so she can feed the little ones. There are lower marks that she has had to overcome. There are many ways that she marks her territory, rubbing her back against the trees, urinating to mark the area, but marking the tree with her claws is her own statement. Léonie cannot reach even close to Mama Bear's mark. Nor can Lucas if he sees the mark. Lucas is not, cannot be, aware of what is occurring in this animal world even though it is in response to him. Nor can Léonie. Bear knows what they cannot know.

A critical moment. Léonie and Lucas are more allied than he could ever imagine even if this were a meeting after years of contact. And yet Lucas knows that they are not quite in accord though he cannot explain why. Léonie is grateful that he understands there is a world crisis but she wants him to care about the Bears in particular or to understand that she does. Later they can discuss the reasons there is such a crisis and how the Bears' situation and the human situation have a common root. But for this moment, she does not care about the humans who always take focus. She cares about the Bears. About these Bears in particular with whom she sat around a fire, all of them sitting on or leaning against the logs. How delicate and precarious human speech is when it matters. Yes, he has to say more.

"Yes, I would like to know what the Bears think, what they would say if we could sit together." He doesn't have it right yet.

"You must be crazed with the grief of it," he begins again hesitantly, determined to cleave feeling and meaning to each word. "Genocide and extinction are the same, that's what the dream is saying, isn't it?"

Who is going to say the next necessary sentence? Will he beat her to it? She is pulling her lips in as if to bite both her lips at once. He leaps off the cliff: "And the dream indicates these are your people." Relief. He has succeeded. This is what she needed him to understand.

"Yes. They are my people."

She doesn't say, "You will see." She doesn't say what he must understand according to the laws by which she lives. Laws of kinship. She also lives by law. They are her people so they will be have to be his people and this will not be an abstract idea. She doesn't know that he understands more exactly than she imagines. She doesn't know he is reeling with the synchronicity of their concerns. Fortunately, the food comes and they yield to the slight distraction, dividing the plates, adding salsa. What is the next move? He takes a warm tortilla from under the white cloth and tears it in two and gives her the first half. They begin to eat. Slowly. Everything has to be digested.

Now it is his turn. She wants to hear his opening.

"It's not right for me to do the work I am doing," he begins, hoping she will listen to the end. He is starting a long way from where her dream has taken him. He is not articulate the way she is and he is awkward in this way of conversing as he has never had such an opportunity, not opportunity, invitation. Who wouldn't be awkward inventing a language that is inter-cultural and inter-species and inter-worlds?

"I had to train to do it and training means…" it's hard to find the words, "training means forgetting a lot, forgetting much of what I value." He laughs, maybe he snorts. The sound is bitter, directed first at himself and then *everything*. He doesn't want to have to say too much and is expecting her to understand what is not said but still he is going to use too many words. His profession is so contentious even though everyone talks about healing—they are armed to wage war against whatever causes disease as they define it. Everything is contentious in the system, patients, physicians, nurses, research, staff, technical staff, housekeeping, hospitals, pharmacies, pharmaceutical firms, insurance companies, government—the list is end-less—all duking it out, looking to have hegemony. But now, he is looking, as he sees she is, for the common field through which everything is instantly, perfectly and happily translated from one personal language to another and it makes sense, the way he listens to a patient.

"I have a degree as a Medical ethicist. Not only a doc, but an ethicist. Imagine." He is rather bitter given this is an introductory conversation. "That's what I meant when you spoke of the four years. I got an advanced degree. I can even teach it. I can join an Ethics department. I am *qualified*." That snort again. He isn't bragging. He is vexed. He isn't trying to certify for a position as her companion. She isn't sure she intuits where he is going but it sounds like he is suffering an ethical dilemma. This she under-stands.

He continues or he can't stop, "Teach ethics? Teach about ethics as part of the necessary humanities training? Yes, we certainly need to balance, to offset science? But teach ethics? Assert what ethical principles are? Advise responses? Create curricula for the down and dirty bloody stuff of life? Such degrees are offered because we don't have elders, because laws and regulations replace natural relationships and because rigorous ethical thinking isn't part of the medical curriculum or, everyday life. We learn about the law … but … maybe that is just learning about limitation and contention. And how even convey what an ethical dilemma feels like, how it sits within the patient, the family and the doc? And the hospital? The hell with the hospital." He can't stop himself. "Because we don't commonly speak of such issues—like who we save and who we let die which, today, may be the way of saving someone." He has to stop here. He is teetering between a lecture and a rant. Each implies disaster.

His voice lowers, softens. "I'm too young for this work. It isn't the job of a professional. It's the right work for an elder who knows what he has lived. Not what he's read, not about the difference between Aristotelian ethics, Christian ethics, Church ethics … Buddhist ethics, Navajo ethics, blah blah blah. Certainly, certainly not about a law passed in a legislature somewhere. Sometimes I wish I could go to my father and ask him what to do instead of referring to certain standards as if ethics could be charted or described in the DSM. I wish I could go to my father." He has slid down from the public controversy to a silence that resembles sorrow.

"But?" She just wants him to know she is listening. There must be a thousand reasons he can't go to his father like the ways she could not tell Melissa her dreams.

"I can't because he's no longer here. Nor is my grandfather who would really know." He has reached the boundary between worlds for himself now. He has come to the place where he must leap across the line. "My father died when I was three. He died of the war." He hesitates and then elaborates.

"He didn't die in the war. He died *of* the war. War killed him."

She does a quick calculation and immediately knows which war. For her, and now she understands for him, Vietnam is the living war that is never ending but for her family, *The War*, is WWII.

"I know such a story," she murmurs quietly, "from my grandparents." Her instinct was to say grandfather, because he had been the one to enlist but he didn't suffer more than her grandmother who, with her people, had nothing, absolutely nothing, to gain from the war, except suffering. Only suffering. What is called Biblical suffering. Which is now commonplace.

He studies her and begins to get a clue to the mystery she holds. "Your people are not from this hemisphere," he suggests.

"Not all of them," she agrees.

"And yours?"

"They're from this hemisphere."

"And your father? He fought …?" She can see his face distort. He does not want the conversation to go down into this crevice.

"Someday, we'll talk about war," he adds. "But not now. Ok?"

Every moment between them is a test, is a dare, requires yielding. She reaches across the table and puts her hand on the fist that is clenched around a knife. He drops the knife which clatters and takes her hand, one gesture.

"No use pretending I am not an angry man," he looks into her eyes and holds on.

"No use pretending I'm not broken-hearted," she answers.

"But I don't hurt anyone or anything with my anger." She doesn't say, "We'll see." He hears what she doesn't say and can go on. "I hope I don't." He laughs sardonically. "I am an Ethicist, after all. And a physician."

"I think you may be an honest man."

"I am already thinking about making you 'an honest woman,'" he says, quickly wishing he hadn't blurted these words out like an adolescent boy trying to make a pun. His hand is on the table in the way it was on her desk whenever it was they first saw each other. It is a square brown hand. It still looks steady to her.

Did this happen during their first meal together or did it happen over several months? Did it happen within twenty-four hours or a year? Does it matter? If it matters, do you want to know how often they met, what they had for breakfast, whether or not he/she smokes or drinks coffee, whether they had sex, when, how was it? What is time really and how do we mark it? Different beings mark it differently in different cultures and different people, what each notes and what is not noted.

He says," Let's take a walk around the block."

They stop outside the restaurant and smile at the yellow cursive neon restaurant sign that augurs a possible miracle in the making and then she moves ever so slightly to the left knowing there is a park around the corner. He is just behind her and puts his finger in one of her golden curls, which wraps around it, glowing. He likes the shine against her dark and his darker skin and the way her golden hair frames a face that has so many histories he cannot distinguish them. He has always wanted to lie next to a body that in another life could have been a tree. The tree again.

He has gotten lost in his thoughts and she panics, afraid she has misunderstood entirely who he is.

"I'm not Goldilocks." It seems it is her turn to blurt out words she regrets. There is no reason for her distrust.

He's undone. He was so far from thinking about a fairy tale. Such are not his references, though, of course, he knows the story. Who does not know the story?

"I'm not Papa Bear," he counters but is dissatisfied with his answer. He still has her hair wrapped around his finger. "I was thinking that your hair has drawn the sun down into it and Leo is a fire sign and one confirms the other. I'm not Smokey the Bear either or we would be in trouble before we started."

This exchange is awkward. There is already an intimacy between them that has erupted out of nowhere and they don't have words for it and ordinary banter contradicts their connection.

She saves the moment and reaches toward his own black hair, waving down his neck.

"If your hair were longer…" she speculates, thinking it could curl like hers does and though black, it shines..

"Lucas means light," she replies triumphantly as she withdraws her hand. They were almost in conflict or almost in an embrace.

There are so many stories happening at once, there are Bear stories, people stories, and, unexpectedly, war stories, stories that shaped them, stories they were determined to forget.

"My grandfather made the most awful war into a love story." She is astonished that she has said this. Not only because she didn't heed his warning not to talk about war.

He looks at her as if entirely unable to understand the words she is saying. "My father did not," he manages. But there is more that he wants to say, that he wanted to say earlier but withheld because there are so many stories intersecting that to say anything is to impose a direction on what is occurring between them. He is a physician of a certain sort, one who listens to the patient's story for what is hidden but could be revealing. Sometimes his intuitions guide him to combine random events to see what emerges. He holds her blond curl on his finger, quickly discerning it is natural and so unexpected in her. "My grandfather made the most awful war into a love story." He can write this war story and his gut clenches as he understands what his father and her grandfather might say to each other. They were both drafted, he figures. They both knew the eastern front or hemisphere, they both knew hell. A universe with ten dimensions makes increasing sense to him as the stories converge. Several hours ago, he had not known this woman at all, now their ancestors are talking to each other.

* * *

"Oh," the Writer utters aloud, though she is alone at her ancestor altar. She has just felt the pathos of Lucas' story as she recorded it, his entire past has entered her like a poisoned arrow or a bolt of lightning. This is what she has been trying to understand and explain at the same time. He has revealed his entire life, its history and its implication as contained in a particle as dense as the particle from which the universe exploded for isn't his life a world and isn't it exploding from this tiny point of understanding? She would howl, the Writer, I would howl if I didn't want to be disconnected from this moment and what is being revealed, including the implications of each one of our stories, if we are willing to know them in their anguished particularities and unbearable immensity, these would be worlds, universes present and inescapable, like torture or ecstasy. Parallel and intersecting universes, vast, infinite, lived and unknowable, as many as there are living beings willing to know. His universe, his father's universe, his mother's universe, which now I must take into myself without any barriers or neutralization for how else will we know what to record, what to do, how to be. His story isn't only his story, as Léonie's isn't only hers and La Vieja's isn't only hers.

* * *

The rough rail scratched La Vieja's palms as she ran her hands over the weathered wood railing of the deck that circled the cabin. Inexplicably she held on tight, as she searched the area below, hoping and fearing what she might see. Her hands, themselves, equally weathering from the time she spends here among the elements.

* * *

I can focus on my own story, descend into my own memories, what it had meant as a child to be born during war. Safe in Brooklyn but still there was a war. So safe, at nine, I could travel the subway alone. The passenger seated next to me by the window, a stranger, as impersonal as the strap hanging overhead for a standing passenger to hold for balance, happened to open the *New York Times* over both our laps. I was drawn immediately, as anyone would be, to the map tracing the progress of Allied troops in France after the second invasion in the summer of 1944. We were in a war. Everyone would want to know where our troops were at this moment. I focused adamantly on the arrows across the map at the very top of the page over my legs while the man, as if illustrating the progress but in reverse let his fingers trace the invasion up my leg.

Approximately 3500 rapes were committed by American soldiers upon French women in the years of the war, but they were less restrained against the German women. Clearly, my story isn't only my story, no one's story is. At this moment, my story is the story of the French, German, and also Polish and Russian women and Lucas' story and Léonie's which dovetail with hundreds of other stories that coexist within us. Distinct, co-extensive and vital. And at the same time, scanning the panorama, now and then, the stories of the Junipers, Jeffrey Pines, Coast Live Oaks, gravely threatened in most forests if not this one, below the Lookout where La Vieja is standing, gripping the handrails.

"My father died *of* the war." This means that Lucas knows what war is without having gone to war. Really knows. And we have to learn too without looking away and without being absorbed into the details of information which distance us rather than providing internal, emotional, spiritual experience.

His grandfather was a bone setter, that is a healer, and his father, the grandfather's son, died *of* war. We don't know yet if the grandfather died before the father died. That will be another story and we don't know if we will ever learn it, but we can use our imagination to enter both scenarios and live out both of them, the father's loss which may have contributed to his death, or the grandfather's loss which may also have killed him for we think the grandfather is no longer alive. Lucas' father, Isai, died in 1978 when Lucas was three years old. Now we know which war killed him and if we have any awareness, we know why and we can guess how.

Resonance, John Briggs and F. David Peat say is … not following or imposing a pattern but recognizing it when it occurs. I take this little detour of referring to these two thinkers and Chaos theory because, to be honest with you, the reader, I have to breathe. But to breathe means to take in everyone's breath, the Eucalyptus trees, both the tree nymphs and the old woman tree, and all the others, and the plumbago where the Quail, Towhees and even a Thrasher lives in what has become interspecies co-housing, and those two Mourning Doves in the bare branches of the dead oak, the hidden Cougars, the Mule Deer, the Lizards and so on, all breathing each other's breath, taking each other in and offering ourselves to the others. Here, tree, is my breath which you take in and then offer me back your breath which is my life.

And just so we don't lose track of this layer as La Vieja is up on the Lookout for a reason, the Amazon rainforest is burning, the Indigenous people are in great danger from the assault on their habitat and from being shot and killed when they act on their essential belief in the value of the natural world. They are also in danger of burning to death because central Africa and South Africa are burning. You can read about it on the computer, or in the papers, if you still receive them, or watch the news on TV, or you can travel to the Sierras and climb up the single stairway to the Lookout and stare out far enough to see the burning, the extent of it and what it means for the planet, for you, really!

That's what La Vieja is doing. La Vieja? Her entire life has led to these moments when she is up there, feeling the heat of a very distant forest fire on her face. Of an apocalypse. Allowing herself to feel it. Unflinchingly. The fire is the kind that melts steel and tires. That dissolves the bathtub and the kitchen sink, leaves the hot tub as a pile of toxic ashes. Turn your head away when the wind blows.

Today, July 31, 2020

The Paraná, South America's second largest river after the Amazon and the eighth longest river in the world, its floodplain a vast delta covering some 15,000 km, through which the Paraná drains towards the Atlantic Ocean 300 km away, is burning. The wildlife are burning. A Gato Montés, a Wildcat, cannot outrun the fire. She is howling in the agony of being burned alive. The essential cause of the fires? Illegal cattle ranching.

Lucas' ancestor's lands, well, all of our ancestor's lands, are burning now too. Léonie's grandmother's land, her ancestors, are long destroyed by war.

This is not really a break from anguish, but it is abstract or general enough to give us a pause through which to look around as La Vieja does, every hour whenever she is awake, and seemingly even in her sleep. This is so we can be with her and with our world, our stories and all the stories, in this time when some of us are in seclusion, here and everywhere, separate and at one.

* * *

They walk around the park and then up and down through the park that is several city blocks long and wide. It is a "nice" park, as she puts it. The paths crisscross at angles but this doesn't erase their regularity. The trees grow at respectful distances from each other, at first glance one is not certain if they were planted or sprouted naturally. No one tree steals shade from another, they are watered regularly, the underbrush is cleared from under their canopies. There are refuse cans along the way for trash and recycling, and benches, benches for the elderly, for mothers with strollers and carriages, for friends having lunch together, for lovers. She leads him to a rock wall in the middle of the park under a towering Oregon Ash. It is a fortunate anomaly for an urban park dedicated to various forms of play and recreation, a free-standing wall of horizontal stones held fast by their own weight and in relationship to each other. The stones which glimmer in shades of bronze or silver, a hint of mineral or metal, are irregular but similar in dimension. Water drips and flows from a hidden source at the midpoint of the top of the wall as if there had just been a heavy downpour that coursed down to a shallow pool, a hint more than ankle deep. The wall, as far as he can discern, has no function whatsoever. She stands against the dry edge of the wall, running her hands over the rough stones as he imagines the possibility of being stroked so, despite the roughness of his old wounds, external and internal, and then he shakes himself as if to awaken again from a dream.

Several circles of stone seats crafted from boulders invite conversation. The wall is most unlikely in this setting except, he begins to understand, the world of forest and rain it conjures. They sit down on the seats across from it. He leans against the stone, stretches out his legs. It is 11 p.m.

There is so much to say; they are both silent. He reviews their conversations. Can he possibly understand that the Bear have become kin through dreaming although humans have made themselves their enemy and that she is making a unique alliance?

But you are a librarian, he might argue, meaning that she is devoting herself to the gathering and preservation of human knowledge.

No, she might answer. No, my mother is a librarian. I am helping her out while she is traveling. Meaning, she is trained, certified, degreed, but it is not what she does any longer.

But she doesn't speak about her waking life. She says, "Once a very light brown Bear, maybe a Kermode Bear, he wouldn't say, sat down next to me in my dream. He never came back. Maybe he was killed. Hunted. They are so unusual and beautiful everyone wants to kill them.

"But," she continues, "maybe he just didn't come back. Maybe it wasn't the right time. Until now. He looked like you. The same coloring."

He smiles. He is trying to avoid what may be a compliment. He doesn't think he looks like a bear. Too thin, he thinks, and frowns as he wards off the images that are crowding in of young thin Bears attached to chains for hours so they learn to dance or perform other tricks upright, or worse fates.

She and he get up from their stone seats as if with one mind and begin walking again, both aware even as entirely engaged in their own thoughts, which are so similar, of the Bears, their suffering, also aware of how unexpectedly comfortable it is to walk with someone, especially someone one has just met, yet without the need to speak aloud. Each one has opened a door in the other and they are free to step across the threshold.

His familiar escape route is thinking. In her presence, he begins to wonder whether his interest in why people do what they do, is his way of staying connected to humans? He only contemplates this for a second before returning to Bears. This is the unexpected gift she has given him. She opened with Bears. And he can respond with Bears. If he identified with the Bears first he would ask other questions: What relationships need to be established to meet the Bears' requirements to allow hunting, to allow themselves to be hunted, to create the conditions where they will offer themselves up? What agreements have been made? What reciprocity established? What is necessary for the Bear people to come to the negotiating table? What intrinsic Bear rights to their land, their habitat, need to be mediated so coexistence, where appropriate, might occur?

He is lost in his familiar state even though he also feels the blessing of the delicate mammalian presence who is alongside him.

Would it be right to refuse to offer medical assistance to a man who wounded himself while hunting? What if he were hunting illegally? He knows the legal answer which is, supposedly, the ethical answer, but is it ethical? And who is to decide? And, again, how would the Bear judge it? There is another question that comes to him because Léonie is with him. What if the Bear is wounded? What if the wounded Bear is a mother with young cubs? Can he offer assistance to the Bear mother first before even considering the hunter?

He's in a whirlwind of questions and concerns. He's back to trees which give him the human legal foundation for his thoughts. About trees having standing. That old case, 1972, three years before he was born, is haunting him. He doesn't know why. He is both exhilarated by her presence and distraught. He lets his mind wander, but it is a way of distancing. He knows it and allows it.

She thinks they are together—she is secretly exulting in it—and they are and they are not. To himself, he is reciting the names of the cases, national and international which aim to give legal standing to animals, those who are imprisoned, for example, in zoos, circuses or roadside exhibits. And then, he thinks, there are Bears who are captured for their bile and tortured their entire lives. He does not know, he realizes, a single international court case to free bears being tortured.

He has completely forgotten how he came to this train of thought, has forgotten her dream and connecting him to it in the presence of the bile Bears whom he can't abandon.

They are having a double conversation that is entirely contradictory and a little maddening and can't be stopped because none of it is being spoken aloud, so in its way, is entirely specious. She wants to make light of where they're going. She must somehow know what he is thinking because she wants to neutralize the issue, saying, "Well, you also look a little like a honey Bear, you know, a Sun Bear."

"I know why honey Bears are hunted," he mutters. Instinctively, he presses his free right hand against his liver and releases her hand which he was holding. He is afraid for her, what she knows, or of her, of what she is evoking in him, as he thinks what agony it must be to be milked for one's bile.

She says, pulling very slightly away, feeling his distancing, not knowing it is anguish, "You don't want to know." But he knows. When she realizes this and that she is not the one to guide him into this knowledge, she is wonderstruck to have met someone who might truly be a partner, even in consciousness. An animal partner.

She doesn't know, cannot anticipate what he is thinking about, what concerns him. She cannot know his preoccupations. Medical ethics, bioethics, responsibility for the entire sphere of teeming life so wondrous and afflicted.

It is part of his work to know about torture and he doesn't limit it to humans who are tortured as it is humans who do the torturing. He agrees as an ethicist and believes as a physician that he needs to know what humans do to each other and to the others. His mind is spinning. He saw a tornado once, from enough of a distance to be safe from it, but close enough to see the dark spin and it felt like his own mind. This is such a moment.

She feels unsteady though his internal state is invisible. "What is happening?" she asks, puzzled.

"Not the chemistry between us, but the physics. Energy fields, colliding and altering each other accordingly. Can you feel it?"

"It seems to me," she considers each word as she speaks carefully, "we have entered a common territory and are submerged in it. I don't think we are shattering. Are we?"

"Ah," he grins, "If you are asking that then, I am in the chaos and you're steps ahead in the transformation. No surprise," he continues, "men carry a lot of inertia, particularly professional men, like a fully loaded eight-axle truck going downhill trying to come to a stop. That's me."

"That's a strange image."

"I used to drive a semi. Got me through college. Good money but not good on sleep."

"What was that like?" she asks. Not anything she would have ever done.

"Challenging," he answers. He knows how she will interpret his answer. He is not lying to her, he is just not saying all of it. He knows that saying a half-truth is a lie and he does not want to lie, not to her, certainly not to her, and not to himself. But also, he doesn't know the whole truth either. Something is arising in him that has no words or clarity of understanding. And it's not about the semi.

So many times in his life, he has had to exercise his will to accomplish something, to protect himself or others. He calls on this skill, takes a deep breath, is resolved to fully return his attention to her. He wants to see who she is and so he must be fully present or he will be blinded by his own distraction. He has an uncanny ability to focus when necessary. Determined not to lose her through allowing old pain, whatever it is, scar tissue maybe, to overtake him and so create new pain, he slows their pace and stops and looks at her, the luminescent golden curls against the warmth of her skin. They look in each other's eyes. Something eases so they can continue to stroll. He is clear about one thing: he doesn't expect a woman to heal his pain but to be a companion as they go on together and so he stops, takes her face in his hands gently, kisses her on the forehead, a gesture which could also be a blessing and turns back to the path.

"Maybe I am about to die," he says, "as my entire life is flashing in front of me, but not in a coherent alignment, more like a fractal pattern, expanding by deepening."

"Sometimes we die to the old life," she responds. She is not impatient and can wait as long as necessary to hear the details of what he is experiencing, or not. They are walking together, but she is also watching, can learn more from her observations than from what he says or does. Her awareness of him takes her attention; she has little interest in herself. In this way, they are exactly alike, but approach themselves and each other differently.

She knows this park, has walked it many times but not with a companion such as he is in this moment. And the moon is rising, it is almost a half moon, waning. There is a slight breeze, enough to rustle some of the leaves. They are in the center of the park as far away from traffic as is possible and so it is fairly silent and they may be the only people walking tonight, though surely there will be some men and perhaps even some women with their dogs. It is a lovely night and quite ordinary when an ordinary night is so rare, and therefore precious.

She can feel a slight burn where he kissed her. Where he marked her. She asks an ordinary question to enter the mundane, relax the energetic bond that is connecting them, loosen a knot and let the rope that is tying them to each other, slacken slightly. "And so, why did you become a doctor?"

He hasn't considered this question for years. Lucas usually has few answers himself, but lots of questions. At the bedside, he acts first on behalf of the patient and the patient's sacred territory. He is supposed to be impartial, carrying everyone's concerns equally but he can't, according to his own ethics, because they don't start from an equal playing field and the patient has not participated in writing the laws which protect and benefit the hospital, the physicians, the various institutions, the government, etc. The patient as an abstract body which has no significant meaning in this real moment to this patient who is injured or anguished and whose sacred life and the body he/she/they inhabit is threatened. Let us not add further threat, Lucas responds. We are called here to sustain, support and heal. And then beyond. We have to let the patient take us beyond to something else, waiting, wanting to be healed. His mind is wandering.

He was never deeply engaged by the mechanism of any particular disease. And still he became a doctor. It wasn't as if he always wanted to cure cancer which seemed like his friends' default answer and he wasn't sure he believed all of them when they said it. His own answer was more difficult to formulate. It lay in the area of the myriad things he didn't understand and believed, again not knowing why, a physician was responsible to meeting them. It wasn't cancer that possessed him but cruelty. He didn't understand human cruelty but increasingly felt assaulted everywhere, as he assumes everyone feels now, and, also, he knows it isn't a psychological, an individual problem. He didn't want to be a psychiatrist. He didn't want to "treat" one person's cruelty or the consequences of such in an individual.

Nothing turned out the way it was supposed to, nor the way he was obliged to think it would. He does not live in a kind country. He is not passionately drawn to easing an individual's pain. He is determined, however, to finding and remedying the underlying causes of that pain.

That's what he is thinking or reviewing when he hears her question and for a moment it is as if he is to answer the question within himself, without words spoken.

"Oh," he says, perplexed, "Why did I become a doctor? And this sets him off again. Everything she asks and says requires him to examine it scrupulously. Did he become a doctor? Yes, he works in a hospital, in a medical office, he wears scrubs or a white jacket and hangs a stethoscope around his neck like a talisman. But is he a doctor if he is wondering, even as he palpates the area of injury, what ultimately led to this wound?

"I am getting lost in the complexity of the answer inside myself. It is as if I were speaking to you but I wasn't, was I? I would have to tell you everything, to answer that question. Everything. How is that possible?" He stops and looks hard at her face again, into her eyes; she does not look away, but is scrutinizing him with the same intensity. She looks kind. He has come to the core of what has been puzzling him his entire adult life. That life is suffering was never a satisfactory response to the extent of torture willfully imposed on other living beings. He always felt drawn and quartered between the seeming requirement to believe in human superiority and cultural enlightenment and his daily awareness of a global descent into violence and depravity. Harsh thoughts at such a time when he was looking at a person who might challenge his darkest assumptions.

His face must look gloomy because he notices her slightest intention to put her hand out to his, but then she returns it to her pocket. Oh, she must think she was responsible for his mood. He has to speak.

"Why did I become a doctor? That's a question I have to ask myself. Does the motivation matter now when years later medicine has changed so much.? My grandfather was a healer. He was self taught. I wanted to be the same, but even better with training. But medical school was nothing like I imagined."

Yes, this begins to be an authentic response. "I have to find a way to doctor that's in right relationship to what called me in the first place. Every gesture aligned with the original intention. Not my intention. Not mine, but medicine's original purpose." He paused and for a moment she wondered if he would ever start again. "Then you spoke about the Bears and that took me to my own connection, more abstract, but also real, and the questions I am always asking started bombarding me, as they do when I'm alone."

They both look away and start walking again.

Aware of the persistent internal legal arguments, he speaks them. "Do animals in the wild have the right to demand a gun-free that is, human hunting free zone? What is my responsibility to life? All life? That can't mean human life alone, can it?"

Of course, it is not what she expected to hear. She is studying him carefully. Is this rhetoric or is he sincere? Words are not validations. She has to know the truth of him the way a Bear would know. The Bear Momma will have only an instant to assess whether the man is dangerous or not. The likelihood is he is dangerous but the Bear, being Bear, wants to be certain, would not want to make a mistake either way—her cubs' lives depend on her judgment. She wants to raise them in Bear mind, the intrinsic Bear mind that prevailed before these current humans, the ones who are unable to think of being without weapons, dominated the Earth. The ones who speak of weaponizing everything now the way the old ones once spoke of Spirit, referenced their lives in relationship to Spirit. Spirit and … Earth.

So in this way, they are both drawn to distinct but similar concerns. Léonie shakes herself out of her Bear trance but is still holding to what she can assimilate of Bear nature in order to determine who he really might be. Without thinking in such terms, she is waiting for a sign, the kind of sign, Bear Momma would need.

He is trying to deflect what he knows to something a little less unbearable so he can breathe and also take her to a safer place. It is horrifically familiar to think about hunting in North America, using dogs, baiting adults and cubs with bacon and doughnuts, killing Bears in their dens, feeling what it is for Bears with drains to their livers confined in tiger cages in Asia. He is back to his dilemma. He cannot accustom himself to cruel and un-ethical actions. As a physician in ER he has seen too much of it and when he does, his task is to bring comfort, which he does, but it isn't his major concern. In such instances as a physician—as his nurses like to say, with a good stitch—he never looks away while focusing his attention upon the patient. But he hasn't solved the problem. He hasn't identified the etiology of the disease, he hasn't brought healing to the plague which is overtaking the world. This is what he may not say aloud, does not give himself per-mission even to think, though it rises up in him, will not be stilled. The ill-nesses aren't, he believes, in the body. They are manifested there but these are only phenomena. The illnesses are of the mind, heart and soul of the desperately injured and distorted world soul. Cruelty and its companion, dispassion, are even in medicine. This is what he dares not think. If such attitudes weren't intrinsic to the current system, and at the heart of research, other ways of discovering, of testing, other medicines and regulations would exist. It hurts him that he hasn't convinced his colleagues that they must attend both the immediate affliction and what is engendering it.

"I can't separate questions like these from being a doctor. I am obli-gated to try to diagnose a rash, tendonitis, a kidney stone passing, a tumor, or to meet a suicide attempt, but I don't think the required interventions and the accompanying proscriptions, let alone the prescriptions, heal what needs to be healed. And that's why I am whirling inside, but grateful for these, for your," he smiles, emphasizing the word that is coming, "provo-cations."

These are just thoughts and he dispels them by actively using his breath as if they were sitting in meditation which brings them both to the calm they felt before. She feels it then, what she needed in order to go fur-ther. Though he is preoccupied, that is not why he is harmless. But he is harmless. She feels that. Not that he is weak but that his strength derives from his strictest intentions to do no harm. It is an activity, a vivid activity, being harmless. Not by one's nature but by one's intention. By restraint and refusal to participate in the common ideology of perceiving danger everywhere and insisting on dominating everything. It was not always this way, one did not have to adamantly refuse the cultural instinct of combat, but now it is a given in most interactions, given the ease, the ubiquity of harm.

* * *

Momma Bear drops to her four legs and goes loping toward the river where the salmon are running, having made it back home despite so many obstacles, some intrinsic to their nature and others foreign, like dams to control waters the Salmon need to be wild, in order for Salmon to remain wild that is, to remain and thrive.

* * *

Two people meet and the unacknowledged field of violence and grief that is the current atmosphere of the entire world reveals itself. He and she have reached a common point. From a common point, a new world can emerge.

They continue to walk silently. He takes her shoulder bag and slings it over his shoulder. She allows it. Then she slips her arm through his as he extends it to her. Their pace is coordinated and comfortable. She leans in against him very slightly to see how that feels. If you squint from a distance and respond to the profiles, you may see two small Honey Bear with broad collars of sunlight around their necks, she more delicate than he, the two walking upright.

They reach a literal crossroad. They can take a new path into another part of the park or they can step onto the sidewalk and then? Then they will be confronted by practical questions, each of which will have consequences—questions of cars, houses, schedules, the future. They have not yet confirmed that they will meet tomorrow and the day after and the next days, most probably for the rest of their lives.

"Let's take another turn," she says moving forward decisively and he follows as she leads them along the same paths they walked before, but at a brisker pace, until they are sitting again on the stone seats before the unlikely wall with the recirculating water dripping into a pool as if it just rained.

She steps out of her shoes and with one hand against the wall, steps into the shallow pool. "Want to join me?" It's an invitation he can't refuse. He takes off his shoes, removes his yellow socks, rolls up his pants and steps into the cold water that reaches just above his ankles. Rather than balance on the wall, she puts her hands on his shoulders which allows him to put his hands on her waist. They begin to laugh as teenagers might without either of them pretending they are not undressing the other in their minds, here in this public place in full view of the world. "A physician and a librarian were caught *en flagrante* in the fountain in Main Street Park last night," the imagined headline reads.

She reads his mind. Of course, she does. She says, "I am not only a librarian, you know."

He waits.

"I built this wall." Now she turns so that she is leaning against the wall, just there where the water is dripping down, puts her finger against his lips obviously to keep him from asking questions and pulls him against the wall so he is wet also.

"You being the architect doesn't give us permission to enact what I am thinking," he says, watching the water from the wall darken her green silk blouse, seeing the outlines of her body emerge as the cloth clings to her. "Not only the architect, but the builder. The architect, the builder, all of it," she says. She wants him to know so he will know who she is. He is trying to encompass what she is saying. She built the wall. This is entirely disconcerting but so is the outline of her wet silk blouse revealing her breasts, naked he thinks, under the green.

Now that she is pulling him into the water, he can feel the truth of it in her physical strength. He has his hands on her biceps and this makes her laugh so he laughs with her.

He wants to know everything about her and he wants to know it the way she wants to convey it, entirely without words, or without the need to ask or state something to which the other will respond. Call and response. But sometimes the call would be silent and sometimes the response equally so.

To read someone's mind is not to hear the words that might have been spoken, it is to grasp what is there to be conveyed, outside the limitation of words, in the way that the full reality of any being is so much greater than we can know in language or from science. But then, because we are ourselves limited, we translate the infinite that we glimpsed for a brief interval into words and are astonished when it mirrors what the other has also reduced into words. For a moment the infinite of one and the infinite of the other merged.

"This wall," he marvels, "this wall. You built it," he marvels. "I don't know anything about you," he says.

"I will tell you but not here and not now. Even though telling won't tell you."

Will touch? he wonders. He is dizzy with wonder.

"Let's go," she says.

He carries his shoes and she carries hers. The wind cools their bodies where the cloth is wet. Each in their own way, they feel like animals who have just come out of a river with the water trickling through their fur and hides. He wants to shake himself free of the water. Finally they come to the corner where they entered the park.

"It felt quite normal to be standing in your fountain with you and yet, it feels entirely unnatural to be standing with you at this street corner with a traffic light and the Ford pickup that has just driven past us with the driver listening to the 11 p.m. news.

"Let me walk you to your car," he continues speedily. He is brash and reckless. "If you give me your address, I will pick you up in the morning and take you to work—what time will that be?—and then we will not have to bother with two cars in the evening."

"I don't work on Saturdays," she says, smiling.

He's embarrassed. Befuddled, he's lost track of everything, including the day of the week, and she knows it and is pleased. "Well, then, let's go for a hike," he quickly counters. "I will pick you up and so you still have to give me your address."

"Very deft," she says. "Very deft."

10

In the southern Cascade foothills, approximately twenty miles east of Red Bluff, California, lies the Ishi Wilderness, a unique 41,000 acre, low-elevation wilderness. This is a land incised by wind and water, dotted with basaltic outcroppings, caves, and bizarre pillar lava formations. This is up and down country, a series of east-west running ridges framed by rugged river canyons.

The Ishi is named for a Yahi Yana Indian who was the last survivor of his tribe, who lived in the area for over three thousand years. Shortly after 1850, the white settlers killed all but a handful of the Yahi. Ishi (the Yahi word for man) and a few others escaped and lived quietly for decades in this harsh, wild country.

US Department of Agriculture, Forest Service

Greetings from the Writer. I am writing outside on the patio. It is 5:28 p.m. on September 17, 2018. It happens to be my birthday and I am alone and have been for weeks. Well, this is my virtual Fire Lookout and company is rare (and will be scarcer in 2020 during the Covid lockdown).

La Vieja is similarly alone, and she interacts with other humans only when supplies are needed, someone is lost, or a researcher wants some information and has, hopefully, brought some Irish whiskey and fresh cream for the coffee it is known she will offer. All non-humans live in reciprocal relationship with the natural world. The hikers who find her when they are in need, and who sought the natural world to restore themselves often illustrate how far we have come as a species from such intrinsic exchange.

On several occasions this summer, even my solitude has been interrupted by hikers who have no idea where they are. We get in my truck and try to figure out where they entered the park that this land borders in order to find their car. Recently, offering water wasn't a mere courtesy, the woman was entirely dehydrated, fainting away. No water left in her bottle, no sun hat, no sunglasses. Little if any knowledge of the wild. None. That didn't stop her from entering the domain as if it belonged to her.

Last night, as I sat here in the dark, looking out, a young Coyote came into the area and began drinking from the Buddha fountain where the bees drink, morning until night, all summer in company of the birds without interfering with each other. She's a hunter with highly developed eyesight, hearing and sense of smell so we know that she had to have sensed me four feet away even though I was downwind of her. But as she didn't sense fear but only welcome and delight, she paid me no mind. She drank, looked around, changed position, drank again and then glided away as silently as she had come, trees and grasses springing up in her wake.

The sun will be going down soon, and the light will turn golden and in that light everything in view comes into startling presence. The golden light is the color of Léonie's hair and she also has that presence. Lucas recognized it. His mother knew that light is the signature of the holy and that is why she named him Lucas.

Melissa was motivated by a similar understanding when she named her daughter, Léonie Augusta. For the wild and for the fierceness of the Lion's light. Each of the mothers detected something in the infants when they were placed in their arms after birth and the names came to them. Neither of them had had amniocentesis. They did not know each other. From their own very different orientations, both believed that nothing can or should be known about a child, especially from data, until you hold her or him in your arms. They both, in their ways, knew that the observer acts to create reality and they didn't want a technology to determine anything about their child.

I have seen Lions in the wild. I have seen them in August. I have seen the tenderness with which they mate. I have seen the old Lion gentle the young female when she is wild, first time in estrus, with fierce desire. I have seen them when the sun is in Leo, have seen that honey light. To understand Lion you must understand that Lion, Honey and Light are the same. That the Lion, the Bee and the Sun are the same. There is an intelligence that is implicit and active in those interactions, in the way one appears as the other. This is something like shape-shifting but it is not. It is a field of consciousness that is formed by who they are and from which they manifest, like the waves rising up out of the sea and falling back.

The Huichol Indians whose territory was in the area of San Luis Potosí, Mexico, say that the Blue Deer, Corn and Peyote are one. They say they all come from the Sun. They don't mean that they shape-shift into each other. They mean they are one, the same but distinct, though related, in their manifestation. It's about essence, not appearance. You understand, yes? When you stand in the east, the Wind, the Eagle and the Moon are one, yes? Or in the south, Fire, Heart and the Mammals are one. And Rain, Fish and Starlight are one. And finally, Earth and Time and Space are one.

Léonie's mother, Melissa and Lucas' mother, Honey, understand this. Melissa and Honey! Of course their children meet. That is how Léonie and Lucas found each other, like far ranging moving particles among the inert, like dancers among the dead. There is a molten rock of fire at the core of this text. As above, so below.

* * *

La Vieja looked down from her perch on the widow's walk that surrounded her little cabin, 13 feet above the ground, 4,800 feet in height and above the trees. A Fire Lookout with the required 360-degree view.

Inevitable symmetry that the two who are claiming our attention had also made their way to a Fire Lookout in Northern California adjacent to Lassen National Park. Lucas had rented an outlook in the rough and remote Ishi Wilderness, dedicated as an animal refuge. They drove North on Hwy 5 until Red Bluff and then headed in.

* * *

Lucas led her to the unoccupied cabin. "I come here when I need a large view," he said.

They had driven to the parking lot below and he got out of the 4 x 4 without explaining, not disrespectfully but as if they had done this a dozen times together, opened the back of the car and began loading far more supplies than any day hike required into it. She watched, inquisitive, but not saying a word.

"I called this morning. It wasn't rented. They know me by now. We have it for today. I'm sure we can stay longer, it isn't rented for anytime soon, so until we run out of water which we may do before we run out of food."

She was pretending she hadn't noticed he was planning for more than a day hike. "You come here often?"

"Very often. Because I get lonely for myself in my daily life, and I find myself here."

"The trees are familiar. They are like those in the place where I first dreamed the Bears. Maybe I will spend a lot of time here as well."

"There are lots of Black Bears here."

"Are we going to spend the night?"

"We can," he answered as he was loading a few gallons of water, sleeping bags, pads, and an assortment of paper bags into the wheelbarrow supplied by the Forest Service to take to the cabin. She hadn't looked around his truck, had not seen what was in the far back. She felt no alarm, rather the contrary, having supplies for several days indicated he was reliable and responsible. It had been a long time since she had been able to rest, truly rest, the way one can only in the natural world and he was providing the means. Scanning him as he unloaded and carried, she detected only kindness. Soon, she would dare to put her head on his shoulder and let herself be held.

He followed her eyes as they landed on the fire pit. "We have firewood," he said, catching himself before he said, "I brought..." *We* was getting easier because it was becoming real. So quickly. "But it is for the woodstove above. Ongoing fire season down here. Best to be cautious."

"This is good," she was clearly surprised and delighted. He saw her body ease, almost imperceptibly, as if a great weight was falling off her or, as he watched more closely, onto her. A heavy grace. Falling off him.

"Where shall we sleep?" she asked.

"We can sleep in the cabin or outside, there are lots of options, but we'll leave the food in the cabin." He was thinking of the smell of food, who it might attract. He was thinking of the food they had with them, their food, no matter who had brought it, stepping over an edge, grateful.

"We'll sleep outside," she said definitively, and he countered slowly working out the structure of the sentence. There would be times, many times when he would refer to himself or to her in particular, but he wanted to be careful about those times when it could be avoided. "I brought us toothbrushes." Maybe she intuited his struggle, his way of courting her, or she was just pleased that he was so thoughtful. "Do you do this often, pack for more than yourself?" It surprised her again that she knew nothing about his life. Nor did he know hers.

How many different ways that question could be understood. "I come here alone," he said. "I always have but it wasn't difficult to supply us. I just thought of everything I was bringing for myself and brought two while also thinking of the aesthetics of it." He held up two wooden bowls. "Easy."

"I brought us sandwiches for the hike," she said. "And baked yams."

"Yams?"

"Yes, we always have yams, just in case. Comfort food. My grand-mother always did so we do."

"And she would mash taro root, right?"

"How do you know?"

"Because I think our families lived half way around the world from each other, but maybe we sometimes ate the same food."

"How does that make you feel?" she asked.

"At home," he paused to nuzzle up to her as he put the supplies down to put in the code and open the lock box and extract the key. It was awkward because both her arms were laden and his were empty and it had to seem accidental though it was shyly intentional. She laughed quietly as she sidestepped him just slightly.

Knowing his answer to the question she was about to ask by seeing his familiarity with her and with the land here, she persisted, "We can, can't we, sleep without a tent?"

He laughed. "Yes, we need to see the stars," he reassured her. "Or we can sleep beneath the trees. We'll look around. You will find the place."

She didn't answer.

"Ok, I will find it for us as I know this site." He was wishing the dark were here, already seeing her hair shining in the night, like the spread of silver light of stars through the trees, her breath mixing with his and the breezes filled with the scent of sap and musk.

Soon everything was set in place, and they settled down against a Ponderosa Pine but not before they each pressed their nose against the bark for the welcoming fragrance of vanilla and laughed because they each knew. Then he turned to her and took her face in his hands and leaned forward. He wanted to smell her breath, he would know her that way.

She took his in as well. "Bears do that," she said. "That's how they are certain who you are AND what you've eaten and so where you've been. Catching up on everything they need to know about the time they've been apart." She paused, took a deep breath of his breath and spoke again. "It will be a long time breathing this way for us to know everything," but she didn't pull away even when speaking. They rested their foreheads against each other and took in what they could of their history that was best spoken this way. "Przewalski's Horses breathe this way," she broached the subject unsure if she would tell him why.

"I love those horses," he said.

"Why?"

"Because I feel so confined by this life and I heard that someone found a number of wild horses in zoos and gathered them up and took them to the steppes and let them run free."

"Where would you want to be let loose?"

"Right here. Right here if we would never have to leave." He was aware, as was she, that he had said "we."

"*We*," she emphasized the word by pausing somewhat markedly before starting again, "we, could stay here."

He paused, and maybe he was surreptitiously pawing the ground. "But why did you mention the horses?"

She had no choice but to answer him honestly. "When you walked toward me in the library, not when you first came in but when you had finished your first round of research, I thought, if he were an animal, he would be a Przewalski's Horse." She flushed because she had revealed her interest in him from the beginning.

"Not possible. I'm skinny and they're stocky."

"Yes, I know, but something about your energy and theirs. In all the time they were in zoos, even born in a zoo, they didn't lose their wildness."

"And you think I haven't lost mine."

"No more than I have. Or the longing for it. One or the other."

"So which would you like me to be, a bear or a horse since I am too skinny for either?"

"A Bear, so we could live here."

"There is so much I will have to learn, then."

He leaned forward and rearranged Léonie against him so that the bark of the pine would not be digging into her back as it must have been because she had been adjusting her position frequently. He did not mind being the one to have to accommodate.

"How will it be do you think?" he spoke quietly, almost whispering in her ear, his arms enfolding her lightly.

"How will what be?" she queried, though she knew exactly what he was asking.

"How will it be when we make love for the first time?"

"It will be splendid. Don't you think? But when will it be, that's the question?"

"That is up to you."

"Well then, we will have to wait until I am in estrus."

"When will that be?"

"When my blood comes in about a week."

"That could be full moon."

"Unless you throw me off schedule, that is exactly when my moon time will be."

"Always?"

"Most of the time."

"My family would be upset if they heard you, Léonie. They would think that's a taboo time."

"Dangerous?"

"Not quite. Taboo, meaning sacred. They might ask me to build you a moon hut so you could go off by yourself, not sure I, a mere man, can handle the powers that are supposed to come at such a time."

"Supposed to come?"

He should have expected her retort. But he didn't want to engage in repartee. They had been in ritual he had felt from the moment they had met. And he had learned ceremony from his grandmother.

"I would like to know the animal in you," he waited a few seconds, checking to see if what he was about to say was true and when it was, he continued, "and the animal in me."

* * *

The conversation had to go this way. They're animals, you see.

PART IV

11

The old stories of human relationships with animals can't be discounted. They are not primitive; they are primal. They reflect insights that came from considerable and elaborate systems of knowledge, intellectual traditions and ways of living that were tried, tested, and found true over many thousands of years and on all continents.

But perhaps the truest story is with the animals themselves because we have found our exemplary ways through them, both in the older world and in the present time, both physically and spiritually. According to the traditions of the Seneca animal society, there were medicine animals in ancient times that entered into relationships with people. The animals themselves taught ceremonies that were to be performed in their names, saying they would provide help for humans if this relationship was kept.

Linda Hogan

L a Vieja sees them, sees Léonie and Lucas, seated below on what she knows is soft earth, needles and leaves, leaning against one of the sugar pines, the one, as it happens, she favors, though she reminds herself this cannot be as when she descends, as she does each day, she sees another landscape not unlike theirs, but still different. They'll all see Ponderosa Pines, Douglas Firs, Spruce and Incense Cedars but in different configurations. For this moment, it is simple; she looks down and sees them in their territory. Close focus is difficult as La Vieja has trained herself to look for fires—that is her task here—and so she has cultivated distant perspectives but now she is looking closely and her equilibrium is shaky. Also she is looking into another dimension and this requires another focus altogether. It may be for this reason, although she sees them, they do not see her.

La Vieja

Here we are. Two people who did not exist some months ago have come to life. Léonie Augusta because of her relationship with non-humans and Lucas Jay because Léonie asked him if she could help him and he really needed help, his soul was longing for it. We have witnessed their beginnings. These moments, the sperm and egg from which they spring. Later we may fill in a history that conforms to our sense of time but those details are arbitrary and may not be requisite. It is a curious experience to watch something entirely unfamiliar come to be totally unexpectedly, and then realize that although they are newly alive, one's own life is and will continue to be intertwined with theirs. Nothing will ever be the same. Like a meteor entering the atmosphere from far away in space, beyond one's imagining and depositing unique life forms that intersect with ours.

* * *

These, you understand, are the same two that La Vieja saw at the foot of her Lookout earlier in this text. She witnesses them. She testifies to their existence. Because we are so literal minded as a people, we can only imagine being on the watch for fires, or storms, or invading armies. For danger, not hope. She is not a witness to something that happened, but a witness to an event that is occurring in the moment while creating its own past, the mysterious and unpredictable circumstances from which it arose and became inevitable, affecting everything and everyone, La Vieja and myself, the Writer included, and ultimately, you the reader as well because any and every new element in the world affects us all, everything being connected.

The enormous chasm between what we are learning about the nature of the world and what we can understand, that distance between the two is not a factor to preoccupy us, because once we touch in any way we are eternally connected, and so nothing is separate from anything else, though each one of us is entirely distinct from all others.

Let me suggest that we give up relying on simple versions of cause and effect, or that one thing leads inevitably to another or that we can trace and measure that interaction. Consider resonance instead. That events vibrate continuously, that we are drawn into a vast harmony with which we can make music eternally, unless we continue being afraid of and overwhelmed by beauty. To be in accord with the true nature of the world, we have to yield. In the perfect dance, we lead and follow each other, and then all others simultaneously. That is how the Elephants live. That is their nature. I yielded to them and so I learned yielding. And now Bears. But not dancing bears, not those tortured to dance for some perverted entertainment we seek, oblivious to another's suffering. That's not what is meant by dance!

Something is being born. I mean this literally if not chronologically. Léonie is not a fiction, Lucas is not a fiction. I am not, this Writer is not making up a story. Look, it is happening, right there. Their manifestation cannot be dismissed as a mere act of imagination. Not when the Imagination is a real world. I am not willing to say that Léonie is a fiction, nor that Léonie wouldn't exist without me. Like the proverbial question: Has a tree fallen in the forest if no one has heard it? You bet it has. The question points to our great delusion that humans are the center of the universe and nothing exists without us. This self-centeredness, this narcissism may partly be responsible for the dire fate of the Earth. Would I exist without Léonie? Yes and no. Maybe in another life. But not in this life, because she calls this life, this moment, into being. Does Léonie exist without me, that is, independent of me? Seems very likely except that you would not know about her existence in the same way. As the Writer, I don't give her life; I give you access to her life. And so I give her access to you.

I presume that is why I have been given the responsibility of recording this as it comes into view. While I am not affecting the action or the story in any way, we are still profoundly interconnected. Is this a mirror of the way life and the natural world really work though we have been given to believe that cause and effect are much more direct and able to be traced?

To what purpose? We can't answer that because we don't know where this is going, only what is appearing, only what is being revealed in the way the Przewalski's Horses entered this text a few pages ago, came out of nowhere, a year and a half after it began. It isn't easy, not only because I don't understand and don't know what is coming but because the forms, shapes, sounds and thoughts in this realm don't translate into words perfectly. And yet it is my task to bring them forth.

Welcome to the mysterious tangle of spiritual intelligence, intent and the unknowable.

I feel compelled to repeat certain words—mysterious, inexplicable, unfathomable, incomprehensible. It is the consequence of standing at this juncture of what is real where events and occurrences are entirely mysterious, inexplicable, unfathomable and incomprehensible, where the nature of reality shifts so entirely that it seems our minds must break from the impact of it. So we shatter and put ourselves together again, but most tentatively and in a different configuration. One we can't predict.

This is the way it was when Galileo asserted that the Earth was not the center of the universe. That was an earthquake! Or when we had to understand that matter isn't solid, and that the laws of physics and the laws of quantum mechanics are different.

Now the contemporary tsunami: the human being is not the center of the universe. The human is not the purpose and pinnacle of evolution; there are other species who carry great intelligence, even greater intelligence than ours. They carry spiritual development in ways we cannot imagine, that we lack the capacity to perceive, let alone judge. Maybe humans are the equivalent of a small if awesomely beautiful Earth revolving in a third orbit around a small sun in a universe of billions and billions of such suns. While it may be that life as we know it, that sacred enigma, is rare in the universe, life doesn't necessarily imply human, or even earthly. There well may be myriad wondrous forms wiser than we are, that we cannot fathom because we are unable and unwilling to acknowledge what is beyond our benighted and very dangerous selves. Because we are not capable, because our minds have not encompassed reality.

I am reminded of looking down while flying in a small plane at about 12,000 feet across the desert in Namibia and seeing patterns on the Earth that I had first seen in the art of Aboriginal people, which I thought then were abstract images until I realized the artists or dreamers understood things I did not and were rendering the meaning of the landscapes they saw, physical and interior, through their visionary art, however it was that they came to be flying, and so able to see the design. The parallels are so exact, it's as if the Aboriginal artists have indeed flown across this territory, or that their desert landscapes look enough like this desert that when they fly this is what the spirit world reveals to them. The physical appearance isn't just happenstance. It develops over millions, billions of years, but physical evolution doesn't explain the configurations. There are other levels that just begin to reveal themselves to seers like those artists whose work we can admire but cannot yet—I don't see any evidence we can—understand. We do not see what they see. Layers missing. Levels of understanding.

But meditating upon their art, I understood things I couldn't say in words. The same for this terrain through which I am flying now. The Aboriginal people will fully understand, no words needed.

I can't ask La Vieja—it would be rude and intrusive—but I do wonder what La Vieja sees. Is she learning to see with the unique perception of the Aboriginal or other Indigenous peoples?

Two San people accompanied us to Chobe to meet the Ambassador in 2006 and while we, the non-Indigenous people were awed by what transpired, because it was the third time we had witnessed Elephants approaching us with clear intent to transmit something specific of great importance, the San were not impressed. They live in such a world of relationship and interconnection that reveals itself to them consistently and, yes, now also to those of us who are willing to see.

* * *

Having just met, Léonie and Lucas are in their own world in a small enclave of possibility, examining each other and their close surroundings, the trees, rocks, wildflowers, but not even those, not yet. Light, yes, the sun will set soon. They are aware of the light, they both seem to move slightly to gather onto themselves what light comes through the trees. They move to the light the way boughs move in the wind.

They arrived in time. Some wind, not much, enough for vitality. A breeze. Soft. Enough to feel and hear the life of the forest. And flashes of blue sky through the slightly moving limbs of the pine and spruce. He is more interested in her than anything in their surroundings, and at this moment particularly her hands. She is, she said, a stone mason.

"I build walls," she had said. "Free standing. So you can walk around them," she said. "They often have free-standing arches constructed without mortar. Always without mortar. They serve no purpose except to be themselves. We acquire the stones from wherever we could find them after they had been moved from their original home. My task is to return them to themselves but visibly so they confront us.

"They stand firmly by the way the stones fit onto and so into each other. Sometimes there is earth between them, softening their edges, but mostly, the stones are simply placed, one on another, skin to skin. No mortar to fix them in place while still keeping them apart. Each time a stone is placed, it has to fit perfectly as if it could not be anywhere else, but where it is, upon the stone that has been waiting for it, and between the stones to the side, each perfectly suited to the other."

She was moving her hands when she spoke as if she was before the wall and placing a stone. She had closed her eyes and bowed her head slightly looking in the dark to see the wall as it might be, scanning the pile of rocks, choosing the one that would go in this place and no other, having been taken once from its original home, she had to find another home for this life that stretched before it. It had been uprooted and she had to set it in place, had to restore and affirm the intrinsic relatedness of the universe that prevails in every quanta of the 7.3 trillion light years of the dimension of the universe. She was building a world.

It is odd, he is thinking, that she would build walls, work with stone, with the unmoving, when it seems she, herself, is always moving slightly, adjusting, affiliate with what is arising, entering, leaving.

"It may not be realistic," she continued, when she opened her eyes and leaned back upon him again, "but I want to find the stone people homes they will cherish forever. Building a wall, means bringing the stones home. That's why I do it."

He determined then to be such a home for her though they had just met.

"The walls you build," he asked, "standing alone, aren't they lonely? Or the stones at the top, exposed as they are, aren't they lonely? Or precarious?"

"They have weather. The foundation has earth and the capping has sky and there are always the birds that land and the squirrels and other creatures who scamper across them. The stones have weather and there is always the company of the trees. They are not alone in the world."

The two of them had been alone in the world and now, it seemed they were not.

* * *

The old woman, La Vieja, looked down upon them, relieved, not because they were inadvertently providing company for her, but relieved that they had found each other and would not be alone. She could feel the energy that was binding them together; it was the force that keeps the planets in their orbits. There was an oppositional force which exuded from them as well that had kept them singular and single until now. It was the force that shielded them from being entangled in the conventional life around them while still always faithful to the central fire around which they circled, always had. La Vieja knew that dance of attraction and repulsion that ultimately became a steady and reliable ellipse around a great sun.

La Vieja was amused that she had come to look far and was looking near and finding the near would have to learn another dance, equally paradoxical. Could she observe without intruding? Was it possible to witness without violating their privacy? At first, she thought this pertained to the two people below but then she realized it pertained even more to the animals. Alone, at a great height away from the ground, she blushed. How quiet she would have to become to view the animals, Bear, Coyote, Bobcat, Cougar, Fox, Squirrel without violating the integrity of their lives. How much quieter so that even Eagle and Owl would be unaware of her. Sure, she wanted to see everything but did she have a right? Did the animals want to be observed by a member of such a voyeuristic species with whom there was no reciprocal exchange?

Colleagues urged me, the Writer, to put up hidden cameras to spy on, to catch the animals at night, or in their nests and dens when she located these. The arrogance and entitlement of two-leggeds. When she had been in Botswana with the Lions who were mating, they had seen her watching them. For a brief moment, when the young lioness had backed off, it seemed that the old man had scanned her and she had, like the lioness, given him everything. He could have leaped upon her and devoured her in one action. As she is a woman, she knew how to open and she did so. In return, he yielded to the lioness who had just risen again on her hungry loins and began to circle him, ravening.

There are two Eucalyptus trees along the patio that I am certain are spirits. One trunk rises up and then bends backwards slightly, displaying her taut belly, one that had never had a child. An equal distance up, she divides into two raised arms. The bark from breast level to elbows has been stripped away and the tree's body is smooth to the touch. Three feet away is another Eucalyptus with a massive trunk and from her very root, two narrower limbs or legs splay up. The two limbs join the trunk at her craggy groin; the old woman is offering the sweetness of age to the world. These two trees are Maiden and Crone. Is La Vieja willing to be so naked? Am I? We were once the one, the maiden, and now we are the other.

La Vieja kept looking at the two below her, but was no longer hiding herself. She knew them, of course, not the ways they knew themselves yet, but in other ways equally intimate. She has observed them directly as if looking down the hundred feet, approximately, of stairs which lead from her small shelter to the earth floor, where, depending on perspective, another set of stairs might appear leading to another Lookout three hundred miles away.

She had learned to look carefully, to note what was familiar and what slightly awry, so that she would not miss, out of distraction, the small signs that might be of concern, a subtle shading in the sky, a slight shift in color in one place while in another an unexpected haze or a shift of wind apparent in the gentle countermovement of branches and leaves that might indicate heat arising from an illegal campsite or fire. Over time, she had become skilled. It is why she had come here. She wanted, finally, to learn to see. Not daring to consider what use might come of what might be revealed but needing to remain clear-eyed without interpreting. What was the visual equivalent of emptiness? Seeing without naming. Observing without judgment. Seeing in a different ways.

* * *

What does that mean, seeing in different ways? How do the lenses of our cosmologies determine what we see? Is it possible to see a fact without looking through a cosmology? Science said yes, but isn't that the illusion of its perspective? I get up and walk to the southeast corner of this land and turn around slowly, examining everything before me, near and as far as I can see. 360 degrees. My virtual lookout. What do I see when I give myself over to this virtual lookout?

* * *

La Vieja pulled herself away from the two below her and traversed the walkway, almost panicked. Fires everywhere. Some were very close, the air dense with smoke, and here and there, toxins rising into the air, black fumes and unnatural colors. If she continued to stare, she would find it hard to breathe and if the firewall moved closer, it would certainly take her down. She had to look away. This is where she was challenged. She was in the process of not looking away, of being resolute in bearing witness. But would anything come from her succumbing to the heat? No, she decided. It would bring the fire closer and much more than her life would be endangered. Yet, she did not rush to call the Rangers.

She cast her gaze further as if a telescope aimed at the sky, the farther away she looked, the further away in time. The fires weren't all current. Some were fires of the last years, Paradise, Australia, the Amazon, Chernobyl, Fukushima were still burning, still smoldering though common sense (another point of view) said they were out and need not call our attention when indeed she had resolved never to look away.

And then the question came to her: was it possible to put out the fires which were still burning in the past because the causes had never been addressed?

She scanned all the directions again, aware that she had successfully taught herself to look far, farther than she imagined it was possible to see. Some of the fires were not from the past, some were burning in the future, but their light hadn't reached us yet. She could see far enough to perceive them but she had no idea yet and might never know whom to call or how to begin to extinguish them, let alone prevent them from being ignited in the first place. Which, unknowingly, had she set?

La Vieja looked from the two below her to the fires and back again and to the fires again. The movement prevented her from being dazed by despair. She needed to know she could look back to that view even as now she scanned the green forest around her where there was at this moment no sign of danger, and then she looked below and saw the familiar footing of her Lookout. Then again, a slight shift, not a filmic dissolve but so rapid a substitution of another reality it was seamless, and there they were again, as if only one hundred and fifty feet away, still as the planets in the night sky, breathing in and out each other's breaths permeated by the breath of the trees, listening, like she was, to merge with them, listening for the Bears.

*　*　*

A film of a tribal village had been made by an anthropologist who had shown it to the tribespeople. The tribal observers had not been able to "see" the chickens who were pecking in the dust though they saw them perfectly when among them. They were not trained to differentiate the pixels in the ways Westerners are trained. The images were merely images, two dimensional moving shapes which interested them not at all. Representations were not real. What then, the anthropologist wondered, about their art? He would have had to penetrate far more deeply into the culture, would have had to take on another mind or understanding, to experience the reality of the sacred images they carved and painted. He and his colleagues had been cautioned against, "going native." Although participatory observation was encouraged, it was to assure those studied of the sincerity of the scientist, it was never intended for the anthropologist to fully accept the world view of the other and live accordingly. Objective observation was the goal, subjective experience the means. The anthropologists must always hold themselves apart. The film proved to the tribespeople how remote the filmmaker was from reality. The image of the chicken was not a sacred image and so it was not real and so it did not exist. How much the Western anthropologist missed by his remove. The tribespeople would not explain what they did see because the anthropologist was the one unable to see. It was the anthropologist who could not organize "the data" to perceive what was real. The anthropologist could not speak the tribal language as a Native and the English language could not hold perceptions foreign to it.

"The image of the chicken was not a sacred image and so it was not real…" La Vieja lifted her eyes from the two below her and then back to them. Something shifted as she changed her focus. Shifted because, it seemed to her she was expecting the shift. But what if she moved her gaze without a change in concentration or tone? What if she lavished the same interest on the Pine that they were leaning against as upon them, as if it were an extension of them, one of their limbs? The tree also urged her heart to open the way it opened in their presence. She stilled herself as best she could. She was not contriving this response: what if the sincere expression of the sensation of love onto the tree sustained it? What if she, bathing the future with her great love for the land, quenched the future fires?

She could do so ritually because it was true in her. There might not be much in her that was entirely reliable, but her love for these great beings, this landscape, was true.

* * *

It felt so heady, though it was not of the mind but of the heart. Indigenous people thought with the heart but now she was seeing through the lens of the heart as well. Time then to close her eyes. To stop. To rest.

She believed she had seen the two before, probably in her imagination because they were so familiar to her and she knew their names and details of their lives, confirmed by the conversations with each other which La Vieja was overhearing. She recognized their stories, imprints more telling than fingerprints..

Now they were here. Just below. Embodied in all ways. She can almost touch them. For a moment as she gazed at them, they tensed a little with anticipation and their muscles tightened, their bodies taut in expectation of the others coming, the Bears, they hoped.

* * *

Turning and turning, walking, from east to west, from dawn to nightfall, from then to now, round and round the boardwalk as if walking the rotations around the sun, walking time and space, hoping the momentum, the passage from past to present, might help her reach the deep connection from which wisdom might arise. The two appeared below her, albeit in another geography, another time, another dimension. She had to keep her focus, the ongoing inquiry, her desperate and perhaps naïve assumption that if she kept asking questions, kept looking farther and farther, further and further, where both knowledge and the past, even the far past resided as one, she would get an answer or a direction. That ancestors would answer, whether it was a short-faced Bear who 11,000 years ago might have walked exactly where the Lookout is now, or her own equally unknown great-great-grandmother, someone or another from the other side to guide her, some voice, some communication beyond herself would finally arrive, some explosion to illuminate these times, like light arriving finally from the ring of fire we call the Big Bang, our own birth throes. Wisdom. Might she hope for wisdom?

They had not built a fire because the continuing and intensifying fire seasons prohibited what had been totally acceptable when Léonie was a child. Her father had built the fire as soon as they had arrived at their hideaway. She stayed by it after he and her mother had withdrawn to their tent. Her father trusted her to be attentive even when she was quite young. The Bears agreed the fire pits indicated a meeting place for Bears and child.

Léonie and Lucas will build a fire later in the cabin woodstove but it was not one the Bears would join in the way Léonie always shared a fire in her dreams. Without a fire, what would draw them? How would they know she was returning to them, now and here? She sniffed, snuggled more deeply into Lucas, rubbed against the roughness of his red and black plaid wool shirt, differentiating his scent from the surrounding scents, waiting for the pungent odor like no other, praying they would come before it was dark.

La Vieja began this vigil with them, looking into the woods for what life might be there. No matter how dark it gets, La Vieja could see them, curious that it was this vision that was given to her during this vigil.

* * *

The Bear sensing Léonie and Lucas upwind of him but down the slope moves toward their Lookout. He is examining the stairs, establishing the fact of them. He knows humans can't climb the way he does and are continuously finding ways to augment their biological limitations. He scratches his back against the nearby sugar pine, not honey, but sweet enough, then turns swiftly and is up the trunk, up, swift to the branches which lean out to the deck and settles into the crook, observing.

They look out from this shelter, he understands, for he has often been in, has taken on their body mind, or if not theirs specifically yet, La Vieja's, and if not hers, many others, even former residents in this cabin. His small brown eyes crinkle and his black stub nose crinkles; sight and smell often fuse for him into a single way of knowing. Why distinguish them? He can scent the two from below and the odor from the cabin verifies them.

From this perch, he can also smell the stream that has carved the valley below, her tireless pursuit of her beloved river that likewise rushes toward the distant, irresistible salt tang, the current that rises from the sea seeking the warming, sundrenched earth. One wind becomes the other, the salt laden wind sinks as it crosses the land and then rises on the exhale of trees to slide down again to the waters, a mixture, a little twirl, invisible turbulence or the spout of a whale bellowing, and then the dissolve into the sea and beginning again. Wind, rising and falling, in land and offshore, warm and cooling, fierce and gentle, a field of actions interpenetrating and dispersing, distinction without separation. Everything is in motion, that is what life is, even the boulders he lies on when he wants to warm himself in the sun, or those which have been formed into the cave he enters to sleep for a winter, are all still in movement, as are even the stones, though so slowly a human will miss it, but he doesn't. Everything in motion, everything. As long as the humans aren't there, all is well. As long as the humans aren't there now or later. He is always seeking exceptions as they are so numerous.

He looks in every direction. But he knows this is no way to see, or for him to see in the manner the humans call seeing; assuming that the visual yields the most significant understanding is remote for him. So much can occur, is occurring between where he is cradled in the tree and the stream he senses and beyond, a world of beings, multitudes in dynamic interconnection, no human being can take it in. The humans must ignore these exchanges for if they were aware of each, they would explode, for it would mean carrying the entire universe, actively, at once. They cannot, will not open to it. Although his way is simple, it is sufficient. Even as sight and smell inform him, what he knows best at this moment is tree, because he knows her, this moment, with his entire being. He examines the deck, the faux timber, and the distorted and altered scents that arise from it. Then another scent rises and descends the tree, each motion releasing an aroma as if conversational. His touch, her response. The two humans are seated a short lope from him and he will loop around a good distance and approach them from the east. They are waiting for him; they are attuned to the proper etiquette to encounter the wild. Him.

Léonie is leaning back into Lucas and he is settling against the sugar pine so that the Bear senses he has the freedom to approach or not as he wishes. As he, the Bear, *wishes*. They consciously open to his choice and this reception exudes from them like an aroma so that even La Vieja can smell it a hundred or more feet away.

Soon the Bear will approach and this is what will occur. Or the Bear approached and this is what occurred. La Vieja won't reveal what has or will occur while it is occurring. She would not dare to influence this event in any way. Having said this, it is best if we learn what happened after the fact.

Imagine how quietly he walked that he was suddenly before them, standing erect, nine feet tall, without either of them, or La Vieja, having heard him. That is an awesome height to confront. Lucas tightened his fingers on Léonie's arms inadvertently but she remained still because the moment Bear appeared, she fell into the dream realm and was calmed by memory and experience. Lucas doesn't have such an experience and further, he understood instantly that Bear was not here for Léonie, he was here to discern who Lucas is. He had smelled the two of them from many miles away. From the moment, they arrived, he smelled them. And La Vieja? Of course, he smelled her in the other realm that she inhabits. No animal has a better sense of smell than a Bear. So let's be conservative, Bear smelled them when they were within 20 miles of him because they had the windows of their car open. This only gives us distance. It doesn't give us time.

Bear had come to see if Lucas is a killer. He already knew Lucas didn't have a gun or a hunting rifle in his car. He would have known immediately, by odor and intuition and would never have approached, but rather sounded the alarm to all the Bears in the vicinity, especially the female Bear who is currently eating and eating because she is carrying his cubs and needs to put on lots of weight to support the three of them in the winter when they will be born while she hibernates. At some point he may compete with the grown males, but not now. Now he wants his gene pool in the world. It is robust.

Bear wanted to know if Lucas has ever carried a rifle. Not whether he has one now, whether he has ever carried a rifle. He has to smell back forty years. A Polar bear can track a scent forty miles but this Black Bear has to track back forty years. He isn't concerned about Léonie, she is a woman and she is a dreamer. But Lucas is a man. A two-legged male. He will have to prove himself. Bear stood his full height, rubbing his back against the closest pine. Then he turned and ran his claws down the bark of the tree, marking it. If Lucas used guns, Bear intended to mark him. This is 2020. Men are exceedingly dangerous. Trustworthiness needs to be proven again and again, and from Bear's point of view, is never certain.

Then Bear perceived something odd. He put his nose into the wind, but that was not the source of the scent. He couldn't place it because it wasn't from this geography but it wasn't alien either—it was distant, it came from miles away. Even a thousand miles away and many decades earlier. It didn't overpower Lucas' scent, but it was a portion of it. Old. Passed on. Female. Had he spoken English, Bear would have said Mexico, then pine nuts, prickly pear, madrone, yucca. He began to ease. It was an old scent, several hundred years old. The Bear couldn't know what has occurred since, and Lucas probably didn't know either. But Lucas came from this hemisphere. He was born here as were his mother's mothers and fathers centuries before the invasion. The Bear dropped to all fours. Lucas passed his scrutiny. Thank his ancestors for this.

Bear looked over at Léonie who did not dare make eye contact, knowing she was in his sight and could hide nothing from him. He could see her almost as well as he could smell her. There was nothing she could hide from him. She went directly back into the dream where she had sat next to the male Bear. He would be able to track her there as well as here and it would protect her. She had fallen onto the mother Bear's body but she had sat erect and cautious next to the male Bear. As she did this moment. In this moment and in the dream, simultaneously. Not worried but not casual about this encounter. She was being scrutinized by a high intelligence whose every sense was extremely sensitive—his awareness from every perspective far more highly developed than hers. It wasn't simply that he could smell her but he understood her from her various and varying scents. Or that he could see her precisely, had far better vision than she did, or that he could hear her so well, he could interpret each of her breaths, even from a distance. It wasn't only that his senses were so very refined and developed, like microscopes, telescopes, finely tuned instruments, it was more the ways he processed the information that he had received, until he felt confident that he could make a valid assessment of how Léonie would affect Bear's present and future. He had progeny, after all. He'd better have progeny. There were two possibilities he was considering: these two could sustain his species' future, or they could kill it. These two were allies or murderers. Only these two possibilities? Yes, only these two!

The Bear perceived Léonie entirely, everything about her now, everything, and her past, as with Lucas, and his origins and so her origins. She knew she didn't comprehend him. Her task was to acknowledge this in all ways. There was nothing she could keep secret and so she opened. Even Lucas felt the flood of revelation as it passed by him to the Bear. He caught the wave of it. The full scent of woman's heart and a wisp of four-legged intelligence flooded his entire being. She would want reciprocity from Lucas, would want him to open to her so fully, but the presence of Bear would not be there to help him yield. He would have to learn the means alone.

12

I know what I want. I want to live in a world with more wild salmon every year than in the year before, a world with more migratory songbirds every year than the year before, a world with more ancient forests every year than the year before, a world with less dioxin in each mother's breast milk every year than the year before, a world with wild tigers and grizzly bears and great apes and marlins and swordfish. I want to live on a livable planet.

Derrick Jensen
Endgame, Volume 1

When I moved to this land, this village sanctuary for a reliable future for all beings, I went to the eastern edge to journey to the spirits of the land. But I didn't know who they are. I lay down on the ground, closed my eyes, and offered myself to the invisibles so that I could serve the land. After a time, I heard a whirr of huge wings and First Bird, Pterodactyl, swept over my head. She was unexpected though I had several times looked out over the land to see the Wooly Mammoths, Mastodons and Dire Wolves crossing the hills and making their way through the Canyon to the sea. From the beginning then, when I looked out, I looked back in time.

We are all seated in the dark. Léonie and Lucas are at their Fire Lookout and La Vieja is at hers and I am too in my way. I look out for hours each day, unfailingly awed by the beauty of this wild parkland of chaparral, the piebald branch and straw hues of the meadows and the dense dark green of the rivers of oaks that I have been observing for almost forty years.

Over the last years, I have settled on this spot where an ancient elder is interred. There are many graves on the land, and one day my ashes will be here feeding the roots of the olive tree that fell and re-rooted when the hill collapsed some years ago. Timber Wolf was buried above and Isis the white wolf pushed the earth onto him with her paws. My old friend, Steven Kent, his ashes are here. Mine will mingle with his, with Timber's, with the Cockatoo who spent her life with another friend, and the doe who was run down on Topanga Canyon Blvd. where it curves away from the Valley at the summit. I look out to the south, the direction of fire and the heart and my mind is momentarily buoyed by that future and the blending of our consciousness.

A medicine person, a *nganga*, Mandaza Kandemwa, says we live in order to learn how to be ancestors so we can return to protect and inform the living. There will be no distinction then between my mind or concerns and the Deer's the Wolves, the birds, the sage and the trees. May this land and all the beings thrive.

As each place is a hologram of entirety, I hope it will yield the wisdom that my heart is craving and that we definitely need. I am determined to do what I can to die here, even sitting at this exact spot, looking toward the field of purple sage, accompanying all else that is also preparing to die, looking through this land to find Elsewhere and leap toward it. I didn't know that the place of dying, of crossing to the other world that holds this one in its arms, is as essential as the burying. Might I be able to cross not from my bed watching the midnight moon crawl through the branches to four a.m., the hour of the wolf, not looking toward the rough crest of the Santa Monica mountains facing west, but here with the ancestors, or on my gravesite, that knoll to the southwest rising out of this wild land which we have left intact except for the olive tree and … our dead.

Cherokee is in the same grave in the orchard, as Tschee Wah'Yah, Love Puppy in Tagalog, her daughter, who preceded her, killed by a car on a rainy morning when she noted the gate had been left unlocked and sped out because she loved to run. And Shoonaq' joined her mother Cherokee and TscheeWah'Yah on June 23, 2021 when her legs gave out from old age. 14.5 years is almost eternity for a Wolf. Isis, the white Wolf, is on the hill facing the sunset, though she would have wanted to be with Timber but the hill collapsed. Owl is by the Eucalyptus tree, Blue and Akasha are in the secret garden under my bedroom window and Cheyenne is under the stupa to the south.

La Vieja

The Indigenous ancestor is here on the southeast corner of the land. His skeleton bones were in a plastic bag stored on a closet floor, after having been used for medical education. When the bundle was discovered, he was rewrapped in white linen, then legally transported with a TSA permit by the physician's granddaughter, Suetta Tenney, also a physician, so we could bury him in a sacred way. Ben Garcia came up from the Museum of Man in San Diego for the ceremony. He held the skull gently in his large hands, turning it carefully as if to examine it visually from every angle, but we knew he was listening to what it would reveal to someone who had learned to discern the language of bones during his years being a caretaker for the sacred. "It could easily be four hundred years old," he suggested in a very quiet voice, waiting to hear if he would be corrected by the spirit of the bones, then continued. "He. I am certain it is a man, also by size and density," Ben spoke even more slowly and quietly. "He could be," he paused here, because he knew the history of colonialism and the wars against the Indians beginning in 1622 against the Pequot. "He could be a Native man." The sadness to which Ben, because of his position, had to accommodate was articulate as he put the skull down on the altar we had created, "He was probably dug up from a grave." Ben sat down among us in the circle. It was through grave robbing, politely called "removing" that the museum had obtained ancestors from Alaska that they were in the process of repatriating.

Several of us, including Cheryl Potts, an Aleutiiq woman from Kodiak Island, had been invited to the museum to perform rituals when the extent of the Native remains had been discovered. But it was only the night before we were to arrive that he telephoned to say that there were ancestors from the Aleutians, her relatives. She began, then, to participate in their return. The skulls were wrapped tenderly in white linen and protected with Bear skin for their journey home.

It is estimated that there are at least 180,000 human remains that need to be returned to the tribes. There was no way we could discover who this ancestor is, or the people he belongs to and so we buried him at dawn just as the sun was rising, creating an ancestor altar at the southeast corner of this land where I am sitting now, praying. And not that he should feel any gratitude for being properly buried, but still I am always hoping that he will answer, that an understanding that is clearly not my own, that I would not have come to on my own, will occur to me when I ask, as I do repeatedly, "Please, how do we meet these times? How can we shift so that extinction and climate dissolution are reversed?"

I have been here, studying the landscape, asking that question for three summers, trying to see differently than I have for the forty preceding years since I gained access to this vista. The essential configurations are always the same, that hilltop that rounds as if offering itself to the sky, that peak, Eagle Rock, that dense brush. It is always the same and yet every variation of season and so of light, every shift in temperature, every breeze or wind alters the vista. It is always, and it is never, the same. This view and my agreement to pursue it on a daily basis is the foundation for reviewing everything I can, our lives, my life to see what understanding might come from a focused and relentless view far in the distance and equally personal to everything that coheres in this moment and place.

I don't spy on La Vieja but I listen to her, as I must, in order to write her story. I try to enter her perceptions but from this perspective which is a different geography and, possibly, the consequence of different goals. And maybe that is why I feel comparably blinded, unable to see the way she sees. The differences seem small, but they are extreme. Except for the days or weeks of imposed retreat, I drive to the market rarely but still as needed, return phone messages over time, and I do read the news. She does none of these and so we inhabit different worlds. Mine may end soon and hers, likely, will not. There is another significant difference, she seems calm, or exudes a deep quiet in her soul with her situation though clearly she is undone by the global disarray and she experiences the suffering of the animals and other beings increasingly. But she does not question where she is, the decision she has made, her circumstances; she doesn't speak of loneliness, doesn't wonder how to spend her days, isn't concerned with her health, finances or her moods. As if having retreated from social life, she also managed to disentangle from the most ordinary and persistent worries. Distinct as my life is now from what it has been in the past, I am not free. The best I can do is relegate perceived obligations to a particular time in the week or month, although actually sometimes, more often than not, I am out of my mind. Our world does this to us and there is no escape, and maybe that's the intention—as long as bills arrive, as food needs to be purchased and then prepared, as the electricity is subject to outages, as the phone rings, as the cell phone offers up news bulletins, I live in constant alert. A helicopter hovers across the land. Is it a taxi between airports or a police or a fire vehicle? That siren: ambulance? Police? Fire engine? But even if all of this calmed, I am here to look out for fires. They are the consistent concern. And then there is Covid, Queen Corona's demand that we stop and consider our lives before all life is over. These two concerns are La Vieja's as well as mine.

But I am also, as she is, looking for the unchanging, for what is stable even under the new grasses that rise and dry and fall away, becoming earth again. I don't mean only what I have seen in forty years of contemplation of these hills, these Oaks. Or trying to understand in forty years something of what this land taught the Tongva people who lived here for 3,500 years until the Church and military decimated them. The land and so the people suffer from that continuous violation that began on this land 250 years ago and on this continent more than 500 years ago. As far back as I can see, the same land grab, the same violence, the same cruelty, and little of it mitigated. Everywhere now, people fleeing their home countries, fleeing war, colonization, famine, drought, extreme poverty, genocide, fleeing the consequences of every possible form of violence against the Earth, fleeing climate collapse as if there is somewhere safe. Fleeing climate collapse as if there is somewhere, anywhere to go. La Vieja knows this, but perhaps her goals are sufficient to protect her from the nervous tremulousness of contemporary life. My hands tremble, hers do not.

March 2021

The hills did not turn green this year. There has not been enough rain.

September 10, 2019

There is almost nothing left of the Abaco Islands of the northern Bahamas after hurricane Dorian.

Events rise up, assume a place in my memory. What presents itself is out of my control.

May 15, 2021

Within hours of opening the land to the community, we have to close it again; the Fire Department has sealed the state park. Someone has set multiple fires in rugged terrain with thick dry brush at the summit behind my house, near Eagle Rock. History, that is human life, is speaking, but the land is speaking as well. It is our task to learn her language because what needs to be understood cannot be conveyed in English or any of the other dominating languages. She remembers. She knows. It's possible that something external to myself has called me to this pursuit, is a sieve dipping into the vast well of the past to bring up what serves the moment. Bringing up not only my own personal past but the concurrent historic and social circumstances of our lives. The parts rise up higgledy-piggledy and reassemble themselves into what is and what is not, randomly taking on form and meaning, each piece thriving from a new relationship with the other.

I'm in the kaleidoscope: different memories, concerns, observations, each holding different threads, not coherent but still consistent with each other, not unlike the different birds at the feeder—they all come at the same time: Thrasher, rarely now, but Mourning Dove, Quail, Towhee, Red Finch, Goldfinch and Scrub Jay, in the way the thoughts cluster together. Blue Jay, Finch and sometimes Towhee go to the feeder itself, dropping kernels down for the Doves and the coveys of Quail. The Goldfinches have their own feeder with Nyjer seed from the African daisy which no one else seems to want. We lured those Goldfinches here with narrow strands of turmeric yellow hemp cloth and now they know there is food for them here, as long as there is Nyjer seed anywhere, because we don't know how long the lives we are accustomed to living will continue.

Hurricane Dorian was threatening Florida where floods may still occur while it makes landfall further north, perhaps at South Carolina and Georgia.

Reading ahead in this manuscript but back in time, as time and space fold in upon each other, I see that I was sitting here and writing almost a year ago, time and weather converging. Chronology has become irrelevant—what matters is the insight that comes from the co-extension of events and the patterns that emerge as each informs the other.

Fog enters the canyon between the hills and a lemon light on this side of the fog turns all things golden. Hurricane Rosa is about to make landfall farther north on the Baja peninsula than is usual. As the fog approaches, I pray warily to Rosa on behalf of rain for the graying Sage bushes and the

Coast Live Oaks increasingly threatened because of the drought by Western Oak Bark Beetle. They need water to be able to resist. The molten gold of the sunset shimmers against black streaks of storm clouds too thin to rain but still Rosa's gift. The winds rise and the prayer flags tear as they flap.

On my late afternoon walk, I note scat in the orchard and along the path, larger, different from the significantly smaller deposits of the Coyotes. It clearly belongs to Mountain Lion. The Lion deposit has lots of fur and bone, while the Coyote scat will have the same but from smaller animals and interlaced with berries and whatever else it finds to eat.

After the 2018 Woolsey fire, my physician began warning me about the Lion's increasing presence. "Don't walk in the hills without a large stick and a companion," he said. But Mountain Lions have walked here for years. They, like we, come to this sanctuary expecting to find water and leave their scat in exchange just yards from where I'm writing. All night a female Lion in estrus bellowed, sounding like a woman in childbirth. Her lineage has been tracked. P-1 was called the king of the mountain as he was the only one documented to cross from the north of the 101 Freeway to the south. P-12 took up residence in Griffith Park. P -70, P- 71, P -72 P -73, are two females and two males, born July 2018 and may well have been guests on this land. P-64 and P-74 died in the Woolsey fire. The Lions lose habitat each day, are vulnerable to traffic, rodenticide, and illegal hunting. We are so afraid of them but we should understand that most probably they identify us as mass murderers.

It's hot and I am ranting. Two hurricanes are spinning at the same time, Rosa and Walaka, September 29, 2018 and I feel as if they are inside me, an internal turbulence, wet and fiery at the same time. It's all out of control and we think technology will subdue it, but the opposite is true. Maybe humans will end up dominating the rebelling natural world through technology and artificial intelligence, which looks like the direction we are going, but only by becoming increasingly artificial ourselves and threatening the survival of everyone else and all the ways that life has formed itself since the beginning. I don't want to be here to see it happen and while I have the ability, I choose to stand with the animals and the natural world. If the natural world can only survive without us, so be it; let all the Others thrive in their complex interrelationships of intrinsic beauty. All of this at once, shifting and refocusing, at this Lookout. Will anything emerge from this boiling cosmic soup?

2018
 We have an 80% chance that rain will come here tonight.

Hurricane Walaka, a Category 5 storm with 160 mph winds is approaching Johnston Atoll considered an uninhabited, unincorporated US territory, similar to the ways Columbus, his sponsors and cronies, considered the US uninhabited and thought they had come upon a virgin land they could rape.

Millions of sea birds live there on what has been designated as a National Wildlife Refuge even though it is the most toxic and radioactive atoll, having been the victim of seemingly endless nuclear and biological warfare testing. Johnston Island will probably experience the right-hand eyewall of Walaka. This will devastate the island's millions of seabirds: the Noddy, the Curlew, the Masked Booby, the Petrel, the Shearwater, the Tern, the Great Frigate Bird and the Plover, the Turnstone, the Sanderling, the Tropicbird and the wandering Tattler, the Red-footed Boobies, and the Brown Noddies. This atoll is currently the only nesting site in 450,000 square miles of ocean. The four scientists? They were airlifted out by the Coast Guard before Walaka will strike. They didn't rescue the birds even though we are responsible for these storms.

* * *

How did I, the writer, come here, to this way of being? Ultimately the animals brought me to this roost. The great mystery is that they come to us, is the ways we're altered by the unexpected. We become who we are through uncontrollable and unfamiliar forces that take us over as surely as the most devastating storm can take our lives in more ways than one.

Yes, I can say the Elephants brought me here in the ways the Bears brought Léonie to life. An unpredictable event occurred twenty years ago. Now everything turns around that event. An Elephant in the wild met with me and my people; he and his people met us in a particular place at a particular time. We returned, returned again and again, to that place and that time, year after year, and so did they. Incomprehensible. Real.

I had wanted to sit in Council with the Elephant people and the medicine man, the *nganga*, Mandaza Kandemwa, whom we were visiting in

Zimbabwe, said "When the people sit in council the spirits are sitting in council with them." And having been with him and the Elephants the year before, I said, "When animals sit in council, they are the spirits."

At the same time—and this is another lost memory surfacing as the sun sets, as the fog comes in, as the hurricanes spin up out of the ocean—as we were sitting in council with Mandaza's people, a young man was on a rampage outside the hut where we were meeting. The African healer had tried to help him, as those of us who had gathered from the States and Canada had as well, but equally unsuccessfully. There was nothing to do but let him go, which is what he wanted, to climb into the Musasa tree alongside the house. It held him easily and hid him in its leaves as he howled his incurable anguish. There was no healing for his agony and the healer knew it. The healer had no medicine for street pain, if he had he would have healed his own sons and daughters, and his country living under Mugabe, (who died in September 2019) the revolutionary turned tyrant, another too familiar story of these times. We couldn't tell if the wailing outside was from a man or an animal suffering the grief of this time. A roar, an inconsolable whoop, an ongoing desolate screech from among the branches, plaintive enough to bring down a dry rain of brown leaves.

The young man's mother had been born in a remote village from which she had walked 400 miles to the city to find work, as the white Europeans had taken all the land under apartheid and it had not been returned to the poor post-apartheid. Her only possibility for survival was to do domestic work for the white man at starvation wages. A dark line of earth, scratched from outside the door of the shack where she had lived, remained under her fingernails. She had never wanted to remove it. It was her real home and so she carried it on her body as long as possible. In Bulawayo, she suffered her son's madness in quiet despair. She was helpless, he was a city boy, without work. He raged. His rage was large. Large as a colonized city.

The neighbors white, black and colored in this mixed post-apartheid suburban neighborhood in Bulawayo, Zimbabwe each called the police after closing their windows and turning up the sound on the only two TV channels, one featuring reruns of the television soap, Santa Barbara, about the very rich.

Red lights flashed onto his tree haven as if setting it aflame. He sidled down the tree that had given home to Leopards for millennia, then leaped across the stone wall and ran full force into sliding glass doors—taking down what he could before the police got him. It was the least, he felt, he could do. Bleeding, he was handcuffed and thrown into the police car by officers who could well have been his schoolmates had he had the money to go to school. The man-child was taken to jail. There was no other place for him. They put him in a locked cell within a locked room with other cells, within a locked building, within a locked fence—a European invention.

But somewhere to the west, to the north and south, in all directions, from the savannahs to the jungles, the young man's cry was received, the air willing to carry it, a cry beyond prayer or hope imparted to his kin who wailed in response. A wretched yowl of lamentation from the four-leggeds of the world who knew his condition although separated by hundreds and thousands of miles, because they knew their own.

We had failed the young man.

*   *   *

Later that year, I visited Angus, an Elephant confined in Bowmanville Zoo in Toronto bringing a letter from the directors of a large South African wildlife preserve requesting Angus's release. He had been incarcerated just after he witnessed his mother killed in a cull in South Africa when he was three years old. We wanted him returned to his own land and his own people. The goal was endorsed by Nelson Mandela who, understanding imprisonment and solitary which was awaiting Angus if he would come into musth in Canada, was hoping to greet Angus as he himself had been greeted not so many years before when freed from prison on 2/11/1990.

At Bowmanville Zoo in Ontario, Canada, an old bull was chained by all four legs to the wall. It was winter. There were patches of snow on the ground and the cement floor was ice cold. The old bull rocked from one leg to another. He would remain this way for one to two months. His musth rumble broke me into a thousand pieces.

Though promised I could speak with Angus to discern whether he wanted to return, and to prepare him so he could participate in his destiny, he had been taken off the premises for the day just minutes before my arrival. I left the letter for the zoo owner, but he did not respond and never agreed to the proposed transfer which would have given Angus the opportunity to journey to villages across Africa teaching about Elephants while advocating for continent-long wildlife corridors, a project of the wildlife preserve.

In 2006, the zoo owner, Michael Hackenberger, did choose to send Angus to South Africa to make a commercial film. "I have no environmental interest," he had asserted in justification. But Angus died of a sedative trial given a week before he was scheduled to return. For other reasons, animal cruelty charges were filed soon after against Michael Hackenberger for violence, and the joy he took in inflicting pain upon a Tiger in his care. The charges were dropped when Hackenberger suffered a stroke in February 2017 and was deemed unfit to stand trial. However, PETA circulated a video made by one of their members working at the zoo with a hidden camera showing Hackenberger during a training session with the Tiger named Uno, saying, "Cause I like hitting him in the face and the paws ... and the beauty of the paws being on the rock, when you hit them it's like a vice ... it stings more."

* * *

In the years that I and a friend, Valerie Wolf, visited the Los Angeles Zoo, Miko, my imprisoned friend, a Gorilla, would come running out to the edge of the moat he couldn't cross from behind the fake mountain setting where he was locked in his cell at night. We visited him for an hour every week the way we might have visited an imprisoned uncle or cousin. Each time we gathered up our backpacks to leave, he railed. We set them down again, turned toward him calling back and forth. But then again, we had to leave. He railed again. We returned for a moment but ultimately we had to walk away. First we went every week, then life set in and we came less often, then could only arrive every month. One day we arrived and he was gone. They had transferred him to a zoo on the East coast so that he could breed. No surprise he died there. Quickly.

After Miko, we always visited Dream, the Polar Bear. As we stood at the railing, we watched her lift her listless, lonely white body from one side of the tiny pool to the other, flopping down like a water-soaked rag. In the summer, it was 98 degrees F. The ice floe on which she might have lived in the Arctic had long since melted, threatening a drastic rise in sea levels. A 60 foot rise followed the ending of the last ice age. The same could happen from our machinations. We tried to communicate with Dream, but she did not respond, ever. Miko died and then she died.

Then Gita the Elephant began failing when her partner Ruby was sent elsewhere. Ruby was brought back but not in time. Then Ruby was alone. Finally, she was rescued by PETA but too late, she died soon after.

Billy the Elephant has been confined and suffering alone for thirty years in the Los Angeles Zoo, his head bobbing, zoochosis, in abject loneliness. Though we came back regularly for a year, he was too traumatized to notice us and, ultimately, there was no reason for us to return to the zoo.

*   *   *

2018

The probability of rain in Los Angeles and Topanga has been reduced to 40%.

*   *   *

The crazed young man went to jail in August 2001. We didn't speak about him because we had failed him. And while we couldn't hear his cries from the jail, we did hear the chorus of animals who recognized his pain, Billy's rumble, the agonized roar of the Sun Bear in his cage smaller than he is long, the Chimpanzees in an American chemical laboratory confined in metal crates alongside each with wire mesh at the feet to allow piss and shit to fall through, and also a choir of an infinite number of Mice, Rats, Rabbits, Guinea Pigs, Monkeys regularly receiving doses of deadly potions to reveal the precise nature of their future suffering and how long they will survive. An opera of common anguish. We all heard it. Acknowledged it. But the next day, the memory was a little vaguer, then quieter the following day, then still, at least for us. But for them…?

The Elephant Ambassador did not show up when we went to Chobe after tending to the crazed young man. The only time the Ambassador did not appear. But also, we didn't, as we did afterwards, wait for him where we had met him the first time.

From an outlook we observe and gather information. I sit in the dark, wondering what story, what conclusion can be reached from this amalgam, Angus, the Ambassador, Nana and Frankie, the Matriarchs, the crazed young man from Zimbabwe, Gita, Ruby and Billy the Elephants, Miko the Guerilla, Dream the Polar Bear, the endangered nesting birds on

La Vieja

Johnston Atoll? What can the events tell us about our common lives?

What do these details reveal about these times? How did we get here? Is there any way out?

Blue skies this morning. We are still waiting for rain.

13

You will know
when you walk
in bear country
By the silence
flowing swiftly between the juniper trees
by the sundown colors of sand rock
all around you

You may smell damp earth
scratched away
from yucca roots
you may hear snorts and growls
slow and massive sounds
from caves in the cliffs high about you.

It is difficult to explain
how they call you
All but a few who went to them
Left behind families
    grandparents
    and sons
    a good life.

The problem is
you will never want to return...

Leslie Marmon Silko
from "Story From Bear Country," *Storyteller*

They had gone into the Lookout as soon as the Bear left. Inevitably, every interaction between them was awkward and they both knew it. No one was pretending otherwise. The contrast between not knowing each other at all and sitting as they had when the Bear arrived, as two bodies that had long ago become one, was disorienting. Standing still in the center of the 16 x 16 loft, Léonie was lost and it was hard to be lost in such close quarters, without her own provisions to attend and no sense of how to negotiate this time.

Lucas, on the other hand, had taken charge. He had brought the food and supplies, knew where they might be stored and what would be done with them. He was alert to whatever question sat behind the expressions that flitted across her face. He was, he had to admit, pleased with himself for seemingly reading her right.

"I left the sleeping bags, pads, etc. down below .... The supplies, are, however, queen size. He hesitated, "We can make adjustments if you prefer…" He didn't hesitate for a moment to allow her to respond but asked, breathlessly, "In the meantime … Brandy? On ice?" He could make chips from the slabs he had brought to cool the food.

"Neat," she answered, glad there was more than tea.

Every moment there was another line to walk between the familiar and the unanticipated, the domestic and the wild, reticence and revelation. They knew nothing of each other. Every word was discovery. Nothing could be assumed and within moments all expectations for both of them fell away.

Then he saw that she was disturbed, standing still in the middle of the room, not knowing what she could do. He saw the steadiness of her stance, and also how awkward it was for a woman such as she to do nothing. She had not chosen to sit down as someone else might have done. She stood there as if waiting for the stone to be passed to her so that she could place it as only she knew how.

"I can put things away," she said, "I am very skilled at sorting and placing. It is what I do."

"And I," he countered, "am good at assessing someone's skills." He appraised her with an exaggerated scan and big smile. Indeed, all he wanted to do was let his eyes survey her, for sight to substitute for touch. Instead, he said, "I assume you can cut, chop, peel, sort and display. Even with limited resources."

She didn't hesitate but went to the bags which had food and kitchen supplies, found the cutting board, utensils, platters, bowls and began. "I am not going to be your sous chef forever, you know." She was grinning.

He brought her the brandy and stood close as she took the all-purpose knife to the cheese with a flourish.

He had brought his finger up again to the golden curls which he allowed to wind around his finger as if a vine in accelerated motion. His dark skin, her brown skin, her golden hair. Her light.

"Your father?' he asked.

"Yes, but primarily my mother," she said, "and before her, my grandmother and before her…. We're dark and we're blond. Our lineage."

He began to respond but not with words she expected. Rather, he blurted, "Do you know this Bear?"

It was as if they had been spun into another language, into another country where another language was spoken with all its singular premises and hypotheses.

"How do you know the Bear?" It wasn't a question, it was an interrogation and yet how much was revealed by his asking. She could discern his history, lineage, beliefs, world view, his blood type and his passport simply by his asking. If he asked this, he understood. She was afraid. She put the knife down on the cutting board. There was no interfering with this slide into such a mind that had been beckoning to her, as if hope were a signal from the universe that had previously offered no evidence it existed any longer anywhere. She understood the question entirely because she was wild, because she could not be tamed or domesticated. His question revealed what she hadn't known about herself. What she now knew.

Does she know *this* Bear? Had she dared to imagine that a dream Bear and an embodied Bear, might be one and the same? He had accepted the possibility.

She stared at him, examined the bone structure of his face, his build, the origins and confidence implicit in his carriage, the way she had examined his stance and movements when they arrived and later in the woods, needing to be certain of his affinities or apprised of his disconnections. Was their connection fate or was it enchantment?

"Do I know the Bear?" She asked aloud but almost whispered. "Do I know the Bear? Do I know this Bear?" Her voice lowered even further because she was querying herself. Is this Bear the one I have met in my dreams? Did I dream this Bear and he is real? She wasn't certain that what she would say next was true but she thought it needed to be true and then she thought there were times, after deep ethical inquiry and consideration, that one was called to allow or yield to the truth, the reality of something that might not be capable of manifesting itself and yet had.

"I dreamed the dream, again and again. Differently, each time, but not so much, but enough to know it was a living event, with the kind of variations implicit in life. Light, temperature, seasonal shifting. I grew older. The Bears in the circle remained, came and went, changed, aged. It was a living dream in which I returned to the same place, time and again. And now a Bear has come, or *the* Bear, to this place, now that we are here, not there, when my parents aren't here and we are here together. It's twenty plus years plus or so later and a Bear or *the* Bear has come. Are we in a dream, Lucas? Are we being dreamed by someone, something, somewhere?"

He waited. He had dared to ask and as he knew, she knew, that the question assumed the possibility of a passageway between the worlds which, would be dizzying at the least and could be maddening and could open to what neither could imagine or predict. It was happening to both of them at the threshold of their coming together.

"How do I know?" He paused. "I don't know how I know," and found himself trembling just enough to be aware of what had transpired, that they had not noted to each other. Within him, a growing disbelief that the Bear had come and accompanying awe that it had, coupled with a vague but developing sense that the Bear had considered striking him, but something stopped it, other than Léonie, an awareness it had about him that he was, himself, faintly coming to recognize.

They were in a passage between the worlds. There might not be a return.

She saw the tremor. She could have laughed to dismiss the implications of his awareness and it would all be over and they would be back in their conventional lives, two people with their biographies intact, their lives and experiences, their professions and successes, their degrees and licenses, all recognized, certified, approved. She didn't laugh.

"If I dreamed him and he came to us, then, Lucas, only the Bears could have dreamed us. It must be the Bears who have manifested us. There is no doubt," she began, running her fingers down his cheek and then turning so the back of her hand, her knuckles, ran down his cheekbone, as if smoothing the hide of a Horse or the thick dark fur of a Bear to see if he was real, if they were real. Unsure, perhaps, she reached out and grabbed his arm where the rolled-up sleeve of his plaid shirt met his muscle. And he twirled and placed both his hands on the sides of her head and pulled her to him, kissing her hard on her furled brow, so she couldn't question one body meeting another and tousled her curls and then pulled them hard and would have pulled her into making love in that moment but that she had said they would wait for the moon to decide their time. But he assumed, and he was right, that his heat was meeting her heat and he would have to awaken his hard-learned adolescent restraint. Waiting for the animal moment, he would have to restrain his very mammalian desire. It was a role reversal. The male Bear did not enact the restraint that the female was able to exercise. But now there were no cubs to protect, nothing to inhibit them except the extraordinary human ability to consider and act on behalf of the future.

Words, then, he could use words to temper the moment while aware he was simultaneously lighting fires. "Well" he said pulling away slightly but not really, "where shall we be when the blood time calls us?"

"Why, here, of course," she said also pulling back to ease the tension, "but inside, not to tempt fate." They hadn't even sat down in the cabin, they hadn't prepared their beds, he hadn't taken the candleholders from his suitcase, so he hadn't lit the candles, and she hadn't laid out the chocolate she had brought. With a decisive gesture, she picked up the knife again, precisely slicing a jicama, then surveying the cheese, avocados, onions, chile, salsa, cherry tomatoes, limes, cilantro and salt.

"Garlic?" she asked, testing for the guacamole she was about to prepare.

"The next bag," he answered, "at the bottom, by the cucumbers and red peppers you will want as well."

"Oh yes," she agreed, "I am full of wanting. As I suspect you are as well."

He grinned. They were finding their way to each other.

"I will drive down tomorrow morning after taking the salmon, which is on ice, to a lakeside and find a place where I can get phone service and extend our lease."

"How long?" she asked to tease him.

"Indefinitely," he responded. And then he had to hold her, had to pull her close, and they stood that way, their heartbeats entraining with each other, slightly fluttering, slightly trembling until the squall passed.

They ate dinner. They washed the dishes in a bucket. They carried the bucket of dishwater down to the plants below. Then the moment arrived when a decision had to be made. Léonie had examined the space. There wasn't much to peruse. Whatever he had brought, she saw there were two single mattresses on cots behind the screen.. "I would like to sleep on one of those on the deck," she said. Her need for quiet was overwhelming. First Lucas had come and then the Bear had come. And if she went out, there would be the Milky Way as well. So many big presences pressing in upon her. They were all getting closer and she needed to push them away, to raise her arms, extend them palms out and create a circle around her that was inviolate, even from beauty, yes, and even, at least now, from love.

Had she dreamed the Bear? Or had the Bear dreamed her? Or both? And who was he and what monumental decision has she just made? She didn't want to listen to music, read or write in her journal. She wanted to go into the dark the way one dives, head first into a lake feeling the cold comb through her hair, one finger at a time, and then spread up in streaks through the rest of her body. Soundless. Moving in the dark waters as in the night until the light of the small fishes became quietly visible like the first light of stars.

"We have lived a lifetime today," she said.

"Tell me what direction you want," he accommodated, "and I will take the opposite."

They took out the mattresses. She took both his hands but did not draw close and looked in his eyes. "I…" she started to say. But he silenced her and she was grateful. "We have a lifetime" he said completely puzzled by what this meant and how it might be possible.

"After a hard day building, especially when working with a team I enjoy, after all the shared strain and effort, the sandwiches, the cold beer, I have to be alone. It's like cutting exactly the right window into a wall. Architects like to plan everything out, know the dimensions, order the materials with the contractor, determine how to create exactly what they have visualized. But, I can't. I have to see the wall as it develops, as it grows like a living thing, the exact nature, color, texture of each stone and their relationship to each other. I build the wall and then … then I open it. Then I take out the stones. Rebalance. Find the place where the wind wants to enter, where the light wishes to penetrate to the other side."

"Are you making an opening for us?" How mysterious she was, he thought happily.

"Yes. But I can only make it alone and in the dark."

She went to the north side of the porch surrounding their cabin and he took the south. In the morning he awakened, he believed, before she did and went to do what he said he would do.

PART V

14

...the animals knew this stalking game too, and they watched us watching them as we listened to Sweet Hunter, and all of us danced our thoughts together across the meadow, talking into one another's minds, human to animal and back, and I realized with a start I'd almost forgotten this simple thing too, so immersed I'd been in that other way of seeing. I shook my head sharply, as though clearing cobwebs from my eyes, and Unole looked at me curiously, so I smiled at him and held a finger to my lips as we watched a small family of young deer stepping gingerly across the forest floor, moving steadily but with big eyes trained on us. They could see my newness, my coming home fresh again from a different world, and they spoke to me, "Did you forget?" They asked, voices echoing in my mind. "You're a curious one," they said, and when I smiled back at them, they looked away and paid us no mind anymore, finally satisfied with my presence, and that I was real, that I could hear them. Blue Jays called back and forth across the open spaces between high branches, and we let the sun move slowly across the sky, as it should be. We let ourselves dream together, and we let the dream grow and expand and become nothing more than the world that lay before us. This was the healing and the promise come together, what we have always known was ours.

Stan Rushworth

Going to Water: The Journal of Beginning Rain

La Vieja was at her Lookout walking the catwalk. In the beginning she had rationed her visits down to the loo, learned timing, a feat for a woman her age. She hadn't imagined this to be a challenge and she didn't intend concerns with her body to preoccupy her. There were two options, reliable self-restraint or becoming agile going up and down the stairs. She thought that if she managed the stairs the self-restraint might follow, but she also valued agility. The results, she kept to herself.

She walked round and round. She was creating a routine. Or a ritual. One which she did not invite the Writer to witness although she herself followed it faithfully. There was the deck where she was visible and then it was as if another deck was below, and only she knew its location, could see it, enter it. That was where the second circling took place. Or, more likely, it wouldn't always be on a deck, but later on the ground, then further away, out of sight of the cabin, of anything that reminded her of her human life. There, finally, she carved an inconspicuous path that was level enough through the grove of firs to circumambulate them again and again until the energy of the rotation began to dissolve the seeming differences between the various beings who lived there, of which she was one. A new way of reflecting on herself. The human with its adamant and singular importance seemed to be dissolving in her, as if a preoccupying pain in a finger was easing in favor of her being a particular manifestation of the life force, nothing more. This is where the seasons she had spent on this land had taken her. Self, human self, and the incessant low-pitched buzz of the ongoing anxiety about survival and satisfying needs dissipated here, as she was molded by light and weather, accommodating without urgency. Especially now, when the forest, because of fires, was closed to humans and so could begin to be restored to its essential nature and she—was it possible?—was a part of this. On the one hand she focused on disappearing herself but not without being increasingly aware of how large her careful footprint was. She carried waste water down the stairs, examined her green companions to see which plant or tree could use the water, composted whatever she could and assisted what might be struggling. She made herself smaller and stiller, smaller and stiller.

Each day, she gently probed further into what the natural world might be thinking, asking permission to participate alongside the others. No, more than permission, she wanted an invitation that would allow her to be integrated into Earth's physics and laws, to relinquish distance and space, to blur the hard edges of her body, mind and heart.

She didn't think anyone should dare to penetrate this realm without knowing it was reciprocally desired, that the Earth was also imagining the return of the human within the natural order. She hoped to cross that barrier, to undo the distinction and separation her ancestors (and mine and yours) originated. She was beginning to understand that this is why she had come here. Just beginning to understand. She was no longer committed to looking far as she had claimed in the beginning, as I, the Writer still attempt to do, but wanted to enter and explore *here* because it's all here in this spot as long as soil and rock remain. Here is beginning, here is an underlying intelligence, the foundation of everything, the bass note, the drone. But it wasn't exploration any longer, it was both being present and yielding, and allowing herself to be penetrated, everywhere, and then, inevitably, penetrating but without dominating. To be another grain of sand in Earth's realm, ruled by Her laws. That was now La Vieja's goal.

Yet awareness and self-awareness didn't disappear. She was attempting to cross to what her culture said was impossible, also said was immature, naïve, infantile, uncomfortable, stupid, awkward and inept. Primitive. But for herself, and these times, she wanted to see if she could dissolve, slow step by slow step, the habits of the body-mind warning against "going native," so that another being attuned with all the other distinct beings could come into existence finally after so many thousands of years apart.

She leaned up against the huge, rough scrappy trunk of the white pine that had become her interlocutor. We used to live here, she said without speaking, thought without thinking. In intimate relationship with each other. We made home here. All with our hands. Her hand was against the bark, her hands on its old body. If we return to the old ways, we can repair the harm we have done simply by the way we will be, the harm we do will no longer be intrinsic to how we live. It wasn't a statement. It was wondering. And hoping the tree would acknowledge her but she hadn't reached that level of connection yet and possibly she never would. If she were a tree, she couldn't be part of this bio-world without being of it and so would be unable to endanger the others because it would be endangering self. If for a moment, she had disappeared herself, she had reappeared. Sadly evident through her knowing and experience that as a member of the current human world, the habit of doing harm to oneself and others remained. La Vieja looked up the enormous height, the pine rushing to the sky, each day as she aged growing faster than the day before, and La Vieja felt for a nanosecond what it was to be rooted when suicide and so ecocide were not conceivable. She had, she understood, come here to know this. And why was it so frightening to be able to know this. No matter why. She was after all the months here, beginning.

La Vieja believed that the Writer had also experienced this invitation for immersion from the natural world but had resisted it. La Vieja rarely thought about me after our agreement which demanded radical independence and coexistence. So her current assessment was no more than a sidelong glance in an odd mirror, as revelatory of what La Vieja was as what I might be. La Vieja conjectured that I had not succeeded in overcoming how shy I am, how timorous, in the face of the enormous presence of the Earth. The enormous demand of possibility. Perceiving its essence I was daunted, La Vieja believed, and so I shrank away. She thought that it would be painful to me if I knew that she, La Vieja, was apprenticing herself to the spirit of this place, to this place in its particulars.

Maybe I have been reluctant. But this is not a cautionary tale. A writer's life is intrinsically different. La Vieja is there, in that cabin, and intends to die there. When she admitted this to herself, the thought shook her foundations but did not change her resolve. I, on the other hand, the Writer, decided on a virtual retreat, an act of the imagination which is also intimidating if adhered to faithfully, but not the equivalent of deciding to live alone 5,000 feet up in the mountains, twelve months a year, winter and fire season. I truly do my best though she thinks the virtual gives me a way out which she will not allow herself. La Vieja wants nothing more than a way into the old ways of being still vibrant in the natural world. And she's right, that door will probably not open unless La Vieja abandons the past, the present, her identity, and her will. Actually, I am speculating now which I don't like to do. "… Abandons the past," stops me. I don't know if she even has a past or what it might be, so how I can I theorize about her? Let me just repeat the last sentence as it calls to be written in the right way: La Vieja believes the door will not open unless she abandons the past, the present, her identity and her will.

La Vieja thought she could think these thoughts without the Writer's awareness. And perhaps that was correct, but then they would not appear in this text. And while I have to accept these perceptions, I do so realizing that they are inaccurate. What she calls my reluctance, or even failure to consider the path she is on, is simply my obligation as a woman and a writer to be where I am and must be, in the world, entangled in human affairs, aware, painfully aware of what is, of what we have become as a species, unable to look away. La Vieja's task seems to be to radically disentangle; my task precedes hers: bear witness, be engaged. The virtual retreat, the commitment to see far means there is no relief, no distraction. There is no way out for La Vieja. There is no way out for this writer. Ultimately, if we are to survive, there will be no way out for anyone. We will all have to bear witness. And then we will all have to step out of the predatory lives we have created by preying, without any reciprocity, on the Earth.

* * *

This morning, La Vieja saw the sunrise while looking toward the mountains. She would see sunset later. Red sky at dawning, sailors take warning. Red sky at night, sailor's delight. And even though she was desperately concerned about the Earth, she was confident the sun will set and will rise in the morning and she can predict the time. She knew, as I do, that the sun will die ultimately, will retract into a neutron star or a black hole, billions of years from now and that will be a minor event compared with the end of the universe itself by endless expansion, accelerated expansion, irreversible retraction or some sudden and catastrophic event like vacuum death. Don't ask me to explain it even to myself she thought, and I echoed the inevitable failure to truly understand these words.

Sometimes these cosmic futures strike terror in my heart but they are distractions from the real, current, present terror from which I must not look away, and what had brought La Vieja to the Lookout originally: everything we love could end soon, if not in our lifetimes, still within calculable time, within a few generations and by our own hands.

She had come seeking understanding that could help two-leggeds change course. Her concerns, my concerns were the same—that is why she sought me out—although her approach has shifted. She felt no relief that she will die before this occurs because the pungent odors of the heat of the two below were rising up as trenchant as any fire. If she was alarmed, it was for them much more than for herself that the human instinct to survive was waning in her as she extended herself to encompass the whole.

She was alarmed and she was sustained because she could smell them, the scent of his stalking her and a similar fragrance that Léonie emitted even as she was gracefully eluding him, but not for long. They were in La Vieja's field; she was heartened by the presence of passion and desire, the life force rising, and who knows, she thought, what forms of regeneration and restoration this energy might inspire. If they were Bears, there would be cubs seven months from now. These two also appeared to have a biologic destiny. Through a rare, sacred trust, they were beholden to the future. La Vieja sensed this as strongly as she sensed the wind arising, winter coming, ice. And somehow they have, we have (all) found each other.

15

It is said that the close study of stone will reveal traces from fires suffered thousands of years ago. These would have been natural conflagrations, waves of flame burning through forests. This fire was not anomalous but part of the cycle of life.

Susan Griffin
A Chorus of Stones

Note: As is frighteningly appropriate, fire season June 2020 has begun.

L a Vieja is pacing as she does and so am I. I am not walking round and round, but pacing, the way I did as a child when I tried to understand something and walked and walked inside my house, up and down the narrow hallway, and then when I was older, round and round the neighborhood, then along the ocean and bays until I had puzzled it out or set it aside. There is no way to dismiss the current enigmas that threaten us all.

La Vieja had come here with a singular purpose to look far. She was searching for fires, not only to give warning, but to bear witness. From this Lookout, I do the same. It is baffling that so many, that millions, follow the news of the ongoing fires, the Amazon, Australia, the American West burning more relentlessly year after year, and still turn toward the television, switch the channels, follow their Twitter titillation and sleep as if they had been merely watching daily reruns of an apocalypse movie: cartoons to follow.

Ladybird, Ladybird, fly away home, our house is on fire .... The Ladybirds are burning, those tiny black and orange beings, who might land so gently on the back of one's hand. I had been hiking not far from her Lookout years and years ago and came upon what seemed like the birthplace of the Ladybirds, great orange and black mounds, like molehills, gopher mounds covering stones and boulders then rising up into the air and going west together, with some sweet purpose, tiny little suns with the tiny spots from which we can imagine a miniature solar flare will emerge, radiating a dark kindly greeting. How are we going to protect the Ladies' home? It is our responsibility to protect it, we have set it on fire.

The way I know the rhyme is: Ladybird, Ladybird fly away home, your house is on fire, your children alone.

My dear friend who had to live many years in exile remembers it so: Ladybird, Ladybird fly away home, your house is on fire, your children will burn...!

* * *

When did I first understand the extreme urgency? It was before La Vieja came and confirmed it.

I was seated in a circle of my students on the patio, before the Eucalyptus trees, the ones so many neighbors, forest rangers, environmentalists want to take down because they think these flammable immigrants should have been stopped at the border, sent back to their places of origin.

There were twenty-five or so students of various ages, some in their twenties and thirties, some into their seventies. I sent them out for an hour to walk the land attempting to feel the danger which is coming upon us, the increasing heat, the sense that all can burst into flame in any moment, and everything can burn: the grass, Spiders, Lizards, Gophers, Mice, Rats, Raccoons, Skunks, Bobcats, Deer, Coyote, Mountain Lions, even the Quail and the Mourning Doves if the fire explodes as increasingly it might. When they returned to speak of their experiences and responses, I felt dismay. They hadn't understood the gravity. "Climate change," I said, "is a fire coming down the hill at us right now. How are you meeting it?" They were removed from experiencing the coming impact; they hadn't felt the imminence. Climate dissolution was still vague, remote, incomprehensible. All the more reason to extend every effort. (They were tired, hadn't had lunch, didn't comprehend and resented that I had said they'd all failed to meet the moment, were still living the way they had always lived—indulging the same desires, the same assumptions, the same ambitions, the same future plans.)

I sent them out again, at least to imagine what they couldn't see. "Climate change is a fire coming down the hill into this narrow eleven-mile long canyon," I repeated. "11,000 people. Only one road from the ocean to the valley."

Reluctantly, they stood up and began to gather their things to return to their quest. A young man who had recently apprenticed at an organic farm, and so was more attuned to what is occurring than the rest, exited the turquoise gate first. A moment later, he flung open the gate, his panic clear, shouting to all of them in shock and wonder, "There *is* a fire coming down the mountain toward the road!" he cried. "There *is* a fire coming down the mountain across the Canyon road, just as you said!" He was shaking as, indeed, fire leaped up into the sky at the ridge and slid down the hill toward us.

Some ran while others went out the gate slowly, dazed. Each went to their respective cars except the few who stayed to help me pack, eyes on the mountain, on the helicopters that had come with their loads of water and fire suppressant, on the road crowding with vehicles.. Within an hour, we all evacuated. It would be close to a week before I could return home. Then, because of another fire, I would have to evacuate again, several weeks later, this time for eight days.

* * *

At every place on the Earth outside of human domination, all the vast multitudes of living beings interact and support each other's welfare without needing a king, a parliament or a police force to regulate their behavior or enforce any laws external to their being. Benevolent interconnection is their very nature. They are all unalterably interconnected with each other. It is instinctual and complex.

The wonder of self-regulation and cooperation strikes me as I focus on the increasing chaos, violence and detachment among humans and the antidote of beauty that presents itself from everywhere outside the human realm. Outside of human control and appetite, sky, earth, light, dark, creature, stone, configure into dynamic patterns unique in every instant. I am speaking to myself, trying to understand. But it isn't self-regulation or regulation. That is the human thinking I am trying to avoid. Everything is simply and intrinsically related to everything else.

Away from humans, life thrived. Indeed, life and the body of Earth thrived on their own. Needed to be free of most human intervention to thrive. Because humans, two-leggeds, or maybe only non-Indigenous two-leggeds, had separated themselves, they are no longer aligned by their intrinsic nature. Is this what is meant in the Bibles that humans had been thrown out of Paradise? Some friends who are Native American laugh at this.

"We live in Paradise," they say, "and always have despite you colonists who are always hunting us down, trying to herd us off our land until there will be no land left. Then," some add, "we may have to leave this dimension the way the animals have left until we can return to live our rightful lives.

"Having lost the essential connection and relationship, you use everything for your own individual purposes, see everything outside yourselves as objects and then place everything outside yourselves; the danger to all life follows directly from that."

* * *

La Vieja looked down to the Pine, Fir, Spruce below. It was more than knowing that they were linked, one organism, breathing each other. It was every organism interdependent with everything else. When Wolves were hunted almost to extinction, Deer and other ungulates multiplied, then the forests diminished and all the animals as well until desert conditions took over. Then unexpectedly, a few years after the restoration of Wolf packs, a cascade of returning life forms resulted in the restoration of streams and rivers, until, finally all the life associated with the rushing waters returned too.

Yes, she had *known* this. It was not about knowing. There was another level of cognition, distinct from thought, knowing and mind. It was not feeling. It was not intuition. It was not instinct. It wasn't different from them. They might be incorporated in the experience but these categories did not explain the irreversible shift in consciousness that occurred when such awareness became part of oneself. One was altered. She had come to the Lookout to be altered and she was being altered.

She had been standing on the deck looking into the trees and she had grokked what she had come to understand. In that moment, her mind was entirely empty of thought and filled with awareness, a non-verbal event. She could only hold on to it for a moment. But in that moment, it was so much a part of her, she would have responded from that knowing to anything that came her way, because nothing that came her way was a thing. Oh, she was trying to understand again.

She had fallen back into thinking.

Left to itself, the non-human world flourishes though humans often judged it differently. To my kind, it looks like the Elephants are destroying the forests and then moving on to the next victims of their hunger, but it appears differently to those who are able to encompass the 200-year migration cycle of consumption and re-seeding by Elephants who leave the emerging meadows to ungulates who return it to the Elephants as the trees begin to re-emerge. A cycle of consumption and restoration. Everything in its own time. Everything in its own time.

* * *

La Vieja paced back and forth and round and round on the narrow deck. She was thinking too much. She was thinking and so she would be thrown out of the Garden. The damned Angels would come to get her as they had Eve. For eating an apple! Really! For wanting knowledge. Aha! Maybe she hadn't understood. Yes, for wanting and honoring abstract, disembodied knowing, for favoring detached mind and thinking and all these disconnections. There was so much more to the story than had been understood.

And now? Well, first, she had brought too many books which only encouraged her thinking. Why wonder what other humans had to say when the species is the problem and she had come to observe the Others. To observe and then to contemplate what was revealed. If she wanted to continue to gorge herself on what humans thought, she could have acquired an academic research card at a major library and settled into a comfortable study to use it online. Why, indeed, had she carried so many boxes of books up these stairs?

Here was the contradiction, the act of eating an apple, open to all that apple is and nothing else, rather than reading about, or thinking about it, might drop her right back into the Garden now. The real Garden where the real Apples grow.

She seated herself on one of the wood kitchen chairs she had placed in the northwest corner of the walkway, her preferred view at this time of year. The sun would begin to set soon, darkly shadowing the bases of the conifers as their upper branches took on brush strokes of amber and golden light. What could explode dangerously were now simply resplendent candelabras swaying in the gentle wind that rose as the temperature fell. Constant movement, steady and shifting, giving and receiving of life. She had had to come away from her own kind in order to know the holiness of connection. She had known she had to retreat but hadn't anticipated what, if anything, would fill the void.

There was just a hint of a coming sunset, a familiar view, summer light, a few clouds that would soon smear shades of pink and pale rose across the sky. How tender a finish to the day it was and equally how unexceptional.

As the light dimmed tonight, it would not become noteworthy. But if one were not ranking, it would provide a soft entrance into dusk. After so many months here, she was beginning to marvel that every aspect of natural life from the seemingly silent and teeming worlds between the roots of the trees she was watching and further down to the solar heat of the molten core of the Earth, to the magnetic energies that determined the relationships between the stars and planets, the visible and the hidden dark, the known and unknown of the universe beyond, from weather to material structure, including the millions and millions of different vital forms and the myriad staid minerals and stones, each unique organic and inorganic changing and unchanging element from which the world is constituted and on which it depends, each innate connection in time and space, form and movement, is in vibrant relationship with everything else. This ordinary day which thankfully revealed no lightning strikes, no trees exploding into fire, no wisps of smoke, no signs of danger, opened itself to her. How simple.

She dropped to her knees in awe. Then as if struck by an electric current, she rose up, threw open the trap door, rushed down the stairs to the green world below, weeping and laughing, wanting to be enclosed in it, by it, to know what it is to be integral to such wonder.

16

Bears don't give a damn about what time it is the way humans do, always checking our watches and calendars. I always wear a good watch. I used it a lot when I was flying to keep track of fuel and things. But, in another way, bears are more aware of time than we are. It all relates to how much fat they have. They comfort from being full. It is not a daily hunger that can be satisfied, but a yearly hunger. Feeling and being full this way is mandated. There is no choice. It is a psychological crisis which can lead an old bear to go after a human. The awareness of death is always with animals. They don't want to die, but death is a fact and they know it. Bears live with change and deal with it, become a part of it, whether it is moving to find some other food when the salmon are poor or sometimes needing to not do something. Bears are conservative. Grizzlies could do a lot of damage to humans, they have a lot of opportunities. They usually see us before we see them and it is easy for them to attack us, but they don't. They don't because they refrain. They only fight when that is the best, last and necessary option.

G. A. Bradshaw
Talking with Bears: Conversations with Charlie Russell

Once enfolded in the darkness the leaves and needles were gathering into themselves, La Vieja would not stay long. These were not her woods. This was called the Trinity-Shasta National Forest as if it belonged to the nation, but it truly belonged to the Bears and all the other peoples who lived here long before the settlers came and took everything for themselves. La Vieja had seen a great Black Bear striding along the bank of the river, his river. This was the Bear's land and river. His ancestors had lived here for somewhere between twenty-five and thirty-thousand years, long enough to homestead by any standards. And also, this was August 18, 2020 and hunting season had begun. Fifteen hundred Bear would be "harvested" and who knows how many Deer. It would go on until after Christmas. Bear understood this. He understood every nuance in the language the settlers used and how it affected him, his cubs and his people, his communities. He lived in jeopardy for five months of every year. Cubs under fifty pounds or a female with cubs or pregnant, were supposedly protected. But a human excited by having sighted a kill, doesn't care, doesn't always check it out, can't contain the thrill of killing. And Bear himself, was "fair game." He did not love these humans though they often thought he did, believed he wanted to teach them, to bring them wisdom. There was absolutely no reason for La Vieja to assume he would spare her if he felt endangered, though the statistical likelihood of a Black Bear attacking a human, particularly a woman, was almost nil, despite the extremity of human fears and assumptions. She trusted Bear's ability and innate reflex to distinguish a killer from a lover. If Bear attacked and killed her it would be a mistake. Careful, La Vieja carried a note on her person that said she was entirely responsible for any attack from any wild animal and the animal should not be injured. Probably no one would listen to her plea if it occurred. But she needed to state it in the event the ranger or whomever had consciousness and the authority to make such a decision.

* * *

Yes, a great Black Bear strode among the trees. He was smelling her presence and the future. He was smelling today, August 21, 2020, three days after permission to kill him had been extended to so many and when the forests of California including the Redwoods were burning and he was running from yet another danger and, again, without anywhere safe to run with so many embers searing his fur, burning down through the glowing hairs scorching his flesh. He shook himself to remove the sparks but without affecting the fire and without the time to stop and roll on the earth, already so hot his paws were beginning to blister. His lungs were overcome with smoke. The red of the flames was everywhere around him, his eyes blazing until all he could see before he couldn't see at all was red, fire and blood. He is in a boiling sea of fire and blood as the embers set his fur aflame. He is an offering, an auto-da-fé, a holy sacrifice to a god who howls in bitter anguish and rage as the divine is forced to receive the burning flesh offering, this divine beloved.

* * *

Time returns to the present moment. La Vieja and the Bear know what is coming. Both know she can't stop the fire. Both know the 11,000 lightning strikes are the immediate but not the ultimate cause. She and her kind are responsible for these strikes, for the heat, for the winds, the climate gone to hell, for the inferno, for the human rampage inflicted on the Mother, Earth.

He howls with a pain so great the sound breaks the barrier of time and the great fires of a few years hence display themselves here, now, among the two of them and burn through his flesh and tear him apart and sear her body/soul. As it should be. Her rightful common jeopardy with him. She burns and she burns and she burns.

* * *

It is getting darker and soon she won't see her way out but she doesn't want to leave because she is a different being here, leaning against a tree that will or won't survive the coming fires. But in this moment, she breathes and the tree breathes. It is one gesture. She has waited her entire life for this.

But she must not stay.

She, a human, must step away, must leave some portion of forest and time to the Bear and so she rouses herself, puts on her boots, laces them, stands, puts on her dark blue jacket—no orange vest for her as Bear has none, and if he did it would become a target. She turns back to acknowledge the Bear, long enough for him to notice, if he is watching her, and begins walking out, reluctantly, of his territory.

A red stripe of cloud cuts across the horizon as the dark approaches. It is thirty minutes after sunset, the hunters are required to lower their bows and rifles. It is not the best time for the Bears to find food, to fatten for the winter hibernation but they have to eat and they have to sleep. They can't sleep in the day and forage at night because the hunters will not hesitate to shoot them when asleep in their dens. so … they attempt to find something in the dark. There is no escape from the humans and the hunters in these times of torture.

17

With words at your disposal, you can see more clearly. Finding the words is another step in learning to see.

Robin Wall Kimmerer

August 20, 2020
August 20, 2021

There is no way to avoid this. The forests of California are burning. The imagination has its limitations and can't avoid the real. I can't pretend I am safe because I can write "I am safe" on a page. I must not write as if I am of another time and place. Must not write as if the 21st century has not come to Planet Earth.

La Vieja begins to consider that she is afraid for herself and for the Bears and all the other beings in the forests.

I, the Writer, continue to be afraid for myself, the Mountain Lions and Bobcats, Coyotes and all the other beings on the land. The land here is endangered again. On August 20, 2020 and August 20, 2021 the fires are burning everywhere. Where I am, wherever she is, wherever we are, all the places where we are, there is only one road, one lane out and when we are out of the mountains, the world is still burning. And Queen Corona maintains her hegemony. We didn't change our ways—the 6th IPCC report has been issued, this one with even more dire warnings: **"It is unequivocal that human influence has warmed the atmosphere, ocean and land. Widespread and rapid changes in the atmosphere, ocean, cryosphere and biosphere have occurred."**

La Vieja

Today, August 24, 2020

Fire weather warning, dry thunderstorms with lightning in effect for higher elevations where La Vieja and Léonie and Lucas are.

The writer will not describe the actual experiences of the three of them in the fire zones during this time. She does not know, nor does anyone, the consequences that might develop when life and literature interpenetrate. She does not want to play with fire.

The heat has not burned away the pandemic. The Writer has no agency here. Maybe the animals have agency but she, I, do not. The animals have no agency, they are burning in the fires, their paws are singed, their fur and skins burned, their lungs scorched, they are dying. Some are rescued and taken to hospitals but most succumb.

La Vieja is outside scanning the bowl of mountains that surround this observatory. They are covered with a patina of ash from the fires in every direction. ~~She wishes the sea waves would rain up and wash the sky.~~ She knows what a dangerous wish this is and cancels the metaphor though it remains on the page.

The epoch Fire Next Time has arrived. Epochs are getting shorter and shorter. The Neolithic, the New Stone Age, lasted about 12,000 years, dating from first signs of human settlements and agriculture in different areas, until the Anthropocene. There are many likely dates for the Anthropocene especially the beginning of industrialization or somewhat later, the internal combustion engine. The next epoch that concerns me is the one I call the Deadly Anthropocene. In my mind it begins with the first use of poison gas (Chlorine gas) by the Germans against two French divisions in WW I on April 15, 1915. Or with Guernica, the first bombing of a civilian population. Or it begins with the dropping of the first atomic bomb on August 9, 1945. In the 75 years since Hiroshima and Nagasaki we have entered the epoch of Fire, Flood, Extinction, Climate Dissolution and Global Chaos—all developed by the dominating Euro-American Imperial mind. *Wetiko* mind for the Algonquin, *Wendigo* for the Ojibwe—a cannibalistic way of thinking and acting, devouring everything and communicating such a hunger for possession from person to person as if it were a virus for which there are no antibodies. Wetiko is the disease that came to this continent with the Conquest and has infected all the colonists and their descendants. A few Indigenous people fall sick with it as well and pass it on, as do the colonists, the settlers, to everyone they encounter. Sometimes it goes dormant in an individual, but can still be communicated as it is highly contagious. It has a peculiar quality, this virus, the carrier does not always know they are infected despite the evidence in their behavior. They may not only think they are immune, but that they possess a cure. Often their "cure" becomes a super-spreader.

Covid and Wetiko as viruses resemble each other but they are also distinctly different. Covid wants us to stop and change our ways. If we listen deeply to it, we will withdraw from our familiar lives of amassing things, valuing possessions, using up all the Earth's resources, and live simply in alliance with all the other beings. Listening to the virus, we will have found the cure. Until we do, it is possible the ways to meet the pandemic will continue to elude us. We are being called to change our lives entirely and every time we return to our former ways of life, new manifestations and new forms arise that threaten our lives as we have threatened theirs. There were eight different strains in August 2020 and we are in a grave pandemic of the Delta variant, August 2021. The Lambda variant was identified in Peru in August 2020 and as of August 2021 has spread to dozens of countries, Argentina, Chile and Ecuador. Since the first documented case of reinfection occurred in Hong Kong, reinfection is occurring everywhere. Increasing fissures are occurring across the globe and particularly violently in the US as the push to vaccinate everyone over twelve years old, and soon children, accelerates and much of the country refuses the vaccine even as the numbers of cases are skyrocketing. And so the virus Covid may be the only antibody to Wetiko as it keeps us restrained.

November 30, 2020
Los Angeles County is in lockdown again and Covid-19 cases rise drastically. 13,500,000 cases in the US. 250,000 deaths. By September 2021 there have been 231,421,601 cases globally and 4,741,914 deaths. In the US, there have been 42,893,199 confirmed cases and 687,670 deaths.

I try to understand what Stop means for me now that I, myself, have seemingly stopped. Haven't I sequestered myself far from social life in a virtual Lookout? Is it virtual or is it real, Lookout to Lockdown. Still I am not close enough to understanding what everyday life should become when we begin to emerge, what lifeways might lead to Restoration?

La Vieja

August 26, 2020

Two hurricanes are making their way to the gulf states. One so close to the other they could become one. The Fire Next Time may not eliminate the possibility of the flood returning simultaneously. Hurricane Laura, as large as the entire Gulf itself, is due to touch down on land with 150 mile an hour winds. A Synthetic Aperture Radar carried by the Sentinel-1A satellite, measured surface winds of 198 mph in Laura's northeast eyewall at 8:10 p.m. EDT the same day.

August 2021

Flooding and frequent hurricanes or tropical storms are becoming commonplace. Haiti has been devastated by the assassination of the President in July 2021 followed by a 7.2 earthquake and then a Hurricane, both in August.

* * *

There was once a rainbow covenant. Judaism and Christianity are obligated to it. But we continuously break it as we break all our treaties. Don't trust them, my Native American friends say, "They break all their treaties when it's convenient, when they want something. There are no antibodies against their hunger."

Social chaos was predicted. It is here. The time of warlords and bandits occupying our governments has arrived.

* * *

La Vieja may, in unguarded moments experience unbidden thoughts of leaving to rise to the surface, but for the most part, she walks the deck, round and round, to spot smoke, able as she is to see 40 km or more on a clear day, rooting her mind here and putting out, as if they were fires, any thoughts of evacuating. The safety of the Bear depends on her fidelity. Her growing determination to protect him and the trees, no matter the consequences for herself, is what makes her a Vieja. I am beginning to glean that I can't write La Vieja truly until I become such a Vieja.

What does that really mean? Am I afraid of the implications, just as La Vieja speculated? I can't communicate La Vieja until I know within myself, what it means to be La Vieja? She transmits but I have to understand what she is saying in order to translate her vision into words. Have I stopped in the ways the virus, Queen Corona, demands? As La Vieja has? Otherwise, isn't everything written here simply speculation? Arbitrary? A fiction? Is this the moment when I must also become someone who is able to be right here, in this spot of land, in order to see? Ironically, because of the real possibility of deadly gridlock, local authorities are giving instructions to those of us living in Topanga on sheltering in place even in case of a fire.

What will be the first step? Or is there no particular first step? Is there only one step without a return?

18

He (my captor) gave me a bisquit, which I put in my pocket, and not daring to eat it, buried it under a log, fearing he had put something in it to make me love him.

from "Captivity" by Louise Erdrich.
Based on the narrative of the captivity of Mrs. Mary Rowlandson,
who was taken prisoner by the Wampanoag

He returns from his foray down the mountain with supplies he loads into the wheelbarrow for the thousand foot trek to the cabin. He's brought a lot of water and he has to bring all the food up as the ranger advised him that the Bears are becoming quite deft as the salmon supplies diminish and human presence increases, at getting what they want even from a car if they need it. He has brought provisions in this way so many times, this routine is as familiar to him as bringing in the groceries in the city. They will have to return to their homes to resupply from time to time, but not at the moment.

In the country store which has everything, he found a plain gold ring, well, gold enough for the moment, he thought, amused as it was in the girl's toy area and he purchased it, and also two simple women's shirts, one bronze color, one silver, and, a pair of black jeans, he was guessing now, size 1. A black sweatshirt, leather flip-flops with bronze studs, he is definitely out on a limb about shoe size. Worst scenario, they will have a giggle. Then he speedily took a box of tampons from the shelf and, as an antidote, stood an embarrassedly long time before the women's lingerie and finally bought 3 pair of bikini panties. What color? Black. (Lace, he admits sheepishly to himself and to us.) There were some sleeping garments, but he preferred thinking of her in one of his chambray denim shirts (He had decided to bring several with him, a few for her too. He couldn't sleep the night they had met, the night before he brought her here, until the surplus shirts were in his duffle.) In the store, he imagined tucking the ring into the shirt pocket before giving it to her. He had calculated correctly the number of shopping bags needed and didn't have to go back to the car. Small achievements to relieve extremely tense moments.

Under normal circumstances we would know where they both live, what their work schedule is, how they negotiate this turn of events, but in this accelerated time indicated by the abrupt shift from one epoch to another, equal to the pace of global dissolution, none of this matters. We are required to change our lives and they are no exception. There were solar rechargers for their computers so they could do their work and he had brought two solar rechargers for their phones although he had no idea what use the phones would be except when they went downhill and then the car engine would serve.

She had gone for a hike and afterwards left her boots at the door and so was barefoot when he came in. He dipped into a bag and with a flourish pulled out the sandals. They fit. This astonished him as much as his thoughtfulness surprised her.

"How long are we staying?" She tried to sound casual as if she was asking what time they would eat dinner.

"They said they had no future bookings."

"And now?"

"And now they are fully booked."

"Do you think we should continue to limit our conversations to these haiku exchanges?"

"I do, if you do," he said. "I want to read your mind and am not at all concerned with your reading mine."

She nodded and approached him and began sniffing. "Fruit," she murmured, "and cheese." Then as she came around his back and went around into the crook of his neck where she imagined laying her head and then around again to his chest where she imagined her head would rest for most of the night, she said, "Man smell." She was weeping but so was he. The night had not separated them from each other.

As if casually, he pushed some bags toward her and the others with food toward himself and watched as she unpacked what would now be her wardrobe. There was a screen between the two single beds which they had returned to their original place, their couches to be, and the kitchen living area and she went behind it and came out in jeans and a shirt. Whether or not she tried the underwear, he couldn't know and tried not to look inquisitive. Everything fit. This satisfied him. As a doc, he knew people's bodies and was glad that his expertise could extend to new situations.

"I can't wait to see what you've forgotten," she grinned, turning so he saw how it all fit, as if they had done this a hundred times. "And I hate shopping…"

He nodded. "I could be recruited," and considered saying more but feeling like a teenage boy, turned instead to the groceries.

He unpacked everything carefully, and if not from soup to nuts, from tea, coffee, half and half to breakfast fixings, orange marmalade and honey. "You know my mother's name is Melissa," she said.

"And my mother's nickname is 'Honey.'" He paused. "Not quite. That was her nickname. Her American name. Her name is Miela. She was very tiny when she was born. Her mother called her Mielita." He was filled with wonder. "Your mother's name is Melissa. Bee, right? My mother's name is Miel, honey. What are the chances?" he asked.

She opened the jar and put her finger in and put a dab of honey in his mouth, feeling the softness, the warmth, his lips closing slightly around her, imagining she would eventually feel this way to him, and then so as not to be lost entirely in wonder and confusion, put her finger back in the jar and took some honey for herself. He took the jar back from her and took some honey on his finger and offered it to her. Then hesitated. He imagined his finger in her mouth, and how overwhelming it would be for him. Without more touch, their bodies were already intermingling. He stopped. Overcome.

"Did you get a newspaper?" She also needed grounding.

"I did."

"And so?"

"The world is going to hell."

"Let's stay here forever then," she said relaxing into the blue sky and the varied conifers visible from every window.

"We may," he said. "It will certainly take until forever for me to know you. But let's begin over coffee." He turned toward the coffee pot on the shelf on the only wall without windows.

Then the obvious occurred to him … knowing they could remedy everything if they needed to, but she seemed unconcerned, "Work?"

"I have no commissions I have to attend to in person and I can design those pending here. As for the library, I had an intuition I wouldn't want to work on Monday and so I called early and said I would be away for a while. It's not a regular job. I just fill in as I was doing for Melissa."

"And you?" Her smile was all knowing. "You called in too, didn't you? You told them you wouldn't be on call for a while, right?"

"Um. Yes."

"And you didn't say anything to me? Have I been kidnapped?"

"White slavery, but you don't pass." Both of them were startled by what he had said. "I'm sorry. Not an appropriate joke. Let's start again. I called work and you called work. Because we know something. But I can take you back tonight or tomorrow if you wish."

"But I haven't slept outside on the ground under the trees yet," she responded and put the chocolate bars on a shelf away from the sun.

"Where did you walk?" he asked.

"I followed a few paths trying to get an understanding of the terrain. I wanted to see what materials were nearby."

He looked at her quizzically and waited.

"When I stay in a place for a long time, I like to build something from what can be found but with the proviso that the only intrusion occurs from carefully moving something from one place to another, but taking pains that the essential patterns of water and wind, the animal paths, remain essentially the same."

He continued to wait. Their haiku style, as she had named it, was interesting to him and he wanted to see how long he could maintain it.

"Well, let's see if we can build a den," she continued. It satisfied her to say this and moved toward the east window where, looking down the slope, she could follow the path she had taken until it was lost in the trees. He followed her gaze, imagining what he hoped she was considering, a stone shelter that opened to first light. By now, he was aware she said "we."

* * *

That evening, he walked her down to the loo, which, of course she had used before. It was beautifully paneled in cedar. There was a compost toilet, some baskets with wood shavings, empty wood buckets near the pump for non-potable water to wash with and another by the outdoor shower that was attached to black piping in tight spirals on the little roof and a container for extra water to warm in summer and sunny weather. Everything beautifully crafted.

"Someone put a lot of effort in this, maybe more than in the cabin. I wonder why. Must be someone who comes here often and so spends a lot of time in this room," she grinned. "Maybe he was seeing if he could get away with it, and if he did, working his way up?" Running her hand across the red-toned cabinet radiating warmth that contained the sink, as a builder might examine workmanship, she said, "Crafty! Oh, sorry for the pun." Her smile was genuine. "Ok, was it you?"

"I was guessing that the Forestry Service was not going to want to keep it up for long, as one after another lookouts are being abandoned. I heard that renting it out and the necessary upkeep was becoming too much trouble, and I thought I would be able to secure it in some way, long term lease, or buy it."

"You have some skills."

"Enough." As he began leaving, he reached to where, earlier, he had stashed the paper bag with the shirt and the ring in the left pocket and brought it forward so she wouldn't miss it, slipped around the back, showered quickly leaving her most of the hot water from the black hoses coiled on the roof, and walked halfway up the hill to wait for her.

Then she appeared. He could not avoid sucking in his breath, so taken was he by her beauty and, equally, by her steadiness. Wearing his shirt was itself like a vow taken. She had placed her turquoise ring on her right hand and the child's band on the second finger of her left hand but made no move to acknowledge it. He had purchased it in the toy department and she was playing innocent. So he took her backpack as he had taken her purse in the park and put it on his shoulder as they began walking to the air mattress and sleeping bag he had arranged under the trees but, as she had requested, with an open eye to where their heads would be bare to the sky.

She watched and listened. Was she testing him? Of course she was. Lust betrays and he had to rein in his instincts. This, at least, bioethics had taught him. Or was it the opposite? That science and medicine had to yield to biology, bypass the mind which could manipulate anything and everything and follow the heart? And the heart is a vast domain that considers in a single present moment the entire past and the future it can access.

But he had already committed himself to this woman and the ring on her finger, though she had not placed it on the fourth finger of marriage, but only on the second finger leading to the heart, still it bound him to her for his lifetime. He had only known her 48 hours.

"I would like to hold you," he said.

She looked to the place on his chest where she had imagined placing her head. She saw that he was offering himself, not taking anything from her. This offering of self in the manner of trees giving of themselves to the others, even in their dying, releasing all their nutriments, and then when fallen, being the ground for new sprouts. Their bodies offered to the last cell for the others.

"I trust you," she nodded to confirm what she was saying, knowing this too, was a test and a bond. Trust had come up between them before. Her grandmother, Mere, had been a war bride (the Writer typed war bridge in error—but that too) whose husband understood the gravity of uniting two very distinct cultures and how the war he/his people had waged had been anything but a moral intervention. But if they were to bond, he had needed to transform it, if it was to be won between them he had to proceed ethically at its core.

Sean O'Malley married her grandmother-to-be before he was sent home, and in the traditional manner before her people. He was not going to violate their trust. It was a long time, then, before Melissa was conceived. Trustworthiness was the thread that was woven into the fabric of the family and Léonie's life. Mere had needed to see if it would be a real marriage from her perspective and that required everything from Sean. He was willing.

Isai knew he was broken and he didn't know if a bone setter like his grandfather could fix an injury that came from another culture. He didn't know if there was any medicine that could heal the war that had settled into his bones and began to metastasize within him. His grandfather could heal the injuries endemic to his land but the Americans were never able to heal the wars they started. They didn't know it was an illness. Honey wanted to try, based on what she knew about healing, knowledge she believed was universal. For a time, it seemed possible but ultimately the pathology was too great to be overcome just by the two of them. And so trust, trustworthiness was the essential issue of the meeting between Lucas and Léonie. This was evident to each of them. He was definitely being challenged. He believed he had as good a chance of meeting it as had her grandfather, Sean. After all, he had traditional ways behind him even if he was born, as

Léonie and her mother, and yes, her father were, in the States.

Lucas was not going to assure her that he was trustworthy. He was not going to say anything about this. Neither being a trained physician, nor a bioethicist was going to help him here. He reached back, far back, to the lineage the Bear had awakened in him by sensing and scenting it. His father had been too compromised, too broken, too maddened by the war to be steadfast here. But Lucas could make amends on his father's behalf by being principled. He didn't even say, "I am not going to say anything." She had nodded and so he nodded. He was simply going to be trustworthy. It wasn't merely a vow for tonight. It was as far back as he could see and like her grandfather's vow; it was, he thought for the future, seven generations forward. It was for eternity.

19

I drove up the Pacific coast and across the Columbia basin into the primitive area of Idaho.... I was so tired that I did not even wash before falling asleep. This part of Idaho is so undeveloped that there is no electricity. It was a dark night with little moonlight. The stars twinkled a universal message and I fell asleep quickly and deeply. I was sleeping on my stomach with my hands on either side of my head when I felt something scratching on my left hand. I moved my hand as I awoke and a little squirrel scampered away. Looking over my left shoulder I saw a deer and a bear standing about five feet from the bottom of my sleeping bag.

I wondered if I should be afraid. Mother told me to be afraid of bears. But I didn't feel afraid. If this bear were hungry wouldn't it eat the deer? A bear that hangs around with a deer can't be that bad. I finally decided to slowly turn over so I could protect myself with my hands if things turned ugly.

It seemed like a long time that we stared at each other. Probably it wasn't. Finally the bear walked on all fours over to me. I remember its paw being next to my arm—not on the arm, not hurting me, but very much next to my arm. I looked up and realized that the bear was so large that if I had raised my arm up I would not have reached the top of its shoulders. I could not tell whether it was black or brown but it was a dark bear. I was still arguing with myself about how frightened I should be when the bear licked the side of my head. Then he/she licked again. I thought, "This is how a salt lick must feel." Maybe six or seven times the bear licked me. It felt incredibly intimate and erotic. I wanted to put my arms around the bear and roll around holding it closely. But I knew my mother, long dead, would not approve.

The Bear walked away into the woods with the deer. ... I felt some shame for the deep intimacy I had felt. I wondered if this could be a dream. I felt the gooeyness on the right side of my head

*and thought that I would sleep on the left side of my head so that
if I awoke with my hair still gooey, I would know the experience
was not a dream....*

*When I awoke the hair on the right side of my head was very
different in consistency than that on my left side. It was dry but
thick and stuck to my head.*

*In my mind I gave the experience many meanings, thought
about it a lot. It was such a private affair I didn't want to talk
much about it. I expected anyone who heard about it would have
doubts about my sanity. I wondered if perhaps I had betrayed my
species. I had never known such acceptance from such an exotic
animal before.*

Fran Peavy
The Bear Story

Being trustworthy is what La Vieja offered to the Bear in the woods.
My time with the Elephant people had prepared me to understand
both La Vieja and Bear. Despite how the Elephant people are
treated, in a sacred universe their laws prevail because they are Indigenous
to the land wherever they are meeting. Their ways agree with the laws of
the land because of their moral rectitude. This connection is inherent in
them, it is inviolable in their being. The secular ways of the two-leggeds
are entirely different because the majority dominate by force of their arbitrary
and partisan laws based on self-interest and their insurmountable
greed.

Trust was what I, the Writer, hoped I had sincerely offered the Elephant
Ambassador when I opened my hands on the rail of the truck as we
were facing each other to show that I carried no hidden weapons while acknowledging
I was entirely vulnerable to his strength. It was what I wanted
to be offering Nana and Frankie when we met each other at Thula Thula.
I was following what I understood about the etiquette of meeting Elders,
the Matriarchs of another People who lived according to other laws, ancient
laws, resonant with the intrinsic laws of the natural world, that is the universe.

The natural world has its own intrinsic laws which cannot be abrogated
or repealed. They are more fundamental than any others and do not depend
in any way on the understanding, verification or approval of humans. They
are. This is where I am seeking a foundation. I want to understand them
sufficiently to coalesce myself, my thoughts, heart, behavior with them.

My retreat or advance to this virtual Lookout is, I realize, to initiate such a process. This is more daunting than seeing.

* * *

Lucas was so startled by Léonie's appearance, a shock wave emanated from him, traveled the several hundred miles and shook La Vieja to her core, awakening memories of her own youth and the intensity of the electro-magnetic hormonal field, which was—how could she have forgotten?—she realized, despite all, still buzzing everywhere on the planet. Indeed, the entire field of life was vibrating. Leaning into the night woods, she could feel the roots, trunks, stems, branches, leaves, petals, all the beings, trembling. Interconnection, inter-relationship ... are ecstatic forms. La Vieja felt a sensation she had not known for a long time, lurch within her. It was ... hope. It wasn't a thought. Hope was a way of being. It hadn't come from Lucas and Léonie alone, it had come from Bear. From Bear to them to her. And ... she leaned further into the tremulous green dark that hummed with a fusion of night songs, from Bear to her.

She pulled back, distrusting her too human desire to want something, to do something. Rather, she allowed herself to be tempered by the subtle withdrawal, albeit still intoxicating, pervading Léonie who was choosing constraint in order to follow her own equivalent of estrus, when, ironically, unlike Bear, she would probably not conceive if they mated tonight, but would be looney with promise and desire.

What were nature's intentions? La Vieja wondered. Was it possible that a blessing of pleasure was always permeating the Earth, a gift from the nature spirits, a paean to joy, a ritual of praise for creation experienced by all creatures? Not restricted to humans? Nor abused by the others in the ways two-leggeds violated the gift, increasingly associating exultation with violence and war. Killing, the drug they couldn't live without. Here, rising up alongside her familiar dark thoughts, something else was arising, a different kind of fire.

She closed her eyes and found herself in her imagination within the core of a Sunflower where a Bee had landed. What was quivering? The florets, the core, or the Bee? When a Hummingbird arrived, she was em-barrassed by the exquisite sensation, the delicate prick of its beak. She shuddered, happily.

Quickly, she stepped back even further and circled and circled on the widow's walk. The name, widow's walk had a bittersweet quality now. Yes, she was alone. But maybe something would be born in her, maybe something would be met.

As her tension eased, she was willing to face the forest again. Though she was not going to invade the Bear's territory unless invited, she did want to be available for whatever the Bear might want to transmit to her. La Vieja felt the force of the relationship with the Bear that she had not seen, but who had seen her in the woods. Perhaps he had sought her out. Perhaps, as she had considered before, the Bear people were deliberately contacting humans in order to communicate the desperation of their plight. She wanted to be available but didn't want to spy on the Bear any more than she wanted to spy on the two of them.

She wanted …. An internal force turned her toward the Bears. She wanted, she felt desire or longing, some sensation that she could not define as sensation or emotion. It was not desire, wanting or longing as she had known these. It was as if a part of herself had literally to yield up her autonomy to another being to correct a deviation that had occurred in another time and was now experienced for the first time, as if a space within her had been twisted by a cosmic force that distorted the emptiness. As if Bear could set it right. She had to be careful so Bear would benefit. The desire to be set things right was greater than eros. This was the desire of the old woman.

* * *

Lucas led Léonie with great care to the bed among the trees that he had prepared. He was afraid his heart would break, it was so full. She could not let her heart break open. In a few days, she would have to take him into herself and she could not be splintering, but she had to be open. She would have to spend the next nights, opening and strengthening, opening and strengthening, so she could take him in and hold him whole.

* * *

And La Vieja, also. She knew she was being prepared for what she could not possibly imagine. She had been brought, she realized, to the sacred direction of the east. New beginnings at her age. The wind came up and she trembled, pretending to herself it was the temperature. She could not take this in at once. She could smell the Bear, his musk. She would not smell it if he had not released it to her. She dropped to her knees, quivering. Weeping. She managed a sob of gratitude as she fell away from all her former knowing.

* * *

Léonie will dream tonight, La Vieja was certain of it. She doesn't see the two of them now, but as with the Bear, is sensitive to other paths of awareness. She doesn't seek them out. However, she can't avoid sensing them. They are like X-rays that penetrate to the bone. They are like a wind that carries the scent of White Pine and Fir to the widow's walk.

* * *

Eucalyptus trees, like the ones in my patio, were planted as windbreaks but the strong winds from the ocean seven miles away slide through the spaces between, sidle along the curve of the trunks, bend the swaying branches, finger the leaves, tangle in my hair. The scented wind is a companion as I write this.

* * *

They have spent the night. The moon crossed in a silver line through the pond of dark sky rippling between the branches of the trees. Hovering above them, it shone down upon Léonie directly as she lay just as she anticipated with her head on his chest until he roused her gently. They were placed exactly as was needed. She did not feel spotlighted but revealed. She raised her head so she could be completely seen by the light. "Thank you," she said to him, to the moon, to everything in the field from which such beauty was emerging. "Spirits are here. You found the exact place for us to sleep. Science or intuition? Don't tell me," she added instantly, her fingers his lips. "They are acknowledging the care you have taken. We will have to make offerings in the morning." She returned to sleep, entirely secure. Whatever would happen would be in the purview of the holy ones.

* * *

When morning dawned, Léonie sat up on the air mattress to lean against a tree as Lucas was doing as well. "A council of animals. A council of animals," she said, "not just Bears. There was a trial. I was on trial. Yes," she said, puzzled, "I was on trial. Only Mountain Lion sitting across from me looked at me with any sympathy."

The dream returned to Léonie slowly. She was leaning against a tree as was Lucas with her legs crossed as they had been when she was sitting in the dream council. "Nothing was said." She pondered this. "I was on trial. But I was also the one bringing forth evidence. I laid out my transgressions in a row like wooden sticks waiting to be placed strategically in the fire before us. I presented the charges. One by one by one." Impatiently, she wiped away some tears as he leaned toward her to pluck some oak leaves from her hair. "Yes, I brought the charges." She was confounded. Why should she be surprised? Of course, she was the prosecutor. She knew. Why leave it to another being to confront her. Though she is a human, is a non-Animal, still, she knew. It was essential that she not pretend otherwise.

"I went to bed expecting the old dream. I wanted to be welcomed back, welcomed here. Like they would celebrate us." The perception staggered her. "Maybe the dream is a rebuke for my pridefulness. She placed her hand on his arm as a Lapis Bunting streaked by, remarkable with its brilliant blue head and back and red breast plate. A momentary reprieve. Then she continued.

"I filed the complaint and I was the prosecutor." She took in this understanding. The dream was vividly in the air. "It is a relief that I was the prosecutor, that I knew the transgressions and crimes. That I didn't try to hide them. That it wasn't necessary for Bear to stand up on her hind legs and accuse me from her full 8 feet and 400 pounds. That I didn't wait for her to say: "You took my land. You took the water from my cubs. You allowed your kind to shoot me and left my children orphans. You did that!"

"I had no argument with these accusations. There was no defense attorney or defense. There is no defense.

"What could I say on my behalf when I had brought the charges? The first thing I said to them was, 'I understand. How could I have thought I was one of you, one of you amongst you, when I have done such harm, while no one of you has ever acted against me in kind.' Then I lay down the sticks, one by one, each representing pain inflicted, harm done, injury and death.

"And what judgment did they offer? What penalty did they impose?" She snorted as she was experiencing the difference between American jurisprudence and the animals' law. "What an interesting sense of justice, they have. There will be no conclusion to the trial, no verdict, no limit to the amount of evidence to be offered, nothing to put behind me.

"Do you know what the punishment is? Awareness is the punishment. Ongoing, unceasing, inescapable awareness. They are aware and so they suffer. And so I will be aware and I will suffer. I …!" she concluded without there being any closure.

She remembered that he was alongside her. "Can you heal me, Mr. Physician?"

"It's not between us, Léonie. It is between you and the animals."

"No," she was considering what he was saying, understood the logic of it but found it incorrect. "No, it is between me and you because you are a human and so you have also done harm.

"Didn't you take a vow, Lucas, that first you would do no harm? Didn't you?"

She was distraught. No one will comfort her, not one will take her in their arms. No Papa Bear anywhere will ease her heart. She was not used to being bitter but the feeling was slipping in and it was flowing from her to her.

"I'll tell you what I am not going to do," she said. "I am not going to send a measly 100 bucks to a wildlife fund to ease my heart. There is no getting off easy on this one." She was crying. "Well, since I said it, of course I am going to send the $100. I can't get off that hook either. But it doesn't have anything to do with the trial. I am sending it because… We know why and it isn't enough. All the money I have ever earned would not be enough to make amends, to compensate and remedy the harm I have done. Money won't do it. Will never do it. Ask the Bears."

He was fully present when she turned toward him, laid down against him, let him hold her. She was everyone in the dream, literally, not as a matter of interpretation, but as the event presented itself. And so he had no role. Could not intercede. But he could hold her as the Stellar Jays shrieked through the trees, also flashing blue. Then she articulated her failures, one by one, her particular most ordinary human failures in relationship to the animals. Why had Mountain Lion been kind to her? She gave him the widest berth. This was the only reason she could imagine.

* * *

They slip and slide into each other, these characters. La Vieja is 40 to 50 years older than Léonie and Lucas. They are each wise in different ways. She has those years of experience. But Léonie and Lucas were born into a dying world and they both know it and are alert; they know who the perpetrators are. Furthermore, they are not colonists by birth, if tainted as everyone on the globe is, by the colonizers' mind, perspective, educational and legal systems. They know from their own experience and from their people.

La Vieja

Léonie's grandmother, Mere, will not speak of what she knows. When she came to the US, she began speaking English, not Pidgin, but formal English, and never spoke another word in her own language. That her daughter became a librarian was no surprise to her. She knew what her people had suffered in WWII and had saved her daughter and her descendants from such a fate. Being innocent had not saved her or her people from the atrocities of the war which was not against them although they suffered it as their *allies* confiscated their land and resources. Just because. She was not going to be an innocent. And though her people only wanted the invaders to leave their lands, wanted nothing else, had resisted being infected by their insatiable wanting, they didn't succeed in rousting them. So as she had had to live among the barbarians since 1893, was relieved she hadn't become a slave, she may as well live among them in the way Sean invited her to do.

He was going to make a home for her. He was going to provide for her, he said. Maybe he was making amends. Or being Irish, he knew something about the British who had invaded her land first and she knew more than she wanted to know about the Australians, Japanese and Americans. His family had come here to escape the famine which was not, according to them, an act of God but an act of the British against the people, his people and the little people. Sean and Léonie's father, Adam, were in agreement on this and Sean always felt Adam, also Irish, could be his son not only his son-in-law. "They cut down all our forests to build their damn ships," he had said. "And they took our food and shipped it home. They ate well; we starved." Sean made certain everyone ate. No one near him went hungry. Ever.

Everyone in this text carries a family history of war and hunger. It wasn't contrived. That is how it is. They all know what they have to know to survive. But they have different roles. Léonie and Lucas are seeking the knowledge of setting out and La Vieja needs to bring it together.

"Go home," is what Léonie's grandmother's people had said after WWII to all the invaders, no exception. And the animals were saying it now as well. Or maybe they always have since the Neolithic, but we have finally developed sufficiently to understand them.

Thirty years after the amphibious invasion of the Solomon Islands, Lucas' father, Isai Baez, staggered home from another war and another invasion. He walked like the drunken man he had become. He came home to no home. He pulled himself together somewhat knowing the animals and Agent Orange blackened trees from Vietnam were celebrating his departure and he was not being welcomed home.

"He met my mother," Lucas said, "at a Canción Protesta concert in '74. Occasionally, he liked to be where some of the people spoke Spanish. It wasn't his first language, but his parents spoke it among themselves. He liked not being in North America for a few hours."

Honey told Lucas that his father had taken her hand and started walking out of the auditorium when the musicians began speaking to the audience after the concert. It was a fundraiser so he put some bills in a collection jar as they left and then they continued walking and that was it. But, he had said, he was afraid he would hear too much about the golpe in Chile which had occurred in '73 as he knew too much about torture and American intervention than he cared to remember.

"The war?" she asked.

"I don't know a lot, if anything. I was three when he died. He didn't tell my mother much. He had come home, he had said, unsound of body and unsound of mind but without any visible wounds by some miracle or irony. He said his heart didn't work and it took her a while to assure him that he could love. He had some skills so he cobbled work together. "

"Like you?" she commented.

"My father was very inventive. He did tell my mother that he would have been a sapper if he were Viet Cong. After a year, they married. It wasn't important to her, but it was to him. She thought it was so there would be no questions asked about her right to the substantial insurance payments after he died. I don't know how he died. Mama Honey never told me. Whatever it was, he made sure it looked natural. He had ischemic heart disease. Terrible pains down his arm and back from lack of oxygen. He said it was the least he deserved. He took up running. She begged him not to. I think he ran himself into the grave. We both got money from his death. We mostly lived on hers and I went to college on mine. That's what he wanted.

"That's my paternal story, my dear. I didn't ask my mother for more information. It pained her greatly. She loved him. She always knew he was broken. But she said, somehow because of it he was very kind. Exceedingly, extremely kind. And always afraid he would hurt her, or me, inadvertently. He never did but it terrified him."

Lucas stopped talking, abruptly it seemed. Léonie wanted to know so much more and prodded him to continue. He flushed with anger but subdued it. "You're angry," she noted.

"No, he was," Lucas asserted. Finally he spoke again, "I will give you one sentence and afterwards you will never question me again. My mother told me she had been afraid to hear it but then she had no choice.

"Isai said to her, 'I have never recovered from seeing with my own eyes the agony that a people will inflict on others, on strangers. My government asked me to do the worst and for a short time I obeyed orders.'"

Léonie wanted to ask him so much more, as Honey had wanted to hear it all from Isai, but Lucas' jaw was set and his eyes were black. Instead, she simply asked, "Is that it, is that your last and only sentence about your father and the war?" Léonie was whispering, afraid to hear his answer.

"It is. It definitely is."

* * *

Understanding she could not pursue it, Léonie stood up and stretched, entirely comfortable in her body, a body he longed to know but it was not time yet.

"It's Monday morning," Lucas said. "Do you want to go home today?" He was trying to be honorable.

She turned toward him, standing in the soft cotton shirt, her legs spread slightly, out of reach if he remained seated and he did.

She waited a long time, seemingly contemplating another question, this one, unspoken. Finally, she said, "No." It was her answer even if she was also teasing him and they both knew it.

Best he could do then was rephrase the question, "When?"

"Full moon."

"But surely it is full moon now."

"Hardly."

"When then?"

"Thursday night. It will be the Sturgeon Moon. The fish will be running somewhere. Maybe somewhere close. And wherever they are running, the Bears will be out in the moonlight. Imagine it, Lucas, the long rays of the moon striking the dark fur and riling the water with platinum light."

20

Whenever I see a photograph of some sportsman grinning over his kill, I am always impressed by the striking moral and esthetic superiority of the dead animal to the live one.

Edward Abbey

Hidden in the forest is another sovereign nation, are other sovereign nations, peoples governed by and living according to the laws of the natural world which are intrinsic, not external, to them. They do not speak the way we do nor do they communicate the way we do. It seems like they live in the same physical world as we humans do, but they may not. We may have done more than withdraw our minds from the natural world when we separated and chose exploitation in lieu of inter-connection. Our dependency remained—it is not possible to be an earthling without it—but we thought we could survive without reciprocation and let everything we didn't consider essential for ourselves die out, and so it is. Only interdependence is more complex than we know and as the Others die out, the system itself falters, the one we cannot survive without, or outside of.

The non-humans become increasingly dependent upon each other, huddling together and feeding each other, living and dead, as their resources dwindle. Now they gather, but that is a misnomer because they don't gather and separate and gather and separate the way we do, they are always inter-connected. The term, gather, is how we try to find our equivalent of what is essentially incomprehensible to us, the way the many are distinct and one.

La Vieja

* * *

It's the next day or it's the next year or it is the continuous present now of eternity/nanosecond time, all at once. La Vieja has learned how to live here entirely alone and isolated in time to be formally engaged in the summer ritual of scanning the horizon 360 degrees and reporting in to the Forest Service. Every fire lookout has been reinstated. There were 53,000 lightning strikes in August 2020 and 1600 in the last twenty-four hours. 500 fires were torched and over a million acres burned, burning. Some of the lightning storms are created by the intensity of the fires and some fires have the potential of becoming firenadoes, the heat and smoke rising up and twisting into a chaotic storm. Some fires are so intense that they create their own thunderstorms with lightning and wind but no rain.

She scanned. When they re-installed this Lookout, a team came up, brought some supplies, checked the communications systems, the two-way radio, gave her instructions, tested her ability to follow them, acknowledged her abilities with some amusement, nodded belligerent approval, added a stash of chocolate bars, and took off. In another time, she would have brought out the whiskey, but they all needed to be on alert.

She was glad they came and not sorry that they left so quickly. She scanned her responses for her ability to be honest with herself. Yes, it is true, she more than adapted to being alone. She prefers it. This is misleading. She is so different a person than the one who first came here, this way is becoming natural. Without being able to anticipate how it would be to become other. She is another being if not yet fully formed or acquainted with herself. So many years of introspection, of self-awareness, continuous focus on herself before she came here when she lived a far more ordinary life, which has become increasingly, now entirely irrelevant.

She expected, no, intended, to strip down, to be stripped down. Still she also expected to be somewhat the same afterwards, familiar, newly born in some way but essentially identical to how she had begun, her nature intact. But that is not the case. There has been an essential alteration over these three years, not simply a return to a primary state. It doesn't seem that her condition is final but is preliminary to yet another, equally extreme conversion, equally unpredictable from this vantage point. What is it, she asks herself? What is it?

Then she feels what it is. She no longer has will. That intrinsic definitive quality which animates humans as she knows her own species, which has directed every action of her life, from turning in her bed to moving to this

Lookout, is not operative now.

Under some direction, with some motivation, she leaves the cabin and is moving toward the woods, as she has done every day since the Bear indicated he is aware of her presence. Walking each day as if summoned, but only a foot or two further than the day before, and remaining there entirely open and without interpretation until released. Blank and attentive. Can the two coexist?

Vague comprehension developed but again, without will and outside of language, absent of the particular indicators of her humanity. What was arising in her was like a change in humidity or a subtle but continuous change in barometric pressure, sensed, not measured. A shift in atmosphere as if breathing water not air, yes exactly, as if negotiating the sea and everything that it requires from twenty fathoms below, instead of walking on land. I have blindsight she told herself, without speaking of course.

* * *

Her experience being the same as what I have been trying to explain to myself since the Elephants came and created a field of awareness in which they communicated across continents and oceans until we ended up in the same place on the same day at the same time. And then again, and the same, with other Elephants, in the same way. And then again, and yet again, another year and then another. Chobe to Mashatu to Thula Thula to Damaraland.

* * *

She felt herself breathing in the oxygen of a field of awareness. In order to truly participate, she has had to relinquish will and so agency. Even the agency to relinquish her will. Even the will to relinquish agency. Even the agency to respond. Something was dawning in her about the energy of perception and the forcefield of natural law. It isn't a concept, it is an irresistible energy, like gravity. It just is. Movement occurring in all the realms.

* * *

I write this, thinking I understand and so am also integrated into its knowing and then I am snapped back into my old self, remembering having read of a conversation between two astrophysicists in an elevator. One inquired about a colleague who had worked on a project with the other.

"Oh, he had a nervous breakdown."

La Vieja

"What happened?"

"He tried to understand quantum mechanics."

My own laughter resonates around me and I calm. What was the state of mind or state of being that the lone bull Elephant experienced moment to moment, or the lone male Bear day after day? Are we approaching a similar state? Wisdom or madness? I ask the question without asking the question. How can I address the question?

* * *

La Vieja's ankle twisted slightly, not enough to do injury, but sufficiently to realize she had been moving forward thoughtlessly, without having developed the keen global awareness of the Others and so had tripped over a stone. She needed to stop and so she did. She saw she was significantly closer to the edge of the trees. Her shadow would reach it soon if she persisted, but persistence was not the mood. Maybe standing still was sufficient if she could allow the Earth to move under her as it spun on its axis while traveling the celestial highway, the moon in tow, around the immobile sun.

She felt an irresistible force urging her forward, but she did not want to invade a territory that is not hers. Occupying a very small area, not taking up much room, had become an essential principle of hers. Her cabin is not much larger than a den or a cave where a Bear might stretch out with two yearlings and two newborns. She hadn't wanted to acquire more territory than she absolutely needed and this path she has walked, which is inevitably marked with her scent, is narrow; repetition has described and limited it. But now she was compelled to extend it and resistance was inappropriate. She moved forward one step. And minutes later, another. This repeated over several days. The same scenario repeated one step further each day. And repeated.

She reached the ecotone between the brush and the trees, between the Bear's territory and her own. No man's land. Exactly, she thought. She stood very, very still and let an authentic smile on her face actively erase all fear that might have arisen. It was inevitable. She had known this would eventually be the outcome. When it occurred, it would be now.

There he was.

She stopped. Over time she had developed the ability to be entirely still. Her heart beat. Her breath came and went. The essential movements continued. But otherwise she was entirely still.

He had come to this place. To meet her here, he had determined the place and the time. Her intention was simply to accommodate as some animals are able to do, to submit to him entirely.

There he was.

She knew the drill. She had taught the occasional visitors to the forest who inquired at her Lookout how to deport themselves if they met a Bear. First do what seems impossible: Dispense all fear. Calm yourself. Feel kindly and move backwards slowly. Make no gesture that can be interpreted as aggression or hostility. Smile, if possible. Smile anyway. Move. Move away. Move away!

She could not. She could not move away.

She could dispense fear and smile. She could feel kindly. What she couldn't do was move. She was not paralyzed with fear, but she was held by his presence and his gaze. This was not a chance meeting and he was not alarmed by her presence. Quite the opposite, he had brought her here, one step at a time, day after day, with the magnetic power of his presence and his intent. She had relinquished will as he had acquired agency. Trust, she instructed herself. It required overcoming a lifetime if not centuries of conditioning and the training she had received. Despite the last years, despite her daily walks, trusting Bear, a wild animal, was ... difficult, was challenging, was ... inconceivable. But Life required it! Trusting Bear could become easy, but trusting herself was not. Would she find the right gestures and responses? The ones, she began to understand, he was counting on her to extend beyond herself ... to him.

He moved closer to her. It wasn't that she held her ground but that she was captivated and without desire to free herself, rather wanting to be bent even more to his will so that her mind would be imprinted and altered. There was a gesture to be made of her willingness to comply with his patient invitation.

She could move backwards if she really tried, but she was not certain it was the right approach. She looked directly at him, taking in his enormous size, six feet she guessed, if he were standing. Five hundred pounds or more. Yet, as he was on his fours, and she was standing, she was taller than he. This was not right.

His eyes were intense, his gaze penetrating. Assessing. He wanted to know what she would do having tracked him all these months. His dark nostrils extending from the pink furless trapezoid surrounding them and his mouth seemed almost like the barrel of a gun, that is, they confronted her. She saw by his expression that he could read her most intimate internal adjustments. There was nothing that eluded him despite what eluded her. She acted against all official instructions. She locked eyes with him trusting that he would see that as an act of submission not aggression. But first she dropped to her knees.

Then she began to perceive herself through those insistent dark brown eyes which indicated wariness and hope—hope for her, on her behalf. He had no fear of her but it seemed he wanted her to have a precise understanding of his strength and willingness to use it and, simultaneously, preferred her not to fear him. Yes, he wanted a form of coexistence to which she was fully responsible but without any sentimentality.

If he had spoken within the limits that she identified as language, he might have indicated that she did not understand him, his people, or non-humans. That she and her breed were vastly ignorant. It would require an extraordinary shift of consciousness for her to begin to meet his ways of seeing, his intelligence, his developed mind which did not resemble hers, and so, how could she appreciate it when her breed was convinced it was distinct in its evolution and could not imagine otherwise.

He was also aware of her fragility, of the species' fragility and the extremities necessary to survive. He easily perceived the judgments her species made in relationship to their own essential weakness and vulnerability. To bolster themselves, they presumed beings who lived in such a den as he constructed, or were dependent on hunting and gathering, who were unclothed, and did not hide or disguise their bodily functions or their eros, were certainly … primitive. (This is a transcription between worlds). Another sign of what she didn't know or understand. But it was also a reflection that she could, perhaps, see in his eyes. He was not transmitting this. The understanding was part of his being and she could take it in and integrate it, or not.

She was on her knees. Her eyes opened to his so he could see within her. This much was clear to her initially—he certainly did not see her the way she saw herself or imagined herself being seen by others. The image she projected cracked, fragmented, crunched halfway between them, the way a Pinacate Stink Beetle crunches when stepped upon accidentally. It required exquisite sensitivity to differentiate one human from another through the energies projected, and he had had to fracture hers. The broken pieces of her being, the way she had been taught to present herself, lay on the ground halfway between them, unable to sustain the performed veneer before the beam of his scrutiny. A millimeter further, his image, her reflection, moved toward her. When it landed, when she could absorb it and integrate it, she felt reassembled and entirely peculiar. (We don't know how long this took—minutes, or hours. No one was consulting a watch.)

Her first shock, despite everything that had transpired between them, was that he did not find her fearsome. In the way she translated his seeming observations, he differentiated the fragile human body from the weaponry he associated with the species. Then she felt his loathing because the armaments were not alive and never had been. She was almost dizzy with confusion because it seemed he thought that humans had crossed a line when they had left the natural world and surrounded themselves increasingly with the insensate. It was not like a crow using a stick, that stick had once been alive. What difference does that make, the human asked? The stick is just a tool now. No, it makes all the difference, Bear asserted. The world the hunters in his woods were creating was not a world of death. Dead had once been alive. This world they were imposing had never been alive, it was insentient, it was null and void, it was *not* and when *not* is activated as if it *is*, then horror enters. Bear perceived the process by which each individual human using the insensate, appreciating it, adoring it, absorbed its makeup and its nature into itself until it, the human, was changed cell by cell into the exact opposite of itself. It was not a man with a gun that came toward him it was a gun moving empowered by the sensibility of a gun. When Bear looked at a hunter, the gun's inanimate hunger is what he saw. The thing he saw coming at him, still claiming to be a mammal, a vital being, was the mechanized anti-life, a mindless, heartless, soulless weapon, a thing, mobilized.

He had managed to disorient her! That alone, aside from the content, confused her. She was undone. Well, what had she expected? Control of the dialogue? The upper hand? Had she had any idea what submitting really meant or had it only been language? Even on her knees, she was unsteady and would have gladly fainted away if she weren't also intrigued by these ideas which, ultimately, were merely sensations or energetic events that were reorganizing her being. It had taken three years of solitude to be open to this.

Increasingly lacking the strength to hold herself up, she let herself collapse, her head finally on the ground. But instead of feeling defeat, she discovered she was unusually sensitive to the particular quality of the dirt, the individual pine and fir needles that her forehead rested against, the snap of some dry leaves, the scent of decay or transformation over the last hundred or five hundred years, the fall of this year's foliage, and the animals that had crossed, Bobcat, Turkey, then an amalgam of feathers, urine, scat, dew, paws, all of it. This also startled her. Everything startled her. She raised her head. At first, she had looked in his eyes as an act of daring but now she needed to hold on to something and they were the only support she could find.

Then, he constructed an image, a true image from the naked elements, the essential qualities from which all mammals other than civilized, that is altered, humans are comprised. It made her tremble to recognize herself in her nakedness as he mirrored it to her. Could she accept the consequences that artifice and human were intertwined with each other and nakedness was mammalian, was animal, was entirely and indefinably natural? Could she allow herself not only to be shattered but to be stripped bare and remain that way?

He did not want to frighten her. He did not want fear, of him, or what was occurring within her, to be in the dynamic between them. He did not want those distractions. He moved closer toward her. There was slightly more than a Bear's length between them. Another step so still all the forest sounds flattened into silence in his tread.

Unexpectedly, La Vieja remembered Léonie's dreams, the way she had scuttled over to the Bears seated around the fire in a circle, the little girl joining them, then leaning against the Bear. The dream took on another quality as the notion of property, that it had been Léonie's dream, dissolved and it emerged as a place and event that she could enter. His proximity began to feel comforting as it had to Léonie and she inclined forward toward him so very subtly, it was almost imperceptible and yet she could feel an internal shift, the ever so slight hesitance, avoidance, had dissipated, replaced by attraction. And attraction was motivated by safety. So much in the world was dangerous but he wasn't dangerous. He was … he was … refuge.

Nothing else was required to allow everything. She wanted to weep for the relief of it. Distrust, an ordinary sentry, conscripted by history to a kind of serfdom, had accompanied her everywhere, particularly alert at the sharpest boundary line between the civilized and the wild. It had meant there would always be a standoff, no matter what she pretended to anyone or to herself.. And now …? La Vieja spoke aloud though, of course, the Bear couldn't understand. (Of course, he did.) She knew she didn't have the ability to communicate precisely in any other way but human language, and had no history from which to accept that he did indeed understand her because of his developed skills of interpretation and not her choice of words. All these thoughts were both her attempt to reciprocate, to meet him in ways that admitted he had reached her. As limited as her under-standing had been, her inability to communicate to a non-human was even greater. But finally, she found some words and stammered hoarsely.

"This is kinship, isn't it?" Her voice startled her and she hoped it hadn't startled him. (He wasn't startled.) She had no capacity left to hold herself as Other to him in order to maintain the hierarchy that he had shattered as if he had swung at her with his paw, which could have killed her with one blow.

"Kinship, Poppa Bear," Poppa Bear! What else was she going to call him?

She felt a great release. How tightly he had held her. How great her need as she had no agency whatsoever. She smiled, she actually smiled, re-alizing, he had been keeping her in check because she, a human, was the unreliable one. Of course, he knew how erratic humans became when they were afraid. He appeared the same, his eyes perhaps slightly softer but still intensely focused while the energetic line between them went slack and she recognized she was to stand up slowly. She did so, waited, observed that his grip didn't tighten. She moved backwards, it remained easy, was permitted, she turned slightly, and then more so, until she was facing the cabin, her back to him, and began to walk toward it. Free. Hmm. Free? Was this freedom? Mammalian freedom?

She'd been on a leash! She! La Vieja, not Bear. Despite his controlling interest as it were, she walked with increasing self-possession. Something unprecedented had occurred and she was altered, was in a different body with a different mind.

Every step was both entirely free and un-self-conscious. And yet, she was aware of each step, of the quality of the new movement. Walking like this, she never would have tripped as she had earlier. She went slowly but as precisely as a Bear running or a Deer, exquisitely aware, entirely spontaneous.

After a while, other senses rose in her. She was confident but like any animal she needed to be mindful, sensitive to what was around her. And as she hadn't developed her ability to hear, smell or sense what was near, she had had to look, to rely on sight. Then, unprecedented, all the senses rushed in like great winds from everywhere, she was dizzy with the force of all the forest sounds, all the creatures singing, each exuding its own signature scent, as well as the sight of them, even those hidden in plain sight. She was aware of every part of the great world, each in its wholeness, intersecting with every other portion. The great hum of ceaseless and continuous creation.

He was alongside her. It shocked her. She had not known but he had known to escort her. To protect her. Bear stopped fifty feet from the house. She went to the stairs, looked back, and went up, one by one by one. When she reached the top, she climbed through the trap door, closed it onto the widow's walk, turned around and looked out toward the Oaks, Pines and Blue Spruce. No Bear. He was gone. He could have been an illusion, she thought, but she didn't believe so. It was already beginning and she had to oppose the inevitable reversal to an old and now unwanted, unwelcome self, mired in doubt.

* * *

She couldn't account for what remaining inside her had been altered, because she still relied on words to understand and again, language would not serve her because there were no words for this, neither of guidance nor comprehension. She would not only have to express herself differently, she would need to perceive differently. She had wanted to think, to perceive "herself" differently but she was losing the identity based upon differentiation. Another awareness, a dissolution of the familiar "I" without creating any panic or loss. While the boundaries were permeable, and while she as she knew herself was absent, there was a recognizable core. Bear hadn't completely transformed her. He had not released her from the enchantment of human form. She was not a four-legged. He was not a wizard.

Had Léonie known this as a child? She had spent many, many hours alone outdoors, experiencing the exit from her house like slipping down a slide into a watery element in which she could breathe and live easily until she heard the call home and felt the jolt of oxygen, house, family and expectations. She hoped such returns would have been vanquished in the woods, but here she was.... One might think this was like those moments in meditation when one was for consecutive seconds or minutes that felt like eternity, without thought. And then...

Thinking. Thinking. Thinking. She couldn't avoid reflection. However, it locked her into her humanity while being inundated by simultaneous awareness of the engaged and connected particularity of every living being around her. Gaia must feel this, she thought. This must be Earth consciousness. But not Earth alone. Bear must feel this. Waves of benevolent appreciation swept through her like particles from the far distance of the universe without drawing particular attention to themselves or rather without taking away the awareness of all the other breathing beings. Yes, Bear must feel this, if this was indeed feeling. All beings must feel such, except those who feared being immersed in this world.

Regrettably, she had started thinking and was falling toward her former self. She consoled herself by considering she had no choice. Bear had to find food. So did she. She had responsibilities.... "Bullshit," she warned herself.

Of great concern, as she began her rounds to check for smoke, was whether she would have the ability to also warn Bear and his people if there were danger, not only the rangers of her species. Where could the Bear people go if a firestorm was on its way? Or how could they put it out?

She couldn't say, "Here, get in my car, squeeze in, take the passenger seat and put the cubs in the back with Mama Bear. Fasten your seat belts, it's the law." The divide, the consequences of it were undeniable, extreme and heartless and would remain.

* * *

La Vieja's experiences spark my own memory. A Con-Edison employee had been startled by a snake on the path of my house as he went to check the meter and with one strike of his machete, severed the head of the garter snake from its uncoiling body. Futile to tell him it was a harmless snake. "Look at it carefully, it has no rattles. For next time." He shrugged and drove away. I continued to stand there as the head reached for its writhing body and the body for its head just out of reach, coiling and uncoiling. They couldn't join and I couldn't reunite them. Where was its sweet and welcome death? An hour away. I stood still as it sought its life at my feet. My reflex was to call 911. But as I was approaching the front door to telephone, I stopped, laughed at myself and returned. No neurosurgeon was going to be helicoptered out to land in the meadow staked out for firefighters in order to do emergency surgery for the guillotined creature. An hour later, I buried it.

* * *

La Vieja walked round and round, more engaged in looking than she had been before though she had never felt distracted. Now, she had sharper inner instruments, needed technology less, could see better, sharper, could continue to detect different odors from a distance. A faint whiff as an old stag stepped on a branch on the ground, broke it, and released a moist scent that enhanced his own scent. A breeze signaled its crossing of a large body of water but she couldn't discern yet if it had come down the length of a river or across a lake. Scat was dropping onto the ground. Some animal in heat. Sweat. Crushed berries.

She stayed motionless, reaching through the air for Bear. If there was a fire, he would know. If there was a fire that she located first, he would know instantly but not because she had transmitted it. Because she had entered the field that wild beings inhabited. Simultaneously, she felt the wound where she, as a human, had been separated from all that is, as she felt the balm of that wound somehow, miraculously, beginning to heal.

21

Out of all that gets forgotten grow stories to fill the ever deep-
ening void. The complete inspiration for a work is not known
until after it's been made. Over time, the fact-littered history of
the building process fades and is replaced by a freshly minted
awareness and viewpoint. The experiences between the time a
thing is made and when it is looked back upon, morph into a cre-
ative intelligence that imbues the object with the power of pre-
science. It is as though it came to being when it did in order to be
there in the future, when a place for the memory of new experiences
would be vital and welcoming.

The ideas that initiate a piece of work in dry stone, and the
processes that take it from excavation through construction, to
completion, hang over the work like decaying fumes, until, even-
tually, they dissipate. And all that's left in place is the over-
whelming and everlasting presence of the piece. The discussions
about siting, access, footing, proportion, scale drainage, stability,
materials, tolerances and grades are what the piece is made out
of, but not what we are left with. What remains becomes an
open receptacle for dreams to fall into. A mass of rock becomes
fertile ground for myth to grow.

Dan Snow
Listening to Stone

The setting sun was burning the sky, a red-hot iron in the increasingly
gray body of the ashen sky from intense wildfires, distant in time
and space. There is no way to keep time separate when events desperately converge.

Why impose an innocence upon the two, one neither Léonie or
Lucas would ever choose? When they met, it was another time but how to
keep what we know about this time out of the text as if they didn't have

foresight, as if their original meeting wasn't a consequence of the future as well as the past?

He led her, she led him, to their bed under the great limbs of the trees that form a bower open at the top where soon the rising moon would cast its own red face down upon them. The smoke in the air will blot out the stars. Now there is only the red glow of the setting sun catching on the density of the air. The glow will continue through the night and into the next day. At first, they thought it was their own passions that were uniting them, then they recognized they were yielding to external energies both invisible and beyond them.

Without planning it, they were walking as if in procession, in ritual. They couldn't have expected a blood moon but there it was, a sign perhaps that the moon had indeed called forth her time and determined their time of joining. There was gravity in this moment. They understood this. Hadn't they designated this night, this time, weren't they prescient? They will bond in this moment exactly as the red moon enters the sacred circle above them in this moment of blood and fire.

They had thought to be careful, to hide the blood scent by entering the sacred ritual within the cabin, but quickly set that idea aside. It was here, on the earth, they needed to join.

Three hundred miles away, the old woman, La Vieja, is praying, an activity she has added to her repeated search of the land. She can sense their ceremonial moment. Age is upon her and an unexpected wisdom. Their presence reassures her, creates an unexpected continuity. The appearance of Léonie's dream as if it was her own memory at the critical moment with Bear had bonded her with them, though they are still innocent of the connection. At least, we think they are.

By the stream below, Bears, a wisdom people, are gathered in council. It is all the protection and blessing that is needed. The old woman, the Bears, and the two lovers are drawn closer as they meld into their common field of knowing which increasingly becomes their habitat and from which may yet arise a future. The two stand between the sun and moon, their clothes and identities dropping away as they reinhabit their animal selves and each hidden level of reality after another opens into the others through their holy ceremony.

* * *

We leave them here trusting our futures to them. This is a dream or this is not a dream. Or both. It doesn't matter how you imagine it., how you perceive it, see it. It is.

* * *

In the morning, Léonie said, "Let's go into the woods after breakfast. It seems right to gather stones today." The moment she roused, she wanted to explore the woods to be sure of the place she had found that very first day they had arrived which had a rock and earthen wall suitable for the den he wanted. She was already ruminating on the stones she had seen down the incline. In her mind, they were already gathered, stacked according to size and kind. "We will have to look long and hard for enough stones here for a clochán but we can start looking. It's not a day's work, it's month's work, several month's work. At the end, we'll manage the equivalent of a thatch roof from what is here.

"My grandfather taught me, you know. And his father taught him. And his father taught him. And grandfather taught my father, he's Irish too, you know, but he only helped out when we needed labor. When my grandfather picked up a stone, the Irish in him came alive. Same happens with me."

"Your grandmother is left out, then."

"Oh no, she knows how to thatch as well as he."

"I didn't expect to see Irish in you," he said, "but I see it now." This isn't a casual recognition. He will ultimately be linked with whatever she carries as she will take in his many histories, every world of its own overlapping with all the other worlds inside them.

They were getting out of bed, she was putting his shirt on again, he had tied an African cloth around his hips as his people did. They were both somewhat unsteady, their ground had shifted. A new undertaking was calling them but he was not entirely ready to enter the next moment of their lives. He was encased in the memory of the night and that was embedded in their meeting. That memory was clear, clear as the water that had been flowing down the wall in the park, as the sight of her hands stroking the wall, as now he knew that she had held every stone in her hands and placed each one. He had felt the craftsman in her hands when she held him, how sure she was with every stroke, both confident and curious every time. Her touch had given him permission to explore her without inhibition; she was grounded in the art of loving in a most earthly way. Yes, he had felt they were building something. Building was her art. This craft meant she created simple structures that could last several hundred years. She could do it if she had to entirely herself without any help or equipment. This would no longer be her option. He examined his own hands, a physician's hands, a surgeon's. He also could open and seal.

He took her hands in his. "I love these hands," he said simply.

"They're rough from stones," she wasn't embarrassed and didn't try to hide them but turned his hands over. "And these hands are soft, they're the hands of a medicine man. These hands heal. I bet you have sewn wounds together."

"Many times," he admitted. "Even babies. They say I have a good stitch. My nurse says I could make a fortune in haute couture. Not really my ambition," he laughed with the pleasure of ease.

He stroked her hands, ran his finger down the life line and then the heart line, as if they were speaking to him.

"Can you read my palm?"

He nodded. "I have been known to do divination. It's a family gift to connect with the spirits."

"What do they say?"

He examined her palms again, first one and then the other with the concentration she expected he would show to a patient in pain or confusion. "These hands," he said, "believe in a future even when the ashes are floating down on us from firestorms not so far away." The tenderness he felt for her shook him to his core. If he wept a thousand years he would never get to the bottom of awe, for who she was, for his ability to see and love her. It was the equivalent of holding a newborn bird, a mountain and the red full moon in his hands at once.

She held his eyes steadily when he looked at her now. Everything she had learned in tending the earth had coalesced in the moment of their union. "The Earth trusts you," he said.

"Yes, that's what it's like doing the work I do. She gives me everything, stone, mud, fire, water. I lack for nothing and then there is a wall."

"You will teach me," he said, a question or request becoming an agreement. Then we will be partners."

"I've watched you, as you have watched me, all this time we've been together. I watched you take up our supplies. Everything you carried was precious to you because you were going to assemble them into the marvelous. And then," she was smiling broadly, "your little foray to the phone and what transpired there. I think you passed a test you didn't know you were taking."

They were getting ready. He was pouring them coffee.

"Stonemasonry is not my 'profession'. It's not how I make a living. Well, I am compensated but I won't ever look at it as a job.

"But I wanted to be a stonemason so I could genuinely live as a stonemason. Not what I was doing, not how I was making a living, I wanted to believe in the mind and body of a stonemason. I knew I had to get back to beginnings. That we have to get back to beginnings. I had to or my life would not matter. Beginnings. As soon as I got my degree and became a librarian and began working in the library as my mother had done all her professional life, I realized I had come to the end."

She reached in a deerskin pouch she always kept near her, and took out a river stone that had been smoothed into an oval, inviting as an egg, and gave it to him. It lay next to the stone she had rolled into the fire in her dream which had come back to her. "A talisman," she said. "For you. I have another. It's a gift from the Colorado."

He put a red grape into her mouth and then kissed her. She had a ring and he had a stone.

"Do you ever think of going to your grandmother's country? Do you ever think of going back home?"

"Never. She isn't there, nor her mother or grandmother, obviously. There's nothing to see. It doesn't look like it looked when she was a girl. It's ugly. The only thing you see there are the ruins of war. And you? Do you want to go to the Island?"

"Oh yes," he said. "We will go. We will find an elder who knew my grandfather and she will marry us in the proper way."

Trying not to be startled or blush, she pretended curiosity, "And what way is that?"

"Not according to the state, but according to the spirits."

She didn't ask which spirits so he knew that it had been the right thing to say.

And so, they went into the woods and so their common lives began.

22

Now, at the moment of species re-unification, we have the chance not only to meet the toothed and clawed in the light of reality, but the opportunity to vanquish the self-imposed fear and ignorance that have held humanity hostage. Seeing the world through the eyes of the carnivore is the first step in learning how to relate with these kindred beings, and ourselves, honestly and responsibly.

G. A. Bradshaw
Carnivore Minds

When it was safer and La Vieja didn't have to be at her post constantly, she began to make her way to the forest again. Smoke and ash had kept her inside and she felt increasingly claustrophobic despite the large windows and the surrounding walkway. But heeding the call to keep watch served her as it meant she would have to be outside for long hours. Yes, she could look around through the windows but it was not the same; she had to be in it to see it.

Finally, when she could leave, she made her careful way in segments each day, down to the forest and stopped at the perimeter. If Bear was at the edge or visible, she paused for instructions, sometimes proceeded and sometimes retreated. Each time she saw him, it seemed as if she was being led, not so much into the woods, but into another awareness. She was grateful.

And so it went on and on for weeks if one could track time in such arbitrary units, rather than by the light, temperature, sky, the position of the sun, the waxing and waning of the moon, the constellations. The day the Geese flew south. When she found berries and she was certain there were enough for Bear and enough for her to have a few. The day the salmon returned for the Bear people. The day the leaves and needles began falling. The day the pile of redwood bark had been clawed down to the foot of the hollow tree and the shavings would soon be swept into the den for a Bear, maybe even Bear himself, to hibernate there. When the summer birds began to migrate. When fire season noticeably waned.

It became quieter in the forest as the Bears fattened. Soon he would disappear. But not yet.

They had an arrangement which she believed had been commonly devised. She had a lightweight red shell which she kept in her backpack and wore only when in his proximity. Seeing her, there was a better chance— but no guarantee—the hunters would not shoot in her proximity and so he could stay by her and forage. The "arrangement" was that he tolerated her presence and refrained from overtly reading her mind when she indulged the illusion she was Mama Bear protecting him. Once or twice, she stayed in the forest several hours after sunset when he was eating heartily, not stopping as was Bear's habit, because he was going to try to eat at night when he usually slept and would hide out during the day when the killers were about. A calculated choice based on thought and discernment. Yes. Because of the fires, there were fewer hunters as the acres that were burning increased. Some National Forests were still closed. The Doves, the Deer, the Bear, all the animals were greatly relieved though they knew it only meant they were momentarily safe from one human danger but greatly imperiled by the other.

Whenever she passed the den in the making, she gave thanks for it. Soon she would avoid it to allow whomever it was who would dream there, privacy and security. He or she was the lucky one. The fires and the reforesting that would occur afterwards destroyed the potential sites to hibernate, the ground cover gone on millions of acres, the hollow trees burned, the rock ledges exposed, the blankets of leaves turned to ash and wafting through the air across the country. It was unending and unfathomable the extent of destruction that the world was suffering. In New Mexico, birds were falling out of the sky in the hundreds of thousands, perhaps from smoke damage. La Vieja was alerted to the die-off through a bulletin from the National Forest Service. Her ability to be entirely free of the world had ended when the Lookouts were conscripted. Hundreds of thousands of birds it was said. Hundreds encountered on hiking trails and thousands on the White Sands Missile Range. The military was engaged in finding the birds in order to study them and determine the cause of the mass deaths.

The world was inflamed in all ways.

* * *

She wasn't aware of the subtle daily changes in her feelings and behavior as the remarkable ease and comfort she felt in the wood was coming upon her gradually after the radical meeting with Bear. Despite everything that had transpired and its aftermath, she had to accept that she was a two-legged and her mind retained its essential biological and cultural imprinting. If it seemed to her sometimes that she could shape-shift, it didn't last. She came back to her rounds and called the rangers on her two-way radio. She cooked the beans she ate on a stove. She slept in a bed. She wore clothes. She spoke English to herself despite its inability to convey or comprehend what had transpired in the forest.

What had changed was that she went into the woods every day. She also admitted to herself that she was seeking him as he was allowing her to be alongside him from time to time. In return, she took whatever opportunities appeared to make some miniscule amend for the ways the humans acted without regard for anything but themselves. Whenever she was called to resolve what could be a conflict between the animals and humans, she unfailingly favored the non-human. If asked if animals had been sighted, she said no. She lied. Asked which were the routes most likely to reveal animals, she sent the hunters in the opposite direction, away from those they wanted to kill. She continuously argued for the forest to be closed and finally those who agreed with her prevailed. She could not forget she was a human; she could only mourn it and be bitterly grateful for the opportunity to intervene on behalf of the Others when possible.

Reflecting back on the first days she had spent at the Lookout, remembering her first steps up the stairs to the cabin and her great ambivalence, even fear, she admitted that she had expected to change but she had never expected to become the person she seemingly was becoming.

* * *

Over the weeks, there appeared small changes to the Bear's den. More of the dry leaves and shreds of bark had been brushed inside the tree and it appeared that whoever was preparing this den was visiting it more often. That meant ... her thought was interrupted by confusion. How was she to refer to him? She couldn't say, her Bear or her teacher or her guide .... Clearly, the possessive was highly inappropriate. How subtly the tendency for humans to dominate. Ownership was embedded in language which then determined everything that followed. Nor could she name him as his name, should the Bear people enter a naming process, it would have to be determined by him, himself. She couldn't call him Poppa Bear. Such a name would be too intimate and worse would name him in relationship to herself. Shameful even to consider. That meant ... a way of identifying him for herself came to her. That meant the Bear who had summoned her.... She paused again as the name came to her, Bear Who Summons was also getting ready to hibernate and would soon disappear in this den or another but she doubted he would retreat before the hunters retreated. If hunting season started up again, it would end on December 27th. The archery season which had only lasted a few days in 2020 because of the fires, would have ended on September 6th. The Department of Fish and Wildlife had set a quota of 1700 Bears to be *harvested*. 1700 of her people.

* * *

When I had met the Elephant Ambassador in Africa, I had said to him, "Your people are my people." Now La Vieja was feeling that the Bear people were her people. I hadn't meant I was taking them as my people, certainly not that I had any rights to them. I had meant I held them like kin in my heart and would be responsible for them in ways that were appropriate to kinship. It seemed La Vieja was holding the same sentiments for the Bears. She was actively crossing over to meet Bear as a peer, more than a peer, as someone wiser than she. A radically demanding task. She couldn't possibly do more.

When she first rented the Lookout, she had not been required to read the California Mammal Hunting Regulations. But now that she was one of those who was designated to look for fires, she had had to read it so she could advise people who came to her as the equivalent of a wildlife officer. She had to force herself to read the list of names of animals that could be "taken," and when, during which days, and which hours, and by what means and how many. Deer, Elk, Pronghorn, Bighorn, Bear, Wild Pig, Bobcat. There were others under different conditions, licenses and permits: Mountain Lion, Coyote, Weasel, Skunk, Opossum, Moles, Rodents, English Sparrow, Crows; the lists went on and on.... She forced herself to take in those particular words and be "accountable" for them. When she was alone in the forest, when she was the only one speaking, whether to herself or aloud, the words rang deafeningly like gunshots. Archery hunting season,

Deer hunting season, Elk hunting season: 1 bull, 1 antlerless, 2 spike, either-sex…. This is how her species marked time. She no longer thought this way. The mind developing in her did not reduce the living to objects, assume ownership or plan annual slaughters.

She stopped wearing her red shell when the land closed. If there were humans in the woods at this time, they were predators and arsonists and would appreciate such an easy target to dispose of before they were noticed. Their mantra: shoot and burn. She huddled closer to the animals hidden around her for safety and camaraderie. Her people, the two-leggeds like herself, were no longer her people and would remain aliens as long as they were killers. What a grievous but essential consequence of having chosen to see from a Fire Lookout.

23

The threads which tie the child to the land include its conception site and the significant places of the Dreaming inherited through its parents. Introduced to creatures and land features as to relations, the child is folded into the land, wrapped into country, and the stories press on the child's mind like the making of felt—soft and often—storytelling until the feeling of the story of the country is impressed into the landscape of the child's mind.

Jay Griffiths
A Country Called Childhood:
Children and the Exuberant World

We cannot measure time. It is not an object to be quantified. Time holds us. We can learn to live within it in the way we are not only of the Earth but on it and in its sphere, and will be returned to it, become of it again, feed the others who come afterwards with our bodies, as we were fed, not only by our abstract legacies should we leave any, but by the bodies of everything that lived before us.

She set out that day with a full backpack containing water, food, birdseed for offerings, a flashlight, sunglasses, a pocket knife, phone, a two-way long range radio, a mask in the event of smoke, a survival blanket, (less than 3 oz), an extra pair of socks, a small book to read (*Carnivore Minds* by G. A. Bradshaw) and a journal. Bringing a book surprised her but she trusted this text. Bradshaw was a hybrid, many animal minds mixed into one body.

La Vieja had made no plans in advance. The call had come as clearly as if someone had telephoned or more emphatically had been drumming for her. The process of packing, both automatic and attentive, advised her she would be gone far more than an hour, maybe more than a day. She arranged for someone to cover her watch while she was gone. "A relative needs me and there is no one else," she lied.

She was already wearing long silk underwear under her sweater and pants, and a vest and so she added a scarf, tucked gloves in the pocket of her lightweight forest green down jacket and tied it around her waist. Her boots were waterproof and lined for warmth. Bear walked around entirely naked and entirely self-sufficient. There was a lot of laughter in the woods as she came by. Not because she was naked which would have amused her peers in the city, but because she wasn't. A year or more had passed. It was November.

Because the pack was heavy, she walked slowly which meant she had time to examine everything. It began to feel as if she was being conscripted and given orders to become very familiar with the territory. Brilliant summer colors had faded to subdued autumn tones. Everything was covered with a tincture of gray from the ash that been drifting down day after night, year after year, settling everywhere, and also from the cyclical dying down, the leaves aging and falling, the cold fronts coming in more frequently, juxtaposed with the increasing and lengthening and intensifying heat spells. What was increasingly lacking were the ordinary days of the familiar cycle. If spring had been pert, the mood was now brittle. Not unlike her own body which was more fragile than it had been. She found a branch on the ground and it was exactly right for a walking stick which helped her carry the weight of the pack.

When she came down to the little stream which was no longer a wash, as there had been some rains up north, she sat down on a rock ledge overlooking the running water, like a small song, sometimes tentative, memory returning as the stones settled into mud. The wind came up and died down. Some birds had remained. Animals, who had not heard or did not believe that hunting season had been postponed or cancelled again, moved with a learned trepidation in the quieter season of bedding down for winter. One night it had threatened storm, but no rain, only the winds gathering in a furious circle dance. It had been necessary to keep a steady watch as the wind could well have roused the smoldering hot spots to full blown blazes. She was so appreciative of the creek's music, the renewed melody of the life force as winter augured dying.

From time to time, she saw Bear moving parallel to her. Was that him, that dark shape in the shadows, spotting her or was she, more likely, unwittingly following him once again, so tuned to his signals, she acquiesced to his invisible directions without knowing she had done so? Or could it be that the interconnection of everything manifested in all the different realms, and Bear had grafted awareness onto her. She would never be free of him, nor wanted to be, and so, likely, he was also bound to her. What could he be thinking? What was she thinking? This was not thought. This was restoration. So fundamental, it was stronger than purpose. They seemed to be bonded by cosmic law, in reality, inalterable.

She cupped her hand and took some water from the stream, assuming she was high enough, that it was running fast enough, there were no humans or cattle living above her between where she was and the headwaters, so it was safe, relatively safe, safe enough for Bear and her to drink. Her thirst eased, she set out again.

The terrain changed, the creek widened, the banks disappeared into vegetation which crowded down hastily to the waters. Mossy rocks, boulders, stone walls, Gray Pine, Blue Oak, Ponderosa, Madrone. She leaned on the walking stick and took each step with care, finding her footing as others had, her prints covering their paw prints. Though she had a compass and a topo hiking map, she did not access them because he was here and trusting him was essential. If she lost faith in the mystery that had cleaved them, she would be instantly, hopelessly, irreversibly lost.

She did not know where she was. That was an understatement. There were no signposts. She had never been here. There was no path except for the waters. Still, she went forward, even more slowly than before and when she came to a juncture with steppingstones, the water burbling white around them, creating a walkway from one bank to the other, she took it. Bear had crossed earlier, somewhere close, she could smell him on the froth of the raucous waters. Now he was moving in front of her, further on, moving her further down as she scratched, unsteadily through the undergrowth.

The soundscape continued to change. There were more sounds, trills and whistles accompanying the timpani, the drum rolls, the tambourine of wind in the trees, limbs rubbing, bruising, the crack of twigs, bird calls, barks and coughs, chases through dry leaves, alarms, hidden fluttering and scampering. The bass of Wild Hog and Mountain Lion.

Oh! The Ishi wilderness. This was a declared refuge. Hunting was prohibited. There were inaudible whispers, communications, acknowledgements, recognitions innate to the natural world and the spirits that sustain it. There was more than what she heard, the press of hidden presences on the composition of this niche. She could sense what she could not see or hear. She left the bank and turned inland to the west. The trees thinned. She proceeded confidently, tuned to his invisible presence.

Concurrently, while she had never been here, she recognized where she was. She had not been here, but she had seen it, she had looked down upon it. From the cabin walkway she had looked down upon this scene where she was now standing. She looked up. The cabin was not there. The scent of a vanilla pine caught her, sharp as a thorn. She knew that scent from that pine, not a pine, that pine. From her own stand she had looked down upon this view. How was that possible?

Now, she smelled Bear, It had to be more than one Bear, the scent like the pine was so pungent it had to be released by several Bears. She had never been able to distinguish the scent of one human from another, but Bear, she realized must be acutely aware of the different spices each Bear released. She imagined them further down the slope where, she recalled, there had been stones surrounding a central slab. Surely, the Bears were gathered there.

As if to confirm her memories, a Bear ran through the brush across the stream, not Bear Who Summons, but a female Bear who plunged through the stream as if it were not another element and disappeared quickly in the direction she had visualized, toward a council of Bears.

She stopped. No, she was stopped. Even if she tried, she couldn't go forward. As if she was impaled on inertia. She had reached the destination she hadn't known she'd reached. Without a doubt, this had been it. OK. She put her backpack down, scanned where she was, found she was alongside the most southerly sugar pine and able to lean against it. She lay her walking stick to the side and settled down in the south. Time passed and she scuttled clockwise to the west and then north and the east. Soon she was back in the south but facing west. Her intuition, or whatever was compelling her, indicated that whatever would come, if anything would, would approach from the west. The food she had with her could last a day or more and there was water.

Her jacket was warm, she had the blanket if necessary. For whatever reason she was here, she would be fine.

She could not discern whether she was remembering or exploring for the first time. Each leaf, each stone, the shape of a limb startled her with either the freshness of memory or the satisfaction of discovery. Over these last years, she had learned to see by absorbing the habit of attention that existed in the four-leggeds and the winged around her. It seemed she knew parts of this land well, exceedingly well, and there were other areas she had not seen before as her vision had been limited by what had displayed and what had hidden itself. She had not been a free agent then but as one to whom a film was being continuously presented: what it was safe to show her; what it was necessary to hide.

She settled in. She felt safe. The environment was pristine; she could assume there would be no humans.

It was later in the afternoon or it was the next day or she didn't know when it was that she saw, perhaps five hundred feet from her, an outcropping of rock backing into a hill obscured by tall grasses, brush, narrow trees above and a fairly smooth stone wall leading up from the ground to a ledge. It was so much a part of the landscape she did not notice that the outcropping might be a substantial roof that was not necessarily a boulder that had tumbled down the earthen wall, but a constructed shelter. How was this possible? She couldn't go all the way to examine it, that was forbidden. Still what she observed indicated that this could be a human version of a found animal den. Where a shape-shifter might want to live. Without approaching closer than she was permitted—as she had been released from her invisible shackles based on her willingness to heed the inaudible instructions to stay within a designated territory—she studied the arrangement of rocks. It was more than happenstance.. A bird might land summarily, even that importunate Steller's Jay with its pointed wizard's hat without requiring permission, but not a human, not La Vieja.

Well, it was a den. And it wasn't. Bears enhanced their lodgings with found materials when constructing its winter shelter and so this could be, but … . At first glance it was a den in a rock wall. But when she looked again…. The rocks at the base comprised a wall that might have formed naturally over time or was formidably constructed to appear that way. What a cursory glance would assume were a random pile of stones gathered together and shaped over millennia by earth movement, rain, wind, gravity, were individual stones fit exactly one into the other, held together with packed dirt as were the rocks that only appeared randomly piled upon each other as from a slide. She edged closer. This aggregate of stones, rock and boulder was certainly not haphazard but ingeniously stacked with great care. This was designed to delude passersby, if any came close. And seemed to have a purpose, to serve something, but what? La Vieja had no idea. The assembled walls supported an arch with a large capstone held in place by companion smaller stones pressing against each other from each side and underpinning what might be a rounded roof hidden in the shadow of the overhang of equally amassed stones. This seemingly makeshift but exquisitely designed hut was far too large for a Bear who would have to pack it full with dirt and then burrow into it to be secure. A human shelter. She did not doubt this was created for the challenge of constructing something that partook of both worlds sufficiently not to intrude, concealed in plain sight by its nature and intentions. If this was the goal, it was realized. Visible and invisible, a perfect hideout. And who knew but that it could be remedied so that Bear might occupy it. He certainly had the skill. Or was it actually designed by a human who was trying to cross a line? Was this created by a human as a dwelling to allow for another way of being?

She was comfortable as an animal might be leaning against the tree, or getting up and walking around in a small circle acquainting herself with her surroundings. Female Bears might range up to 10 miles and males even up to 59 square miles, although the needed territory was rarely available in the current times of grossly narrowing habitat. She sensed the Bears to the southeast seated among the boulders of a stone circle and so she did not go further, did not want to encroach. She had walked many miles, how many she could not assess. Now she was being asked to confine herself. A simple and most comfortable restriction that informed her nevertheless of the endless restrictions on non-humans whose range and need for freedom was so much greater than hers.

It was a remarkably warm day in November. She was able to repose with ease. Apparently, her presence was not alarming the others who lived there as they cooed, snorted and grunted, growled, whistled, hissed, squawked, bellowed, roared and chirped unreservedly. Here at least, and maybe only momentarily, seemed to be the animal orchestra in symphonic fullness. She leaned back and relaxed even further, breathed in the tones, sang back to them in her mind.

Then another sound at variance with the rest. More studied and careful. A sound modulated by caution. La Vieja did not want to turn her head to identify what resembled human footsteps to the west, definitely not animal treads. The steps had a distinctive beat but also frequent hesitations and alterations of pace and place. La Vieja assumed she was listening to the complex tread of a human negotiating an unknown territory, engaged in assessing each movement before stepping next, unlike a four-legged mammal simply making her confident, most graceful way. As they approached, yes, they, it had become clearer that there were two people, probably of similar height and build, fairly light and lean, she sensed. One's stride was steadier, more confident than the other. One was more delicate, somewhat unsure, but also heavier, and leaning upon the sturdier one.

Instinctively La Vieja stood up, maintaining the steadiness of her gaze and her refusal to move toward or away from what was nearing. As she would now with wild animals, she waited for the beings to determine what would occur. Still, when they came into view, La Vieja was startled. Once again she was thrown into the improbable; she knew the woman, she knew her intimately. She recognized the man. How long had it been since she had seen them? The woman hadn't been pregnant which, clearly she was now, thus accounting for her odd gait.

As La Vieja had learned how to practice the animal art of invisibility, becoming so still that she dissolved into a haze of surroundings, it took a long time for the woman to sense La Vieja's presence and turn toward her albeit without fear or tension. The man turned too, curious and vigilant as he did not recognize her. Though awkward physically, they seemed, like La Vieja to be comfortable among the wild.

"I have seen you," La Vieja stammered because something had to be said and it was for her to reassure them. "I know you." That was ridiculous. This encounter with words was so different than the no words that had engaged her in the last months. She searched for the right words, searching for a common language and the appropriate decorum.

"I see this is your territory. It isn't mine. I don't know why I'm here." She was blabbering but also speaking what was true. Overcome with enormous feelings of … love? … she only wanted to reassure the woman. "Something called me here. Do you understand? Has that ever happened to you? It didn't call me, it transported me, even though I walked. I don't know how far. Or how many miles. Or how long it took. Seeing you is not the result of anything willful. I wasn't prying. I am not prying now. I am not hunting you down."

The woman looked at her kindly the way a pregnant woman learns to care for everything that comes into her tiny dominion.

More than anything, La Vieja wanted to embrace the woman, to fold her into her arms and, and, and what? Praise her? No. Bless her. She wanted to embrace and bless her. "I don't know, it, they, something called me, brought me here, stopped me, nailed me to this spot. Then I looked and here you are!" Short staccato sentences, simple as any animal vocalization. But awkward as animal's aren't and their approach had not been. Finally, she had the right phrase: "I think I was brought here to meet you." It startled her more than anything had in this time when everything she knew and understood had been transformed.

As with Bear, she hoped she would be understood but why assume anything in the slip and slide of realities in which they were immersed. This was a human La Vieja assumed, but the woman could equally have been a Kermode, a Spirit Bear, with her almond color skin and golden curls or a Sun Bear with a golden breast plate. Maybe she and the bear were the same species, maybe the true relationship between beings was based on factors that have not been determined, maybe phylogenesis and taxonomy are benighted studies, oblivious to true kinship which cannot not be predetermined and should not be.

The man, who remained somewhat behind the woman, was supporting her ever so lightly, no more than was needed as the invisible bond between them had high tensile strength. They must have been living in the woods for a long time, as they carried the intrinsic poise of the myriad living ones around them.

Now they were both directly before La Vieja and had taken on the same posture that La Vieja had assumed. The mirroring was reflexive and exuded calm and acceptance.

Then the woman began speaking as if the conversation had started a long time ago, when La Vieja had first seen her, had overheard their original communications, as if they had been directed toward her from the beginning.

"We were going down to the Den. We put it together against the rock wall over there. You might have missed it, but coming here, sensing you present, we hoped you hadn't, though we hope, equally, that other people will. We weren't certain it was the right place as we couldn't determine its character by appearance alone. Structurally it will serve, will drain well, is stable. We couldn't know immediately who had lived there before, what its history had been. We started with something that was already beckoning to be occupied in the right way. We didn't want to dispossess anyone, and it didn't appear as if it had been occupied recently, nor did we want to birth in a dark history where pain had saturated the foundation. But, if it were possible, we wanted a legacy.

"One day, when we were leveling the floor, we had to dig down further than we expected and then dig some more and then we came upon some bones, and then a bear skull." Lucas watched La Vieja carefully to see her reaction. Understanding that they had to agree intuitively, La Vieja also waited until it was certain to her that she was being invited into a dialogue.

Finally, she said, "I think it is right to birth where the Bear ancestors can watch over the children and bless them. A birth chamber in a death chamber is a wheel of life."

"It was what I was thinking," Lucas interjected, "and strangely it reassured me that if I had to leave Léonie and the babies for any length of time, they would be protected."

His response indicated that she had passed the test. If they weren't so steady, La Vieja would be reeling. All conventional assumptions were obliterated. But she couldn't dwell on it as he was continuing.

"We returned the bones to the ground, smoothed the surface, offered Juniper berries to the old ones and began constructing the den in earnest. I consulted my grandfather, of course, and my grandmother and Léonie listened for wisdom from her old people. They were all agreed. Maybe they are already meeting with each other and the Bear people on the other side."

There was a pause. La Vieja said nothing. Then Léonie resumed speaking, "Lucas and I come down to it regularly to ready it. As we are doing now. We can't come every day. We add or subtract something and it has to settle, all the parts need time to come into relationship with each other. Then we return and look at it again and see what is needed." She looked so sharply at La Vieja her gaze pierced what was left of La Vieja's composure entirely. "We didn't know if you would actually arrive today. Or ever. But we proceeded as if you might." Léonie paused to allow La Vieja to comprehend everything implied.

"When the Bears begin to hibernate, I will enter it. It will be winter and I want to deliver the babies into the dark. Lucas will deliver us. There is no one else in our families who can be there."

La Vieja saw that it was her turn to step forward. And maybe it was because her own green eyes cast a light upon them all that even she could see. "I will come," La Vieja said. She was absolutely certain she was being asked and equally certain she would attend. She didn't know if she was responding in this straightforward manner to a less than straightforward situation or if she was being spoken through.

"My name is Léonie," the woman said, "I dreamed you would be coming. You will know when the time is right as we have no means of contacting each other."

La Vieja nodded and maybe she was weeping. The first and only time she had been met in such a manner was by the Bear Who Summons. This was the second time in her rather long and solitary life. "Whatever brought me here, will bring me again." La Vieja said, or didn't. Because there it was, a great mystery had been spoken wordlessly. She had, or Bear had, dreamed these two but what she hadn't understood was that they had dreamed her too. They were emerging out of a common seed of possibility, out of an incomprehensible, invisible and inscrutable reality, coming to life, for the first time, here and now, with their pasts and futures ruffling around them as if they were emerging from watery depths, entirely unfathomable.

"I know who you are, Vieja. We will definitely birth in the Den. I will go in early to be sure the time doesn't surprise me. Lucas is a physician but we will need your help as there will be two babies." The agreements were made most casually and outside of the previously known world.

There was nothing else to be said. Léonie began to turn away and La Vieja understood she was to turn away too, turn back in the direction from which she had come. As mysterious as the way down had been, the way up was clear. She would walk alongside the stream to the stepping stones across and then up again onto the path until she passed the other den for the last time until Bear Who Summons would rouse or Léonie called, as she believed Léonie's need would wake him too.

Far from her now the two made their way to the Den. Léonie dropped to all fours and crawled through the narrow passageway to her bed of leaves, bark and soil within. Lucas followed her in, closed the entrance with branches. The sleep they entered was a different sleep. In their sleep, they entered the centuries past and future from which their cubs were being fed. Below them, to the southeast, a circle of Bears was meeting around a flat stone still blackened where a fire had once been kindled in the days of an unbroken climate. When the cubs would be born, they would nurse on Bear milk. Léonie dreamed the Bears or they gathered together while she dreamed, or abided in her dream, or all.

La Vieja made her way back to her cabin. Somehow, she expected to traverse the three hundred miles by nightfall which would occur quickly at this time of the year. Three hundred miles. There was no way for her to know where she was and its distance from her cabin but she knew. She knew so many things she had not known before, nor in this way.

What had happened? She had crossed a threshold and so had they. She had dreamed them but they were real. If she were real. She was not going to pinch herself, that was not the test for being of a time, space and place. Somewhere in another dimension, a writer was getting this down. That was fortunate. She felt considerable affection for the woman who was occupying her own parallel post, watching for fires, listening for these words, being faithful. They were indeed a very unlikely cadre. How would the writer explain it? She would say, "These times …. These dark times demand it." That is what she would say.

The Writer must have heard this in her way for she felt a twinge of companionship like a sudden breeze. It eased and encouraged her in a moment when the news was increasingly unbearable and she didn't know where to look or focus as everything, everywhere was collapsing. In such a short time since she had met La Vieja and had been enlisted as a sentinel of global breakdown, there had been a terrible quickening, the way objects nearing a black hole spin out of control. GentleBoy, the Husky, got up and pressed his large head against her thigh, wanting something and soon she would go through the routine with him: water? food? walk? Generally, he was specific and articulate and infinitely patient with her as a two-legged who didn't understand very much. Maybe he didn't want anything but their communion. She put the computer aside and stroked his head and when that bored him, she drummed on his rump. There was no smoke in the air at the moment.

* * *

The Bear Who Summons would soon enter his den to sleep. "I'll meet you here, when it's time," La Vieja indicated when she came to the tree with the high scratch marks that would not be covered by snow. The California hunting season that had been cancelled because of the fires would officially end for the year very soon. Winter would come. No one could predict what might be born in the dark. The fires continued raging in the wild but would probably not engulf them this season.

* * *

La Vieja didn't know when the shift had occurred. It had probably taken the entire time from coming to the cabin to this moment of becoming the old woman. It was not something she had aspired to or worked toward. But it had happened to her and she did not refuse it. She had known she had to inhabit the Lookout. Nothing more but nothing less. Many thoughts were coalescing as she walked, not hesitatingly as an old woman might but aware and with an unexpected confidence. The land was familiar to her as if she belonged to it, as if she had been born here of people who had lived here for hundreds and hundreds of years, the way Bear's people shared their origins with the trees. She was observant of every detail, but in a different way from what she had known. What was it? She was walking among relations, everything she saw was alive and beckoning? Greeting? Wanting, no, expecting in a wise way, to be recognized. To be known. The Earth did not want to be observed, it wanted to be known in relationship to her and all the others.

As a child, like the Writer, she had read about old women who lived alone except possibly with their familiars. Maybe Bear would eventually be her familiar, or was it the opposite and she was his. The name familiar given for such a connection was because of being family. The words she was thinking were opening and closing doors in the same instant. They only served what people who originated and lived within this particular language knew. But she was knowing something else and it had no English words or any words she had learned. To preserve this state of mind, she would have to still language altogether and know in other ways. "Bear, be with me now," she called silently. He did not appear. For this season of hibernation, she was on her own.

Now as she was walking home, yes, home to the cabin, she found herself wondering why she had brought all these supplies in her backpack when, even though she was an old woman, she probably didn't need them, not enough to warrant the effort and its preoccupation with things and supplies. Yes, she was the old woman. That must be how Léonie knew to call her La Vieja. She had stopped caring about so much she had thought so essential, it had absorbed most of her earlier life, only to become entirely irrelevant.

The path narrowed. Brambles scratched at her. "Hello," she said aloud.

When she came home, she could sign in that she had returned to her lookout shift which had continued as had the fires. Or she could wait until her shift officially began again and spend the time in her own way, not thinking about anything but the approach of the just waning gibbous moon. She climbed the stairs. This mundane activity seemed so strange. Set her backpack on the deck, untied her jacket, dropped it and her sweater, scarf, turtle neck, everything.

What mattered most now was lighting a five day glass votive candle, setting it inside a metal fire pit, knowing she would tend this light until she was called to the twins. Getting as free of encumbrances as temperature allowed, she stood there, the animal she was becoming, until she was fully saturated with moonlight as she longed to be.

When a cloud passed over the moon, she noticed she hadn't closed the trap door. She did so with a great unnecessary bang which startled her. Rightly so.

24

C rash!

The sound reverberates through the realms. It startles me. That's the end of it. La Vieja has removed herself from my view. Wherever she was, my ability to see her and record her story depended on her consistent transmissions, on a continuous process of revelation. When she shut the trap door, that was it.

It is very odd being without her and still feeling her presence as with a phantom limb whose pain is constant.

La Vieja left at this critical moment in history, one of some continuing possibility and so much danger for all of us. Who will she become now? I wonder this, of course. And the same for Léonie and Lucas. What of their lives?

Snow will fall soon, and it will create a deep silence that extends into the future. In the afternoon, when the sun is overhead, there will be the patter of melting snow on the banks that bury so much in their whiteness. Perhaps the figures formed will be a code that other beings who do not ask, "And then what happened? Who did they become? What is the rest of the story?" will read on behalf of knowing what we cannot grasp.

Léonie, Lucas and La Vieja didn't want to answer such questions which reduce the myriad distinct coexisting possibilities to a banal certainty. "Oh, that's the ending! Oh, that's the conclusion! I thought it would be ...."

Alas, I fail the text. I am not supposed to ask, to pry, to wonder, to have preferences. As the writer La Vieja chose, I am to hold and protect all the prospects, nascent and imminent. But I was also drawn into outcomes and expectations.

* * *

La Vieja

As we come to the end, the Dixie Fire is burning on the Plumas National Forest, Lassen National Forest, Lassen Volcanic National Park, and in five California counties: Butte, Lassen, Plumas, Shasta and Tehama. This is only one of so many fires it is impossible to name them all. We do not know if La Vieja, Lucas, Léonie, their cubs, and the Bear Who Summons will survive.

* * *

For almost four years, La Vieja and I inhabited a Field that emanated so fluidly from the consciousness we shared with each other and other beings, that time, place and event dissolved therein as well and we were shaped into what we might become. The Field is constituted from, cannot exist without, the full submersion of the specific and individual. Also, the Field depends on the exact effect of its diffused energies on everything within. We were simultaneously immersed in it beyond definition and equally never lost our particularity and then La Vieja did and that, in itself, was her distinctiveness. The Field is composed entirely of what we were and what we are and will be. Singularities within and consequences of myriad potentials. I think I am speaking here of how particle and wave are one and coexisting, forming and reforming themselves and the world. And such is Story, isn't it? We are created from its intelligence in the telling of it.

La Vieja, Léonie and Lucas disappeared from my view, and with them The Bear Who Summons and the other Bears. So the Field vanished from my sight and the sensation of its existence. Extinction takes many forms. We cannot ignore the mystery that the living depart in one world but in another they manifest, they thrive and wait for the opportune moment to return.

* * *

The pandemic seems to be easing in some places as increasing numbers receive a vaccine and then explodes, particularly, but not entirely, among those unvaccinated, and there are many in this country, and too many around the globe. Different variants are emerging and millions of lives remain threatened. Borders open and shut. Hospitals empty and refill. The number of patients overwhelm the staff and facilities, then ease. The violence around masking and restrictions is unprecedented and ugly. I do not recognize my country or my state of California. Queen Corona still rules.

The slam of the trap door echoes like a drum roll as people begin to spill onto the streets, masked or not and warring about it. Will anything restorative be gleaned from this time of sequestering? I continue my watch as the hazard of our presence on the Earth looms ever more darkly. The pandemic, sequestering, stopping and listening and trying to live accordingly to these alerts may have shaped many of us but not sufficiently to transform the time. Too many want nothing but to return, thoughtlessly, to the former conditions that have done so much harm. Areas of the Amazon release more carbon than they captured as the areas are cut down, violated. The violence against the Earth and all people and beings increases each day. I feel it in my body.

* * *

There was almost no rain in Topanga this winter. I have not lit the sacred fire outside. What are the consequences when the sacred fires cannot be lit?

* * *

I place kindling, pine cones, logs, all from the land, carefully in the wood-stove. I say the prayers that have come to me and light the fires on behalf of La Vieja and all her kin. Then I go out to my perch and try to see as far as she sees. Perhaps I saw the man who was driven to arson in the heavy brush between this roost and Eagle Rock only a few acres away. I saw him in ways distinct from those in helicopters and those watching with drones who still couldn't apprehend him for days. I saw his madness and fiery grief and could only bear witness. I beg that it be sufficient.

* * *

Once a month, I leave this post to carry boxes of supplies, including some bottles of mead and newly filled gallon containers of water to the foot of the stairs. I take back the empty ones she has left; she does give me that. I consider honking the horn of my 4x4 to alert her, to catch a glimpse of her, but decide not to jar her with such a sound, relying instead on her heightened sensitivity to all that is, suppressing my own need. The supplies will end up with her and or the Bears; they will decide conjointly given that they know I am always adding birdseed and honeycombs for the winged, four-leggeds and all. When I can no longer accommodate La Vieja, Lucas will provide.

Of course, she needs supplies. But that is not the only reason I do this. Admittedly, I am trying to mitigate the reality that La Vieja having withdrawn is no longer vital and present in our lives. What does that mean for me, the Writer whose awareness was influenced each day by what she transmitted?

Didn't she indicate that to write about La Vieja, I had to know La Vieja myself from my own being? There are scores of ways to be a Vieja. It may not mean that I, we, each have to find a cabin on a summit and keep a lookout in that manner. But it may mean that I am required to fulfill her calling to see into all the dimensions and not look away. Bear witness, relentlessly, to our own culpabilities. I can't bear the heartbreak of it.

La Vieja's absence insists I stay here at this perch, that I stop pretending it is virtual. I note each fire and evacuation because these are not statistics for me, this is not data, this is the fabric of my life. Your life too, if you don't look away.

I walk back to the lookout at the edge of this land in the southeast, the same direction as the council of Bears, and look far into the rugged chaparral of Topanga State Park, trying to see it as it is, and how it was once—remember?—and all the possibilities of how it can be.

* * *

I am already intensely lonely for her and … for you. However, let us imagine that you and I will not be separated by the closing of this book. Haven't we also formed a field of interconnected awareness and vision that need not evaporate into the cosmos? Might we continue to spin around each other, creating a dynamic field, attracting other energies into our vortex? Again, who knows what will begin to form out of such minute but vital particles of love?

* * *

Try to keep a small sacred fire lit. This is the beginning or the end of the world.

September 25, 2021
The Village Sanctuary for All Beings
Topanga, California

DEDICATION

To White Buffalo Calf Woman

In June 2020, White Buffalo Calf Woman came in a dream to a woman whom I scarcely knew, Adina Kaplan, just after she first attended our community Daré online.

In her dream, she was participating in council, sitting in circle with others telling their stories, as we do here on the patio in Topanga. Unsuccessfully, I was urging the speakers to focus on the subject—Extinction. "Extinction," I said, repeatedly but no one paid attention. Then I was no longer leading the circle. I was replaced by White Buffalo Calf Woman, who exclaimed several times, "Focus! Extinction." And then again, "Extinction. Extinction, Extinction."

Adina Kaplan did not know who White Buffalo Calf Woman is, she did not know she came to the Sioux and brought the sacred pipe, the ceremony of the *Hamblechya*, the Sundance, the Lodge and more.

I believe White Buffalo Calf Woman came to our Council, to our community, came to me, came to all of us, to you, the reader as well, because we must focus on Extinction and everything leading to it, also Climate Dissolution and the social and political chaos we are creating everywhere on the globe by imposing, as we have on this continent for at least 528 years, an unsustainable, violent, voracious, and imperial culture.

We must change our lives radically.

We must reverse extinction.

I dedicate whatever merit there is in this book to White Buffalo Calf Woman and her sacred teachings in such a time of the Earth's and the Peoples'—all the Peoples, non-human and human—-great suffering.

But, White Buffalo Calf Woman would not have come if it weren't possible to reverse climate dissolution and reverse extinction.

I offer this book to you the reader, that together, we may change our minds down to the cellular level, divest ourselves of the dogmas and assumptions of Euro-American and imperial thinking and live on behalf of a viable future for all beings.

AFTERWORD
by Laura Simms

La Vieja is "not a novel." It is a living story. It is a spiritual autobiography offering experiential instructions from characters who summoned the author to write their story into existence at this time. It is to be heard as one would attend to a great myth being incanted by an elder who makes visceral and real what needs to be known before it is too late. Just as the sound of the voice of the myth teller evokes trust and draws us close, the braided stories of the author speak directly to our own La Vieja, wiser than ourselves, but within us. The book is constructed of a myriad of interwoven personal stories told throughout a larger mythic story. Myth, memory, dream and reality in our minds as it was for tribal peoples for thousands of years. It is more than a book of narratives. It is a ceremony. We are witness and participant. La Vieja becomes the vehicle through which the heart-mind of the reader is released from the tyranny of a way of thinking and being that is destroying our planet. Deena Metzger has answered a call on behalf of ourselves and our world. She is our elder guiding us to see what we have forgotten—how to be of this world.

There is a very old Inuit myth about a wife and husband, and their three sons. They live apart from other people, and cannot find food. The two eldest sons travel far in search of prey. On their journey, an eagle circles above each young man and alights on the cold earth beside him, turning into a man. The eagle/man requests that they accompany him to his mother's realm in the sky. Each one refuses. They become lost. They do not return home. The third and youngest son goes out. He sees the eagle and agrees. The eagle said, "Good. Your brothers refused." Like the youngest son, Deena accepted the call of an old woman, perhaps spirit, more and more real to her and to us.

The young man was flown to a place beyond the sky, to a mountain on which there stands an old lodge. He heard the sound of a drum. But the sound was low, faded, barely audible. He entered the lodge and encountered an aging, feeble, near-to-death Eagle Mother. It is her heart that he heard hardly beating. She instructed him to build a ceremonial house, to make a drum and learn to sing. Eagle Mother then told the young man to sing the songs on the earth, and invite all the people. The young man said, "We do not know any people." She answered, "This is the sorrow and problem of human beings. You have forgotten celebration and ceremony.

If you do as I instruct, you will have food. You will know joy." The young man followed instructions. Many people arrived. They danced all night. They danced the way that our author danced in an early part of La Vieja during a conference with the Bushmen in California, and brought rain. They gathered in ceremony the way that our author gathers others in her sanctuary home in Topanga Canyon. He saw an eagle turn into a man the way that characters in the story meet Bear in dream and in reality as knowledgeable relatives. The young man in the Inuit story followed instructions the way that Deena responded to the requests from elephants to sit in council in Botswana.

In the early morning as each person left the lodge, they bent down, and turned into animals. Many people came to live nearby the small family. Food became abundant. They remembered joy. Days later, the youngest son sought out the eagle man in order to be carried to Eagle Mother's Lodge to thank her. On his arrival the sound of the drum was loud. The lodge was beautiful. Eagle Mother was young and radiant.

La Vieja is an immersion into this primal authentic way of being. It opens our eyes with heart-aching stories of a world on fire because of our forgetting. The old woman character who requests Deena to record her journey to a fire outlook is not fantasy. She is the essence of reality unobstructed by the bias that we humans are above and separate from others. The old woman takes us through a portal, dissolving false and dangerous walls constructed out of fear, greed and ignorance. We see intimately, and from far above. Stories change us. La Vieja changes us. We begin to know our fundamental relationship to the world, a felt-sensed relationship of interdependence and consequence. Those who listened to myths long ago were reassured of the truth of birth, life, death and regeneration. Today the myths still hold great power, but we have lost the capacity for the immediacy of their experience as truth. La Vieja helps us relearn to construct a ceremonial house in our world, in our heart. The process of engagement in the stories restores the eyes of our heart. We realize our connection to everything.

Deena breaks ground for a new and urgent literature of restoration. Page after page reveals the working of an artist deeply committed to the responsibility of the writer at this time of climate extinction, increasing violence, greed and pandemic to more than remind us—to open us to the full capacity to feel the devastation of the world. At the same time, the book provokes us to fall in love with the world, regardless.

We are living in mythic times. Fire, plague, violence, earthquake, drought and an awful blindness to regeneration. Myths of the end of the world caused by human greed and violence—like Ragnarok, the Norse destruction of the human world—is no longer a story we hear as an unreal and exciting epic. The isolation, physical and spiritual hunger of the couple and their children in the Inuit story without nurturance is our painful dilemma. La Vieja drops all pretense of explanation in order to restore within us a different capacity—our birthright of being. Throughout, we become bear, elephant, earth and each other. We see the way a medicine woman sees, a poet observes, and a great teller of myth sings us back to life with drum and incantation. Yes, we trip over ourselves, as Deena reminds us, humbly realizing how fragile our connection to knowing in this way has become.

From the moment La Vieja, through the words of our author, leaves the ordinary world that is on fire to become the caretaker of a fire station —above a forest, an outlook, a place of refuge, a possibility of unobstructed encounter with reality of what is happening in our world and to us, to animals, to trees, the damage and the beauty—we surrender to the palpable intelligence of heart and imagination.

Deena has offered a powerful memoir of a writer in her 80's who is not stymied by the limits and delusion of chronology and logic alone. She has gathered all that she has learned about the power of language, and spirit-trusting story, garnered over a lifetime to save us, gift us, awaken us. Reading Deena's writing is a "holy ceremony." Like all great tales it is participatory. The alchemy of a story is its power. As we read, or hear, we become everything through the imagination that lets us become, create, and feel again. La Vieja is our cauldron.

I was struck by the love story that threads throughout, a young man and a young woman, Lucas and Léonie, who are drawn irresistibly to each other. They develop as La Vieja develops, through the writing. They return to the natural world to create new life, as La Vieja remains in her outlook until her death. It is a great fairytale. Not in the achingly foolish analytical or self-involved psychoanalytic interpretation way, but in the rooted archaic symbolic sense of a story that is ritual transformation. It is a story that repairs the destruction and imbalance in the world, first in us so we can discover what we each need to do at this time.

I was drawn into the music of the layered fugue-like stories, and the den of her words. La Vieja's encounter with Bear, and Deena's encounter with elephants, melted away a false veil of fear-based separation. Everything in the book is in service of awareness and the restoration of our abiding connection to the earth, to spirit and to the renewing source of our own dreaming mind.

The book does not end. We become part of the story. In the introduction Deena wrote, "I understand now. I have been brought here through La Vieja to witness a possibility and give it language without retreating from the motion, like the possibility of an expanding universe retracting on behalf of restoration, seeking an equilibrium that had been bypassed in error. We are here within the manifestation of a synchronous moment. How can we make it real?" It is through our engagement in the new ancient mythic story that we remember it is real.

We are enabled to make our way "toward the song that has been absent for so long." We are carried to Eagle Mother's lodge and learn to construct a sacred ceremonial house in our selves. La Vieja speaks to us, through Deena, as the Great Mother spoke through myth and ritual. A language shared by all creatures is lament and communal renewal. "We live in a world entirely different from the one we are trained to accept as real."

Deena asks, "What does an old woman do at the end of her life?" La Vieja is the response, the gift, the doing. "The job of the elder is to remember how it was once before we destroyed it. To remember and to restore. To remember and to restore. I am trying to live up to it. It is a hard task." Deena has done just that for us all.

Laura Simms
Manhattan
October 7, 2021

ACKNOWLEDGEMENTS

To write a book is to engage in a great mystery. The story came as a surprise and maybe all stories do. *A Rain of Night Birds* had just been published and Carolyn Brigit Flynn arranged for me, Stan Rushworth and Carolyn to read together. Stan read from the soon to be published *Diaspora's Children* (Hand to Hand) and Carolyn read from her forthcoming *The Light of Ordinary Days*. The next day, sitting in her lovely garden, flush with the deep joy of our shared work, she suggested that we write together. I declined. She smiled and skilled writing teacher that she is, dismissed my objections and insisted that I confront the blank page. Having myself imposed such a demand on many writers, Carolyn included, I submitted not knowing what, if anything, would appear. Hours later, I had the first shadowy glimpse of La Vieja, of an old woman who had decided to spend time in a Fire Outlook as had so many writers—which is how I knew about it —including Edward Abbey, Jack Kerouac, Norman Maclean, Gary Snyder, Philip Whalen and Phil Connors. La Vieja was not a writer, but she presented herself to the Writer soon after and that is how the book came to be. I do not know if it would have been conceived without Carolyn's intervention and her encouragement when I did not know what could possibly arise from those first awkward pages. Deep, deep gratitude to you, Carolyn.

As the book developed, I became curious as to whether there were, actually, any women stone masons like Léonie Augusta and so was pleased to find and study the extraordinary work of Thea Alvin, albeit from a distance, as best as I could. I thank my friend, fellow writer Joseph Mackenzie who, building a house in Vermont and digging up many stones from the land, agreed to visit Alvin, where he arrived as a veterinarian was castrating two goats which he observed, but which made it impossible to discuss stonemasonry or to see her remarkable stone structures. I am also grateful for the work of Dan Snow as documented in *Listening to Stone*. For both Alvin and Snow, stonemasonry is an act of beauty and spiritual practice. As it happens, I learned of Snow's work when doing research for a trip to Ireland, another gift from Carolyn Flynn, where I was able to spend time among the sacred stone works and to observe the ancient tradition of stone walls.

Thank you to writer, Pami Ozaki, my spirit daughter who, when hearing about Léonie Augusta, knew her lineage immediately, which I had not, and from her knowledge I could deduce many of the circumstances of Léonie's life and her family's. Similar gratitude to my son, Marc Metzger who directed me to what I needed to understand about the Pacific Theater of WWII. To Lise Weil and Kristin Flyntz of <u>Dark Matter: Women Witnessing</u>, who read and published some pages of an early version of *La Vieja* and whose questions helped me in the editing process.

Without friendship, it is difficult to face the many challenges inherent to writing such a text. Sharon Simone and Cheryl Potts consistently encouraged and supported my efforts. Ariel Dorfman, with whom I have been fortunate to be friends for fifty years since we met in Chile in 1972 before the golpe against the Allende government, read the manuscript several times and his notes and perceptions have been invaluable. I am grateful to him for his wisdom, consciousness and companionship all these years. In like manner, I am so appreciative of the friendship with Stan Rushworth who has been willing to transmit to me his unique and profound understanding of Indigenous ways. I am honored by their support. Similarly, Laura Simms, a master of myth and story, is a compatriot in the journeys across the thresholds to the different worlds. Additionally I wish to express my deep respect for the radical and compassionate work of Anna Bretynbach, a true communicator with the wild.

Immeasurable gratitude to Cynthia Travis, founder of **everyday gandhis**, who recognized that the stories of the Elephants are central to the peace building activities in Liberia and who made many of the journeys to meet with the Elephants possible and has been a constant visionary companion as we traveled together in Southern Africa and Liberia.

I thank Gay Bradshaw for her exquisite understanding of Elephants, their nature, intelligence, and the wounds they carry. Also the wisdom she had transmitted to us about Bears from her long companionship with the incomparable Bear whisperer, Charlie Russell.

My dear friend Stephan Hewitt has held and served the vision of Hand to Hand Publications for twenty years. Publisher, editor, designer and more, he has accompanied the work in a remarkable way. Without his exacting eye and open heart this book would not exist in this form. In these dark times, it is a rare gift to have such a friend and skilled companion in bringing such a work into the world.

I am thankful to all my friends, colleagues and students who share my anguish about extinction and climate dissolution and inspire and encourage me with their devotion to the work of imagining and so creating a culture from which a viable future for all beings might develop.

And finally, gratitude beyond words to the radiant Spirits and the Beings of the natural world.

ABOUT THE AUTHOR

Deena Metzger is a writer and healer living at the end of the road in Topanga, California. Her books include the novels *A Rain of Night Birds*, *La Negra y Blanca*, (winner of the 2012 Oakland Pen Award); *Feral*; *Doors: A Fiction for Jazz Horn*; *The Other Hand*; *What Dinah Thought*; *Skin: Shadows/Silence, A Love Letter in the Form of a Novel* and *The Woman Who Slept With Men to Take the War Out of Them*—a novel in the form of a play. The latter is included in *Tree: Essays and Pieces*, which features her celebrated Warrior Poster on its cover testifying to a woman's triumph over breast cancer.

Her books of poetry include, *The Burden of Light*, *Ruin and Beauty: New and Collected Poems*, *A Sabbath Among The Ruins*, *Looking for the Faces of God*, *The Axis Mundi Poems* and *Dark Milk*.

Writing For Your Life: A Guide and Companion to the Inner Worlds is her classic text on writing and the imagination. Two plays *Not As Sleepwalkers* and *Dreams Against the State* have been produced in theaters and various venues. She co-edited the anthology, *Intimate Nature: The Bond Between Women and Animals*, one of the first testimonies to the reality and nature of animal intelligence and agency. *Entering the Ghost River: Meditations on the Theory and Practice of Healing*, and *From Grief Into Vision: A Council* examine the tragic failure of contemporary culture and provide guidance for personal, political, environmental and spiritual healing.

Deena is a radical thinker on behalf of the natural world and planetary survival, a teacher of writing and healing practices for 50 years and a writer and activist profoundly concerned with peacemaking, restoration and sanctuary for a beleaguered world. She has been convening ReVisioning Medicine—bringing Indigenous medicine ways to heal the medical world—since 2004, and is imagining a Literature of Restoration as foundations of a new viable culture. She was instrumental in the introduction of Daré to North America in 1999. Daré and the 19 Ways Training for the 5th World, are unique forms of individual, community and environmental healing based on Indigenous, contemporary medicine and wisdom traditions.

Made in the USA
Las Vegas, NV
20 December 2022

63617677R00164